Simmer and Smoke

A SOUTHERN TALE OF GRIT AND SPICE

Peggy Lampman

In memory of Mama, Ann Allen Stewart
(1931-1997)

ACKNOWLEDGMENTS

To my husband, Richard, who believed in my ladies and me even when inspiration came at three a.m. To the thoughtful advice of Lucy Carnaghi, Mara Brazer, Tania Evans, and Judy Harvey; to the watchful eyes of Jane Rosenman and Marlene at First Editing. To my inimitable son, Zan de Parry, whose name and poetry I borrowed; to my gutsy girl, Greta de Parry, who taught me how to get back on the horse that threw you; having raised such magnificent kids is my greatest triumph. To Betty Lampman and Nan Hoaglin—you both know why.

To the immigrant workers who perform the most demeaning and dangerous jobs in our country for the lowest pay; to the Southern Poverty Law Center for promoting tolerance, and to which I'm honored to donate a portion of book revenue. And, finally, to the young woman and child I watched one chilly December afternoon near the cemetery in Stewartville, Alabama, where my Scottish ancestors are buried. Although we never exchanged words, I imagined your world; how would you escape a town of poverty, crack houses, and racism? To every Shelby and Miss Ann in today's American South: Thank you for inspiring me to write this book.

A NOTE TO OUR READERS

Ten percent of net profits from the sale of this book are donated to the Southern Poverty Law Center. All of the recipes may be found at the end of our story.

Shelby Preston & Mallory Lakes

If reality is an illusion,
then is self-perception a deceit?

Contents

Contents

December 31, 2010

Shelby

In the cemetery tucked behind First Baptist Bible, next to the broad-leaf tobacco patch twelve miles south of town, scrawled-out writing on a buckled, tin sign reads: "NO BURIAL'S WITHOUT WRITTEN PERMISSION". Those words piss off Mama—dead men don't need no rules—but she obliged.

Last night, she mended the zipper of her darkest dress. She put the permission slip, alongside eight, crispy-new, one hundred-dollar bills, into a manila envelope. She hid it under the mat in her hatchback Chevy, and checked that car half-a-dozen times to make sure it was locked.

Uncle Watley's funeral is in thirty minutes and we'll be late. Mama's right hand trembles as she leans into the mirror, fumbling with her eye-liner; a freshly lit menthol balances across the rim of her coffee cup, a slug of ashes threatening to fall. I tap it on the saucer, hand her the cig, and then dump the pyramid of soot into the trash. The ashes puff into a cloud before most of them settle on the floor.

"You said you'd stop smoking in the house." I brush my hands together. "What a mess."

She responds with that cocked-brow, pursed-mouth look and then takes another drag. Moving to the dresser, she digs in the drawers, fists thrusting through nylon, searching for pantyhose without a run. She slides and wiggles into her last wadded pair. There's a tiny tear at the ankle, but I don't speak.

"Fetch me some polish, Shelby."

I scurry to the shoebox with *Manicure* written on the side. There's no clear polish to stop the run, only a bottle of Cherry Bomb Red. Mama dabs the tiny bristles at the rip, that laurel sprig tattoo peeking over the nylon's waistband like an easy grin. Straightening her back, she places the brush on top of the dresser. A drop of scarlet drips onto the wood.

Screwing the brush into the bottle, I feel the skin around my jawline tighten. "I could spend my life cleaning up your trail." I wipe the mark with a tissue, smearing it deep and dark into the grain.

Mama glances at the splotch. "I'd best be following you."

What's this? She's telling *me* that *I'm* the cause of this chaos? I want to lash back, but we've got to keep moving. A sick headache's coming on, and an image of that stain keeps looping across my vision.

She slips into the two-sizes-too-small dress, a deep V cut down the front. "Zip me up, hon. Careful so it don't catch the gauze." Arms clamped around her paunchy midriff, she inhales, sucking in her gut. I pinch the fabric together, slick cloth sliding between my thumb and forefinger, and inch my way up, the zipper straining against the seams.

"Finally," I say, as Mama exhales, rasping and coughing. "You wouldn't have stood a chance without the control-top."

She smooths the shiny fabric over her hips. "I've gained near eight pounds since you started foolin' in my kitchen."

"And no one's complained about mealtime since." I blow her a kiss.

Shrugging, she regards herself in the mirror, tilts her chin, and continues. "Still. Not bad for forty-four." I admire her reflection: quick blue eyes, chiseled jaw and fine-tuned profile. My mood softens. This woman is finely made. Mama is *fine*.

She rings her head in some no-brand hairspray; it smells like pesticide. I open the bedroom door and fan away the stinking fumes. Television laughter floods the room. Mama crushes out the cig, craning her neck through the door.

"Miss Ann, young lady, turn off that TV and *scoot*. Get your butt in the car." We slam through the back door, pile into the car, and screech off to the cemetery. Halfway there, I remember the most important part.

"Sweet Jesus, Mama. We forgot the ashes."

"Damnation, Shelby." Her words sound irritated, hissed between teeth, as if I were the warden of those ashes. A purplish-gray vein snakes up her neck as she lights another smoke, then she makes a hasty U-turn, roadside gravel spitting up to rattle the wheel wells. We backtrack home to get the ashes. We'll be late now for sure.

She scurries into the house, and then returns walking slowly, clutching the funeral urn to her chest. Handing it to me through the passenger window, she trots to the driver's side and slides behind the steering wheel. She busts up the speed limit retracing our route, knocking against curbs, jolting around corners, and racing along the stretch of highway. I hoist, shift and clinch the urn between my thighs; I'm worried it'll fall, or that the top will be knocked off, spilling the ashes between my legs.

At last we arrive at the church.

"Lord, Shelby," Mama smirks, giving me the once-over, "smooth your mane. You look like a wild-eyed dugout soldier."

"Whatever. I'm just grateful we're alive." I twist my hair into a back knot then turn and wink at Miss Ann, my child.

Mama retrieves the envelope from the trunk and secures it under her armpit, I hand her the urn, and then we tread toward the cemetery. Moist weedy grass grows in clumps, dampening my feet and scratching my ankles. I wrap my fingers around the rickety iron handle and push open the graveyard gate. The hinges make a high-pitched creaking whine, and this sound and all this nervousness scares Miss Ann, who whimpers, "Maa...ma. Maa...ma."

That word: *Mama.* Settles my soul. Links in a chain that life can't break. The rusted clasp of the gate cuts a sliver into my palm so I spit on it, pick out a metal splinter then grab her tiny fist.

Uncle Watley's widow, Aunt Mama, is facing the preacher with her head bowed. Cutting her eyes in our direction, her lips curl into a faint smile, as if relieved we finally made it. Mama places the urn and envelope on a table next to the shoveled-out grave, gives her sister a tight hug, and whispers something in her ear.

Aunt Mama chuckles. Then, remembering her role at the gathering, she frowns, swipes fingertips under dry eyes, and directs her gaze to the preacher.

We stand next to Uncle Watley's skinny-boned, slick-haired poker buddies and sing "Walking with Jesus." More sober than I've seen them in years, the men try to settle themselves, hitching up trousers and appearing uncomfortable in their ill-fitting, saggy suits. Swaying to the refrain, I push my daughter closer to Mama so she won't smell those rank wafts of mothballs. The men's whispers of belch are bad enough, stinking of sour whiskey and pickled eggs. Miss Ann's hand is yanking at mine, raggedy nails curling into my wrists. She hiccups back tears, trilling, "Who-whip, who-whip," mewing like an unweaned coon. Hoisting her six-year-old body onto my hip, I stare her quiet.

I can't wait to hightail it out of this backwoods churchyard but the preacher, Reverend Thomas, hasn't even begun. He's a nice enough man but he is aware we aren't in his flock; no flock for that matter. The crematorium gave us his card. Truth is, I admire the mysteries of Jesus, a flesh-and-blood man, but I can't wrap my mind around something as big as God.

The preacher's eyes squint in the dazzle of the high-noon sun and dart across our group, not judging, but searching, blinking, seeming confused, as if he's misplaced his Bible. He clears his throat.

"We commend our brother to you, Lord Christ, splendor of life eternal."

He proceeds to sketch a picture of Uncle Watley's spirit like a white-winged dove flitting off to heaven. What a joke; my uncle was a bat out of hell. Reverend Thomas never once met Uncle Watley but that's not why my stomach's in knots. I'm worried he'll lift the urn and realize it's a good bit heavier than the one he delivered to us from the crematorium.

Mama's used to pinching pennies. Says it's the Scottish in her but the reality is that she's been broke her entire life, so when she had to figure a way to provide a Christian burial for her boyfriend, Sam Cox, she relied on inbred Georgia wiles.

Shelby, really, who'd ever find out? she had asked me, the words rolling around her mouth like sausage balls in flour. *Why not combine Watley's ashes with Sam's? Believe me, I've checked, and there ain't nothing in the Bible that says it's a sin. Just makes horse sense.* I wondered where she'd been keeping the Lord's book all these years, much less reading it.

I told her no. That was a terrible idea. That the church expects payment for every soul dug into its property. Besides, we both knew Uncle Watley despised Sam; the men had quit speaking after Sam shot off Uncle's brand-new Remington 700 without asking his permission. It wasn't the gun itself but the fact that Sam borrowed it and nailed the largest buck ever recorded in Jeff Davis County history. Why, I'm talking the biggest whitetail *ever*. That animal sported a twelve-point rack.

If Watley hated the sight of him when he was alive, I said to her, imagine how he'd feel about Sam poaching in his ashes.

But we couldn't get our heads around the cash problem, and a proper burial for him might give Mama some peace. The trouble began last spring: Sam stepped on a rusty nail, developed blood poisoning, and died two weeks later from complications.

He left Mama crazy as a hit dog—wild-eyed and bumping into furniture, limping around the house—she lost the car keys for an entire week and paid it no mind. At last she slumped into a chair and sat heaped at the card table, face filling her hands, with that teased red hair swaying back and forth; she looked like some split overripe tomato, swollen with late-summer heat, heavy on the vine.

He also left behind a wallet full of credit cards, maxed-out to the limit.

Mama had Sam cremated with funds provided by the State then, gray-faced and empty-eyed, she crept back into the shadow of her life before she'd met him. The preacher brought us his ashes in a plastic-lined cardboard box, no sturdier than a Happy Meal so she scrubbed a two-quart pickle pot with bleach and kept his remains bottled up in the cellar. After a spell, he latched onto the aroma of Clorox, scented with vinegar, garlic and dill. Last month Uncle Watley died from heart failure. His death, followed by a life insurance check for ten thousand dollars, spelled bingo for Mama. At last she could send Sam off in style.

Aunt Mama, Watley's newly flush, not-so-grieving widow, was more than happy to let Mama tend to the burial details—she was busy shopping for a new car. The Veterans Administration provided $255 dollars for the grave marker, and Mama spent $1850 from the check for everything else: $650 for the cremation; $800 for the preaching, grave-digging and burial plot; and $400 for the urn. We decided not to tell Aunt Mama our plans for Sam's remains. *Let sleeping dogs lie*, Mama said with a wink.

The day before yesterday, carrying Watley's urn, we crept down warped plank steps to the cellar; the air lay thick with a wet burlap smell of boiled peanuts and sweet cured tobacco. Pulling webbed threads from my hair, I watched Mama light the lantern.

Sam's bottled-up ashes, outlined in the flickering glow, were sand-wiched between Mason jars packed with pickled okra. Slowly, she inched the pot towards her, embracing him into her chest. I steadied her arm as she knelt onto the crumbling floor. She unscrewed the lid. I squatted down. Resting our eyes on the Heavenly Range Eternity Urn, we admired the handiwork: an orangish-brown ceramic jug decorated with oak trees and deer; she bought the extra-large size so both men would fit. I pushed a funnel tip into the spout. With trembling hands, I held it steady as Mama poured Sam's graveled bones, resembling stone-ground grits, right on top of Uncle Watley. I picture those men, antlers locked on that heavenly range, dueling it out until kingdom come.

I reckon the pearly gates aren't gonna open a crack for mean Uncle Watley, but maybe Sam stands a chance. I whisper a prayer for his soul just in case. His family wrote him off years ago, which puzzles me. He never once raised his voice and always kept a Hershey's Kiss for Miss Ann in his pocket.

When Mama cut butter into flour, he'd shush us quiet, creep up to her back then nip her neck and swat her playful on the rear. *Noreen, sweet Noreen, my beautiful biscuit queen.* There was adoration in his voice when he said her name, *Noreen,* as if puzzled that such a glorious woman would ever let a man like him into her life. And the tales he'd tell around the table; who cared if they were fact or fiction? He spun words into gold. Then, after helping with the dishes, he'd rub baby oil into Mama's split-veined and calloused feet. At his touch, a misty shine flooded her eyes. Bone-tired weary, at last she had what she'd always wanted: someone who loved her as much as she loves Miss Ann and me.

The preacher catches me up, asking us to reflect on the kindness Uncle Watley showed to others in his life. All I remember was his simmering anger at Aunt Mama, threatening to boil over if she so much as scorched a butter bean. Mama and I comforted her the best we could, heartsick knowing that under her long-sleeved dresses lay the handiwork of his nastiness, but mostly we felt ashamed because we were afraid. Messing with Watley was like stoking the fires of Hades. He's gone for good. I am rejoicing. Yet my spirits sink, along with my five-inch heels, into the red clay soil.

Reverend Thomas lifts the ash-packed urn to heaven. His biceps bulge under a stiff bleached shirt; even in the late-December chill, sweat beads pop across his forehead. His brow furrows as he lowers the jug to the table; his pupils dilate, drilling into mine. Holding my breath, I shift my eyes, smooth Miss Ann's curls then moisten my lips.

Mama leans into my side, lips barely moving, and mutters, "A dime doin' a dollar's worth of work."

Here we go, at it again. Hustling, sneaking, scrambling to make people, people who couldn't give a flip, think we're something fine. And if no one discovers our messy little secrets swept under the floorboards, well then, they never happened. None of that business was real. Here's my truth, the lesson life has taught this girl: We can sweep our floors as much as we want, but the grime still stains.

The preacher's mouth opens, then shuts. An emotion hard to read, something like irritation, passes his face, but if he thinks there's more in that urn besides Uncle Watley, he keeps it to himself. Expression distant, he drums the urn with his fingertips searching for inspiration, I suspect, from the King of Kings himself.

I relax, breath settling, and my mind wanders to the rice and pea dish, *Hoppin' John*, I'm making tomorrow. When following a recipe, I escape this life, and it pleases me to no end watching smiles creep across folk's faces when they eat my cooking. Mallory Lakes writes about food upstate in Atlanta, and when she features country fare, I can make the recipe because the ingredients are stocked at The Pig. I clipped her column, along with a Piggly Farms coupon for bacon, from last Thursday's *Atlanta Sun* Food Section.

Miss Lakes wrote the dish is supposed to bring good luck, but only if you eat it on New Year's Day. Lord knows this family could use a pot of something good. Miss Ann squirms, wiggling off my hip, and scoots down my leg. I stoop to straighten her dress; another year slipped by and I'm still drooping into dirt.

"In the midst of life, we are in death."

Startled by the thunder in the preacher's voice, I scurry from my daydreams. Why, that is the coldest sentence I have ever heard. I re-tie and double-knot Miss Ann's shoelaces in quick yanking thrusts. Such a tragedy is this life, if the very meaning of our existence lies in the bottom of a hole.

His head yanks to attention, as if awakening from a trance. His arms flail. His hands wag. And his fingers are spread wide feeling the spirit at last, shouting: "We are soldiers in the army of the Lord!"

"Sounds like he's auditioning for Gospel TV," Mama remarks. I narrow my eyes and shake my head, warning her to keep a lid on it.

"Amen." The poker buddies nod, feet rocking, hands stitched into pockets. The preacher places the urn into the metal box, and then he bends down, lowering it into the grave.

His voice, now hoarse, rumbles, "Dust to dust."

Ashes in a box vanished into the ground. All my life I've yearned for something more, something I struggle to define. An image lies in wait, appears in a flash, then gone. It's in the brushed edge of a dream that leaves behind no memory, only a warming prickle of joy. It's in the smell of fresh-turned soil after a frost, ancient and newborn. It's in the taste of honeysuckle nectar—what the wood nymphs drink, I tell my child—that we dot onto our tongues every spring.

I place my palms upon her shoulders and give a little squeeze. Maybe I'll add a slab of fatback to the peas while they simmer; it's not in the recipe, but peas taste better cooked with fat.

Two black birds hover above our small raggedy troop. Their wings stretch out as Jesus on the cross, painting shadows on the earth. Do they welcome fresh souls rising high or sinking down low?

"Praise the Lord," I exclaim, louder than intended, more relieved the service is over than struck by the divine. Glancing at Mama, I figure she'd be annoyed by my outburst but she doesn't notice. Her eyes flutter across the open field of low grave markers like a gypsy moth searching for a mate, at last resting upon the box in the fresh-dug earth.

"Hallelujah," she sighs. She braids her fingers. She clinches them as shovel by shovel, dirt fills the hole. Bowing her head as if in prayer, she closes her eyes and whispers, "Two souls for the price of one."

I smile. Yes. Mama's done Sam proud.

Mallory

The peas are rioting in boiling water, dodging lashing bubbles as if to warn me that one more minute in the tempestuous brew and they'll turn to mush. I stop scribbling, secure the pen behind my ear, and reduce the heat. Cooking the beans inspires more agitated prose. Retrieving my pen, it tangles in a strand of hair. I yank it out, and then grab the pad of sticky notes.

Clutching the pen like a woman possessed, the words unravel with a mind of their own. *You plunged me into boiling water. Burning, heartbroken, I cry your name.*

I peel away the note and stick it on the fridge. So that's it. Another chunk of life I've sizzled to cliché. Maybe I'll switch careers. The crazy melodrama is so loud in my head, I should market it; write overwrought banality for daytime drama instead of culinary dribble for the *Atlanta Sun*. The pay would be better. I glance at the bills stacked next to my computer.

Dropping the pen, I press my palms together and focus on my breathing: *Whoa, girl, simmer down. In through the nose, out with a sigh.* My shoulders relax, and I regard the fridge, plastered with sticky notes; I notice some of them are curling at the tips, threatening to dislodge. I'll secure those with tape, never mind adhesive leaves marks on stainless.

Memos from the edge, self-help hieroglyphics, throwaway lines galloping off paper, most of them unfinished. These are the words I should have said to Cooper the day he left, bade farewell, adios, arrivederci—however you say goodbye. Itchy, my dearest friend, is returning a platter and will ignore them, assuming they are recipe scribbles. But if these tourniquets had a voice, their banshee wail would rant, rage and scream, shaking the foundations of Atlanta.

Dearest Cooper. What a splendid feast you made of me. A sprinkle of salt, a grind of pepper, you chewed me up then spit me out. Was I that abhorrent?

Visceral, grisly, teeth-gnashing words; much better script. I write, post, then return to my cutting board. Chopping furiously, I collect, examine, and discard words much too ordinary to assuage my grief. Words...words...I need more words; what words can I write that will ease the pain of what you've done?

With the blade of the knife, I scrape the peppers into a bowl and the tears begin to fall. Burning the back of my lids, they leak into the dish. Tears. A novel ingredient. Easy enough to extract; I'll reduce the salt in the recipe. Face into hands, I collapse into a chair and sob.

Several minutes pass until the timer dings, jolting me out of my sniveling misery. I rub my eyelids then drain the peas into a colander; mascara-streaked eyes stare back from the stainless pot. Why did I put on makeup for the New Year's Eve party this early? And what made Cooper bolt without warning, triggering such histrionics? Am I a shallow vessel that only he can fill? And witness the mess when filled over capacity, spilling across the counter, dripping onto the floor. Regard the chaos after the final scene.

The intercom buzzes; it's Itchy, christened Catherine Leigh Coleman. We were raised in Buckhead, a swishy suburb in uptown Atlanta—*born with a silver spoon*. Literally. We each inherited a set of Wallace sterling, the Grand Baroque pattern, from our grandmothers, who were also best friends.

I could continue crying on her shoulder, but she's ready to drown in my suffering; time to dry my tears and switch channels. We made a pact: She'll listen to me, commiserating, for three weeks then we'll stop the pity party and return to Boot Camp, our health club's bi-weekly workout guaranteed to cure what ails, as long as you can survive the adrenaline-charged instructor, her infernal push-ups and whistle. Itchy's sensitive best-friend wisdom also means she'll never say *I told you to take things slow* but *I haven't a clue as to what got into that man; Cooper adored you. Aside from Phil, men can be so heartless.*

But Cooper's not heartless, and I linked my heart to his with abandon, even changing my Facebook status to *In a relationship* before he changed his. But was I too intense? Should I have been more cautious, measuring out love by the teaspoon? Perhaps I shouldn't have dismissed that silly bestseller that defined how to bag a man by playing it cool. But under-the-sheets tactical planning is dishonest and could only lead to a bad outcome. Besides, Cooper said game-playing was a deal-breaker.

And it was more than his sincerity that trapped me in a snare; I've never before witnessed a more alluring arrangement of attributes on a man. With his killer smile and glossy black hair, Cooper smells of cedar and fresh-cut lemons. Green-eyed, cardigan-clad, Irish-witted Cooper is as irresistible to me as plump seared scallops on a bed of truffle risotto, washed down with a Burgundian Chardonnay. Gentle, understated, smoldering and hot—testosterone in a teacup—he is one beauty of a man.

The love of my life has left without explanation. He wounded me, he is destroying me, and I'm supposed to shore up and paint on a smile? Fine. Let her see I'm still grieving. I buzz her in, open the door, and the essence of Itchy wafts through my misery on cue to perform.

"Precious Mallory, lov-e-ly-li-cious lady," she purrs in her refined drawl of elongated, exaggerated vowels. "Happy New Year. You holding up there, girlfriend?" After placing her bag atop my platter on the entry hall table, she envelops me in a tight, muscular embrace then rests her hands on my shoulders, shaking them. Concern is reflected in her gaze, and I blink back the tears steaming behind my eyes.

"Your three-week hiatus is up, hon. Stand up straight, it'll take off five years." She pulls up my arm, and then drops it as if I were a rag doll. "God, girl, you're skinnier than a string bean; skinnier than *haricot verts*. Those are the skinniest green beans in *your* language, right? Don't you ever eat any of those divine dishes you create?"

I dab my eyes with an apron tie. "I've been on the Twenty-One-Day-Break-Up Diet—a weight loss program you'll never have to enlist."

Itchy and Phil dated while attending Georgia Tech, married the week after graduation, and have twelve-year-old twin daughters. Phil's a class-act gentleman—a nurturing, kind person. A mortgage broker, he's been hammered by the economy, is hanging on to his job by a thread, and takes night classes with plans to switch careers and become a certified financial planner. Like so many of us, Phil and Itchy lost most of their savings in last year's Georgia Finance fiasco, but if he had only five dollars and I needed four, that man would give them to me without a blink.

At first glance, Itchy appears a vertical line, confident and poised. In truth, she's an exclamation point, words spoken in underlines and italics. Never a dull guest, she enlivens every social gathering; weaving narrative, she captivates, casting spells, while examining, then heralding, some minutia of her element. Out of my mouth these insights would sound pedantic; out of her lips, plumped from a life of decadence, brilliant. Itchy needs four to my eight hours of sleep, and still has a restless energy that inspired her moniker as a child.

Mallie, *precious little angel*, never stuck on me, the nickname soon rubbed to a dull patina, incongruous on such a serious child. Mallory suits me and I wear the name proudly, as I wear the thin straight nose that I also inherited from my grandfather on my mother's side.

I dramatize and muse—an off-balance question mark, that would be me. My auburn hair, trimmed four inches below my shoulders, is streaked with gold and hangs, as do folds of heavy drapery. I wear it pulled back on each side, cinched with a clip in back. My bangs are side-swept and fall just above my eyes, amber-colored and flecked with brown; eyes Cooper said reminded him of two shot glasses of Johnny Walker Red, side by side, just begging to be drunk.

Since he left, my wardrobe—a once-vibrant array of dresses, jeans, shirts and shawls in a tapestry of autumn foliage—now reminds me of decayed leaves swept into the gutter. My copper bracelets and necklaces suit my coloring, but have impaled a slight green cast to my wrist and neckline. It's said that copper draws impurities from the blood, but these days ornamentation is a bother. Itchy disapproves of my discolored fair skin.

Her signature is the collection of pearls she wears, roped around her neck and dotting her earlobes. She rotates among inherited antiques, Tiffany and freshwater pearls she purchased at a pearl market in China when luxurious vacations were no big deal.

Working outside the home was never on Itchy's radar, and she amused herself with family, social events and volunteering in various Junior League projects. After the financial fall-out, she acknowledged another paycheck was necessary to help rebuild the family nest egg. *Just a hiccup*, she'd said, while mining job sites that would suit her disposition. The search halted after discovering the job listing for an assistant wine buyer at Grasso's, even though until that moment, she hadn't the slightest interest in expanding her vinological horizon beyond a daily fix of whatever-you're-pouring Chardonnay.

Grasso's, a family-owned grocery chain of six stores in the Atlanta metropolitan area, recently began the transformation to appeal to the city's moneyed gentry. Throwing in the towel to discount, big-box warehouse groceries, the Grasso's board of directors believed the only chance they had of surviving the cut-throat grocery industry would be to differentiate from cookie-cutter chains by calculating, rebranding and marketing to those left clutching a buck.

First to vanish were the red-and-white checked Grasso's Groceries signs. All were refaced in antiqued bronze slate, the cursive script of *Grasso's Fresh Market* subtly lit in a muted shade of olive green.

The produce, meat and deli departments were thence remodeled to suggest a Tuscan country kitchen, a nod to the Grasso's family lineage. Salamis and prosciutto now hang from ropes affixed to open-beamed rafters, and dangle above customers weaving their carts around wheels of Parmigiano-Reggiano—aged, certified and stamped—rich, nutty, crystalline crumbles perched atop for grazing.

Towering pyramids of the South's beloved Duke Mayonnaise and Krispy Kreme Donuts were reassigned to bottom shelving, replaced with oversized wicker baskets piled high with glistening produce, placards boasting this family-owned market offers vegetables as fresh as any Georgia farm side stand. Pâtés replace pickle loaves in gold-rimmed deli cases, swiped with Windex on the hour to squeak and shine. Gooey macaroni salads were banished making room for dishes such as Pappardelle in Basil Sauce and Stuffed Veal Bundles, alongside splashy arrangements of grilled baby vegetables.

Well-stocked, lavish wine departments are *de rigueur*. The company owner and president, Anthony Grasso, demanded his wine sets reflect his self-proclaimed sophistication, indeed, his keen interest in any luxurious hobby new money can afford.

Though Itchy knew little about wine when she applied for the job, she did inherit the patrician, polished air of aristocracy. *To the manor born*, as my mother described her. She also majored in French and can pronounce the label on a *Chateau Haut Brion*, a first-growth Bordeaux, without provoking a wince. Itchy embodies the sleek blonde class appeal that Grasso's, a family of short, dark, shadow-eyed Italians, is betting their marketing dollar will keep their chain afloat. Anthony Grasso himself hired her on the spot.

Her new job personifies her refined tastes, yet her custom-fitted suits hint of wantonness as she navigates through aisles of wine, taking inventory and learning the trade. I liken her to a well-tuned concert piano before opening night; or a sumptuous wine, uncorked, breathing after years of containment. Reinvented, racy and rare: that's Itchy.

I watch her, transfixed, almost forgetting my wretchedness as she rhapsodizes over the crushed strawberry and silky tannin of a 2001 Barola she recently imported with plans for us to share. She becomes quiet, gives me a long look, and then reaches for her handbag.

"Here's a late Christmas present." She digs into her purse. "The twins made you a hair clip from shells they found on Sea Island."

I reach for the piece and admire the girls' handiwork of sand, tiny shells and silver beads affixed to a barrette.

"You don't know how lucky you are," I murmur, throat tight, touched by the gift.

"And you have no idea how difficult it all can be." She presses her palm against her chest and sighs, closing her eyes.

I wish I did know. I've always dreamed I'd have two or three kids by now. After all, I'm thirty-eight. I think of the twins and feel a surge of tenderness, as if they were my own. I'm their godmother and have been a part of their lives since they were infants. I purchased a baby carrier after they were born and Itchy and I would take walks and run errands together, each of us carrying a baby strapped to our belly. But these are Itchy's daughters, not mine.

Yet. Maybe there's a chance for Cooper and me. Perhaps I was over-eager, but so was he. The night before he left, he said that when we were apart, he couldn't quit thinking about me, and when we were together, the heat was explosive. Our relationship was tight; we'd been discussing marriage and children. What went wrong? Must I become the type of woman who calculates, strategizing plans to entice his return?

"Here's another gift to cheer you forward. And Mallory, you will move forward even if I have to shove you myself." She hands me a small box that contains two strands of copper-colored freshwater pearls connected to sterling silver loops. "It's your color but won't tarnish your skin."

God, I love this woman; how would I cope if Itchy—the woman who shared my playpen, the woman woven into the fiber of my being—wasn't in my life? I grab her shoulders and plant a fierce kiss on each cheek. She pulls me into her arms with a laugh, patting me on the back.

"You'll be back to the old Mallory in no time." She pushes away with a grin. "See? You're smiling already." Hanging her bag over her shoulder, she opens the door. "Gotta scoot. We'll toast the new year at midnight."

We link pinky fingers—our ritual since grade school—then she swoops into a curtsy, closes the door, and a dust ball spirals through the air as an orbiting planet then vanishes in search of her galaxy.

I fasten the pearls around my neck. The gift reminds me of a poem by Emily Dickinson. I grab the pad: *Her breast is fit for pearls.* Pearls symbolize purity, love and commitment; longing tugs at my heart. The Gospel of Matthew: *Don't cast your pearls before swine.* Checkmate.

Scribbling the notes, my hand quivers and a bead of sweat trickles down my neck. Where to stick them? I'm out of refrigerator space; I'll move on to the cabinets. Breath unsteady, I lean into the counter, pressing my palms together in an attitude of prayer. *Why did you leave me, Cooper, why?* Goodbye is the saddest word I know.

I glance at the time: three o'clock. The deadline for my article, recipe, and photo is in two hours. A cloud hovers over the sun, casting a shadow, and the light falls flat, perfect for a photograph. Survival instincts kick in; get a grip, girl, and *focus.* Trading pen for bowl, I whisk the vinegar into the oil then stir the peas, peppers and tomatoes into the vinaigrette. After spooning the salad onto the serving platter, I place the dish on the butcher block, press the viewfinder to my eye, release the shutter—bracket the F-stop—shoot again then turn my mind to my readers.

A diverse citizenry populates Georgia, and the circulation of the *Sun* extends from the eclectic diversity of Atlanta to the far reaches of the rural south, the very soul of Southern culinary tradition borne of this farmland. My writing must reflect the varied tastes of the paper's readership, which is challenging. Just an hour's drive from my loft, it feels as if I've traveled decades back in time, the pace grinding to a screeching stillness.

People appear boxed into small, closed landscapes of sagging roofs and crooked mailboxes, living in towns prone to trouble. Pinched faces and slow eyes follow me from porches as if I were a polecat then dip to the ground if I meet their gaze. But, as in Atlanta, the food they enjoy embraces their culture like kernels of corn embedded into cornbread. I vary the tone of my articles to keep everyone amused.

The Sun has been testing a new digital format, with plans to go live tomorrow, New Year's Day. If the site meets corporate expectations, it will operate in tandem with the *Sun's* print edition. Last week the paper published my recipe for Hoppin' John; a dish country, as well as city, people would enjoy. My editor requested I repost the same recipe and anecdote today, with photograph, online. Sitting at the stool, tucking my knees under the cool granite counter, I open my laptop and fingers fashion words, following thoughts as they glide across the keyboard. *Happy New Year! Here's wishing you a heaping pot of....*

Hoppin' John

by

Mallory Lakes

Happy New Year! Here's wishing you a heaping pot of good luck, prosperity and happiness in 2011.

I hedge the prosperity odds by eating a dish of Hoppin' John, a rice and pea dish typically served in the South on New Year's Day. After the Revolutionary War, rice and peas were companion crops harvested on the coastal paddies of Georgia and the Carolinas. It's said this old plantation classic got its name from the way children hopped around waiting for it to cook. Earliest memory recalls my tiny fingers plucking out the peas and avoiding the peppers. "Peas for pennies," my father would laugh, handing me a real penny to drive home his point.

Not only do I insist my family eat at least one bite of this regional specialty, I also hand-deliver a Tupperware container of the seasoned peas, festooned with a ribbon, to my neighbors.

There is an art to cooking dried beans, and the main ingredient is time. Not active time on the cook's part, but time nevertheless. Time to soak, time to cook, and time to allow the beans to sit in their cooking liquid absorbing all of those savory flavors. In past years, I've saved time by substituting frozen peas for dried, but this year, time is on my side.

On New Year's Day, I double my chance for fortune by serving Hoppin' John with a side of turnip greens or collards, the greens said to symbolize dollar bills. Imagine that--a recipe to change your reality. Shop early; there's sure to be a run on peas and greens this year at neighborhood markets, especially in this economy.

Make a double batch so you have leftover Hoppin' John, which is referred to as "Skippin' Jenny." Eating leftover beans demonstrates frugality to the good-luck gods, reassuring them you are sincere and deserving of prosperity.

Part 1 | Chapter 1

Shelby

Mama's made a New Year's Resolution. She's decided to open a so-called beauty shop, do hair in the cellar, and is broadcasting her plan to everyone in Coryville; at least anyone polite enough to listen.

A couple of days back, she caught a ride with Lester—one of the skinny-boned, slick-haired pack—to Atlanta's recycle center. While looking for a back screen door, her eyes lit on two chairs with attached drying hoods that you plug into the wall. The tangerine-colored vinyl was ripped at the armrests, but Mama said she'd fix that with duct tape. When she saw those chairs, old dreams must have choked up, like the feeling she had imagining all of those babies—sisters and brothers for me—she said she wanted and would have loved. Maybe she thought a magician placed the chairs there with a note: *It's not too late, Noreen.*

She spent the money we'd put aside to replace the broken door on the chairs, and even borrowed extra from Lester, who had to attach a hitch and trailer onto the back of his Zeplen sedan to haul them home. With a super-charged V8 engine and only a couple of dings on the fender, two-toned tan and beige, that car's the pride of his life. As they pull into the driveway and step out of the car, Miss Ann and I walk outside to watch the circus.

"You and Miss Ann will have to be extra careful opening that door now," Mama says.

We gape at the chairs. Our splintered, warped door is hanging on a broken hinge. These chairs should have been a door.

"Lester, could you get the dolly and wheel them into the garage?"

I don't know why Lester can't keep them at his house. His front yard and garage are graveyards of broke-down cars, split in half and welded into something else. These ugly chairs won't make any difference to him. Now they'll be hovering in our garage, like those hump-backed dinosaurs in Miss Ann's schoolbook, till Mama fixes up the cellar.

Mama has three Coryville lady friends with bone straight hair, whose parts show thick white roots like stripes down a skunk's back. They told her they'd love affordable services, and Mama is revved to deliver. Last night she dusted off her beauty school license, and chose a frame large enough to cover the 1992 expiration date.

I should be happy for her, a dream keeps one foot following the other, whittling away at everyday miseries. I know; I have my own dream: to make a decent life for my daughter and me by escaping this town, moving to Atlanta, and becoming a chef. Grasso's, a fancy grocery store in the city, just posted a listing for deli cooks in the Classifieds, and I'm dying to apply. Benefits include a tuition program that would reimburse me for classes towards earning my associate's degree from chef school—as long as I work for them full time.

The commute from Coryville to Atlanta is three hours each way so if I get the job, there's no way around it, I'd have to find a rental. But what about Miss Ann? I can't leave her behind, but how will I care for her while working in the city? She's also blind in one eye and has a prosthetic fitted in the socket, which needs regular cleaning and attention. I regard her cherub face, arms flapping like a bird testing out new wings. Touching her cheek, a sour taste of helplessness fills my throat as my gaze slides to Mama.

"You are living in the past. Blow dryers and flat irons are what Atlanta salons use these days. No one sticks their heads under those hoods anymore." I especially dislike her calling the cellar a beauty shop. "And no one calls them beauty shops. They're *salons*."

"How 'bout we change the word salon to saloon," Lester jokes, trying to keep the peace, rightly sensing I'm spoiling for a fight. "We'll call it *Noreen's Saloon*. I'd go there for sure."

I glare at him.

"Now don't get lippy with me, Shelby." Ruddy brown splotches bloom on her face and her neck bones flare, high and rigid, like they do every time she starts to unravel. "Before you were born my career was in *beauty*, I have a beauty school license, and I-"

"No one goes to beauty school anymore," I interrupt, nipping at her ignorance, stomping over her words. "They go to *cosmetology* school. You take a full class load an entire year then must pass extremely difficult tests, including one on hair correction chemistry. Sandra graduated from the Altrua Academy in Atlanta and was trained in styling, cutting, color and repairs, plus nails and makeup. But *most* important, she's *young*."

I crossed the line with that last word; heat prickles my face.

Mama points a razor-sharp fingernail at my face. "I ain't *that* old, Shelby. Sandra may be some city-slick, hotsy-totsy, but she don't have no family to look after." She eyes me as if I'm snitching a ten-dollar bill from her wallet then smiles sweetly at Miss Ann. "Most folks I know appreciate a twelve-dollar cut, or twenty-dollar color and curl. Not everyone can afford to go to some swishy Atlanta *salon*." She pronounces the word—*say-lon*—, thinking she sounds French. Placing her hand on her hip, she rolls her eyes, now brimming with tears, and her thrust chin quivers as she turns her head from me. I've hurt her feelings and regret my words. Strange this thing called family; even the love tugging our hearts can't keep us from picking on each other. Her dream was to have her own shop before I was born.

Mama blew it when she had me. She'd just received her certificate from The Georgia School of Beauty when she found out she was having a baby, and before she showed, she got a job washing hair before color treatments in downtown Coryville. But she had trouble adapting to pregnant life, and the combination of morning sickness and hair dye, which smells like rotten eggs, made her run to the toilet, heaving, moments after she arrived at the shop. That didn't go over well with her boss; her job lasted a month.

It didn't go over well with my daddy either, and he left Mama three months before I was born. He did leave her this home, which he inherited after his folks died. It may be some tinned-roof stick house—satellite dish and mesh catfish traps littering the side yard—but it's got three square bedrooms, a den, separate kitchen, and is paid off in full. We haven't heard from my daddy since. Mama gets by with cleaning jobs and as a weekend nursing assistant at Centerline Eldercare.

She met Sam Cox several years back. He worried two women raising a child alone in the backwoods of Georgia smelled like trouble so he put bolts on our doors, made us feel safe. After a spell, Mama let him move in. First thing he did was make a sign. Using stencils and red paint, he wrote, WE DON'T CALL 911, on a two-foot piece of plywood then he spent the better part of a week carving a revolver beneath the words. This sign is our warning: If you break into our house, get anywhere near my daughter, we'd have no choice but to shoot you. Coryville law enforcement's been cut to bare bones, and these days we must fend for ourselves. I centered the sign, holding it in place, as he hammered it into the front door.

After Sam, my opinion about men shifted; maybe they weren't a pack of rabid dogs. I must have picked from a bad litter. The house yawned empty after he died. I've always wondered what happened to Daddy, never even met him. Just as well. Mama said he was selfish and unkind. I've no feelings about that man one way or the other. I'm just grateful the divorce wasn't finalized until after I was born. In those days I'd have been branded *bastard* and *illegitimate* if Mama was single—damning words you don't hear spoken today.

I never tied the knot with Buck, Miss Ann's father; not that he asked. Nowadays a single girl getting pregnant with an accidental baby is no big deal; at least not until after the baby's born.

Buck's the only man I've ever been with in the physical sense, and he told me not to worry, said he knew how far was too far, and he wouldn't go there. I wasn't even certain I was pregnant until the third month; I dropped out of school in my fifth, as soon as I showed. Buck refused to visit after her birth, said a half-blind baby disgusted him, said she was cursed, said he was washing his hands of the both of us. That stings my heart because the blue sky in his eyes—a winter sky, pale to almost silver—is the same blue sky in hers, at least the working one.

Miss Ann carries my last name but I made bloody well sure Buck's legal name was written under *Full Name of Father* on the birth certificate so there'd be no trouble collecting child support. Monthly checks are garnished from his army pay and the military pays our insurance. Money's all I want from him now. Back then, though, he was the only boy that made my stomach churn. It was his smell, like cinnamon and new fallen leaves; I felt dizzy when we touched.

I sensed he was a mean seed threatening to grow, but he was one good-looking son-of-a-gun, and could sweet talk a rose into blooming. Said I was prettier than a rose, said he loved me. Not having a daddy, I craved to hear a man say those words. I mistook the sex for love, but what I really learned of love, the love's that's as clear as the head of a creek, I learned from Mama and Miss Ann. Men are a long upstream to paddle.

Mama made up for Buck being gone. She held my baby tight in her arms, loving her up, protecting her against all the suffering she'd see soon enough with her good eye. It was her idea to name her Miss Ann, though we didn't write "Miss" on the birthing papers. "Miss" makes her special, lady-like. We wrapped and cradled her in a soft cotton blanket, which matched her eye, and stroked those sweet precious fingers, those tiny little nails. Cooing like doves, we inhaled her new baby scent, touching our lips upon her corn silk hair.

The first year of her life we developed a rhythm, my baby and me, bonding to each other and forming a shield, warding off the crazy the world deals in spades. Hearing her lusty wails, my breasts tingled as the milk fell, soaking my bra. Nothing could get in the way of my cuddling her, having her lips latch onto my breast, and as she suckled I felt a glow, something sacred, pulsing through my body. Watching her grow plump through the months, I thought, *I did that. Me. Alone. No one else in the world could nourish her so well.* Such a wonder, nursing my baby; satisfying both of our hungers. She will always beat the rhythm of my breath. I would slay dragons for my child.

After she was weaned, insurance covered an artificial eye, the size of a marble, matching her real eye to a tee. Every couple of years, she gets a new, larger one, which sits in the socket—still and staring—but besides that, you can hardly tell it's fake. Problem is it's irritating and she'd rather not wear it, so her blindness rests crimson with a silken sheen; a fire truck's wail of calamity, a red bird's cry of love.

I look at Mama, now climbed onto the trailer, and cringe as she sits giggling in one of those tacky orange chairs; you'd think it was her throne. She lights a cig and cocks her wrist to the side, like she's waving to a crowd. I close my eyes, shaking my head. Who does she think she is—Kate Middleton fixing to marry the prince? But her happiness comforts me; this is the first time she's laughed since Sam died. I open my eyes and relax my brows, working up an apologetic expression to replace my scowl.

"I'm sorry, Mama. I'm not sure where those mean words came from. I know your beauty shop will be a huge success, and I'm happy for you, truly I am. I'm just worn to a frazzle and need to get to The Pig to buy fixings for supper." I blow her a kiss and try to smile, but my mouth feels as heavy as a crusted-over cake refusing to rise. Miss Ann and I walk into the house, careful not to jostle the dangling back door. Miss Ann flicks on the TV while I thumb through the *Atlanta Sun*, looking for Mallory Lake's recipe for chicken tenders. I find it and tear it out.

I would never abandon my daughter like my daddy and boyfriend did me, but my ambitions would surely lead to better opportunities than tight perms. Mama's forty-four, and when I look at her face, splintered lines spreading into copper freckles, I'm reminded of our cracked, stained vegetable platter. She should help *me* with *my* dreams. Maybe she could take care of Miss Ann here in Coryville until I'm situated in Atlanta; it would only be for a short while. It's too late for her. I just turned twenty-four, and it's not too late for me.

I'd make enough money to give Miss Ann opportunities no one in this family has ever even dreamed. On my days off, I'd fetch her and bring her back to the city for the weekend, when she doesn't have school, and guide her, proudly, through the Atlanta Children's Museum. We'd stop at the dinosaur exhibit, and I'd stoop to her level, pointing to the bones, explaining dinosaurs, like chickens, are hatched from eggs. Folks passing by would look at us, notice my arm around her tiny shoulders, and admire how I educated my child. It would give me satisfaction knowing they thought I was a good mother. I'd clip a ribbon into her butter blonde hair, waves combed straight and parted on the side—they'd surely notice the comb tracks. Her socks would be starched white, folded down, and I'd press them to her ankles with a warm rag so they wouldn't droop.

People say I'm pretty, as lovely as my daddy was handsome, although I'll never know since Mama burned every picture of the man. Daddy's grandfather was native American, a descendant from the original Creek nation, and the tribal's distinct in my features. My complexion is smooth and tawny, and my long jet hair is thick, straight and shiny. I have wide-set russet eyes, gold and beige—eyes like the wings on a sparrow. My lean strong legs could carry me far, if only circumstances would allow. Although it's said I'm the spitting image of my father, praise Jesus I have Mama's kind soul and not his black heart.

Miss Ann turns from the TV. The soft down on her curved cheek is streaked with rust clay soil. Her prosthetic rests still, while her good eye works around my face, as if she's wondering what I am thinking. I'm thinking I love you, little red-dirt girl; I'm thinking I love you to pieces. I drop the recipe, wipe the dust from her face, and cuddle her in my arms, nuzzling into the cotton candy stick and sweet of her neck.

Mama says even the sparkliest jewel is tarnished in the face of goodness; that a loving heart is what makes you rich. But if that is so, tell me how a loving heart will provide a decent education for my daughter. From quarters found under the cushions of our threadbare sofa? If that is so, how come my heart—bursting with goodness and love for my child—breaks when I watch her scratching at dirt where a green grass lawn should be growing?

One day I'll be a chef; it's our only way out. I'll be an example for Miss Ann proving to her that when you set your mind to do something, to be something, you can make that something happen. I'll buy us a house with shuttered windows and put a swing set out back. She could even go to college. What mother wouldn't want the best for her child?

I kiss her forehead, warm and pale as ivory candle wax, above blonde wisps of eyebrows, then stand and get the keys. Walking to the car, I take another look at the recipe. Before I had my baby, each night I'd fall asleep while watching Food Broadcast TV. I dreamed of food—not everyday food—but perfect food, magical food, gussied-up food I've never before tasted, all arranged on granite counters. I'd be standing in front of a eight-burner gas range, juggling pots, pans, spatulas and whisks glittering beneath the hum of recessed lighting, only to wake up in my reality of roach traps, kinked electric cords and bare bulbs screwed into ceilings.

These days the channel is set to Disney, and I only have time to read Mallory Lake's columns. Her writing amuses me, and when I make dinner from her recipes, I'm happy, forgetting my dead-end life. But I wish she wouldn't use so many hard-to-find ingredients. The Pig doesn't carry *panko*, those foreign breadcrumbs, so I'll have to use the American kind. I've got a crock of bacon fat so I'll switch out her oil with that, and I'll use ketchup for the dipping sauce. At least I have a spice bottle half full of rosemary. Mama thought I ruined a dish the first time I used it, but now she says she enjoys the flavor.

Walking to the car, I watch Lester wheeling the chairs into the garage. He's not as funny as Sam, likes his liquor, and wears his pants cinched high above his navel, but he treats Mama with respect. Most important, he adores her, and Lord knows she's not right without love from a man. I'd best make peace.

"Hey, Lester, I'm making chicken tenders from the paper." I wave the recipe above my head. "I bet they'll taste better than the ones you bring over from McDonald's—even KFC. How 'bout staying for supper?"

Crispy Rosemary Chicken Breast Tenders
by
Mallory Lakes

I confess. I've stolen food from the mouths of hungry babes. Fried chicken tenders are the temptation and here is how I operate. When the child is not looking, perhaps laughing at a clown or a puppet on a string, I eye their little grease-stained bag and snatch one, stuffing it into my mouth. I can't help myself.

Generally the child is none the wiser. Occasionally I've been caught and their wail of dismay is embarrassing. I suppose I could go through a drive-through and buy my own bag of tenders, but I tell myself I don't eat fast food; I'm a made-from-scratch kind of woman. When I've confessed my story to others, they nod guiltily, bowing their heads in shame. It's a consolation knowing I'm not the only chicken-tender thief in town.

Perhaps you are a French-fry snatcher. If so, your crime is no less heinous, even if there are more fries in a bag to pass around.

I've developed a grown-up version of chicken tenders to sate my appetite, far superior to the fast-food type that has up until now been my unsavory downfall. Children can once again feel safe to pass me by, clutching their little bag of tenders without fear of hijack..

CHAPTER 2

Mallory

I slide into the chair behind my desk in the newsroom; it's nine o'clock sharp. Swallowing a couple of Excedrin with my third cup of scalding coffee, I burn my tongue. That bottle of wine shared last night with a pal from work has rendered me cotton-mouthed and nauseous. Correction. Tommy wasn't drinking wine; bourbon was his choice of poison. No matter. I remember his anger, unleashed in the ritual of lighting a smoke.

I was a few minutes' late to our favorite watering hole and dragged a stool next to his at the bar. He nodded at me while smacking a pack of Reds, topside down, into his palm.

Wiry yet broad in the shoulders, Tommy's had his share of women combing their fingers through his sandy blond hair, but not a one had what it takes to corral him. Unkempt with a three-day stubble, he has a streak of indifference to keep a girl interested, and is roguishly sexy, as if he'd just walked away from a fight. I sat silently as he removed the plastic wrapper, peeled off the top layer of foil, and rolled it into a ball. Then he flicked it down the length of the bar's wooden counter as if he were kicking a football across a playing field. His teeth, bared like a ferret's, wiggled a cig from the pack and it dangled between his lips, blue flames darting about the tip of tobacco as he clicked the lighter, inhaling in short bursts.

Leaning his face into mine, Tommy's words smelled of whiskey and nicotine, rasping as the soothsayer predicting the downfall of Caesar: *Beware the Ides of March.* His chest swelled as he took another drag, exhaled one perfect ring, and then swiveled to face me. His eyes, flashing gunmetal silver, bore into mine. *My message, Mallory, bears repeating: Beware the Ides of March.* I flinched at the crack of ice hitting glass as he tossed back a slug of bourbon.

Pursing his lips around the filter, he inhaled, brows drawn, with the intensity of a child sucking milkshake through a straw. Holding the smoke in his chest, he sputtered, *The Sun...will then...be history,* his words spat in a fit of coughing, a plume of smoke. Shivering, I clasped my forearms together thinking of Caesar's fate, relating it to my own.

The Sun is folding, he'd growled—*in debt and out of cash*—and I sat sickened, listening to his hoarse, dry voice, downing my wine. Losing Cooper and my job within a span of six weeks. Bad news comes in threes. What next has life up her sleeve? He continued to explain the plans were to reopen under a new media product, the digital news site we've been testing; a one hundred percent about-face from pulp to screen. As he spoke those words— smoking hisses from the corners of his mouth—I felt some relief that my job might still exist, yet bummed a Red, reigniting my unsavory habit.

He said the Human Resource director, Cindy Pritchard, met with him last week and informed him they would be making...*significant changes to the culture.* For starters, the historic limestone and granite headquarters of the *Sun* had been put up for sale, with plans to set up shop in a pared-down location on Peachtree Street. After the *Sun's* parent company dismantles the paper, all employees will be *dismissed, displaced, detonated,* and a much smaller staff will generate the site's content.

Slouching into the bar, he leaned his mouth towards my ear then lowered his voice to a whisper: *Some of us may be invited to reapply at the new company, AtlantaNow. But we'd have to accept a pay cut and re-invent our jobs to sync with new media and social marketing structures.* His breath felt hot inside my ear as I sat stunned, speechless, tobacco burning between my knuckles.

Then he quietened, straightened, and rolled his head back. Mouth agape, he appraised the smoke clinging to the back wall, eyes sliding up and down, as if the billowing sponge of clouds were the Miss January centerfold.

I should have guessed that's what they've been orchestrating. Traditional newspapers, like the *Sun*, are folding faster than you can say *frantically wired world.* The steady drumbeat, that deafening march of the cyber-junkies, is stampeding traditional media, quickening its pace with every Google click. It's the Internet, the seductive temptress of shortened attention spans, that holds the bait. Light on her feet, she thrives, voracious, feasting on change. How can the tedium of newsprint possibly compete with the nimble goddess?

I told Tommy he was lucky. He was the *Sun's* most fearless, articulate crime-beat writer. His job was safe. Crime scoops, the grislier the better, drive readership. The woman who writes about *Grilled Pizza with Caramelized Onions* is not a valued commodity. He didn't reply, only raised his brows at me, eyes hard-boiled and clear, then stubbed out his cigarette.

Leaving the bar around eleven, I took a cab back to my loft, staggered up the stairs, then stumbled into bed. I drank copious amounts of water hoping to dilute the alcohol, but the additional fluid kept me awake peeing through the night.

Tommy hasn't showed his face in the office today; I wish I'd called in sick. I tap the calendar icon on my screen. Holy crap. Human Resources scheduled a meeting with me this afternoon. Only a half-day warning? Jerks. My fingers hit the keyboard, beseeching the Google gods to help me draft a plan that might save my job.

Three o'clock finds me standing outside a closed door. I knock and Cindy opens it then ushers me in. She closes the door and offers me a seat, facing her, at her behemoth, mahogany desk. A photograph of Cindy and her husband on their wedding day is placed, at a right angle, facing me. Her wedding dress appears cheap, too much stiff lace; it looks as if paper doilies were supporting her head.

I notice a box of tissues, next to the picture, close to my side. Here we go. I'm known as the newsroom drama queen; she's expecting histrionics. My armpits moisten and bowels cramp; trapped animal fear must radiate through my pores. She introduces me to Richard Wright, the content editor, recently hired from the outside to navigate the new media dot com through the choppy waters ahead. He sits in a corner chair behind Cindy's desk, gives a half-smile nod then lowers his gaze to the electronic tablet resting in his lap.

"Water?" she offers.

"Sure. Thanks."

She opens a bottle and slides it over the desk. "Been cooking up some tasty treats?"

"I keep my knives sharpened." Hands trembling, I pick at a cuticle. That sounded arrogant, not like myself. I *must* settle down.

"You may already know the plans for the *Atlanta Sun*. Hopefully the rumor mill has not distorted them out of proportion."

You're selling a one hundred and seventy-year-old building, dismantling the iconic *Atlanta Sun*, firing the staff, and now talking portion controls. Keeping these thoughts to myself, I smile. "Yes. I've heard. *AtlantaNow?*"

She clears her throat and nods at me, expectant, giving me an opportunity to elucidate. I ravage my brain trying to remember the speech I'd prepared. Nothing.

She regards her lacquered manicured nails, drumming them in that annoying rat-a-tat-tat habit of hers, tap-tap-tapping nails into coffins. She looks up, and then offers a square smile. Crimson lipstick is smeared on a front tooth.

"Plans *are* to include *Food and Beverage* on the site. We're currently brainstorming a unique posture that will distinguish *AtlantaNow* from the masses of other food sites. Any thoughts?"

Hallelujah, they're keeping food is my first thought. The moment is now. What I say next, if words come, will determine my fate. *Steady girl. In through the nose*—I summon the gods of articulation—*out with a sigh*. My shoulders relax, fists unclench, jaw releases and words bubble to the surface.

"The problem with food sections in papers or magazines is they can't directly ask the audience what they *want* to read about and eat." My voice emerges choked, warbled. I take two sips of water, uncross my legs, cross my ankles and straighten my back. I take a third sip, swallowing hard.

"Traditional media doesn't understand how to entertain the audience or position food trends into consumers' busy lives. It operates in a vacuum." I look at Cindy, who nods her head. Emboldened, I clear my throat.

"By taking our media digital, we can foster ongoing conversations through comment sections and chat rooms with our readership. These days the audience is in charge, and they want us to listen."

I raise my brows, risking a peek at Richard. Head down, he taps on his pad.

"Actually, they've always been in charge in their decision to renew subscriptions or not, but now they have an active voice. *AtlantaNow* will not only be in the information business, but it will be in the business of creating an online, interactive community. Anytime you read or listen to the news, it's depressing; the world's a dismal place. My readers see my articles as an escape, an escape with food, something that is readily accessible to them. Reading my stories and recipes, even if they don't have time to cook, may be a beacon of light they can't find elsewhere."

Richard's eyes meet mine; his turn.

"Do you, Mallory, have any novel ideas for taking this insight to the next level? How would you ensure *your* work would help create a community that would generate the traffic required to satisfy financial realities?"

"If *AtlantaNow* gives me the opportunity, I could be your real-time food writer. I'd write a daily food blog, weekends and holidays included, about what I was eating." I glance at Cindy. "Of course I'd include the usual recipe and photo. Since my audience would be online, I'd upload YouTube, mini-cooking classes as a part of my recipe, showing the readership precisely how to julienne, for instance, that parsnip on the ingredient list."

Cindy's hands, for once, are still; Richard adjusts his glasses. Good. I have their attention.

"Grocery ads generated considerable revenue for the *Sun*. Can you imagine the instant coupon-click dollars they'd yield on a *Food & Beverage* site?" I cock an eyebrow indicating (faked) insider knowledge.

"I'd shop at different groceries across the city, particularly those that buy our ads, alerting the readers to seasonal goodies and exceptional offers, and incorporate them into my recipes. I assume there will be software to track the number and profile of visitors to my blog. I've several ideas on how to build a substantial fan base. For starters, I'd post mini recipe tweets on Twitter."

I'm yammering so clamp my mouth shut. The room is quiet, except for the dull tapping of Richard's fingers hitting the keypad and a clock ticking on Cindy's desk.

"Twitter-feeds?"

"Interesting," Richard says then stands, clearing his throat, tucking the pad under his arm. He wears a brown and black plaid shirt. I've never liked plaid shirts on men over thirty, especially short-sleeved like the one he's wearing.

"We'll get back with you."

I stand, shake their hands, and then retreat to the newsroom. A beetle scurries in front of my feet into a crack in the floor. Those bugs have been around since the dawn of civilization, they'll be here long after us humans have vanished. Collapsing into my chair, I rest my forehead on top of my desk and close my eyes. Effete metaphors are all that's left: Hit by a train. Hung out to dry. Rode hard and put away wet. The chorus of my life.

Sighing louder than intended, I open my eyes and clasp my forearms across a nauseous stomach; food would serve me well. Co-workers keep their distance, pecking at keyboards. A few furtive glances in my direction reflect concern that I'm the latest casualty. Managing a survivor's smile, then giving a perky thumbs up, I decide to get the hell out. I'll stop by Grasso's on the way home for dinner provisions. On Mondays, Itchy works late in the wine department and can suggest a *hair of the dog* Chardonnay.

Reaching for my satchel, a deep unsettlement, a sense of foreboding even surpassing this newsroom drama, shivers down my spine. What is this feeling? Agony over Cooper to compound my misery at work? It's something else, something more threatening. I try shaking off this feeling of doom, rationalizing I'm hung over, uptight, and the past several weeks have knocked me off kilter.

But my instincts are seldom wrong.

CHAPTER 3

Shelby

I gotta meet Miss Ann's school bus; it's dropping her off down the road in ten minutes. I mix the vegetables and cheese into the ground beef, like the recipe instructs, then spoon it into a loaf pan. Mallory Lake's recipe is different than my usual meat loaf because it has cheese in it. The Pig doesn't stock her recommended Farmhouse Cheddar, so I substituted Cracker Barrel Sharp, which is as good as it gets. I splurged on the cheese, but this dinner must be special.

Pressing the raw grinds into the corners of the pan, coolness squishes between my fingertips, calming my nerves. Cooking relaxes me; there's logic and order when following a recipe, untangling life's chaos. Scrubbing my nails to remove the meat bits, I wrap the loaf in Saran, shove it into the fridge, then shout down to Mama in the cellar.

"I'm going to meet Miss Ann. Making meat loaf for supper. There's enough for Lester, if he's here when it's ready." I preheat the oven then bolt out the door.

Mama's been cleaning out the cellar, cramming everything into double-strength bags day and night. There's more than thirty years of garbage down there so her job's cut out for her. Lester stops by most afternoons and hauls it to the dump; Old Crow whiskey bottles filled with rusty nails, Farrah Fawcett pin-ups from the eighties, supermarket tabloids picturing babies born with double heads or to eighty-year old hags.

Each time he brings up another bag, I think *white trash*: folks to break down, ball up then throw away. I've heard every *you know you're white trash* one-liner that's ever been written and understand that we are the living, breathing stereotype of a white trash family; as common as pig tracks, especially if you use our cellar as a yardstick.

But better white trash than taco jockey garbage. We may have to rub nickels together to pay for satellite TV, but at least we have it. Used to be most folks in this town unleashed their venom on blacks for stepping out of their so-called boundaries, but these days they seem to hate Mexicans worse, claiming they take all the jobs. But that makes no sense; they take employment no one else wants. Two years back, a poultry plant was built ten miles outside of town where many locals got work only to quit within a month. One neighbor's line job was folding forty chicken wings per minute. That's eighteen thousand, prickly, pointed parts a day. He complained his wrists and hands ached, the ammonia smell was nauseating, and the hours were unfair. The Mexican population in Coryville has skyrocketed since they built that chicken plant.

I haven't spoken with any Mexicans, except for the brief nod, the *how's it going* when you pass them on the street, but my heart is free from hate. Black, brown, beige or yellow, on the six o'clock news our miseries are the same. Well—that's a lie; no one's color-blind. My white skin has made life a lot easier for me in this town. Mama says Georgia's way of treating immigrants is mean-spirited—may as well spit on the flag for what America stands. Lester disagrees but keeps his mouth shut; it's not worth getting on her bad side.

Like everyone in Coryville, Mama's cheap looking, speaks as if she's ignorant, and doesn't have a clue. Sometimes I wish I didn't know better myself, but that's another lie. I was lucky to get a decent education, even if the most important thing it made me realize was that we live in the armpit of America; not to say Coryville smells like sweat, just the stale air of boredom.

But even with her bad grammar and redneck ways, Mama's graced with goodness, and raised me believing hate's what's messed up the world.

We don't need a Bible Trailer sermon to apostle that lesson, no snake-eyed preacher pressing our heads under water shouting *Heal!* Religions are just different paths leading up the same mountain and at the top, we're all God's children. As long as you *do unto others*, the Heavenly Kingdom is yours. I was hoping a black president would turn folks around, but all that's done is incite the racists.

Lester just drug up the last bag of trash so the next step will be to get the electricity and plumbing working in the cellar. He's good at that, won't bother with a permit. Has a buddy who'll help him install laminate paneling on the walls and pressure-treated flooring. Guess Mama's shop will be opening sooner than later. She's been mixing up perm solutions and begging me to let her experiment on my hair, but I draw the line; I'd look a sight with curly hair. I did let her trim my ends, and admit, they do lay even. I tell Mama now, more than ever, to lay off those cigs. Chain-smoke stench and sulfur-smelling hair fumes will kill us all.

I still haven't worked up the nerve to discuss my thoughts about interviewing at Grasso's, but tonight's fragrant meat loaf should set the stage. Lately, I've been helping Mama whenever I can, trying to get on her good side. Her feelings were hurt a solid week after the argument over her *beauty shop*, even though I apologized a dozen times and was surely sincere.

Life's unfair. She's old, but following through on her dream. I'm young, with my own dream, but my feet are stuck in muck and going nowhere. I never even made it through eleventh grade before I had a baby to tend. When I think I can't stay in this town a second longer, I wonder how on earth I could I ever leave my child. But it wouldn't be for long, and what chance does she—do both of us—have for a decent life if I stay and raise her here? My dreams won't go away.

I get to the bus stop just as Miss Ann comes barreling out the door. Once again, she's popped out her eye; does it to get noticed. A neighbor boy circles her, whooping, "One-eyed Ann from Cory-land" as giggling children cluster. I walk towards her, frowning, narrowing my eyes at my tow-headed, prancing child. Miss Ann smiles, not noticing me, loving the attention, mistaking disgust for popularity.

"Why do you do that, honey? This isn't your pretty self." She quietens and her smile disappears. I shouldn't have said that; she needs to know I love her the way she was born. I try another tactic. "If you lose that eye, insurance won't cover a new one until second grade."

She throws back her head, casual-like, and returns the eye to her socket. She'd hate losing her one claim to fame. The kids yelp like hyenas and her smile returns. Pain swells between my eyes. Sweet Jesus, don't let her hurt when she discovers the meanness in people.

We walk home, kicking at pinecones, dead leaves crunching under our feet. Squatting down, she examines a tiny puff of yellow feathers hopping beside the road.

"Mama, look. A baby goldfinch."

"What a smart girl you are; you've been studying your picture book." I stoop to examine the fledgling. "I believe this is a pine warbler, but with its cute little beak and sunshine feathers, it does look like a goldfinch."

"Where's the mama bird?"

"Gathering seeds from the cones to feed her child. She'll return as soon as we leave."

"You sure? What if a cat comes? We'd better put it in the tree."

"Then the mama won't be able to find her baby."

"But what if she forgets?"

I crane my neck to the top of the pine tree to a tangle of needles and boughs and the sound of a high-hissing *seeeet*.

"Ssssh. Listen." I press my forefinger to my lips, giving her a solemn nod. "That's the mama bird. She's straightening up her nest and warning us to leave her child alone. She'll return to her wee one soon, honey. Mamas always do." She looks at me, eyes wide, swallowing each word like a baby bird gobbling up nourishment from a parent's beak.

We stand and walk towards our driveway; she points at the neighbor's yard. "Those doggies sure love jumping on their trampoline. That black one's a nigger dog. I'm glad my color's white."

Anger flashes through my veins, tingling my fingertips. Last week I heard her teacher say that hateful word at the grocery store; the very woman I entrust the education of my child to. These small-minded people breed bigotry that spreads like a virus. Raising a child in this town is a battle I can't win.

"I will wash out your mouth with soap if I *ever* hear you say that word again. I don't care who says it, even Miss Marie. It's no-count, low-rent and mean. Understand? You take that word back to wherever you found it and throw it away."

"Yes ma'am." Her eyes fill with tears. Even the prosthetic seems to cry, tears squeezing out the sides. The hardest thing in the world is to scold my child, but she's got to understand the cruelty behind that damaging word. Filling her heart with love and tolerance before the rest of this town stuffs it with hate is a full time job. My voice softens.

"Skin color is not what's important. No one can, or should ever even *want*, to change their skin color. But you *can* change what you say, how you act, and how you treat people."

"But that's a lot of changing, and I'm just a little girl."

I tuck her chin into the cup of my palm, raise her head and look into her eyes. "If you believe, truly believe in your heart, that a person's good-ness is the only thing that matters, you're changing yourself already." She takes my hand.

My eyes shift to the neighbor's dogs, bouncing, growling and nipping each other's neck. They freeze, knob knees quivering, and their ears perk then press back, flattening against their skulls. Beady black eyes watch us pass. I'm scared of dogs, especially pit bulls, but those dogs don't scare me as much as the man who lives there. He grunts his greetings then looks at me through the slits of his eyes like some old junkyard dog ready to snatch a bone. His caked dirt yard smells like cat piss, even though there's not a feline in sight. Aunt Mama says he's divorced, lost custody of his daughter, and that's what makes him mean. Mama says he's not mean, just quiet. Says we might be kin so leave it be. Three men regularly visit his house, usually at night; Lester says they must have a card game going.

We walk inside our house and Miss Ann flicks on the television. "Don't you have homework?"

"No ma'am, I already done it."

"You already *did* it. And I don't want you watching *Lana Lantana* again—you'll grow up into one of those teenyboppers. Please change the channel to the Animal Planet."

"Yes ma'am."

Returning to the kitchen, I remove the meatloaf from the fridge, slide it into the oven, trim the green beans and put them on to simmer with a slab of salt pork. As I peel potatoes, my mind goes quiet and I'm not so hard on myself. At least most nights I make sure Miss Ann eats a good supper. I hope Mama doesn't get too busy with her hair business; I hate imagining my girl eating supper from a box or can. Placing the peeler down, I gaze out the window, heart in my throat. So this is it, my mind's made up; for us to move forward, I must leave her behind—but only until I get my bearings in Atlanta. I'll talk to Mama after I put her to sleep.

I walk to the card table and run my palm over the oilcloth, the black-khaki color of a mess of collards, and it glistens as if slick with fat. Peeling it from the table, I fold the cloth into a perfect square. Last year I bought a Martha Stewart tablecloth designed with cut lemons and edged in scallops of lace that I bring out for special occasions. Like tonight. Lester's joining us for supper so I unscrew his quart jar of Shine On Harvest Moon. I could use a little hooch to work up my nerve. Putting the jar to my mouth, I gag; smells like decayed duckweed from the swamp out back. How can he drink this crap? A beer will have to do. When I move to Atlanta, I'm going to start drinking wine, like the chefs.

Setting the table, I notice the jackalope's muddy eyes following me again. Uncle Watley gave Mama the preserved creature's head for Christmas when I was a child, and she mounted it above the card table, on the wall with the white brick wallpaper. He told us it was a rare, near extinct, species of critter, the offspring of a young mule deer and jackrabbit. I figured, knowing him, he'd shot something off the endangered species list.

It wasn't until Buck started getting me into bars that I found out it was fake. Second Chance had a jackalope head stuck on the wall by the beer tap, and I told everyone in spitting distance that it was endangered, thinking I sounded so smart. The guys hooted, and Buck grabbed me tight around my waist, loving me most when I sounded dumb. He explained they're just rabbits with their ears lopped off and antlers glued to their poor frizzled heads. I try to ignore our jackalope; his gaze unsettles me.

Walking to the cellar door, I open it and shout down to Mama and Lester, "Hey y'all, dinner'll be ready in a few." They come up after a spell, laughing at one of his silly jokes. Miss Ann turns off the TV.

"Pour me some home stock, would 'ya, could 'ya, please, please, please." Lester elbows Mama then winks.

"Only one for you, Mr. Life-of-the-Party. You were a might liquored-up after last night's poker." He gives her his dejected, hangdog look, and then his eyes slide to the stove.

"Mmmm...yummy yum yum. Gal's got a way in the kitchen; something smells mighty fine." He rubs his palms together and makes lip-smacking noises. Goose bumps shimmer up my arms whenever anyone compliments my cooking.

"My, oh my, aren't we fancy tonight. Thank you, Shelby." Mama scrubs her hands, pours a short glass for Lester, then pops herself a beer.

"You can open one for me while you're at it."

"Are we celebrating something?"

We are celebrating a better future, I think, giving her a smile instead of an answer. I brace the meatloaf with my fingers and slice it into precise, three-quarter-inch pieces. Mama's in a good mood, must be excited about her shop. Who knows, but tonight's the perfect time to tell her my plans. I set a plate of food in front of Lester's outstretched hands.

After dinner, I encourage them to have another drink while I put Miss Ann to bed.

"Don't mind if I do." Lester nearly knocks over the table as he bolts towards his bottle, grabbing it before Mama can snatch it away. With a weary sigh, she shakes her head.

"Can I stay up too, Mama?"

"No, sugar. Children need more sleep than adults, and a good night's rest keeps your mind sharp at school. I'll read a story until you fall asleep."

I take her hand and we walk to her room.

"Tell me a story about when you were a little girl."

"You've heard those stories a million times. I'm sick of my life. Let's pick out a book."

She selects our favorite story from *Uncle Remus*, where Brer Fox is trying to kill Brer Rabbit. I sit on her bed and she worms into my arms, thumb in mouth. And so I begin. "There's other ways o' learnin' 'bout the behind feet of a mule than gettin' kicked by 'em, sure as I'm named Remus..."

Miss Ann's eyelashes flutter sleepily as my words wander and weave, blazing a trail to the part where Brer Rabbit tricks Brer Fox into throwing him into the briar patch. He tells Brer Fox the thorns would surely kill him, but in truth this is the rabbit's home, the place he loves best. With jubilation, the fox tosses the rabbit into the briar patch, expecting him to die. I always read the last two sentences slow.

"'I was born and raised in the briar patch,' says Brer Rabbit, giggling Tee-hee! Tee-hee!...And the giggle broke into the loudest laughing you ever heard."

Her eyes are closed, one eyeball rolling beneath the lid while the other rests still. Guilt gnaws at my stomach as I stare at her face. Bowing into her neck, I exhale a soft whisper of breath then inhale, catching her little-girl scent. I straighten, trace a heart on her forehead and look down upon my angel, asleep in my arms. Untangling myself from her limp warmth, I tiptoe out of her room, soft, sad, and close the door.

Past the hallway in the den, Mama sits on Lester's lap watching TV, a tray full of ashes and a crumpled pack of almost-empty cigarettes on the table by her side. Her fingertips, stained yellowish-brown, tremble as Lester lights her cig.

"Hey y'all, I need to discuss something important." I'm so nervous I can't sit, and I tuck my hair behind my ears then fiddle with my earrings.

Mama's eyes thin, cigarette poised mid-air, smoke clouding her face. "Oh God, Shelby. Don't tell me you're pregnant."

I think about this as silence fills the room. Maybe what I'm planning to say won't sound so bad if she thinks a baby's on the way. Pressing my lips together, I count to ten, real slow, just looking at them, blinking. Mama fidgets, sucking in smoke with long, deep inhalations as if she were taking her last breaths.

"Now, Mama, really. When was the last time I even had a date? Grasso's, a grocery chain in Atlanta, is interviewing cooks for their downtown deli, and I'd like to apply for a job."

"In *Atlanta*? Why Atlanta? They're always looking for cashiers at The Pig right here in town."

"I don't want to be a cashier, not even a deli cook. I want to be a chef, Mama, a trained chef, and the Grasso job description says they'd pay for chef school."

Hot air bellows up from my stomach and a wave of heat rolls up my neck; my face feels like it just caught fire. Try as I may, I have never been able to control my beet-red blush, and anyone who looks at me can always read my emotional state—nervous, ashamed, fearful or excited—at the least provocation.

"Umm, I'll just interview with them. Probably won't get the job. Then I'll turn right around and march back home."

Mama regards me, eyes crinkled in concern, and then stares at her cig, tapping it in the ashtray, rounding the ashes into a point. Lester pretends not to pay attention, one hand fiddling with the remote, the other rubbing Mama's neck.

"But if I *do* get the job, I'd have to live in Atlanta and will need you to care for Miss Ann. It won't be for long, though, and I'll visit whenever I can." The words tumble out of my mouth, catching in my throat like I'm choking on a wishbone.

"At least once I'd like a shot at...at making a better life for us." Lips pressed under my teeth, those last words hang, dangling as a fish on a line before it's scooped into the net.

Mama raises her head to the jackalope and the glint in his eye catches her gaze. It's as if that mangy creature is putting in his two cents and Mama is interested in what he has to say. Inhaling the tobacco, her brows crease then unfurl on the exhale, and she sighs, shaking her head. "I'm trying to make things better for *all* of us, Shelby. Right here at home, with my new shop, in Coryville. Taking care of that little girl is gonna put another strain on my time."

A minute passes as she smokes in silence right down to the filter. Then, crushing out the cigarette, she directs her words to the ashtray. "But you're my baby too, and you should have a chance to catch *your* dream. I suppose Miss Ann can do her homework in the shop whiles I do hair. Aunt Mama can watch her when I work my shifts at Eldercare. If you *do* get the job, we can try to make it work. At least for a while."

She looks up and gives me the once-over, head to toe, then rolls her eyes, smirking. "Here's my only advice: Keep your mind open and your legs closed." Lester snorts. I don't find her funny at all; those words were trashy and tacky. I smile at her anyway, grateful she's willing to take care of my child, yet sick at heart knowing just how much I'm leaving behind.

Walking out of the room, I take a good look back at the jackalope, whose shiny eyes also mock me, a-laughing-and-a-laughing like Brer Rabbit at the Fox: *You just try to get away from here. Come on, Shelby girl. I dare you. Try.*

CHAPTER 4

Mallory

Kaleidoscopes. Only a little twist, and the patterns change, re-emerge, each design as vivid as the last. So too memories, defragmented, drilling down to childhood's threshold.

In my earliest memory I'm three years old, riding the kiddie train at the Atlanta Zoo. The crimson, olive and yellow boxcar chain clatters behind a chugging engine, punctuated by the whistle's fierce hissing blast. A pigtail is sticking to my brother's cotton candy as I decapitate animal crackers with fierce bites.

We weave past camels, elephants, zebras and peacocks separated and framed into chain-link fencing. And then there are the giraffes, whose necks bend around trees like pipe cleaners; endless tongues circling branches like eels sampling leaves. The train gathers steam as we swing into the dead smell stench engulfing the lion house. Pinching our noses, our hearts begin to pound; the tunnel's mouth is next, which swallows us like a slithering caterpillar as our shrieks ricochet off the narrow cement enclosure.

One sweltering afternoon, the train breaks down in the tunnel, whining and shuddering to a screeching halt. An infinity of darkness and echoing screams. A damp sour smell swelling the air. The conductor admonishing us to choking silence as he tries to work a sputter from the engine. And I, gripping the hand of my brother, imagine the walls crumbling, caving in, smothering me...I can't breathe.

I felt as if I were in that tunnel for days, and haven't ridden a train since.

Writers suggest the sound of a train whistle as a call to adventure in far-flung places, but for me, it's a siren from hell. Visualize Edward Munch's painting, *The Silent Scream.* Trapped in that tunnel was the first time I felt sheer terror, the same sensation cramping my gut now. I pour another cup of coffee and resume my post at my desk; this waiting is interminable. The Ides of March is upon us; the *Atlanta Sun* is greasing its wheels with a skeletal crew, regurgitating a newspaper, if you could call it that, growing skimpier and less newsworthy by the day.

Most of my comrades have been dismissed in a flurry of after-hour send-offs overlapping in waves of shrugs, tears and carefully divided bar tabs. Tommy counts as one of the fortunate few invited to apply for a job at *AtlantaNow*, but I haven't heard from Human Resources since our meeting in January. Sitting at my desk in the newsroom, a faceless drone, sipping from my *You Go Girl* coffee mug, I stare out the window, avoiding eye contact with the other drones in the office.

I try forgetting I don't have a Plan B. At least I paid cash for my loft, own it outright, and it's located in an area close to downtown. As long as I pay the association fees and utilities, I'll have a roof over my head. Itchy asked me to join her at Boot Camp this evening, but I have no energy, not even the stamina for yoga. Depression over Cooper and malaise about my job has been replaced by a dense blanketing numbness. I go to the bar or invite friends over to my loft to eat, drink and critique the recipes I make. These days I prefer drinking to eating. I taste the food, correct the seasonings, and serve the rest; food is such a buzz kill.

I never imagined I'd arrive, two years before forty, no children to nurture or husband to love. As a young girl, I was certain I'd grow up a noble woman, revoking the wrongs of the world like erasing misspellings on a chalkboard. I'd work side by side with Mother Teresa, sponging the backs of the sick and cholera-infected. Or, more sanitized, Julie Andrews as Maria in *The Sound of Music*, accompanied at popular venues with my string of singing children. And, like Maria, I'd never have to perform the unspeakable act that produced the adopted offspring.

Unwittingly, I landed my first assignment when I was six years old. A black and white photo I'd snapped one morning was used in a national campaign for muscular dystrophy, and proved fortuitous, pointing my ked-clad feet towards destiny's path. Memories of that day are like a reel-to-reel playing an eight-millimeter home movie marked *Summer, 1979.*

My father had given me his Polaroid Swinger, a popular instant-photo camera from the sixties, and his last roll of film. He warned me to be careful with my selection of subject because the film was obsolete. With utter delight, I unlatched the white plastic housing, placed film into the canister, snapped the back shut, then looked across the yard for a suitable subject. Our family dog and Mama's dahlias were too pedestrian for the coveted eight photographs.

The previous year, our most recent minister at Saint Luke's Episcopal Church, Tom Elliot, moved to Buckhead with his wife and daughter, little Lacy Elliot. The two had just stopped by to give Mama a copy of last Sunday's sermon; she'd been too ill for church service as the prior night's party stretched way past midnight.

Lacy, so tiny at four, sat on the top stone step of the back porch while our mamas drank a cup of Red Diamond in the kitchen. Her eyes were as round and blue as the buttons on her smocked shirt, and in the thick humidity, damp ringlets clung to the nape of her neck. Her feet were clad in Mary Jane sandals, a small bow at the buckle, but what struck me, as

I practiced holding the bulky camera to my eye, was the Band-Aid she'd stuck on one knee.

On Wednesday afternoons, Mama took me to the Elliot's for Bible study, and I'd sneak into Lacy's bedroom and watch her lying with a respirator, entombed in a plastic bag with tubes sticking up her crusted nose. Lacy was the first person I remember loving, without reservation, except for my parents, grandfather and Itchy. Looking down at her, a bluish cast to her face, I felt guilty. Guilty because I was glad it was Lacy in that bag. Not me.

I walked to the porch, aimed the camera in her direction, and squeezed the red button as she smiled into the viewfinder. After peeling the photo from the backing, I sponged wet, sticky fixer over her image, which bloomed like a daylily in the sun. Blowing on the picture, I ran inside, gave it to Mrs. Elliot, and she stared at the photo with glistening eyes. I'd given her a gift as vast as heaven, more precious than the Last Supper painting that hung on the wall in her living room.

Mrs. Elliot showed the photo to the director at the local chapter of the Muscular Dystrophy Foundation, and the picture was blown-up, reproduced en masse, then displayed across America. Lacy, the poster child, the cardboard girl who kept fighting for a cure long after her fragile body wore out.

One little Band-Aid on such a sick, desperate child.

Today finds me thirty-two years later remembering Lacy Elliot, my heart hurting as if a bandage had been ripped from the wound. Tears prickle my eyes; those little girls live in me somewhere innocent and sweet, faded photographs in a forgotten scrapbook.

Years passed, and photographing people became too poignant a subject. I focused my lens on food, landing my first job out of art school as the culinary photographer for the *Atlanta Sun*. The marvelous creations chefs whipped up for my camera, however, enticed me to leave the *Sun* and attend chef school. In the heat and frigidity of the classroom kitchen, I drew inspiration from my surroundings.

It was here bubbling cauldrons of salted water sat atop gas-lit flames waiting for just-harvested leeks to complete their journey from ground to plate. It was here, in the freezing meat lockers, we butchered a lamb on stainless steel slabs, roasted the loin, then carved into it into medallions. It was here we arranged this food with the deliberation of a surgeon, dotting thick aged balsamic vinegar around the edges of bone-white plates, napping leek purée around circles of lamb, then garnishing the final composition with nips of goat cheese and microgreens. It was here, in chef school, creating these plates of perfection, I fell in love with cooking.

After graduating and earning my *whites*, barely passing that knuckle-biting series of exams, I landed a line-cook job at top-rated Fleurion. I did every task possible to ingratiate myself to the executive chef, but, try as I may, I couldn't advance from low chef on the totem pole.

Days would begin with my head down—same place, same station—for hours, carving mushrooms into precise shapes, mincing shallots just so then breaking for a staff meal, often standing at my post. I'd resume my prep work with the focused intensity of a race horse until dinner service began. This military professional kitchen environment, with no promise of promotion, was grueling, backbreaking and mind numbing.

My parents helped subsidize my education, lack of direction, and ill-compensated ambitions. Daddy worried about his emotional, dramatic and headstrong girl, but Mama said I'd eventually find my way, and if I expected the worst, I'd never be disappointed. But that's a lousy mindset to adopt while you're living your life. I expect a great deal from myself, and my accomplishments bring me pleasure. She said life was like stepping down a ladder—a sequence of lowering your expectations. I try to dismiss her pessimistic philosophy but it haunts me; I worry she may be right. First it was my divorce, while I was working at Fleurion.

David, a Vanderbilt grad from an Atlanta blue-blooded family, and I met while I was in chef school. We married because matrimony seemed the next logical step after great sex. His pale eyes always seemed surprised and his lids blinked furiously; allergies, he claimed. My theory was he was just astonished he could fall in love with the likes of me; a feisty photography graduate from the Savannah College of Art and Design, a student at the Robert Russell Culinary Arts Academy.

The fact that I could extract a proposal from a guy like David was reason enough to marry him, and Mama agreed. But after securing the job at Fleurion, I wouldn't allow David's needs to compete or interfere with the restaurant's demands. Explosive sex morphed into no-sex, and my twelve-hour-plus workdays wrecked our marriage. It was a clean break; no children or money feuds. Within two years of our split, David was remarried and a father. He could have been a father to *my* children if I weren't so absorbed in my career.

I stuck it out at Fleurion for two years before breaking, realizing— *finally*—that I didn't have the endurance, the driving talent, and the blinding ambition it takes to succeed in the industry. So, armed with a chef's culinary background beefing up my photography skills, I once again applied, and was hired, to be the primary food writer and photographer for the *Atlanta Sun*.

The fickle nature of food trends turned out well-suited to my dilettante approach to career, and a couple of years later, a stroke of fate brought Cooper into my life, a hunky package of leonine grace, so well-suited to my commitment to passion.

I squandered those never-ending days, reveling in big love, a close-knit family and amusing job, recognizing today that those days were the best. But back then, who knew? The good times always seem the best times when regarded in hindsight.

Of course the worst blindsided the best, Mama's *expect-the-worst* wisdom, once again, prophetic. I was a fool not to expect it. Maybe if I had expected it, *it* never would have happened. But it did, the worst came to be: Mama's last years on earth were spent with esophageal cancer. Before we learned the correct diagnosis, we marveled at her weight loss. *You look fabulous, Mama. How are you doing it?* Next came the pain; always misdiagnosed. Our family doctor said it was a broken rib and the specialist said it was a hiatal hernia, but Mama disagreed.

Just look down my damn throat, she choked. And he did. Squamous cell carcinoma—mutant cells gone wild—patterned as a brick tunnel running up her swan-like neck. We blamed it on her love of spicy food and the ensuing reflux, shushing the fact that alcohol and cigs were probably the culprits. Any reference to a self-induced smoking gun was strictly taboo in our family.

The remainder of her life was only about the pain. How could this be? *Do you mean to tell me, Doctor Vincent, that with all of the medicine in all of this world, all of the pills she's inhaling every hour, there is not one drug out there that will crack her pain?* A pain so beyond belief she'd stare wild-eyed, wild-haired—*fit to be tied*—she would have described herself if she could have seen herself, if she were granted one moment of relief.

Shocked into numbness, I sat at her bedside, my hand over hers, and sang. Before the cancer, Mama had a rich gorgeous voice, and a knack for writing lyrics, her lusty full-throated alto accompanying compositions she played on the piano. Her songs cheered children in hospitals, the elderly in nursing homes; her songs would stoke my father's passion, and put us kids to sleep. She'd write over-the-rainbow songs, only-a-mother's-love songs, songs of dreamland, songs of angels, and those were the songs that I sang to my mother—her voice, my voice—coaxing, begging her to sleep.

But sleep ignored my pleas, allowing only tattered shards of drugged unconsciousness, and then her ravaged head would rise an inch above the pillow, so desperate to speak, the effort causing her to gasp, head crashing back, rasping:

Mallory...blessed child.

How could this be? My beautiful, fifty-eight-year-old, unflappable mama. You were supposed to sing to my children. *Hang on, Mama, hang on. There must be another way, some cure on the horizon*, stunned eyes spoke to hers. *Just let me go, let me die*, fluttering lids pleaded back to me.

She spent her final days delirious, her last words accusing the doctors of pouring wine into the medication bag affixed to her veins. Her anger was puzzling; past predilections indicated wine would have been a much preferable alternative to drugs. Before she became ill, cocktail hour stretched way into night, accompanied by an ever-ready pack of fresh-tapped "lights." *I'm getting through this life, Mallory, the best way I know how.* Really, Mama, really? Even when it killed you and your death is killing me?

A patter of raindrops splashes against the window in the newsroom. I close my eyes. *Oh dear God, hear my prayer. Let her look down from heaven, or up from the cradling roots of earth, wherever eternal love exists. Let her enter my soul and help me cope with all of this loss—simmering, smoking—this dragging heartbreak. Oh Mama, my dear precious mama; how to bear this life with you not in it.* I open my eyes as the clouds bloom into a grayish lavender mass, burst in a flash of light, then release a torrent of rain laying siege to sidewalks and smoldering memories.

The night Mama died, after the hospice team left her to a morphine drip, our family gathered and we took turns visiting her bedroom to stroke her hand and kiss her damp cheek. Later in the evening, there rose a fearsome storm—much worse than the weather outside today—rumbling the foundation of our home. A lightning burst cracked the sky and Daddy looked up, startled, from the family Bible. His knit brows loosened, shot to heaven, and he exclaimed that this was a sign, God's way of celebrating Mama's return to health. At that minute, my brother Clay walked into the room, crying like a baby. God had other plans.

We tried comforting Daddy, telling him the storm was God's way of saying: *Here she is at last. Let's break out the fireworks and welcome her.* He suffered a massive coronary and died three weeks after Mama's funeral. It was March, almost spring, but there were no smells in the air, nothing growing in the ground, only the sounds of suffering, a damaging tornado, of wind whipping and howling through branches hurling me fists over fists. And there you have it. Pure Grief. Large, wet, and shuddering. Words—fail.

Clay and I were left to divide a hefty portfolio, weighted in Georgia Finance. He diversified, advising me to do the same. I cashed out enough stock to buy my loft, recently remodeled after the leveling storms, but with Cooper refueling my emptiness, re-investing the remainder was an easy task to defer. Then the bank crashed and fortunes collapsed. So be it. Cradled and nurtured in my lover's arms, losing the money wasn't as devastating to me as it was to others, but the price I paid for Cooper's love, well, that's another story.

Is there a lesson in the rubble that might lessen the pain of his departure? Some tonic to soothe as I wait for him to call—or not. I've been debating giving *him* a call, suggesting we meet. I'd wear those tight skinny jeans he said made my butt look great. Reeks of desperation. There's got to be another way, something subtler. I peer into my almost-empty coffee mug as if the answer could be found in the final dregs then retrieve my umbrella from the bottom drawer of my desk; it's time to call it a day.

How to bear such loss. My writing, recipes and photographs are now my lover and family, and tonight we're craving a simple supper, uncomplicated and reassuring, comfort food to conjure the past. Perhaps a pimento cheese sandwich; I'll give a twist to that stalwart of the Dixie kitchen. You see, it's the taste of pimento cheese, oh yes; it's the taste of this cradle-to-grave favorite that dredges memories of Mama. But it won't bring her back. It won't change the fact she's gone.

Pimento Cheese Sandwiches
by
Mallory Lakes

One of Mama's staples was a pimento cheese sandwich. And like a little black dress, she would dress it up or down, depending on the occasion. When friends came for bridge, she'd cut the bread into circles, spread pimento cheese on a round, and top it with another round. Then she'd skewer an olive onto a frilled toothpick and pierce it, dead center, into the sandwich.

After an afternoon of bridge and several vodka gimlets, she'd make the same pimento cheese sandwich for us kids, though she'd skip the olive and omit the circle shape. The bread Mama used was soft, plushy and white, surrounded with a thin caramel line she referred to, with disdain, as "the crust." One thing she always did was remove that crust, gimlet or no gimlet.

Growing up, I had a pimento cheese sandwich every day for lunch, which was my primary source of calcium and protein. I've tasted many versions of this spread through the years, some remarkable and some best forgotten. I am what I am today-the good and the bad-because of pimento cheese.

Today, Atlanta chefs conjure their own riffs of this Southern regional food. They roast their own peppers, substitute crème fraîche for mayonnaise, for example, and season the spread with chipotle powder or smoked paprika. The bread they use is moments from the oven, crusty and dense with yeasty flavor.

Switching out Mama's bread for a fresh-baked artisan loaf was the only change I made to her simple recipe. I initially left the dense, chewy crust on the bread, usually my favorite part, but the crust-on version didn't taste as memory recalled. So I cut off the crust and bit into the sandwich again, uttering a sound of pleasure only spirits are privy to hear.

Chapter 5

Shelby

Apatch of rain fell early morning and a heavy moist fog hung low in the valley, clearing into a pearly-gray mist as Mama drove up the long piney hill to the bus station. My pelvis bears into the hard splintered bench in the waiting room under the heaviness of Miss Ann burrowing into my lap.

"Tell me again, Mama. Tell me where you're going."

Sniffling, thumb in mouth, she twirls my hair between her fingers; tonight will be the first time in her six short years she won't be tucked in bed by me, her mother. Biting my lip, a dull pain throbbing my temples, my mind repeats a refrain like a cuckoo, in, then out, of its clock. *For her. For us. For her. For us.*

"Atlanta, honey, I'm going to Atlanta. Heavens child, I'll be back tomorrow night, no matter if I get the job or not."

"But what then, Mama? What if you *do* get the job, then what?"

"We'll cross that bridge if we get to it. Remember how the mama bird left her baby to find the seeds? I'm doing the same thing, the exact same thing as that mama pine warbler, searching for seeds to make us a better life."

I lift her hand, my hair wrapped around tiny fingers like a black spool of thread, and kiss it. A double image of myself is reflected in her eyes; the prosthetic mirroring me as a vanity glass, the other falling into something deep inside her.

The creaking moan of number 517 wheezes into the lot. Mama peels her from my lap as I unspool my hair from her fist. It would be so easy not to get on that bus, forget this crazy scheme, and stay home. So, so easy. *For her. For us. For her. For us.* Pressing them into my chest, our hearts hammering in unison like tin drums, I lean away, pick up my bag then walk towards the bus, tears burning my lids, willing myself not to look back, each step more determined than the last. Climbing three steps up, I hand the driver my ticket, and my feet travel down the aisle, collapsing into the first set of empty seats.

The bus ride from Coryville to downtown Atlanta, give or take, is four hours. Lester offered to drive, which would save a good hour, but I replied: *No thank you, Lester. A jiggling bus always calms my nerves*, sugar-coating my voice so's not to hurt his feelings. It's hard enough finding words for him at supper, much less on a three-hour road trip.

I've got plenty of time to think about the interview. I checked out a book from the Jeff Davis County Library, *The Job Interview: Putting Your Best Foot Forward,* written in 1999 by Linda Dover. I know times have changed, and I could have checked out a recent book, but *A*, I like the fact it was written by a woman; and *B*, her photo on the back jacket resembles me. At least through the jawline. I like to think of her as kin, steering me in the right direction.

Ms. Dover writes the first impression's critical: I must look professional, so I'm wearing the black dress and sweater set I bought for Uncle Watley's funeral. At the wake, Miss Ann fell asleep in my lap, and the shiny, slick material never so much as took a crease. I never leave the house without painting dark lines around my eyes, then smudging them—Lindsey Lohan's trick, but Ms. Dover advises to keep makeup low-key, just a brush of mascara and neutral shade of lipstick. Perfume's a big no-no, so I refrained. Buck once surprised me with a bottle of Paris perfume, almost two fluid ounces. I told him he was a crazy fool to spend that kind of money on something so small. Seems like a lifetime ago.

I've been brainstorming questions they might ask then compose answers that would make me sound smart. I'm guessing the first question will be what kind of professional cooking experience I've had, which is zilch. I'll say I follow Mallory Lake's recipes in the *Atlanta Sun* and everyone raves about my cooking.

I'm sure they'll ask about my education. Coryville schools were far better when I was attending, but two years back they lost much of their state funding. I loved school and the days flew by in the classroom. My English teacher, Mr. Phillips, paid me special attention, helping me to speak and write proper sentences, and assigned bonus books that he said I'd love.

Mr. Phillips was right. Carefully chosen words threading into a sentence, paragraph, then story—as colorful patches sewn into a quilt—comfort me, weaving me into a bigger life, a life that matters. I'm slow to finish my favorite books, sometimes leaving the last chapter unread so I don't have to leave their world, them leaving me to mine. He encouraged me to write about my thoughts, my feelings, and see where they'd take me, if I could turn them into a story. I'd jot down notes, study the words then throw them away; there's never been a heroine with a dead-end life such as my own.

The summer before my junior year, Nina Bradley came into my life. With her neck craned towards me darting glances at her computer, and those wide-set eyes glistening with light when she spoke, her fingers flickered over the keys of her laptop with a startling quickness.

She was a graduate student at the University of Georgia and spent three months in Coryville working on her dissertation. The goal of her project was to demonstrate the effectiveness of an education program she was developing for low-income, high school women who had demonstrated promise in the classroom. Mr. Phillips selected me to help her develop and test her proposed teaching model.

I worked hours that summer with Nina Bradley at the Jeff Davis County Library. She explained that the groundwork of all of her learning tools would help me develop effective communication skills and build my confidence. I would be the yardstick in her pilot study; her way of proving to her professors, even to the world, that the program that she was developing with me—vocabulary expansion, writing, and computer skills—would help other women like me. She helped me understand that my environment didn't have to control and reduce me. She said that if I worked hard, was brave, and had an open mind, I could grab the reins and take control over my future. She explained ways that I could earn a scholarship, land a good job, and not depend on anyone but myself.

I'd never known a woman like Nina Bradley. I lived to please her, learning the meaning of more than a dozen new words a day, pausing several seconds to think before I spoke, and keeping a journal about my feelings. I gave her my opinion of her teaching methods, what was working, and what didn't make sense.

Nina Bradley said my spark was burning so bright, she could see the fire inside of me. I felt it too. After she had returned to college, she left me with a learning program and goals. The first three months I e-mailed her my lessons from the library, and we often spoke on the phone.

But life smoldered in her absence and the fire went out. I got pregnant, dropped out of school. I quit sending her my completed assignments and refused her calls. She didn't fail me; I failed myself. I idolized Nina Bradley and can't bear the thought that I failed her, too. But look at me now on the path to a better life. She'd be proud. She left me with skills my situation can't destroy: knowledge.

Mama gets ticked when I correct her grammar, says I'm sassing her. I was a straight-A student up to the middle of eleventh grade, but when I started to show, I dropped out. Earning my GED after Miss Ann was born was a cinch. I passed all five tests, even math, with flying colors.

Sandra says twelfth grade exams are much harder to pass than the GED, and advised me to say I graduated from a real school. But I can't begin my new life with a lie. If it comes up, I'll say I had to leave to help the family, which is the truth considering there was a new addition to the roost. But I don't have to tell them that; to say I left because I was pregnant. Ms. Dover says they'd be breaking the law if they even asked personal questions.

She says to repeat Three Main Points that are positives about yourself. I've decided my Three Main Points will be: I am, *Number One*: a good cook; *Number Two*: energetic; and *Number Three*: a quick learner. I'll also throw in I'm punctual and never get sick. At all times during the interview, I will sit straight, cross my ankles, smile, and act *professional*.

I glance at my watch. We've been traveling over two hours and must have stopped at every cow pie junction on Route 6. When one group of folks rolls off, another piles on, looking more bedraggled and saggy-eyed the closer we get to the city. I take this as a bad sign. Then the bus revs up, jiggling like the fat on Mama's underarms when she's sopping and scrubbing the floors.

Yesterday I purchased the February edition of *Home to Hearth* magazine and a pack of spearmint gum at The Pig. My jaws are sore from all this chewing, and I've read the magazine twice. The pages are filled with Louisiana dishes for Mardi Gras parties alongside Valentine's Day recipes for children. Sick sinking guilt swims through my gut; *Miss Ann*. I fold a corner on a heart-shaped cookie recipe with pink icing and red sprinkles. I'll make her a batch the day after tomorrow.

I turn my mind to the cooking magazines they'll have at the Atlanta bus station. They don't sell the fancy cooking magazines at The Pig but they have outdated copies at the library. I'm aching to buy the latest *Bon Appetit,* which I can read at the motel. Sandra said her studio is too small for a guest bed, even an air mattress, and recommended The Troubadour—cheap but clean—so I booked a room for the night. I'll have a bed, a shower, and it's in walking distance from the bus station and Grasso's.

I scheduled the interview as late in the day as I could, ensuring I'll have time to freshen-up. I sniff my pits—whew, ammonia—even though I showered and sprayed with a double shot of deodorant this morning. I look out the window and see the city in the distance; from here it looks tiny, reminding me of Miss Ann's Lego play city. I check the time, twelve-thirty; three hours until the interview.

The bus jolts to a stop and belches exhaust, smelling like burnt matches and old cigars. Standing up, my stomach somersaults, the same giddy feeling I have at the top of a roller coaster right before the plunge. I pull my bag from the overhead rack; there was no need to pack more than a change of clothes because tomorrow I'll return home the same way I got here. I spit my gum into a tissue and wedge it in the ashtray. Guess this is it. *Atlanta.*

In a swoosh of body heat, elbow knocking and *excuse mes*, my feet move with the current of people as if trapped in their wave from the bus into the station. The passengers disperse as ants scurrying towards their next assignment, but I stand frozen in a corner until the terminal empties. Walking within the dingy square, I follow the edge of the room, trying to get my bearings; this place isn't fine like I'd hoped. A business card stained with an impression of someone's pink lips lies on the floor, and I step over a Burger King wrapper next to a flattened foil package, squirt ketchup seeped out the sides. I don't see a magazine stand but an information table is situated by the exit sign; I approach the woman sitting behind the counter.

"Excuse me, do you have directions to The Troubadour Motel?"

She could be thirty, she could be sixty; reading glasses attached to a beaded chain dangle around loose folds of her chin. She lifts the frames and adjusts them over her nostrils, which expand, pink and moist, as she snatches a tissue and sneezes—*ah-choo*—into the tissue. "Allergies," she explains, offering a tired smile. She blows her nose then pulls out a map, placing it on the cracked glass counter. In red ink, she circles the location, even draws little arrows in the direction of the motel from the station.

"Here 'ya go, miss. How long will you be staying?"

"Just overnight. I'm applying for a cooking position at Grasso's."

"Grasso's; that grocery chain?"

I nod; she gives me a hard look over the rim of her glasses. "Well. No offense, but their prices are ridiculous. I mean, who do they think they are charging that kind of money for food in these times?" She shrugs. "On the other hand, their downtown store is always packed. Someone out there must have a buck."

"Since you know the store, would you also draw arrows from The Troubadour to Grasso's? How long do you think it will take to walk there from the motel?"

"It'll take a solid thirty minutes, hoofin' it." She eyes my heels. "You can't wear those, they'll cripple you. Did you bring other shoes?"

"Yes," I lie. "I've got flats in my bag." I don't mind walking in heels; Buck said they made my legs look great. This woman's negative attitude is wearing me down. She's one of those sad and sorry people who finds everything in life a disappointment, probably imagines the world conspires against her. On the other hand, working in this soot-scarred station must be depressing, and it was nice of her to draw the arrows. I smile. "Thanks so much for the info. Have a nice day." I put the map in my bag, turn then walk out the revolving door.

Outside the terminal, next to the door, a woman who appears to be my age sits behind a small metal table. Her right nostril and brow are pierced and her waist-length hair is dyed raspberry and white, striped and wavy like a candy cane. Long fingers, tattooed with stars, extend to squared-off fingernails. They are painted black, which I know is the style but in this environment they look sinister. She pulls a chain from a basket in front of her and dangles it towards me. I step back, my forearm lurching across my forehead, afraid she's going to sling it at me.

"Bottle openers. Made 'em from recycled bike chains. Cool, huh?" Her eyes squint, crinkling up at me, and her voice is gentle, her expression kind, contradicting the way she appears. "Buy one and it'll put you back ten bucks. Buy two, and I'll only charge fifteen."

"No thanks," I say, forcing a smile. "Maybe later." (Lesson number one: Don't judge folks so quickly; looks in Atlanta can be deceiving.) Glancing at the arrows on my map, I turn right.

The sidewalks are packed with people, eyes to their phones, pecking at keys. They bump together like cattle being herded, anxious to get someplace but not knowing where they're going. A saxophone wails through the open door of a dark-lit bar, and a rusted Budweiser sign hangs crooked in the front window. Flickering neon letters follow the burnt-out *B,* as dilapidated as the woman leaning into the doorframe. Beneath my click-clacking heels, putrid smells of sewage waft up from drain water grates—maybe something worse. Mama warned of pickpockets snatching my bag so I hug it to my chest. Staring up at tall, skinny buildings, I jump at the sudden blast of a horn like a bullhorn by my side.

Walking the short distance to the motel, I feel small, invisible. Then, a young man—dimples even—blows me a kiss. I catch my reflection in a storefront as the wind lifts a tuft of hair, like a curtain blown back from the window. Lifting my chin, confidence returns. A little.

My room at The Troubadour is what I expected. Air freshener hangs heavy and fresh-sprayed, the acrid Citrus-Meadows scent Mama uses when she's trying to blanket stale smoke smell. The cream plaster walls are puckered like cottage cheese, but it is, as Sandra said, clean. Clean, in a worn out way.

I open a window then place my watch on the chipped black nightstand by the bed and undress. A hot bath always calms my nerves, but after settling in for a good soak, the water runs cold after a couple of inches. I swat my armpits with a soapy washcloth, climb out, and then wrap a scratchy towel around my torso. Imagining all the sorry souls who slept here before me, I remove the nylon bedspread and drape it across a chair—snuggling under some natty community quilt that's never been laundered makes my flesh crawl. I slide between the sheets; my nerves might settle if I rest a spell.

Fidgeting, checking the time, I can't calm down, so I get up and put on the same outfit I stepped out of a few minutes ago. I reapply lipstick, comb my hair, grab my bag and map, and then walk out the door onto the street. After five minutes of following arrows, a man slides next to me. I dare not meet his gaze but feel his hand fluttering down my back. My neck hairs prickle.

"Sweet angel, where you been hiding?"

Shivering, I jump and bolt towards a policeman down the street; the man scurries away, his soiled, full-length slicker flapping about his legs like a cape. At least he didn't pull out his chicken neck thing like the trash skulking around Coryville's Five and Dime. Perverts. I glance at my map; did I miss Poplar? Nope. Next street down. Maybe that woman was right about these shoes. My feet are killing me and a blister has rubbed onto my right back heel. Band-Aids, I need Band-Aids. I recall what that woman said about Grasso's prices, but at least I should be able to afford Band-Aids.

Finally the sign—*"Grasso's Fresh Market"*—lit glittery and green like the city of Oz. It scares the starch out of me and my ringing ears drown the traffic noise. I'm going to throw up. I'm going to turn around and run back to the motel. I'm going to forget my dreams of becoming a chef and catch the next bus back to Coryville. Who do I think I am, leaving my child like this.

Through the window, a basket is filled with oranges, and hams affixed to ropes dangle from ceiling rafters. I turn my mind to happy thoughts: Miss Ann's Santa stocking filled with oranges, Aunt Mama's ham biscuits on Christmas morning, and I imagine Mallory Lakes smiling, nudging me ahead. Taking several deep breaths to calm the clatter in my chest, I walk three steps forward, and the doors slide open like the heavenly gates.

I've time to spare, and wander down the center aisles to calm my nerves before filling out the application. Picking up a bottle filled with inky liquid and decorated with a maroon and gold label, my fingers slide down the neck. What does it say…*Bal-sa-mic*. Mallory Lakes says this is her favorite vinegar for making salad dressing. I decide to buy it, look at the price, and then return it to the shelf. If I get this job, after my first paycheck, I'm buying balsamic vinegar.

I turn and walk to the wine department, spying a woman prettier than Miss Georgia Peach weaving through acres of bottles, scratching off names from a clipboard. Like me, she's dressed head to toe in black—dress, stockings and heels—but the fabric on her outfit is muted, not shiny like mine. Her blond hair's pulled back like a trophy-horse's mane, and long strands of pearls tap against her board in sync to her step. Pulling a bottle from the shelf, her eyes narrow to read a label. I walk closer; her Grasso's nametag reads, "Itchy." Why on earth would a mother name a beautiful child *Itchy*. I'm reminded of poison ivy and scratch my arm. She notices me.

"May I help you select a bottle?"

"No, thank you. Just looking."

I turn and dart to the deli, cheeks burning, panicked to be talking to someone so classy. Refrigerated cases are decked out with purple and green ribbon for Mardi Gras, their insides tiered with dishes and signs reading *Chicken Bordelaise, Andouille-Smoked Sausage Dressing* and *Crawfish Etouffée*. I can sound out the names in my head but wouldn't trust myself to say them out loud. One lady, hair tucked under a spider net, hands out samples of red beans and rice made up from a box. I make mine from scratch.

The smells are making my jaws sting. Long skinny bread is pulled from an oven, and racks of chicken rotate on spits like they're riding a Ferris wheel. A worker ladles reddish-brown soup into containers, and a peppery scent trapped in a waft of onion stings my nostrils; I pinch them to stop a sneeze. Must be gumbo. Mallory Lakes just wrote an article about that soup, and I can't wait to make it myself. I'm hungry, starving, in fact, since the only thing I've put in my mouth since yesterday's been spearmint gum. There's a self-contained unit beside the deli where a China guy is rolling sushi. I've read about that. I watch him slice off a rectangle of ruby-fleshed, raw fish, place it over rice, and imagine putting it into my mouth. Nausea replaces my appetite.

I study the workers and see myself as one of them, wearing a white chef coat, or a baseball cap and kelly green shirt—the Grasso's name stitched in gold—a black apron cinched around my waist. That shade of green flatters me, complementing my honey-toned skin. Zydeco music crackles on the sound system. Buck and I used to tear up the dance floor two-stepping to that hotter-than-Tabasco rhythm, but I can't even walk in a straight line now because my blisters hurt. I head to the area marked *Guest Services*.

A big-boned woman with tiny hoop earrings sits behind the counter pushing a pencil; her black frizzy hair could use a good trim. She looks up, eyebrows raised. "May I help you?"

"I have an appointment with the deli manager."

"I'll buzz her. Did you complete the application online?"

"No ma'am, I did not."

"Here 'ya go, then. Take a seat." She motions to a chair and hands me a pen and several papers affixed to a clipboard. "Please fill this out. She'll be here in a few."

I pretend I'm Ms. Dover as I answer the questions, trying not to misspell anything. Everyone says I have beautiful penmanship, and as I'm writing my last name—*Preston*—adding a curly-Q to the *n*, a young woman saunters up, raking her fingers through short spiked hair. She looks to be a few inches shorter than me, and Mardi Gras beads hang from her neck, draping her chef coat and sparkling like tiddlywinks.

"Hi there. I'm Tracy. Good to meet you."

She grins, and then asks if I've had enough time to complete the application. A gap between her two front teeth gives her a little lisp, and I nod, *yes*, too frightened to introduce myself. I stand, and a blister on my right toe pops. Wincing, I shake her outstretched hand, and my other hand trembles as I hand her the clipboard.

"Follow me to the break room so we can talk. I wish I had a quieter place to interview. You'll have to ignore the chit-chat."

She leads me to an empty table and pulls out a chair, beckoning me to sit then slides onto a stool. Giggling women sitting nearby pass a bag of Fritos as a woman reads aloud a nanny's confession about some movie star's badly behaved children. A couple of razor-buzzed guys swipe cards under the time clock. Tracy scans my application.

"Hmm...well now." She looks up. "You're a day late. Just hired my last cook."

Face hot, fighting back tears, I suck in my cheeks, chewing on the inside of my mouth; I'm sure she's lying but trying to be polite. Who'd hire someone too dumb to even introduce herself. I imagine the word *loser* tattooed in neon crimson across my forehead as she regards me then her cloudy gray eyes brighten as if a flashlight turned on.

"Come to think of it, we *do* need someone to run rotisserie chicken operations. Just lost my girl." She leans her head towards me whispering, "It's not a job for sissies. We generally hire someone with rotisserie experience, but I've a feeling you'll catch on fast."

That's it? Hired? No questions? After all of my fretting and rehearsing? What about the *Three Main Points*? Do they hire just *anybody* off the streets?

She must have read my mind. "I trust my instincts when hiring. That usually works, but time will tell. Grasso's has a three-month probation period, and you won't be eligible for health insurance or tuition reimbursement until mid-May. We start rotisserie operators at eleven dollars an hour."

That's four dollars more than I'd make cashiering at The Pig. I don't need insurance so I may make even more. I didn't get the job I wanted but I'm close; I'll be roasting chickens. I'll be working in the deli.

We stand and shake hands. Untangling a strand of purple Mardi Gras beads from around her neck, she loops them over my head. "Congratulations, Shall-be. Do you mind if I pronounce your name...*Shall-be?*"

Her lips twitch, and I'm not sure if she's mocking me or making up a nickname to remember my name. She gives a little laugh, a tingling giggle that sounds as if she's kidding. I smile as if I get the joke.

"Of course not. Ummm...thanks so much for giving me the job." The first words that have left my lips.

"Here's an information sheet, which includes the number for Human Resources." As she hands me a sheet of paper, I notice her nails are bitten off in ragged edges, a red splotch smearing the end of each finger.

"You'll need to schedule an orientation and sanitation class with them before I can put you on the schedule. This only takes a few days, so I could start training you at the end of next week if you hop to it." I nod *yes*, and then my eyes drop to my feet, swelling past the top edges of my heels.

In a daze, I leave the break room to locate Band-Aids. My toes and heels are rubbed raw, and I stagger, zigzagging down aisles, towards a sign to the pharmacy. I choose a box of extra-wides, which are next to a magazine rack, then locate the latest edition of *Bon Appetit*. Imagine that, still February and March on the stands. After selecting peanuts to settle my stomach, I grab a cold can of Co-Cola and press it against my face to cool my burning cheeks. I pinch my forearm—I got a job.

After making my purchases, I exit Grasso's and walk behind the store, looking for a place where no one will see me sticking on bandages. I spy three large metal dumpsters next to a small parking lot, a glistening luxury roadster filling one of the spaces. Geez Louise. That must be the sweetest car on the planet. I walk closer to get a better look. The name *Anthony Grasso* is written on a sign in front of the car, and the license tag also reads *Grasso*. In the distance I see a man, medium-height with a solid build, in a dark brown suit. He's walking in long strides towards the car, with a woman trotting beside him like a well-trained pony. I slip between two dumpsters, hoping they didn't see me then peek through a slat on one of the open lids. Sour smells of rotten meat make me gag.

They're close to me now, next to the car. The lady is Itchy, the beautiful woman with the pearls. And the man must be Anthony Grasso, the owner of Grasso's. He opens the passenger-side door for her. When she sits in the seat, her skirt slides up, showing off muscular thighs, which she crosses and arranges into the car. Her stockings glisten in the afternoon sun and, as she fastens her seatbelt, they shimmer and shine. I can't help but stare; Mr. Grasso stares too, hesitating before shutting her door.

I finger my dress, now despising the fabric. And would you look at me, hiding between stinking dumpsters wearing plastic beads and a cheap dress. I shake my head, embarrassed; there's a world out there I know nothing about. But I will soon enough, and for the first time since giving birth to my child, I feel proud of myself. Proud, courageous and strong. I found, and am opening, the door of opportunity for me and my daughter.

Mr. Grasso's car pulls out of the parking lot and glides away. I remove my shoes and stockings, stick them into the shopping bag, and then paste Band-Aids over my blisters. I walk barefoot to the motel—even though it's winter, even though the pavement is gritty—and the sidewalk feels plush, soft, as if paved with squares of Wonder Bread.

Night creeps through the window as I relax in bed, glossy photos of lobster risotto spread open across my chest. I think of how Tracy pronounced my name, and keep whispering it over and over, the way she said it, with an emphasis on the *be*...“Shall-*be*... Shall-*be*...” as if I'm lying in wait, creating a new story—“Shelby's Story”—and the best of me is around the bend.

Chicken Gumbo Ya-Ya
by
Mallory Lakes

Gumbo is not so much a recipe as it is a state of mind, complete with secret language and license. "Gumbo" connotes one-too-many hurricanes. One, a cloud-funneled storm, the other, a rum-based drink experienced in a feverish pitch of shiny beads and parades. "Gumbo Ya-Ya" recalls chattering women cooking in the French Quarter or a noisy party.

My mom followed a gumbo recipe loaded with okra in her Baton Rouge River Road Cookbook, and told me if a recipe didn't include okra, you couldn't call it gumbo. But when I add okra, my Yankee friends object to the slippery, slimy texture us Southerners adore. I prefer okra in gumbo but omitted it in the recipe; if you're an okra fan, return it to the pot.

Like any food you may have been raised on, gumbo's left a footprint on my soul, recalling a chain of kinfolk stirring up a palette of earthen browns in cast iron skillets. Making gumbo is conjecture. It's leaving the recipe behind, and opening your palate to flavor, perhaps, you never knew existed. Magic is sure to happen.

This be some fine gumbo. Mighty fine. Serve with white rice, Tabasco and a sweet Southern smile.

CHAPTER 6

Mallory

Last night was chilly for early April, so I opened the window next to my bed only an inch. Bracing air swept through the crack as I pushed table scraps onto the outside ledge to quieten the wails of a feral cat; soon he will be up to enjoy his feast.

I crawled into freshly laundered, one-thousand-count, Egyptian cotton sheets, which tickle my skin like feathers, then curled into my usual fetal pose, pulling the quilt over my shoulders and positioning a plumped goose-down pillow under my neck, another between my knees. The wind chime's ring with its sonorous drone, sounded like the chanting of monks in a faraway monastery, lulling me to sleep.

Dreams were strange and marvelous; I've mastered the choreography for dancing through Cooper. In past nocturnal sojourns, we were trapeze artists, crashing into one another above a hissing crowd. Last night found me a ballerina, alive to everything, in exceptional form. I pirouetted to a standing ovation, twirling over a splash of dappled slate paint; his shadow, in fact, elongated and distorted under stage lights.

I'm awakened by crisscrossing patterns of light across my eyelids; rubbing them, the apparitions disband. I yawn, roll out of bed and struggle to open the hefty window, which always sticks when cracked through the night. Weekdays I leave it closed, blocking out the discordant traffic of a spirit hammering workweek, but today the weekend sounds of Carroll Street are soothing and sneak into my loft like a sigh.

My Turkish quilt, fallen from my bed, languishes in folds on the floor, splattered with yellow light. I'd purchased the coverlet with Cooper while traveling in Istanbul a year after we'd met. The shopkeeper told us the hand-stitched fabric was created by a bride-to-be, a tapestry of enchanting scenes for the marital bed. A quilt of irony, to be sure. Yet, still, last night, I lit a candle for him, praying he'd call or text; even a few words would be a godsend.

A Japanese screen, red and gold leaves hand-painted on pigmented sand parchment, separates my bedroom from the living room and kitchen. I look around and inventory my eclectic surroundings, remembering each whim that prompted a purchase. The chips on the black and gold patterned Deco plates, circa 1927, must have witnessed raucous, extravagant parties; parties I, too, would have enjoyed. I keep them stacked in open cupboards. Depression-era wine glasses and goblets, lined next to the plates, stand rose-colored and regal.

The walnut Biedermeier sofa from Mama's bedroom is placed against the weathered brick walls. Mama loved the clean lines, arched back and scroll carvings on the arms and feet, now worn to a dull, grainy patina. The nubby beige material needs reupholstering, but if I do, may God strike me dead; I smell her powdered scent in the fabric and a drop of coral color, the nail polish she always wore, stains the armrest.

Sunlight streams through the living room's floor to ceiling windows, exploring every angle of the inviting, open floor plan. Earthen-flecked granite counters pull high wood ceilings, brick and mortar walls, and past lives together. Dried crumbs from last night's baguette scatter the teak cutting board; I swipe them away with a damp cloth. The focal point of my kitchen, the six-burner range, glistens and shines, a Trojan horse ready to conquer the next meal. Last week I removed the sticky notes from the fridge and cabinets, and placed them in a maroon velvet box filled with other peculiar mementos.

I call Cabbagetown home, an eclectic, artsy neighborhood a couple of miles from downtown. As a food writer impressed with quirky names and curly-leafed vegetables, how could I live elsewhere? My condo is sandwiched within a cluster of brick lofts known as The Stacks. Architecturally dramatic, they're situated in the remains of a former cotton mill built in 1875. The mill burned down years ago, and foul weather and fire have wreaked havoc on the structure since, but the smokestacks remain as soaring crucifixes abutting a well-tended cemetery of poetic decay.

Smells of burnt coffee permeate my loft, yesterday's Ethiopian Harrar. Drat, I forgot to turn off the timer on the coffee maker; I make a fresh pot. What joy, what absolute bliss to have such a glorious day in front of me. You may note my glass is half full for a change. Yes, *yes.* I was offered a food writing position at *AtlantaNow*, the expected cut in salary offset by an increased food budget. Since my hire, I've been linking daily blogs to *AtlantaNow*, my subscriber's feeds, Twitter account, and Facebook Fan Page.

You'll find Mallory Lake's recipe blogs anyplace that's wired, and my life has turned into a performance, each post a reminder of who I am, or at least who I believe myself to be. I'm *on* all the time and respond to tweets and comments within minutes. Inputting articles, YouTube videos, recipes and photographs into the blogging platform is as routine as feeding the cat. I have bi-monthly meetings at the office and, aside from that, my work can be done in pajamas. I'm building a fan base, and keep my followers on a short leash, communicating with the rapidity of a tennis match, the immediacy of each return serve an adrenaline rush. I feed my readers and they feed me. A cozy symbiosis.

My readership demographics reflect Atlanta's growing diversity. Yesterday a reader requested I make a hot pot recipe similar to the one served at the Korean Noodle Cart. Today I've planned an outing to the International Market in Franklin, just outside the city, to purchase ingredients for my version of this soup. I hope my follower will be pleased.

Itchy is tagging along, looking for exotic produce for the twins' next school project, so we're meeting in thirty minutes at Carroll Street Breads. Sliding into a pair of chestnut skinny jeans and brown leather boots, I pull an oversized cashmere sweater over my head, fasten Itchy's gift of fresh water pearls around my neck, and slide copper bracelets up my forearms. Makeup is minimum: a streak of eyeliner and slash of lipstick, Nar's Apricot Nectar—lipstick is never on a budget. Gazing at myself in the full-length mirror, I strike a pose, cock my head to the side, my hair piling over the side, and practice my crooked pirate smile. I'm almost happy.

Bolting the door with two heavy locks, I skip down the stairs under a fluorescent glow, the chocolate-brown, rubbery steps giving a little squeak under my weight. My loft is as close to a New York City walk-up as anything you'd find in Atlanta. Leaving the building, I stop and inhale the damp sweet hyacinth of early spring, savoring the moment, sunshine warming my cheeks, feeling new, rescued, alive, given a second chance to make good.

Within minutes, I arrive at the bakery, gulping the heady perfumes of salt-rising bread saturating the air. I can't revel in this fragrance of fermented milk, sugar and yeasty steam because Itchy is standing by the door, arms crossed and tapping her foot as if she's on edge. I check the time.

"Hey, I'm only ten minutes late. That's great for me."

"Actually that is good for you. I'm just jumpy. You see, Mallory—and I hope you don't mind—Tony Grasso is coming along too. He regularly checks competition, and rumor has it this market is big competition."

"The Italian stallion who owns Grasso's? Your boss, right? You on the clock?"

"No. At work yesterday I mentioned our plans, and he seemed eager to review their sets."

Frowning, studying crumbs scattered about the floor, I shake my head. I was looking forward to spending the day with her. *Alone.* I miss our girl-talk.

"Have sympathy. He signs my paycheck."

"It's just we haven't had a one-on-one in ages. And Tony Grasso? Seems cozy. This OK with Phil?"

Itchy gives her *don't-ask-don't-tell* pursed-lipped pout, her eyes darting from mine to the street.

"He'll be picking us up any minute; I was worried we'd have to wait for you. Oh, here's his car."

Like an ice sculpture wheeled out at a gaudy, pretentious ceremony, a silver-white luxury two-door pulls up to the bakery's door. Right blinker flashing, Tony Grasso emerges from the car, indifferent to the honking horns, the traffic he's halted in the right lane.

He wears jeans, sharp-ironed creases lining the front, and a black ribbed sweater. A gold chain loops around his thick sinewy neck, which supports a wide cleft chin. His crooked nose—broken in a fight?—protrudes from a leathery face lined with taut tiny fissures, like barbed wire. I note the calculated twenty-four hour stubble, the dark hair combed back in precise lines. I suppose some would call him suavely handsome, even sexy, if you go for that type, but this overt display of alpha-male embarrasses me, and I duck into the back seat before he has a chance to open the door. He doesn't notice and his eyes slide over Itchy, as she straps herself into the passenger side. She's wearing several strands of pale pink pearls, as is her style, but *really*, a tight skirt and heels on an off day?

"Good morning, ladies. Thanks for letting me tag along." He fastens his seat belt then swivels around. As he extends his arm in my direction, cologne wafts over the seat, provoking my sinuses. I sneeze.

"Excuse me." I fumble for a tissue in my bag.

"I don't believe we've met. I'm Tony."

He thrusts his outstretched hand further towards my face, armpit now hoisted over the seat. I blow my nose with my left hand, and then take his hand with my right. The tips of my fingers graze humped knuckles and matted coarse hair, and he pumps hard, crushing my fingers; shaking hands with this man is like scrubbing a burnt pan with a Brillo Pad. I wiggle from his grip.

"I feel I know you, Mallory. I read your articles and appreciate it when you mention our stores."

Schmoozer. He can't be an idiot, though. He's made a bundle with his grocery chain. I'll at least be polite. "Thanks for driving."

"You're very welcome. A talented lady such as yourself in my company; I'm delighted to have an opportunity to get to know you."

Yeah, right.

Franklin is a twenty-minute drive outside of Atlanta. Conversation is batted between Tony and Itchy regarding Grasso's wine sets, a sexual charge coiling each word like a spring. From time to time, they remember I'm in back and direct a question my way. Do I consider lemongrass, for instance, mainstream? I understand my role in this little field trip: I'm their cover. Sickening, just sickening.

The old Itchy was all about the girls, how they're ready for their first bra. Or Phil, who'd make her elaborate dinners on festive occasions. He barely sleeps between his day job and night classes, and still makes time for his family. Since working at Grasso's, she's been cold to him, distant. She turned her cheek when he tried giving her a midnight kiss at the New Year's Eve party. If she lived one day in my shoes, she might appreciate the man she has.

The old Itchy would have laughed at Tony Grasso's splashy persona, his inflated ego. But Itchy has shifted. Poor Phil; I'll bet he's clueless. How I can relate. Such a ruse, this ruinous love. Why bother committing to someone in the first place? You always emerge battered and bruised, less of a person than when you began.

Pulling into the parking lot, I fight my irritation; I've work to do. Walking through the front door of the market, I'm overwhelmed by the bustle, the fragrance, the sheer magnitude of food divided into ethnic sections. I look around, unsure how to make my approach. Itchy and Tony are nowhere in sight. Better they're gone, I can focus. I've ideas for my hot pot recipe scratched on a sticky note, but I'll save the Korean section for last.

The Indian aisles are my favorite; transparent cylinders filled with red, green, yellow and black lentils, pungent orange curries, all dry goods sold in bulk. I salivate, remembering the earthy exotica of a black bean dal, the legume spread I made last week. Leftovers await in my fridge. A few beans are scattered about the floor; a worker notices too and he excuses himself to sweep around my feet.

Raw mango powder? I've never heard of this. How fun. My fans will love it; the perfect tweet. Grabbing my smartphone, I peck at the keys:

Hey y'all. International Market stocks mango powder. Rub over swordfish, sear, serve w/ coconut risotto; #swoonfood #Mallorylakes.

I drop my phone in my bag and ladle some of the gold-brown powder into a plastic bag. This market stocks at least half-a-dozen garam masalas from different regions of India. Inhaling their sultry scents of cardamom, cinnamon and cumin, I smirk. I tried to buy a generic version of this classic Indian spice at Grasso's, and the clerks didn't have a clue as to what I was talking about.

I turn right and walk three steps into the Mediterranean section. Stiffening, stifling a gasp, I take two steps back. I hope they didn't see me.

Itchy is leaning against an end cap packed with extra virgin olive oil, her black lizard bag splayed open at her feet, and Tony is facing her. His fingers, folded down at the joints like a muscled pink ham, are close to her lips, which are coiled into a smile. His sweater is pushed back, revealing a chunky platinum watch studded with diamonds, and he is holding a strand of her pearls to the light, his thumb and forefinger working one pearl, rubbing it back and forth.

Heat crawls up my neck and spreads to my cheeks, and moisture shimmers across my face, dampening my vision. I jerk around and move forward, ramming into a customer's shopping cart. Muttering, "Excuse me," I zigzag between carts and skim down aisles towards the back of the store, retreating as far away as possible from that creepy scene.

Noticing a table with a hand-written sign: Coryville Organic Hog Farm, I stop, swipe my brow with the back of my hand, and breathe deeply, trying to compose myself. A woman, with a nametag reading Martha-Mae is selling pork chops, loins and sausage from a large cooler. I prefer *this* brand of swine.

"Pardon me. I always purchase beef and chicken from local farms. I wasn't aware there was an organic pig farm in the area. Is Cory a family name?"

"No. Coryville's the name of the town where we have our farm, about three hours south of Atlanta. Our farm and animals are certified organic by the Department of Agriculture and are Animal Welfare Approved."

"I appreciate your contribution to ethical meat options."

"The hogs are fed an organic mix of barley, oats, corn and vitamins, all free of hormones and antibiotics, but their lifestyle is just as important as what we feed them. They're pasture-raised with an access to forage—rooting around is a pig's favorite sport. That and shooting the breeze with their clan. We breed Heritage Duroc with Berkshires. Unlike those skinny factory pigs, which try to compete with the chicken breast industry, our plump porkers have incredible tenderness and marbling. It's a flavor you may remember from childhood."

"Pork's not on my list today but I'll come back when I'm craving some juicy chops. I'm glad I ran into you, Martha-Mae. My name's Mallory Lakes and I'm a food writer for *AtlantaNow*." I fish out a business card and hand it to her.

She fastens it to a ledger with a paper clip. "I read your articles. We'd be thrilled if you wrote about our farm. We've been wholesaling our pork to Atlanta's finest restaurants for six years. This will be our second year retailing to the general public, and you can purchase our products online. As I'm sure you're aware, a happy pig is a healthy pig, which makes our pork a healthy option."

I pick up a pamphlet lying on the table: *You buy the pig. We'll do the rest.*

"What does this mean?" I point to the words.

"Some folks, like yourself, want to know exactly what they're eating, where it comes from, and how it was raised. Especially their meat. Our customers purchase piglets from us now, in the spring, and we raise them. After the weather's cooled down, sometime in November, they come to the farm the day their animal is slaughtered, say goodbye to their hog, then help with the butchering."

I perk up. Purchasing a live pig would be a way of acknowledging and reconciling my disconnect between the animal's death and my gustatory pleasure. Maybe I'll become a vegetarian after buying an animal then facing the reality of turning it into dinner. Or maybe I'll just feel better about eating humanely raised meat. It'll be interesting to learn what my followers will think about this purchase and my intentions, providing tantalizing fodder—the antidote to reader boredom—for future blogs.

"How much does a piglet cost?"

"Five hundred and fifty dollars. That may sound high, but remember you're paying for a pig that lives a happy life, socializing and roaming freely with access to clean water and nutritious feed. The fee also covers the butchering and the packaging. You'll leave our farm in November with two hundred pounds—give or take—of organic bacon, sausage, ham, ribs, and roasts. Believe me, you'll need freezer space."

"Do you take plastic?" If that porker cost a thousand dollars, it would be worth it, though my food budget will be strained for the next couple of weeks. I'll revisit the Indian section and buy rice, lentils and spices to make cheap vegetarian meals. She takes my credit card.

"Here's your prize. Her name's Lilly-Belle, a precious spotted gilt." She returns my card and hands me a photograph of a wee little polka-dot piglet; one ear pink and the other one gray. When friends pull out photos of their children, I'll trump them with my adorable pig.

"We'll e-mail you regular updates on your animal, and when it's scheduled for slaughter." I flinch. *Slaughter.* Such a brutal word.

I thank her and wander to the Korean section to purchase ingredients for the soup. Musing over their selection of kim chee, I remember reading that in parts of Korea they eat dogs, believing canines give them sexual strength. Disgusting. Yet many Muslims and Jews find slaughtering and eating pig despicable, the Bible references it as unclean. Cattle are considered sacred in Hinduism and Buddhism, so there eating meat is taboo. Animals mean different things to different cultures so who am I to judge. Still. *Dog meat?*

I remember the twins' school project and purchase a bag of Asian long beans that look and taste like green beans but are long, like fettuccine. I wonder what Itchy selected for their assignment? I think of her, Tony, and their seediness then bite my bottom lip, texting her, asking if she's ready to meet at the front entry. She arrives with Tony, empty-handed. I hand her the beans.

"Long beans," I say, words tight. "The girls may find them amusing."

Her face reddens, starting at her streaked gold hairline then runs down her neck. She opens her mouth as if to say something, and then shakes her head, turning it sideways towards the street. We walk to Tony's car, not saying a word.

She's got a husband who adores her, Tony has a wife. I don't know if his wife adores him, but they've got a second home in Tuscany. Sweet consolation. They both have children. So much, and never enough.

Tony tries engaging me, offering a humorous anecdote about a dog in customs sniffing out some truffles he was bringing back from Italy. I try smiling, but my lips fade to a frown. Pressing the pad of his smartphone, the car beeps to attention and I flinch as locks click on command. My eyes moisten with despair, knowing there are no children waiting for me at home, no man to love, desiring my touch. The afternoon has soured.

At the end of the day, however, this consolation remains: I have my readers, and as long as they keep following me, I'll never be alone.

Kim chee Hot Pot with Chicken and Soba Noodles
by
Mallory Lakes

Some tightly wound, ancient, DNA thread must still exist in humankind, beckoning and weaving us together around a simmering communal pot of soup. And when a tribal or family member, or friend, ventures forth tossing a new ingredient into the fragrant brew, it's a reminder we're not alone.

The origin of Asian Hot Pot traces its roots back over 1000 years ago to northern China. Hot Pot may have been primitive mankind's version of sedatives. Through the bitter hardship of winter, the consistent demands of an active fire would banish negative thoughts; the hot soup rekindling and nourishing spirits until early buds appeared in the spring.

This recipe is a mosaic of favorite flavors from several versions of hot pot I've tried. If one were pressed to pinpoint a particular region where these particular hot pot ingredients would be served, it would be Korea; Korea because of the kim chee. If dining in Korea, most likely your meals would be served with this ubiquitous pickled cabbage accompaniment.

Invite your tribe to warm up around your version of hot pot. Encourage them to bring an item-spinach, shrimp, pork-to toss into the bubbling brew. Double the recipe; leftovers are a bonus.

Chapter 7

Shelby

I suspect most folks don't realize what goes on back-stage in a fancy deli. Well, I am here to inform. I've been working at Grasso's for nearly six weeks and am fully in charge of rotisserie chicken operations. It's no walk in the park, believe me.

In sanitation class, I learned if raw chicken juice drips down, say, in a deli salad, it's *cross-contamination*. A customer could get sick off a pasta salad because of one splash of misguided chicken dribble. And if the chickens aren't cooked long enough, that could let loose a *food-borne epidemic,* just like those tainted burgers from Hamburger Heaven that killed that poor child. A chicken epidemic would shut Grasso's down in a minute.

Tracy wasn't kidding when she said it wasn't a job for sissies. Three long red and black scabs run down my arm from when the heavy spits slipped off and burned me. Each morning she rubs ointment on the sores and wraps them in a fresh bandage.

She's working me up from rotisserie to gourmet deli. Last week I made *Curried Chicken Salad with Mangos and Cashews.* Tracy said it tasted like dreamland, the best batch ever. After sampling it to customers, two hours later, a twelve-pound batch sold out; I was right proud. In seven weeks, I'm eligible for tuition reimbursement, and I'm counting the minutes. Tracy's a good boss, but if she were like the rest of management around here, I'd hightail back to Coryville, chef school or no chef school.

Most mornings I clock-in at eight, sanitize my station, wash the chickens then skewer them on spits according to flavor: *Plain, Barbecue, Chipotle, Lemon-Garlic, Lemon-Rosemary* and *Cajun.* It takes one and a half hours to roast them, and the first batch must be packaged, under the heating element and on the sales floor, by ten forty-five. As they roast, I skin and bone the chickens that didn't sell, and chop the meat for salads. Then I start the second rotisserie batch.

I'm supposed to take two fifteen-minute breaks and a thirty-minute lunch every day; this is the law, but I never have time to take breaks and often skip lunch, giving Grasso's a free hour of my time. On skip-lunch days, I hide in the cooler and gobble down a chicken leg that got stuck on the spit. If someone asks me I lie: *Sure, I take my breaks.* Because if I don't, Human Resources would nail Tracy. But if I took the breaks, I wouldn't get the chickens out in time. Tracy pays hell when those chickens aren't rotated off and back under the heating element every three hours and she is written up by the store director, Humpty Dumpty.

His real name is Paul Davis but we call him Humpty behind his back. His doughy cheeks just clear my shoulder line and with that swollen gut, he looks six-month's pregnant. Thin strands of sandy hair are combed back over a balding scalp, and he's always glancing over his shoulder, worried Grasso might be storming up to rip another asshole into him. (Tracy's words, not mine.)

Tracy explained this store is *Grasso* headquarters and workers are divided into *Grocery* and *Corporate.* Grocery are us worker-bees on the floor, while Corporate sit behind fat-cat desks in the offices upstairs. I don't know what they do except frighten us with nasty looks when they come down. Humpty's considered Grocery, but he tries to dress like Mr. Grasso, always wearing a natty dark suit and white shirt, hoping one day he can escape the floor by getting promoted to Corporate. When he gives Tracy a hard time, I know Grasso's behind it.

But she pays him no mind. Tracy's slick; thick-skinned. Tracy could give a rat's ass. When Humpty turns his back, she gives him the finger, winking at whoever's watching. She says if he eats another donut, he may burst into pieces, just like Humpty Dumpty, then she'd sweep him up and throw him in the dumpster. Have a beer to celebrate. But I feel sorry for the man. Times are tough and he has a family to support. Humpty reminds me of that straw-colored dog back in Coryville, neck strained sideways and tail tucked between hind legs. The poor thing wanders the town with strap marks across his back and instead of a bark, he gives a high-pitched yip.

Tracy gives me a forecast, her prediction of how many chickens we'll need to cook that day. She's like the weather girl, but talking birds, not rain showers. Today she got the forecast wrong, but it's not her fault. Mallory Lakes is putting all of the chickens in her cart, and this isn't the first time she's done this. Tracy asked her once, real nice, if she could phone us in advance so we could make a double batch and have enough rotisseries for the mid-day shoppers. But she never does.

She used to shop at Grasso's, stopping to chat with her pal Itchy, several times a week, but I haven't seen hide nor hair of her in over a month. I've missed watching her from the kitchen, the glint of her dangling bracelets, how her hair falls and covers her face when she looks down to read her phone. Whenever she came to the deli, I couldn't use a knife because of my jiggling hands. Last time she was in, I grabbed an order pad to get her autograph but Tracy stopped me, said it might irritate her. Surely it's not a big deal, introducing myself. Now or never. I wash my hands, straighten my apron, and walk towards her.

"Oh. Hey," I say, cheeks scalding, voice coming out a squeak, "may I help you with those chickens? Roasted 'em myself, just slid 'em off the spit." I can't hear my words over my hammering heart.

"You're sweet, but I'm arranging them into the cart, just so, so they don't tip over."

Digging my nails into my palms, I take a deep breath as words tumble from my lips. "OK then. Well, my name is Shelby. But there's no need to say who you are; you're Mallory Lakes. I've read everything you've written and I'm always trying out your recipes."

"That's nice," she says, tucking the last packaged chicken into the cart, giving it a little pat. She pulls her phone from her bag and studies it. When she looks up, her eyes widen, as if surprised I'm still standing there.

"It's a pleasure meeting you. Thanks for following me; I appreciate that."

She's friendly. I'll bet she'd shake my hand if she weren't clutching that phone. I can't believe I'm talking to Mallory Lakes. I don't want our conversation to end. "Don't you just love the Food Broadcast? Don't you?"

She gives a little half-smile but remains silent. Sweet Jesus, maybe she thinks I'm talking about Sandra Dean.

"Oh. No. I'm not talking about Sandra Dean. Not Sandra Dean," I stammer. "She takes too many shortcuts. That's what I like about your recipes. You make all of your recipes from scratch."

"Yes. Well, yes. Nice to meet you." She glances towards the wine department then back to me, giving another crooked smile. "And I must say your roasted chickens are the best in town."

The best in town? As she pushes her cart forward, I decide to press my luck and ask for her autograph, but now she seems rushed and irritated, trying to navigate around a table pyramided with chocolate biscotti. I lose my nerve; next time.

My heart's stomping through my chest like a herd of cattle. I just had a conversation with Mallory Lakes. I may have sounded like a crazy fool, but she did say my chickens were the best in town. I catch Tracy's eye from behind the counter. She doesn't have to say a word, but I know it's time to get busy. I scurry back to the kitchen.

"Well, Miss Shelby, Miss Shelby. Mmm-mm. How did Ms. Lakes earn those scarlet cheeks of yours? I hope you told her we'd appreciate a call next time she decides to buy all the chickens."

"Yeah, right."

"Her blogs are funny and her recipes great, but in person she seems girly-girl stuck on herself. Her buddy Itchy's no better; got the morals of a jackrabbit."

"We'll get nailed if we don't get the chickens out by lunch," I say, changing the subject. I don't like mean-spirited things said about Mallory. I take deep breaths and ball my fingers into fists, trying to control my shaking hands. I just spoke to *Mallory Lakes*.

The adrenaline scooting through my veins helps me skewer chickens faster that you can say Jack Robinson. Praise the sweet Lord Jesus it's Wednesday, Humpty's day off. The only bummer is that when he's gone, Mr. Grasso checks on us.

It's twelve-fifteen and Mr. Grasso and Itchy are heading towards the deli; on Wednesdays they arrive at work at noon, meet for lunch, then drive to the other stores to check out wine sets. They're both married with children but with those sly, secret smiles and sideways glances, they seem mighty friendly towards each other. I have nothing more to say on *that* subject.

Out of breath, I roll the last of the packaged birds onto the floor while Tracy washes her hands then situates herself behind the counter, painting on a fake smile especially for him. "Good afternoon, Mr. Grasso. Is there a deli item that tempts you?"

Tracy's lisp is cute and her accent's almost as country as mine, but girls like Tracy are of no interest to guys like Grasso. He nods but doesn't reply, just raises his caterpillar eyebrows, like *who was she to be talking to him.* He walks into the prep area holding a seaweed-lined cutting board topped with a cylinder of rice, arms thrust in her direction. Tracy's cue: Sicilian sushi.

She slides the back door of the deli case open then, with wide-jawed tongs, grabs an oversized meatball and plops it onto the rice. He places the board onto the counter, smashes the meat with his thumb so it collapses and fills the roll, then—with thick, furry, papa bear hands—rolls up the seaweed, rice and meatball, cigar-style. He slices it into thick disks then Tracy shimmies a spatula under the concoction, slides it into a Styro box, ladles marinara sauce over the top, and snaps the lid shut. Taking the roll, he glances at the rotisserie chickens, says something to Itchy, and they walk towards the wine department.

Tracy catches my eye, tipping her head to the kitchen. My signal. We meet at the sink behind the back wall, hiding from the public eye, and she slaps me a high-five. "You are one hell of a worker bee, Miss Shall-be. Way to bust your ass, girlfriend."

"I'm just trying to steer us clear of trouble."

"Hey, team-player. What 'cha doing after work? Clare and I invited some neighbors to stop by Squash Blossom for a potluck. Wanna join us?"

My face feels hotter than it does under the chicken pit. "Where's Squash Blossom?"

"Squash Blossom Farms, the place we call home. We live in a community twenty miles south of here and share a farm with our neighbors. We grow vegetables, herbs, fruit, and, of course, squash. Georgia, in fact, grows more squash than any other state in the country. Their blossoms are our favorite."

I didn't come to Atlanta to go traipsing across the county to some potluck; I must stay focused on my plan. An excuse comes easy: "That's nice of you to offer but I don't have a car."

She grins. "Where 'ya live, hon?"

I hang my head; I'm still at The Troubadour. I don't have money for even a studio, much less an apartment with an extra room for Miss Ann. *Miss Ann*. I've only had time for three short visits since taking this job. And what will happen after I begin classes? I call her each night then lie fitfully awake after we've hung up, loving her so; a piece of my heart is missing. Crawling out of bed each morning, my legs feel stiff, hollow, like a rusted-out pipe. I bite my lower lip, not answering her question, staring at my shoes.

Tracy rests her hand on my shoulder. "Wait till you sample the Squash Blossom Honey we make at the farm. Hoo-wee. Kids love it, most folks do. Elixir from the bees cures everything that ails 'ya. I'll give you a bottle to take home to your girl."

How did she know Miss Ann was filling my head? That woman reads my mind. Her palm feels comforting on my shoulder and I raise my chin, catching her eye; a kind person, even a friend.

"For the time being I stay at The Troubadour Motel. They give me a discount, which makes it cheaper than an apartment if you count utilities."

"I know the place. Leave work early. I'll cover your clean-up and will pick you up after my shift, say five-thirty? I'll drive you back after supper."

I'll bet Miss Ann would love a jar of homemade honey. Maybe a bit of socializing would lift my spirits. "Are you sure it's not an inconvenience?"

"Heck no. The more the merrier." She glances at the clock. "You'll have just enough time to change out of that charming little deli outfit and wash the chicken guts out of your hair."

"But I don't have a kitchen so I can't make a dish."

Tracy folds her arms across her chest, chewing at her thumbnail, looking at the ceiling. "Here's a thought. Mallory Lake's latest chicken salad recipe is penned to the task board. Make that and spoon the salad into endive leaves then arrange them on a platter, just like her photo. I'll charge your labor to R and D. The girls will love it."

I smile, feeling nervous, but flattered to be invited. "Thanks, Tracy. I'll be waiting in front of The Troubadour."

At five-thirty sharp, Tracy pulls up to the motel in a black Ford pick-up, rust-colored dirt plastered to the sides. Her front license tag is decorated with yellow and orange blossoms with a curling green vine circling the cursive words *Squash Blossom*. I wonder how she got the State to do that.

She climbs out of the truck wearing a teal sundress with navy spaghetti straps matching a tie that cinches her waist. She must have changed in the ladies room. Who'd ever guess that underneath that chef coat were Miss America hips and a tapered waistline. She gives me a tight hug and stones on a massive necklace press against my chest.

Climbing into the truck, I notice the platter of stuffed chicken leaves on the floor in back. They must have had a rough ride because even wrapped in Saran, their pointed tips are going every which a way. Tracy, as usual, reads my mind.

"Sorry about your arrangement, Shall-be. We'll straighten up the leaves before serving."

"That's all right. Thanks for picking me up."

As she heads out the parking lot and follows signs to the expressway, I notice a bottle of wine in a skinny *Grasso* bag pressed against her thigh. I've been meaning to try some *Grasso* wine, it's gotta be good. Shoppers spend a long time in the wine department consulting with Itchy and studying the bottles before putting them into their cart.

Tracy follows my gaze. "I'm invited to several wine tastings each year. Corporate wants me to suggest wines to customers when they're putting together a special meal. I'll take you to the next one."

"A wine tasting? I'd love that. I want to learn as much as I can before starting chef school."

"You're going to be one busy lady." She merges onto the expressway. "What about your daughter?"

"Her name's Miss Ann and Mama takes care of her in Coryville. She just started a business doing hair in the cellar. My girl stays with her down there or upstairs watching TV. My aunt helps too." My voice catches, lowering to a whisper, "Meets her school bus. Stuff like that."

We pass a "Jesus Saves" sign, the words written on a black and yellow crucifix. An insect smacks against the windshield with a sharp clicking thwack of blood. Tracy changes the subject. I'm grateful; when

I think of my daughter, my stomach churns and tears push at the flood gates.

"I've called Squash Blossom home for close to six years now. Clare inherited her folks farm after they died. She divided it into eight homestead sites, most of them ten-acre parcels. We live in her family home, and kept twenty acres of farmland for our own organic enterprises."

I nod, pinching my nose to stop the tingling and keep from crying. Rubbing my clenched jaw, I make a little grunt, a sound I've never before uttered. It feels like pinecone scales are lodged in my throat. Who could forgive a mother leaving her child. I should be home with my daughter instead of going to some party with strangers. For a long second, Tracy stares hard at me sideways then her eyes connect back to the road.

"Clare hand-picked the buyers, all women, and sold the parcels at sliding rates based on what they could afford. Practically gave two lots away. Making sure our neighbors share our social and environmental values is way more important to her than money."

I swallow twice before trusting myself to speak. "Can't wait to see it, Tracy. Sounds like paradise."

"It's the life we always fantasized. The neighborhood—we call it our hamlet—shares a common house, which has a library, entertainment space and a meditation area. I never wanted to work away from the farm but that last flood combined with the screwy economy forced me to take the Grasso position. Hope it's temporary. I worry one day I'll scramble Humpty for breakfast." I smile. Tracy always puts me in a better mood.

We exit the expressway and pull onto a street. Large patches of farmland lie on each side of strung-together storefronts. It's a small town like Coryville, but the hardware store, diner, ice cream shop and grocery store aren't weathered and boarded-up. Tracy turns right on a dirt road lined with pecan trees and pulls up to a farmhouse painted lemon-yellow with tangerine shutters. A large field behind the house is filled with tidy rows of vegetable shoots.

Opening my door, I hear goats bleating in pens off to the side of a barn; I also smell their nasty musk stink. Tracy giggles at my scrunched-up nose. "Shoulda warned ya'. We've got a passel of goats. Those two bucks in the far pen give off the stench. Gets worse when the does are in heat. We're thinking about getting into the goat cheese business next year."

We climb out of the truck. I lift the dish of chicken leaves from the floor and follow her up a stone path to the house. The rocks wobble beneath my feet and I worry that if my heel catches an edge, I'll fall; I take tiny steps, gripping the platter. Several rocking chairs, painted to match the shutters, are scattered across the front porch, which is deep enough to accommodate a family reunion and wraps around both sides of the house.

A woman with a thick silver braid pulled in front of her shoulder sits in one of the chairs. Bending over a bucket peeling potatoes, she wears cut-off jeans and a faded green T-shirt reading *Make Cornbread, Not War*. I feel overdressed in my white poly-blend slacks and ruffled pink shirt, a set I bought at Walmart. The words Squash Blossom Farms are carved into the front door, under which a squash blossom is etched and painted into the wood.

"I made that," Tracy says. "Like to whittle in my spare time. This is my partner, Clare." She turns to the woman in the chair. "Clare, this is Shall-be."

My brain cracks open like a hickory nut. Her partner? Tracy's more of a woman than I thought. She's a *lesbian*. I know all about the actress Helen D'Antonio and her gay-lady lifestyle, and wondered if Helen, like me, just hadn't met the right man. Like dark-skinned folk, I don't wish anything bad on them, or homosexuals, the male version. But I have never met, much less had a conversation with, a real lesbian. I can't believe I've known Tracy this long and never figured it out. Holding back a smile, she looks at me like the cat that swallowed the goldfish. Best be careful, woman's a mind reader.

"Hi Shelby." Clare straightens, brushing her hands together. "Tracy's spoken about you." She doesn't pronounce my name *Shall-be* like Tracy but says it the normal way. Her olive skin is smooth and her eyes are the same shade as the sky before it fixes to go dark; she is what you'd call a handsome woman. I wonder why she'd let her hair go gray. Mama'd love to get her hands on that mane but it's so long and thick, it'd take all afternoon to get the color through.

"The girls will be here in an hour," Clare says. "Why don't you put your dish in the fridge till they get here? I'm making potato salad and need to get these peeled." She tries to smile but it twitches on the sides then fades to a frown. "Make sure you close the door; flies from the goat pen are patching up the sky." She makes a waving motion with her hand then pushes her braid back with the flat of her palm, bends over and picks up a vegetable peeler and potato. She digs out the eyes then her hand moves quick, working that potato like she's skinning it alive.

Tracy holds the door for me as I walk into the house. "Clare runs the farm. She plants, harvests and schedules the workers. This is her only job, so she does the bulk of the work. Between all that plus crop rotation, composting and ensuring the soil's healthy, it's enough."

We walk through the living room and the sun shines through old-fashioned warped paned windows, painting squares across the floor.

"We sell our produce to the finest Atlanta restaurants. We tried selling at farmer's markets, but it's twice the work and half the cash. You wouldn't believe how much the chefs pay. They visit the farm and make a big deal on their menus about our vegetables being local and organic. Farm-to-table is important to many people. We're part of a group of vegetable and livestock farmers reclaiming our Southern cooking traditions through our work in the fields."

"Do you sell to Grasso's?"

"That's a joke. They'd never pay us what we'd need to break even, much less turn a profit. What they call *organic* is also a joke. Factory farms across the world do the absolute minimum to be able to use the word organic as a marketing tool."

We enter an airy, spacious kitchen filled with with the tart and sweet smells from a strawberry-rhubarb crumble cooling on a rack. The walls are painted a whispered shade of green, the same color as the chopped celery that fans across a butcher-block counter. A large pot of water is bubbling on the stove, waiting, I'll bet, for Clare's potatoes.

"Our neighbors, the women you'll meet tonight, help in the field. We trade labor for vegetables." She shrugs. "It works."

Tracy walks to a Mason jar filled with cream-colored flowers on a table, and moves them slightly to the left into a crack of sunlight. "You know these? Charming, aren't they? Elderberry blossoms—*Sambucus nigra*—early this year. Pillows of tiny stars. They'll be twinkling everywhere in a few weeks, clustering into purple berries in the summer." I nod. "The women use the flowers for making cordials. Clare pickles the berries before they ripen and we use them as capers. You can also turn them into wine, syrup, vinegar...there's a zillion ways to use them."

I'm glad the chicken leaves are a mess. Arranging them back into a circle keeps my hands and eyes busy; right now, cat's got my tongue. But I don't want her imagining I think poorly on her and Clare—I mean, their lifestyle.

Giving her a side glance, a tip of my chin, I smile, just as a breeze captures the scent of the flowers, pulling their sweet fragrance towards me. I wipe my hands on a towel and walk to the blossoms, lowering my head into their buttery clusters. Their smell changes into an unpleasant fish-like aroma. I straighten, pinching my nostrils, my eyes darting to Tracy.

She takes several steps back, rests a fingertip on her dimpled chin, and stares at the blossoms. "Funny about elderberry, you must be mindful. Their leaves are toxic." After a spell, she returns to the table and slides the jar to the right, into a spot where a cloud has made a shadow.

"A storm's brewing along the Chattahoochee, heading our way. Goats are skittish. I'll get the honey from the pole barn before the rain sets in. And, oh, care for some wine?"

CHAPTER 8

Mallory

Most people don't have time to cook. You know this, no revelation. What's left of you after a not-enough-time-to-breathe workday collapses over a menu at the next swabbed table. Other evenings find you and your child studying for tomorrow's test as the car idles, waiting for dinner to be handed through a drive-through window.

But the less time you spend cooking, the more time you spend fantasizing about your next home-cooked meal. *Food Broadcast* ratings are skyrocketing. You're downloading recipes faster than McDonald's makes fries. I puzzle over this dichotomy: the desire to cook and actually pulling out a pan. I conclude as humans we're hard-wired to nourish ourselves and those we love. If you can't manufacture the time to dice, measure and sauté, you watch Mario flambé the scaloppini. Tonight, in fact, finds you piercing dinner's cello casing, popping it into the microwave then clicking on your screen to see what I'm cooking.

My exploding fan base, built on the readership I developed at the *Atlanta Sun*, has gone viral—even outside of Georgia—indicating that I, Mallory Lakes, can claim celebrity status. On *AtlantaNow* my blog's in the top percentage of hits, rivaling crime and sports. I had over eight hundred thousand site visits last month; a number even impressive to the new boss, Richard Wright, and we're brainstorming a collaboration for an e-cookbook.

My food writing was recently described as sexy. *Underground Atlanta's* words: "Mallory Lake's photography is non-censored gastro-porn. Each day we share her sauté pan and intimacies as we hand her the olive oil. Her seductive blogs simplify the daunting task of preparing inspired cuisine.... her amusing anecdotes make steaming rice an orgasmic experience."

Orgasmic? Really? If home cooking trickles into erotica, maybe more people will pick up a spatula. Flirtatious ditties pop like corn onto my screen. My vanity's stoked but get real, second-hand media is always more flattering; the pictures enhanced, the heavily edited scripts having nothing to do with reality.

Most days find me smudge-eyed and pajama-clad, my disarrayed hair pulled back so it doesn't fall into the stock. You don't see that version. You see the photoshopped Mallory Lakes, shopping for persimmons, or my dolled-up YouTube stuffing the sea bass with herbs.

I'm relishing this fame in an age that glorifies the electronic manipulation of our lives. Facebook, YouTube, Twitter; we sketch ourselves into what we want others to see. Ego reincarnation, if you will. And reality shows? *Ha.* There's nothing real about people, myself included. It's as if I've cast myself as the main character in a play I'm writing. And if I'm playing a part, I'm not a real person and neither is Cooper, making his absence less painful. There is no flesh-and-blood other to distract me from my constant smartphone pecking, tweeting a terrific deal on lamb shanks, or the location of the tamale truck on Peachtree and Adams. It's just you, our next meal, and me.

AtlantaNow has sophisticated analytics that delivers me your profile. My fan, my follower—*thank you*—you're a loyal friend. Your comments inspire my next musings and meal. You advised when the Chicken Biryani ingredient list was too long, and when I overdid the garlic in the Pistachio-Kale Pesto. You appreciated my simplified version of Braciole Ripiene from The Roman Kitchen. When you *do* carve out the time to cook, it's generally during the holidays, or other celebrations. These are the recipes with the most hits; they must be your favorites.

Today's a Mexican holiday, May fifth, Cinco de Mayo, that insists I break out the tequila and respond to your tweets for Mexican cuisine. At the moment I'm scurrying to meet a close friend, Marselina, at Bandaras, which is a Latin grocery, to gather ingredients for a chicken mole. She'll be lending authenticity to what many consider Mexico's national dish.

Marselina was raised in Mexico and while on an exchange student scholarship, dated, then married, an Atlanta native. Granted American citizenship, she's lived in Atlanta for twenty years. We met many moons back while working on a committee creating a Southwest menu for a fund-raiser. Marselina is finishing her last year of law at Emory, and volunteers time, honing her knowledge on pro-bono immigration issues. She maintains close ties with her family and friends in San Pedro Atocpan, a district in Mexico City famous for moles, and to the Latin community in Atlanta.

She's my height, five-six'ish, and curvaceous without sliding into the plump category. Her black hair falls in waves, one layer cut to accentuate chiseled cheekbones and a straight nose, the second layer grazing full breasts. Smooth agave-colored skin and vast dark eyes of chocolate brown are testimonials to the superiority of Latin genetics over my watered-down English blood. Her eager, hot-witted passion and sparkling humor are the perfect foil for my moodiness, but more than anything, I admire Marselina's generous spirit, which is contagious.

Marselina's been divorced over a year, and, like me, has no boyfriend to phone up or children to tuck in bed. After cooking dinner and posting today's blog, we're hitting a hot new Latin club, La Cueva, celebrating the holiday with Gaspar Salvador, a world-renowned Mariachi group. I spy her sorting through baskets of chili peppers.

"Hola, Marselina. Today's the day you teach me and my readers how to make your mother's mole."

"Oh, right. That would take my lifetime. It's incredibly complicated if we make it from scratch; we'd never get to the club."

"I figured. I made a complex mole many moons ago. It was divine, but I thought I'd never be released from the kitchen. Perhaps you've a short-cut?"

"Actually, I was hoping you'd go for that. Let's purchase a ready-made mole paste; the one they sell here is quite good. It has the consistency of peanut butter and tastes like nuts, spices, chocolate. Best of all, it's loaded with assorted chilies."

"What kinds?"

"Oh, you know, mulatas, chipotles, guajillas, chihuacle negros....."

Her eyes glisten, mesmerized by the baskets brimming with fresh and dried chilies in front of her. It's as if she's studying a map of her home country: green, orange and red peppers appear waxed with shellac, as exotic birds and fauna of the Yucatan peninsula; dried peppers rest flattened and stacked, their leathery black and wrinkled brown skin as wizened viejos combing the Coahuila desert for cacti. Marselina's fingers, emblazoned with silver and turquoise rings, shake a basket of heart-shaped ancho peppers. I remove my camera and snap several photographs. Adjusting the F-stop, I alternate wielding her and the peppers in and out of focus.

"Slow down, chica," she says. "We don't need to *buy* the chilie's, they're already incorporated into the mole."

"But they're so lovely." I pose her digging into the basket of long lizardy pasillos, and then take another couple of shots.

"I'm going to purchase an assortment for my terra-cotta bowl." I hang my camera strap over my shoulder. "You remember; the crackled glazed one I bought in Oaxaca? If I don't use them in mole, maybe I'll stuff them with Chihuahua cheese and bake them later."

"Oh, my mom did that whenever my brother...."

"Excuse me. I don't mean to interrupt you ladies." A middle-aged man steps in front of Marselina. Cloudy moon eyes scrutinize me from behind thick lenses, his face inches from mine. His tongue, moistening cracked, chalky lips, darts in and out of his mouth like a salamander catching flies.

"Are you Mallory Lakes?" His breath smells rank, like something dead, and I step back, pushing against a basket of peppers.

"Yes. I am."

"Could you tell me which of these peppers is the *hottest*?" I'm often recognized when shopping and asked for advice, but this question sounds obscene coming from his parched and peeling mouth.

"Hmm. The hottest." I pinch the stem of a mushroom-shaped orange pepper and remove it from the basket. "I believe the habanero has the highest heat index. Right, Marselina? My friend is the expert."

Slithering away from his gaze, my flesh crawls as I brush inadvertently against his unmoving torso while trying to navigate the baskets.

"Ick," whispers Marselina. "Do you have to deal with creeps like that on a regular basis? Poor Mallory. Hey, let's pick up a couple of rotisseries from Grasso's. It'll save us from having to roast chicken for the recipe."

My breath catches. Today's Thursday; Itchy inventories wine at the downtown store on Thursdays. "Let's go to Southern Green. It's a further hike but their chickens are from local farms." I pay for the chilies and mole paste, and we exit the store.

Marselina and I return to the loft, loaded down with bags. Removing the papayas from my bowl, I replace them with the chili peppers. We spend the next several hours prattling, sipping blender margaritas, and exchanging confidences. "...he begged you to wax off *everything*? Ouch."

Marselina shares tidbits of wickedness with me, prying out my naughtiness. I confide erotic adventures, Cooper's predilections, things I'd never confess to Itchy. I haven't returned her calls since our outing to the International Market. I also quit sweating it out at Boot Camp and returned to the safe haven of my yoga practice at a neighborhood studio; I've been missing the repetition of salutations and focused breathing, so nurturing to my sense of well-being. Besides, Itchy would never show up there; yoga bores her to tears. I remember the way Tony fingered her pearls. She was so selfish, so arrogant, to use our outing as an excuse to be with that man.

I feel betrayed, and I'm sick for Phil and the twins. I've only shopped at Grasso's once since that day out of desperation. I'd promised *AtlantaNow* six casseroles of Roasted Chicken Lasagna for a workshop that evening. Grasso's always stocks an ample supply of rotisseries before noon, and it was Wednesday; Itchy arrives at noon on Wednesdays.

As Marselina promised, the mole comes together quickly; my readers will be appreciative. Marselina washes the dishes as I place the finished dish inside my photo tent, adjust the lighting and take several shots. Finishing the blog and recipe, I upload the photos then post them on my site. I glance at the clock; time to switch gears and get to the club.

"Marselina, what size shoe do you wear? I've a pair of fabulous orange and red spikes that would look far sexier than those clogs you're sporting. They're a size seven, and I've never worn them, not my colors, but they'd look great with your top."

"I wear an eight but will force them to fit. Holy Mary, Mother of God. I need to check out your entire closet; I'm a mess."

I crawl into a skin-tight pair of olive jeans and select strappy brown sandals with a stacked heel. The evening air is warm, so I slip into a sleeveless coral top with sequined-stitched palm leaves. The thin fabric drapes my torso and flutters around my hips like a curtain caught in a breeze. I loosen the straps that tie in back of my neck and the shirt plunges into a décolleté. Oversized copper hooped earrings are the only jewelry the outfit requires. Marselina borrows an orange shawl and I gift her the heels, a token of my gratitude for lending her expertise. We reapply lipstick then catch a cab to La Cueva.

Guitars, trumpets and violins spill from the front entrance, electrifying the air outside the club. Two gorgeous dark-skinned hunks in Italian suits stand as sentries outside the open doors. La Cueva, packed like a meat locker in Mexico City, gyrates in a mass of primary color, and we sit at a café table, hanging our beaded bags on the chairs.

I look at the stage and count eleven band members. The lead vocalist, having just belted out an impassioned song, hands a member of the audience his microphone. The young man places one hand over his heart, winces at the flickering sequins on a violinist's vest, then sings a Spanish song, his expression drenched with loss. His melodic tenor melts into the microphone like chocolate into mole, and I close my eyes and drift. Inhaling a familiar lemony scent, my nose twitches. Some presence, a bobcat vibe in the air, jolts my subconscious, causing my arm hair to electrify, my heart beat to quicken. *Whoa, girl, steady.* And there he is— Cooper. I haven't seen him in five months, not since the evening he left my loft.

He's dancing, limbs entwined, with an unfamiliar woman, and his lips lean into her long neck as if ready to take a bite. Giggling, she twirls into a half-spin, her back to him now, pulling his forearms into her waist. Pressing her hips into his groin, she sways to the music, her damp, ivory skin glistening under the swirling strobe. She appears Nordic. Scandinavian? A high, polished forehead and cheekbones, sharp as daggers, dominate her face. Her long white-blond hair is slicked back, pulled severely into a ponytail, and slanting eyes stretch towards the tip of her ears. Wearing a slash of fuchsia lipstick, her smile reveals tiny teeth, like shoe peg corn, misplaced on such a tall woman.

I break into a sweat, the walls of the club crumbling, caving in on me. A wave of revulsion rises though my stomach, the mole threatening to make its second appearance of the evening. I'll bolt before he sees me or I'll get sick on the floor. Marselina used to hang out with us; she knows our story and will understand. *Hang on, tighten your grip.* I grab my bag at the exact moment a waitress appears at our table.

"The gentlemen two tables down want to buy you ladies a drink."

With a cocktail napkin, I dab the tears from the corners of my eyes, glancing in their direction. It's Tommy with a friend; this town is growing smaller by the second. I swallow the bile rising up the back of my throat.

How could I have been so wrong about our relationship? Cooper may as well have hurled a brick in my face with an attached note: *I wasn't that into you.*

Threading my fingers, I press my palms together: *In through the nose, out with a sigh.* I'm walking a tightrope between survival and crazy-land and can't let Cooper make the final call. *Through the nose*—my fingers unfurl—*out with a sigh.* My face relaxes. At least if he sees me now, I'll be with men; and he'd remember Tommy, drop-dead handsome, albeit hard-bitten, rough around the edges. I rehang my bag on the chair, wave the men over, and order a double shot of their smokiest mezcal. They pull a couple of chairs to our table.

"Well what do you know, Mallory Lakes." Tommy looks at me, cocking his head. "Huh. Your color's funny."

Marselina swivels to face me then places her palm over my forehead as if I had a fever. "God; you're damp and on fire. What's with your eyes? They're bloodshot. You OK?"

I bite my lower lip; no more tears will be wasted on that man. I'll fake nonchalance until the pain, if it ever, subsides. "Oh yeah. Fine. I'm fine." I'm not fine, not in the least, and my head shakes involuntarily, as if discounting my words. "Oh y'all. Don't fuss. One margarita too many, that's all." I press the napkin to my forehead blotting the moisture. I turn to Tommy, forcing a smile. "Or maybe I just need another. Thanks for the drinks. I'm afraid I broke the bank with the shot I just ordered. This is Marselina."

"The pleasure is *mine*," Tommy murmurs, kissing Marselina's hand. "This is a buddy of mine, Nick. Reports for *Atlanta Alert.*"

Nick regards me, smiling, with a curious look. A nice-looking man; time to brush off my knees and re-enter the game. Pulling my hair to the side, I tilt my head and lift the left corner of my trembling lips: my crooked pirate smile.

"Crime?"

"How'd you guess?"

"The company you keep. Same with me. I'm a food writer, and Marselina is *my* partner in crime. She's a fabulous cook. We just made chicken mole, her recipe, and it's scrumptious."

"Any leftovers?" Tommy asks, lighting a cigarette and passing it to me across the table.

"You betcha; I've got a casserole loaded with the tempting goodness."

I inhale, appreciating the calming effect tobacco has on my tattered emotions. As the band takes a break, my eyes slide across the dance floor, now empty, then towards the bar; is there enough alcohol in this club to make the memory of Cooper and that woman vanish?

Exhaling the smoke towards the ceiling, I try attaching to normalcy, realigning my thoughts to work and world events. "So, gentlemen; we finally nailed the bastard. Your impression of the Bin Laden coverage. *Atlanta Alert* versus *AtlantaNow?*"

"This will be interesting," says Nick, smacking his fist into his palm, turning to face Tommy. "My man. Your team devoted an entire page to Binny using his wife as a human shield. Ever heard of fact-checking?"

Tommy smirks. "You trumped us on that one, bro; your marketing department's in full swing. I revved up scanning ads in your last edition: Bin Laden shield protectors deeply discounted at Isabella's Lingerie. Myself, I'm looking forward to your upcoming Sunday night special: *Laden's Last Stand.*"

Nick spits on his palms and rubs his hands together. "You're closer than you think."

"Hit it with your best shot, boys," I say. "So far it's been sloppy journalism across the board. Embarrassing. I'm just glad we finally put that..."

The band starts up again, drowning my words. The waitress brings our drinks as I inventory the dance floor. Cooper and the woman are gone; I hope he saw me with the men.

"This group is phenomenal," I say, my voice amplified over the music. "Does anyone know anything about them?"

"Gaspar Salvador is singing; it's his band," Marselina replies. "The songs are from *Los Cruces Fronterizos*, a collection of music about crossing borders; actual borders as well as figurative ones." She taps her forefinger to her temple. "The borders in our head. It's emotional for me, painfully Mexican."

Sipping the mezcal, the rich agave elixir doing an admirable job of numbing my heartbreak, I watch the ashen smoke swirl up from my cigarette like a vanishing dream.

"The music is lovely, magical. I'll download the songs."

"They've just released a Mariachi opera. The story has to do with a family crossing a desert, and one of the children dying in their attempt. All of Salvador's work evokes the extraordinary lengths humans beings will go to make a better life."

I speak only a few words of Spanish but in the music sings prayers of thousands of souls crafting bargains with God, negotiating their cross into America. My misery is meaningless compared to the rest of the world's suffering. I must get over myself. Volunteer. Donate my time. Cook at a homeless shelter. Rock AIDS babies. Something.

Tommy interrupts my thoughts; I tune into his conversation with the waitress.

"You're kidding me. No food of any kind? A Mexican club without tacos; not even salsa and chips?" Tommy winks at Marselina and pulls on her sleeve, pleading and puppy-eyed.

She giggles, a tinkling shiver of notes. "American chauvinist." She glances at him sideways, her tone, each twitching nuance a teasing invitation. Moistening her lips, she kicks back her head, shaking it at the ceiling.

Their chemistry, muddled into my drink, emboldens me. I finish the mezcal in a gulp then raise an eyebrow at Nick, elevating the erotic tension a decibel. "We've got that chicken mole at my place."

"I ask you, Nick, what man in his right mind would pass up an invitation to sample Mallory and Marselina's most recent masterpiece? Lemme take care of the tab." Tommy's hand thrusts into a pocket as the other one beckons the waitress.

We leave the club, pile into Tommy's two-door, and he drives us to The Stacks. The smokestacks appear gothic, night clouds cloaking them in darkness, and small lights twinkle from nearby dwellings.

"I'm as high as a Georgia pine," Tommy shouts, flinging his arms to the skies, and we giggle, swaggering from the parking lot to the front entrance. I turn the key and wiggle the door knob. Pushing it open with my hip, we enter then climb the steps, clutching the hand rail, our breathing labored under the veil of booze. Unbolting the locks to my loft, I open the door, and dim the overhead lighting.

"*Su-weet*," whistles Tommy. "Nice digs, sister. What a jewel box. *Whoa*, look at that stove, what a monster."

"It even breathes fire. Take a seat at the island; the stools are cushioned and comfy." I remove the Saran-wrapped mole from the fridge and put it in the microwave. Handing my guests a shot glass, I push the peppers aside then arrange a bottle of tequila, lime wedges and salt on the granite.

"The thing about mezcal...or rather...the thing about tequila is..." I stop, winded, scrunching my forehead. "What the hell...I forgot the difference between mezcal and tequila." I plop into a chair. "And what the hell was I going to say next? Oh yeah..." I wiggle my brows at Nick then wink. That's a first; I've never winked at a guy I just met. Man, I am stinking, stinking drunk. But enjoying the feeling immensely.

"The thing about this liquid gold that separates it from other intoxicants is that it creeps up on you, worming its way through your system." I stand, give a stumbling little shimmy then slump towards the bottle, tapping at the swollen worm, lying stiff, prone at the bottom. "Like that poor creature. One minute you're fine, and the next, blotto."

"I've an idea," Marselina says. "Let's have a chili pepper tasting. We can play chili pepper roulette." She fingers through the assortment of peppers. "We'll start with the pasilla, the mildest of the group."

"Marselina, those chilies will give us third-degree burns." With wobbly hands I fill shot glasses—half the alcohol missing the glass— then retrieve disposable plastic gloves from under the sink. "Here. Wear these. The placental material next to the seeds gives chili peppers their heat. Put on the gloves and scrape it out with your fingers before you eat them."

"Oh, nurse," Tommy whines, cocking his head as he pulls on a glove, "I'm here for the examination." He wiggles his plastic-covered fingers. "Be careful with the placenta."

Marselina snorts. "Stop making me laugh. The tequila is coming out of my nose." She pinches her nostrils.

"Here, Mallory. You first." She hands me a serrano; I bite into it.

"Kinda sweet." I wait a few seconds, staring wide-eyed at my audience. "Oh...here it comes. I'm feeling the heat...pass the tequila."

"You've got cojones, girlfriend." Tommy laughs.

"Cap...Cap-sai..." I slur, giggling. "Cap-sai-ci-noids spark pain recep-tors, then kick off endorphins. Like buckshot on your backside. And man oh man, that burns." I down a shot of tequila. "Fire me up another."

"Eating a hot pepper is like having sex," Marselina observes, munching on a jalapeno. "A spicy balance between pleasure and pain. You gotta have more." She hands a squat orange pepper to Tommy.

"Don't you dare," I shout, laughing. "Not a habanero. He'll ignite."

"Just remember, *you* started this." Tommy smiles, slides off the stool, and pulls off the glove as he approaches Marselina. Cupping her chin into his hands, he bends down to kiss her. She doesn't push him away. Indeed, she drapes her arms over his shoulders, enjoying his advances.

I'm too hammered to be embarrassed, but sweat is trickling down the sides of my neck from that pepper; I need fresh air. Dizzy with the spins, I sway against the island, hip thudding the edge, then weave towards the bedroom, knocking against the screen. I struggle to open the bedside win-dow. Nick comes to my side and, with a guttural sound, offers a final heave. Cool air pushes into the room. Our bodies collide.

We stagger the few steps to my bed. Our arms grasp each other as we fall onto the quilt. His hand pushes my hair back, ripping out an earring. My fingertip touches the earlobe. Blood.

"You OK?" he murmurs into my neck.

Untangling from his embrace, I roll out of bed and stagger to the screen. Peeking around the frame, I see Marselina and Tommy lying sandwiched, face to face, hips rocking in tandem on the sofa. Her legs, still clad in jeans, are clamped around his waist, and her feet, like weary warriors, rest on his back. Only her toes remain wedged into the pointed tip of the heels. She could have used a larger size. Tommy struggles to wrest his arm from his shirt; I return to bed.

"Yeah, I'm fine." Brushing the blood from my forefinger into my jeans, I pull him into my mouth. His teeth bruise my lips, as he peels off my clothes, as I exorcise Cooper, as I give up the fight.

The wail of the cat, the one who expected and missed the evening table scraps, awakens me. It's three-twenty. I pull the dead weight of Nick's arm away from my breast then sit, curling myself into a ball. Clutching knees to chest, I consider this man as he sleeps. I don't know his last name or where he grew up. I never noticed the dot of gold piercing his ear, or that his nut brown hair is streaked with gray. My copper earring is bent, trapped under his shoulder, the fastener caked with dried blood. *Copper draws impurities from the blood*; last night I should have worn a copper sheath.

I wrap a sheet around my torso, hold it in place, and stumble to the kitchen. Tommy and Marselina are passed out on the sofa; his shirt half covering their naked bodies, and their clothing is scattered nearby. I open the microwave; the mole rests untouched. Face burrowing into hands, I drop the sheet and it slides to the floor, fanning my feet as a coral shell. Images of Mama, her long neck bent, painting her nails on the Biedermeier sofa...Tony's fingers fondling Itchy's pearls...Cooper twirling through lights with another woman, spiral, collide.

Grabbing the sheet, I stagger to the bathroom, kneel over the toilet bowl, lift the seat and heave, big tears splashing into vomit. I flush the toilet, rinse my face, brush my teeth then wrap my body into a fetal position on the floor, the tiles cooling my heat.

I see you, Cooper, right now I see every way you are making love to that woman, every way you use to make love to me.

Love is a plague, the symptoms are the same, and never have I felt so depressed, ashamed and alone, *ever.*

CHAPTER 9

Miss Ann

My school bus is stopping in the usual place by the crooked fence post to let me out. Each time it jerks to a stop, Serenity and me crash into each other, laughing like we're fixing to die.

Serenity is my best friend and each day we try to sit next to each other on the bus. I fall over backwards trying to get two seats together, always beating Serenity because her legs are fat. Sometimes Mason beats her and steals the seat next to me. He's mean. Says I got cooties. Once I put my books on the seat to save it for her but he pushed them off and they went flying everywhere. I lost my homework and Miss Marie, who is my teacher, whopped me across my knuckles with her ruler.

Mason smells like stinky socks. His eyes are skinny and his fingernails are crusted with dirt, which he digs out with an army knife. My granny MeMaw's fresh-dug carrots look like they grow out his head. He says my fake eye makes me look like a cross-eyed monster. He says bad words, makes fart noises with his tongue, and pushes his fingers into my stomach. It hurts.

I don't cry or say nothing 'cause he has a big brother and I'm even more scared of him. I worry that Mason is going to tell his brother if I don't let him sit in the seat, and Lord knows what would happen then. Once he tied Nattie up to a tree and threw rocks at her, and nobody found her till the next day. Mason days are bad days, but I try to be nice. Mama says the bravest thing in the world is to always stay nice when someone else is mean.

Today's a good day 'cause Serenity got the seat, and we discuss our secret code until we get to my stop. Then I pull at her sleeve and point out the window.

"Serenity. Look. See the doggies jumping on the trampoline? I told you." She never believed me about the doggies but she's got two good eyes and can see for herself. One doggie has a tail that twists and turns like the jackalope's antlers.

"Nuh-uh, Miss Ann. They ain't jumping. They just standing there. Dogs can't jump."

I get so mad when she says that, I want to pinch her wiggly pink arm. Last time I did that she cried and MeMaw gave me time out. I hate time outs, but it's better than a switching. The bus driver looks back at me like he's put out so I grab my books and scram.

I stop at the steps, turn and shout back to Serenity. "Maybe they ain't jumping now, but Mama and me sees 'em jump all the time."

When that word *Mama* slips out of my mouth, it tastes like lemonade with no sugar. She left me a long time ago and I only let my toys see me cry. She says she's gone to make things better for us but everything's worse and I miss her. She say I'm lucky to have MeMaw and Aunt Mama. They're sweet, and I love them, but my life has turned upside down since Mama left home.

Good days are when MeMaw lets me bring Serenity home to play, and for dinner we eat Cheerios with chopsticks. But that's only when she's not working on hair so she has time to watch after us both. On MeMaw's hair days, Aunt Mama, who is her big sister, meets my bus. Her husband's gone to heaven so she has time to kill, but today she's seeing the doctor for female trouble. She never could have babies with that female trouble of hers.

I told MeMaw I don't need anyone to meet me. Serenity walks home most days by herself. MeMaw said OK, but be sure to look both ways when I cross the street. I already know that. My mama has told me that a hundred-million times.

I climb down the bus steps then wait. I turn my head towards the crooked post side of the road. Coast is clear. Then I turn my body to the right, my blind side, so I can see the other side of the street with my good eye. This low I only see the doggies' heads popped over the fence, tongues hanging out and panting. No cars, so I run across the road then the bus drives away.

I love playing tricks on people with my fake eye. After recess today I took it out and put it on Miss Marie's desk by her pencil sharpener. When she sat down and saw it, she screamed. Everyone laughed and laughed but she was madder than a wet hen. She yelled at me, saying I'd better work harder at being a good girl to make up for my bad eye. She made me stand in the hall for fifteen minutes, but it was worth it. It's fun making people laugh.

I can't wait to get to my room and play with my Woody puppet. I love Woody, who is the most important person, I mean *toy*, in the *Toy Story* movies. Mama took me to see all of them shows at the Hollywood Showplace. We love puppets in our family. MeMaw has a Howdy Doody puppet in her bedroom. She had it when she was a little girl and says it belonged to her daddy. She says it's worth a lot of money and I'm not allowed to play with it.

I walk six steps forward then stop. Then, I start all over, counting six steps forward then stop. Six is my secret lucky number. If I do that all the way home, I'll shoo away the devil and have good luck.

Walking into my yard, I count to six, stop, then look at the dogs. The man who lives in the house is sitting on his front porch smoking a cigarette. Mama and MeMaw told me to never talk to him, but his T-shirt is clean and white.

"Hey Mister. Can you make your dogs jump?"

His eyes stretch scared like I'm a ghost, and I am sorry I said something. I want to run, but I would mess up my numbers and have bad luck. Then, his eyes squint small and he smiles real big.

"You mean Ren and Stimpy? Why, Ren is stubborn as a mule and Stimpy, here, all he thinks about is his next meal. I can't make them dogs do nothing. I tried to train 'em but they rule the roost, don't mind nobody. Brothers from the same litter, which I 'spects is the problem."

"How'd they learn to jump?"

"When they was pups, my little girl use to bounce with 'em for hours. She's long gone but they got use to jumping around. Even like it."

"My mama is scared of dogs but I'm not. Can I pet them?"

"No, child. 'Fraid not. These dogs are the biting kind."

"Do they eat dog biscuits?"

"On special occasions. Like Christmas."

I laugh, thinking about Sanny Claus coming down the chimney and filling up a doggie's stocking with biscuits.

He smiles again. "I do have a stuffed animal dog that you can pet. It used to belong to my girl. She named the dog Pouch because she has a litter of pups in her pouch. Lemme go see if I can find that critter."

"OK. Thank you, Mister."

He smashes his cigarette under a big work boot and walks into his front door. His boots are untied. I learned how to tie my shoelaces a long time ago.

I walk in the same place and count to six real slow. Then I stop. I keep counting my lucky sixes until I see him come out his door. That was pretty quick. That doggie must have been sitting on the sofa in his front room, maybe watching TV.

"As I said, this dog belonged to my little girl; her name's Tiffy. She's all grown up now, moved away, and I 'spects she don't miss her. I'm gonna just give you this here dog; I'll bet Tiffy'd be pleased if there was another little girl to love her." He turns the doggie over, unzips her stomach, and pulls out a baby puppy. "See here now, if you unzip Pouch's stomach, she's got them here little puppies. There used to be five puppies in there but now I only count four."

He puts the puppy back in the mama doggie, zips the doggie up, stands on his toes and drops his arm over the fence to hand it to me. "Here you go. Pouch belongs to *you* now, child."

"Thanks again, Mister. I promise I'll take real good care of her and won't lose any more puppies." He smiles, turns, walks over to his porch and lights another cigarette. Good luck musta' kicked in something fierce. I'd never have gotten a doggie with a pouch full of puppies if Mama or MeMaw were with me.

I don't have time to unzip Pouch and look at the puppies. Not yet. If I don't call MeMaw down in the cellar, she'll come looking for me. I already know I have to keep this doggie a secret 'cause if she finds out I talked to this man, it will be worse than a time out. I'll bet there'll be a switching. I've been switched once and it hurts awful. Mama never switches me but MeMaw did when she caught me playing with her matches. Said I could burn down the house so she was driving away my foolishness with the rod of correction. I yelped and danced to the sound of the limb whistling through air in time to the swats across my legs. At least the stick didn't have buds, so the hurt wasn't as bad.

I open the front door; no one around. I run to my room and push Pouch under my bed. Then I trot through the kitchen, open the cellar door, and shout down the stairs. "MeMaw, I'm home. I'm going to play with Woody."

"O-key doke. You wanna fried bologna sandwich?"

"No, thank you, MeMaw. But I need to take two rolls of toilet paper to school tomorrow. Miss Marie said the school's broke and can't afford extras."

"OK, sweetie-pea. We got a case in the garage."

I go to my room and close the door. When I'm in this room, I'm so happy 'cause I know I'm the luckiest girl in the world. My room's not big like Serenity's but I don't have to share it with a mean big sister. I have a little kitchen set with real pots and pans, and a bookshelf filled with books Mama and MeMaw read to me at bedtime. Mama likes *Uncle Remus* stories the best but Brer Fox scares me. I wish she'd read my *Toy Story* books more. I don't tell her that 'cause I like it when she holds me, no matter what she reads. Mama's gone away and that's way more scary than any 'ole fox.

When I stand on my bed, I can look out the window and see the doggies. My window curtains have pink ribbons on them and Mama painted all my walls pink. She painted my chair and the table next to my bed pink, too. Coming into my room is like falling into a can of pink paint.

Woody sits on the table next to my clock. Mama bought me a clock with a long hand and a short hand so I learned how to tell time the right way. I also learned how to set my alarm. Every night before story-time, I pull out the silver stick in back of the clock. In the morning at seven o'clock it sounds *ba-ring, ba-ring,* and I push my finger on the stick to make it stop. I don't need anyone to ever wake me up again.

"Woody. We have a new friend who's come to live with us." I crawl under my bed and grab Pouch. Sliding out, I pick the fuzz balls off her. Pouch will be safe there; MeMaw never cleans under the bed. "We can't tell MeMaw about Pouch 'cause I might get a switching. Cross your heart, now." With my finger I draw a pretend X across my chest.

I put Pouch on my bed to get a better look. She has light brown fur with white spots and two eyes like chocolate M&Ms. Her nose is pink. I pull a floppy ear back. Also pink. I turn Pouch over and unzip her stomach, pulling out the puppies. I lay them out in a row on my bedspread and count... one, two, three, four. They look just like Pouch but are teeny-weenie.

Aunt Mama says I have the same cute face as my Mama, too. I push my nose into Pouch's pouch and wish I could crawl into it. I love Pouch and her babies more than Woody. Woody glares at me from the table. Oops. I have to be careful 'cause he gets jealous. "Woody, I love you too, but Pouch and her puppies need my attention right now."

My socket burns so I lean my head back and pull out my eye then put it in a glass of saline by my bed. Pouch is looking at me with her candy eyes. Why, she wants to be like me. I grab one of the buttons and work it round and round in circles till it comes off. There's an itty bit of stuffing where the eye was. I bet Mister would be mad at me if he knew what I did to Pouch's eye. I hide the button under the clock, next to my eye.

MeMaw's clop-clop-clopping towards my room. I push Pouch's puppies back into the pocket, zip her up, jump down and push her under my bed. I grab Woody and play with his arms, making them go up and down as she opens my door.

"Hey, baby doll. I got some good news for you. Want to guess what it is?"

"Are you taking me to Dairy Queen?"

"No ma'am. Better than that."

"A sleep-over with Serenity?"

"Even better than that, sugar plum." MeMaw sits next to me, takes Woody out of my hands, and cups my head in her hands. "Your Mama called and said she's coming home for one whole week over the Fourth of July."

"How many days away is that, MeMaw?"

"Well, May's about over and you're done with school in two weeks." She ticks off her fingers, just like I do when Miss Marie asks me a numbers question. "She'll arrive at the end of June so that means she'll be here..." Her fingers are all spread out, wiggling like tadpoles. "Ummm...never mind, sugar. She'll get here as soon as she gets here." Her eyes shine like blueberries in cream.

I am so happy I like to die. Last visit she could only stay two days. This is the best news I've heard in my life. So why is my chin trembling? I turn from MeMaw so she don't see my wet face. She pulls me into her chest, holding me so tight I feel her heart thumping against mine. She smells like hair dye and cigarettes. I don't know why my mama hates those smells like she do. To me they smell better than hot cross buns on Easter morning.

Chapter 10

Shelby

Today is Wednesday, the next to last day of June, and I'm taking the bus home to Coryville. This bus must be hitting every pothole in the road; bumping around in my seat, I clutch the armrest so I don't fall into the aisle. Something's wrong with the air conditioner, the windows won't open, and I'm fixing to suffocate. I rip off the back cover of *Bon Appetit* and fold it into a fan. Swishing it back and forth under my armpits, I praise Jesus I wore sleeveless.

A man in front of me is eating a chili dog, and between the onion odor, motion sickness and sweltering heat, a queasiness swells in my gut. Pressing my lips together, I put my head between my knees, willing myself to keep from heaving. A baby in the back of the bus lets out a piercing wail, and I rub the temples in my head, feeling a sick headache coming on.

A red light's ahead so the bus shudders to a stop. I straighten my back then grab a pack of gum from my purse. Sliding out a piece of spearmint, I peel back the silvery aluminum and pop the stick into my mouth. The cool gum and minty saliva squishes through my molars, easing my nausea.

Tracy let me have the week off, unpaid, so I can spend time with Miss Ann over the Fourth. The Troubadour wouldn't let me off the hook for this week's rent; I'll manage but it will be tight. I'm off my three-month probation at work and have enrolled at the Robert Russell Culinary Arts Academy. Grasso's covers all tuition costs as long as my grades are C or better. I was disappointed because I thought I could start right away, come to find out I have to wait until early September.

Tracy says at the rate I'm learning knife skills, juggling pots and pans, and balancing flavor and texture, I'll be light years ahead of the other students. Concentrating on cooking, I can also squeeze Miss Ann from my thoughts, at least until her face bubbles up, steaming up tears.

I'm miserable missing my child, Tracy understands, and it was kind of her to give me time off even though the deli will be slammed over the holiday. There's a wine bar close to Grasso's and a couple of times we've gone there for a glass after work. Tracy explains what she tastes and smells when she sips the wine: berries, grass, tobacco, vanilla. It tastes rank to me, like I'm chewing moldy mushrooms, but I keep my opinions to myself. Like so much I've been experiencing since I left Coryville, appreciating wine represents a better life one day I'll understand.

I haven't been to Squash Blossom since the potluck. Tracy says Clare's been crazy busy working the farm; Atlanta is packed with chefs who can't get enough of their produce. One day I hope I'm a chef buying vegetables from her.

Plans for their annual Squash Blossom Festival are underway. The event, which is held in early August at the farm, is open to the public. Artists sell their work and musicians perform. Tracy says it's about celebrating life and *sustainable* living, which means using resources without damaging the environment. They pass plates of food created from various squash blossom recipes, and Tracy asked if I'd help in the kitchen. I told her of course I would, pleased she asked; cooking for a crowd will sharpen my skills and boost my confidence before I start classes.

She also invited me to a wine tasting in two weeks at the Fox Hills Country Club. Tracy attended one there last year and says it looks like Tara in *Gone With The Wind*; the fanciest club in the South. I've never been anyplace like that but I'm fretting because I don't have money for a new outfit. I'll figure out something; I donated that shiny black dress, a reminder of the old Shelby, to the Nearly New.

The bus is pulling into the Coryville station and my stomach's righted itself, providing space to get excited. Lester spent over one hundred dollars on illegal fireworks, and I have a zillion things planned to do with Miss Ann; I especially look forward to getting back into our bedtime story routine. I check my face and pat it with powder, trying to buff the shine. Burning spots creep up my neck. Heat rash. A bag of frozen peas should calm it down.

Mama, Lester and Miss Ann are waiting for me, sitting on the bench. Miss Ann shakes a Pixie Stick into her hand then licks her palm, and when I see her little foot tap-tap-tapping on the floor, my arm hairs prickle. She sees me, and hops from her seat. I drop my suitcase, stoop down, and she runs into my arms. Why, she's shot up like a sprig of salsify. Her damp, sticky hands pat up and down my bare arms—*my baby*. She's been out of school three weeks now, and I know it's hard on Mama, trying to do hair and keep her occupied. I'll make it up to both of them this week.

Lester picks up my suitcase and Mama gives me a hug. "Miss Ann caught a cold and has a cough. I'm surprised me and Lester didn't catch it, nuzzling her like we do."

"Oh no, honey." Her good eye is as red as a berry. "A cold in this heat? Why I never."

"Surely she's past the contagious stage by now."

We walk to Lester's Zeplen; he's driving because Mama says her car's making clunking sounds. Lester says he thinks the problem's with the exhaust and plans to work on it over the weekend.

"Well, Shelby, the car is as old as Methuselah. You know the old saying: If it ain't sand in your bathing suit, it's toilet paper on your shoe." Mama chuckles, smoothing down the wrinkles of her dress; this is her favorite expression.

She looks pretty. Her peach skin tone is complemented by a lime shift, which hangs straight so her belly roll's not noticeable. Her hair's calmed down, too. Not as ratty and the color's a subtle shade of auburn. But most important, her smile comes easy, softened by old heartache and fresh hope. I have a new appreciation for Mama and the sacrifices she's made for me and Miss Ann. I'll be sweet and helpful to her this trip, even when she's annoying.

Miss Ann wiggles her hand from mine and skips over to Mama, wrapping her arms around her legs. "MeMaw, can Serenity come over? We've almost finished working out our secret code. We're putting lucky numbers in it."

Mama frowns. "Why sweetie pea, of course not. All you've talked about is how excited you are to see your mama." She glances at me, her lips pressed together in a nervous, apologetic way. "You told me so a million times. I know how hard y'all been working on that code but Mama's home; it's family time now."

My feelings are hurt, more than I can rationalize. She wants to squander time with her friend when our time together's so precious? I glance away so no one notices the tears swimming in my eyes. I'm also unsettled that I'm clueless as to her latest interests; secret codes and such. I bite my lower lip then change the subject. "How's business, Mama?"

"Noreen's got a knack for hair. Why, half the town's knocking on your mama's door. She's got close to thirty, cash-paying regulars, which includes me and seven other men." Lester rakes fingertips through his steel gray hair, slicked back on the top, grown longer and combed back wavy on the sides.

"Use your comb, Lester," says Mama. Her tone is scolding but she gives him a flirty smile before turning to me. "I only count men as half a customer 'cause they don't take much time. Their hair's not fussy and they don't yak your head off like my ladies."

"Noreen's Salon is gossip central in Coryville," boasts Lester, regarding Mama with admiration.

"So far my work load averages eight customers a week. I even took a leave from Eldercare; I make twice as much money styling hair than greasing bed sores."

"Wow, Mama. That's great."

"I may start taking children, but they're fidgety so it's hard to cut straight. Except for my granbaby." She looks down at Miss Ann and rumples her curls. "Sits as quiet as a church mouse when I trim her ends. I made a corner area for her beside my styling table; she's got her own little desk and a shelf stocked with books, crayons and paper."

Miss Ann and that cold bothers me. School's out for the summer so where could she have caught it? I'll bet cigarette smoke and hair chemical fumes are wearing her down. Guilt tightens my chest, but what can I do? At least she's safe under Mama's wing.

"Aunt Mama is coming over this afternoon in the car she bought with Watley's insurance," she continues. "She's going to drive us to a pig farm so we can hog call; one of my clients said her granbaby just loved the little piglets there. After that, we'll come home and she'll fry up some chicken."

That's exciting news because Aunt Mama makes the best fried chicken I've ever tasted, *anyone's* tasted, really. No matter your politics or what faith you keep, everyone gets along when eating her chicken. At first I thought the secret was her cast iron skillet; she says something's off with ours, it isn't seasoned right. But that's just one reason. Coating the pieces overnight with her onion-salt and pepper mixture is another, but that's not everything. Last year she let me in on the top secret and warned me to keep quiet: She pushes sweet, cold butter pats under the breast meat skin before the buttermilk dunk. No wonder her chicken's so dang good.

Pulling into the driveway, the dogs' grizzled snouts are visible above the fence, their heads bobbing like those dog figurines you see affixed to a car's dashboard. They watch me, eyes twitching, necks stiffening, growling *rrrrrrr* then quick as lightening, they flash towards us, barking vicious, baring sawed-off teeth.

"Good doggies," says Miss Ann, smiling and waving.

My jaw stiffens. "Stay away from those mongrels; they're dangerous. Scare the starch out of me." I walk in the front door and frown at the nasty jackalope that follows me with his gaze.

Well, hello Mr. Jackalope. I've been gone quite a while, haven't I? Who's laughing now? That creature and those dogs represent everything I despise about this town.

I go to my room and put my clothes away as Miss Ann tugs at my hem, begging me to push her in the swing. It hasn't rained in weeks so the swamp's low and doesn't stink. The chiggers aren't biting as bad, either, so I agree. All the same, I have her close her eyes and hold her breath as I spray insect repellent over our legs and arms; their numbers may be down but they're never gone for good. Lester must have fixed the hinge on top of the broken door, and it slams shut with a *whack*, registering a shock that shivers up my spine. I sense the jackalope's eyes blazing across my back.

Hoisting Miss Ann through the tire swing, strung up on a limb of the black gum tree with a scratchy hard-braid rope, I begin pushing, not too high to scare her, but high enough to make her laugh. She pumps her legs, in and out, to the rhythm of our special poem: "Up, up, up in the air, up in the sky so blue...oh I do think the most joyous of things that ever a girl could do."

I watch our warped and rippling reflections stretching out then contracting into the surface of the swamp, which shimmers with dead leaves floating on the surface like tiny boats, some sinking into a muck of rusty pine needles and black pitch bark. My feet settle into the muddy bank oozing with cicada carcasses and frizzled moss, and they make a sucking sound when I lift them. Miss Ann's happy squeals feed my soul, but this wretched humidity's like a wet blanket and sweat trickles down my chest. At least the air conditioner's fixed. Miss Ann starts up with another coughing spell so I hold the swing still.

"Sugar plum, let's put a cold towel around your neck then we'll get a watermelon at The Pig. Doesn't that sound good? It'll make your throat feel better. It can chill while we visit the farm. Mallory Lakes just published a recipe for watermelon salad." I look down at Miss Ann and smirk. "She tosses the melon with onions and cheese. *Yum.*"

The edges of her smile turn down and she looks up at me, pinching her nostrils. "That sounds yucky, Mama."

I laugh, pulling her out of the swing. "I didn't think you'd like that. In this heat, I'd rather have melon straight up myself. We'll see who can spit their seeds the furthest."

Minutes after we return from The Pig, Aunt Mama drives up in a car that is sky blue, almost as big as a hearse, purchased second-hand from a local dealership. She put eight thousand down on the car, and pays two hundred a month. Mama says she was crazy to buy an expensive gas guzzler but she doesn't say that to her face. Aunt Mama had a fearsome life with Uncle Watley so now that he's gone, we encourage her to grab fun wherever she can find it.

In a chalky fog of grit, the brakes screech and whine as she stops in front of the house. Climbing out of the car, she hollers "*You-hoo,*" her hand fans and flaps about her face like a shaking dishtowel. She opens the back door then pulls out her skillet, wrapped in paper towels stained with patches of brown flecked grease. She's lost weight; her face looks gaunt, which makes her nose seem bigger, and it's lined with pale purple veins like an old turnip. Her hair's died orangey-red, the shade of a rooster's comb, and it's done up in tight curls fitting her head like a helmet. Mama told me she's been sitting in her chair, so I compliment her.

"You sure look good. Love your hair." I aim my eyes at the ground so she can't read my real thoughts.

"Why, ain't you sweet, baby doll."

She's been walking funny since her hip operation. Her right leg swings out to the side as if it were made of wood, and she lumbers up to the porch like a lame giraffe. One of these days I'm going to teach her how to put on lipstick. It's spread over the outside of her lips like a clown.

"I done missed you, hon. Here, lemme get a look." She lays the skillet on the porch table, hangs onto my shoulders then slides her eyes up and down my person. "You are one pretty thing." She gives me a hug.

"Your new car's mighty fine, Aunt Mama. What you up to these days?"

"Last night I tossed and turned. Dreamed Watley sprung from the dead and lost us twenty-thousand dollars in a poker game. Had to sell the house and my new car to pay off his debt. He seemed so real, and was meaner than ever, and I woke up in a sweat. But that ain't *nothing* like the water dripping off me now in this heat. May as well fry the chicken on the ground. Mercy, we could use some rain." She mops a handkerchief over her face, smearing her lipstick worse.

"That man's still haunting you, eh?" Uncle Watley's heart failed him last November in hunting season. He'd yet to track a deer, and was off to the races, blaming Aunt Mama for letting Sam borrow his gun to shoot the prize. Mid-sentence, while slapping and cursing her to hell and back, he clutched his chest, fell into her, and knocked her broadside. She broke her hip. But he died.

Aunt Mama shrugs. "I'm getting back in the car and turning on the air conditioner. You tote my skillet to the kitchen and round up the troops. I'll wait for y'all in the car."

Aunt Mama and Mama grew up on a hog farm some sixty miles southwest of Coryville. Aunt Mama considers herself an expert hog caller, and I suspect that's the real reason for this trip: She wants to show off her God-given skill to the rest of us. I take the weighted skillet to the kitchen, shout out for them to hustle then join Aunt Mama in the front seat. Aiming the vents to direct cold air at my neck, I turn on the radio. Lester, Mama and Miss Ann pile into the back, Aunt Mama turns the ignition and then taps the gas pedal.

"Turn up the radio, Shelby," says Lester. "That's my favorite song."

"Mine, too," pipes Miss Ann.

They sing the refrain: "Where squash blossoms bloom, and the honeybees fly, in the sweet ole' land of Georgia."

I'm reminded of that evening at Squash Blossom Farms; I've never been with a group of women whose laughter came so easy. I'm flattered they invited me to be a part of their festival, but a part of me feels ill at ease, wondering if they want more from me than friendship.

The hog farm's a short drive down the road, and a hand-carved sign stands at the front entry before the circular drive.

CORYVILLE ORGANIC HOG FARM.
ORGANIC. SUSTAINABLE. LOCAL.
VISITORS WELCOME.

"I just read about this farm. How come I've never seen this place before?" I ask.

"They just opened up to the public last year," Mama responds.

"This is a mighty fancy hog farm," Aunt Mama comments, cracking her gum. She wheels the car into the packed dirt lot then turns off the ignition. "Whatcha think, Noreen? Think our daddy would have made some money if he'd called his farm *organic* and *sustainable*?"

"First you need to explain what them words mean," Mama replies in a puff of smoke. She stubs her cig in the metal holder on the arm rest. I know what those words mean, but I keep my mouth shut. I don't want them thinking I've turned into some hifalutin hotshot since I've moved to Atlanta.

Mama coughs into a tissue. She must have gone through half a pack of smokes since I've been home; she can't speak without coughing. How many times do I have to hammer in her head the dangers of second-hand smoke; couldn't she have managed that five-minute ride without polluting us all, especially a sick child? But I remember my resolution to be pleasant so my lips remain sealed.

We climb out of the car and walk to a pen; no pigs. Lester cuts a black gum twig from a tree beside the pen, pops it into his mouth, and chews.

Then he spits and grips the fencing, rubbing it between his fingers. "This here is thick-gauge hog wire. Guaran-damn-tee they know what they're doing at this place; my buddy Slats used chain link and his hogs done bent it to hell and back."

Aunt Mama faces the pen, hands cupped around puckered lips, wailing, "*Woooooo...*" the volume increasing and gathering momentum, then exclaims, "*Pig!*" sharp as a knife. Hips swaying, she folds her hands at her mouth as if in prayer then opens and shuts them, screeching, "*Sue-we, sue-we, sue-we,*" squealing like a sow, followed by grunt sounds, "*Hnunk, hnunk, hnunk,*" snorted through her nose.

Her face is mottled crimson and pink with all this effort, and patches of sweat cling to the navy dots on the back of her housedress. Then, out of the blue, a mass of hogs stampede towards us, like horses in one of those old western movies, hooves shaking the earth, dust clouding the air. Most are medium-sized but some are humongous; we must be past the season for piglets. Miss Ann squeals with delight, laughing so hard I worry she'll pee in her britches.

"Lemme try, lemme try calling 'em," she says. I lift her onto my hip, snuggling her into me tight as if her fairy-dust essence were cradled in the crock of my arms. In a tiny, soft voice she says, "Here little piggies, suewe-suewe little piggies." We chuckle but the pigs, slobbering over their swill, don't even look up from the slop buckets.

"Why I reckon, Miss Ann, that you have inherited your great aunt's hog-calling talent." I kiss her cheek, damp as the morning's dew, so relieved to be right here, right now, with my child curved into my body.

"Aunt Mama, I'm taking you back to Atlanta—what they call fried chicken up there's a joke." We've cleared the table and there two thighs left so I put them into a Tupperware container. I try shoving it into the fridge but there's no room for them with that melon. "Let's crack this beast and see who can spit their seeds the furthest." I roll the melon out of the fridge and lug it, pressed against my stomach, towards the door. "I'll cut it open over newspaper on the porch."

"Me too, Mama," yelps Miss Ann, pushing my butt towards the door.

"I'll set off a few of them firecrackers I bought," Lester says. That man can't wait to start popping off his arsenal. His leg's been wagging under the table, jiggling the plates all through supper. "We'll have us a little Fourth of July warm-up."

Returning to the kitchen, I put the chicken in the fridge and select the sharpest knife from the top drawer. I take it to the porch, wiggle it into the melon and it cracks open like a wide, yawning mouth, sticky red juice spilling from its jaws. Perfect; packed with seeds. I cut off four wedges.

This is my favorite time, right before dusk, the sweetest slice of the day, when the clock quits ticking in a dimming of the heat and the clouds melt away in a ripe peach sky. But not for long because here comes Lester, yanking apart cellophane packages filled with red, yellow and orange bundles now toppling across the yard. I declare he's like a little boy at Christmas ripping at his presents. Mama, Aunt Mama, Miss Ann and I sit, shoulders pressed together, on the top porch step. We sink our teeth into the cold red flesh, chewing and swallowing, sucking up the juice. Then, our tongues, curled and poised through pursed lips, fire off seeds like a pellet gun. We let Miss Ann win every other spit.

"Careful now," Aunt Mama says. "If you swallow a seed, a watermelon will grow in your belly." Miss Ann yanks her head at me in alarm and I elbow her tummy and wink. All is right with the world.

Lester makes a pyramid with empty beer cans on the edge of the street. Pushing cherry bombs under the cans, he lights them with a match then runs back to us. They burst in loud *boom-boom-bangs* and red, white and blue aluminum explodes across the sky. Screaming and laughing, we clap our hands. Then stop. At that exact moment, seeming to come from nowhere, a four-door silver sedan inches down the road like a creeping tiger following his prey. Our mouths clamp shut and hands fall into our laps.

"Y'all recognize that car? It doesn't belong to any neighbors." There are only a few houses on the street and I'm familiar with everyone's vehicle.

"I reckon I don't," Mama says, jumping off the porch. "Shelby, quick now, help me clean up this mess afore some aluminum busts a tire." She drags the trash can to the road and scoops up handfuls of the splintered cans, throwing them away. Lester gathers the fireworks and trots to the garage. Some of the smaller packs fall behind him, and Miss Ann, thinking they're sticks of candy, runs to pick them up.

"Don't touch them." I drop a shattered can and run towards her, hoisting her onto my hip. "They could explode." Lester rushes out, picks up the fallen explosives, and then returns to the garage. As he's walking out, the car stops half a block past our house and backs up real slow edging past us, stopping in front of the neighbor's house. Something fishy's going on. This car's creeping us out, even Lester's concerned, but he tries acting brave, pulling Mama into his chest.

Three men get out of the car. Soundless. Leaving their doors ajar, they wear ordinary clothes and identical navy windbreakers, the word *Police* written on the front and back. Hunched down, sliding guns from holsters, they sneak up into the neighbor's yard. Then, fast as greased lightning, two of then stomp up his front porch steps. With the heel of his shoe, one of the men smashes open the door, shouting, "Police. Get down on the floor!" like you see on TV. The third man runs to the back yard and stands in front of the trampoline, his gun pointing at the back door, and the sun, now a burning orange ball, watches the commotion perched on the edge of the horizon, glowering like a jack-o'-lantern.

Fierce, crazy barks, a wild lash of *wuff wuff wuffings* collide with gunshots exploding from the house. At that instant, a cop car comes flying down the road, siren blaring, with the speed of a roman candle. It screeches into a stop of spinning dust that makes a rutted wheelie on the neighbor's front yard. Two uniformed officers, also holding guns, get out of the car then run into the house.

Clutching Miss Ann into my side, pressing her head against my chest, I bolt towards the door. On the porch, I slip on a melon rind and careen into the floor, with my child toppling over me. Lester hoists us to our feet and pushes us inside; Mama and Aunt Mama follow. We slam the door, turn the lock then Mama slides a chair under the door handle. The front window is large enough for all of us to peek out but I push Miss Ann's head under the window in case there's a shootout. Her little chin quivers as she fights not to cry.

A minute or two passes with us staring at the neighbor's front porch outlined in the violet of early dusk, pieces of splintered door littering the entry. We can't hear a thing over our chorus of heaving pants. Then, the uniformed officers drag our neighbor from his house in handcuffs, shove him in the back of the police car, and drive away. The car remains, doors open, in front. Neighbors walk up the road, and Miss Ann wiggles her head up between Mama and me. It's safe now so I let her look.

"I'm going to find out what happened," Lester says. "The worst must be over."

"I wanna come," wails Miss Ann.

"No, Miss Ann, no. You will *not* leave this house. You must stay with me. But, here," I pull the chair away from the door so Lester can get out, "you can stand on this chair to get a better look." I lift her onto the chair.

Two of the men, silhouettes in the halo of an early moon, drag plastic bags from the house towards the car. They pop the trunk, hoist up the bags, wedge them inside then slam it shut. Lester purses his lips and makes a hissing whistle sound through his front teeth. "Those must be the dogs." He walks out the door, kicking half-eaten watermelon pieces and damp newspaper into a side bush. Mama and Aunt Mama resume their post on the front porch.

Miss Ann's fists are knotted and her head is a mass of quivering curls. "They shot the doggies, Mama. They killed them doggies." She brings her hands to her eyes and sobs through tiny red fingers.

I should be relieved they're gone but stifle a heartsick wail, trying to remain calm and console my child. "Settle down, sugar. They've gone to doggy heaven; they'll be happier there." I take her hands and kiss away the tears that are spilling out, streaking her face. My knee is stinging, skinned raw from slipping on the piece of melon. One black seed is sticking to the wound; I flick it off with my finger then, sitting on the floor, pull Miss Ann into my lap and rock her quietly in my arms.

Minutes pass. Then, breaking the silence, the doorknob jiggles, swings open, and night as black as a sightless eye frames a man. My heart skips a beat as my eyes adjust to the dark then my shoulders relax. It's just Lester. Lumbering in, he heaves into a chair, which sags, metal legs scratching into the floor under his weight.

"Meth. All this time our neighbor's been cooking crank in his basement. Those dudes that stop by must have been buyers." He yawns and his jaws make a cracking sound. "I knew he was an odd duck, shoulda' figured it out myself. In his defense, them meth labs seem to be the only way to make a buck. At least in this neck of the woods." He shakes his head, retrieves a toothpick from his shirt pocket, and picks at his dentures. "At least he wasn't using; that stuff makes folks off-the-wall bonkers."

"Meth. Crank. Ain't that the same as crack-cocaine?" My grammar's gone to hell but I'm too numb to care.

"I don't know, Shelby. It's all bad shit poison. We should be thankful he didn't screw up a batch and blow the place up. Wonder who tipped off the cops?"

Disgusted, I shake my head, spitting out pieces of hair stuck between my lips. It's a good thing he's gone, but who'd a guessed? Miss Ann is hiccupping in between sobs, crying as if her heart was busted into pieces. This is no place to be raising a child. Thank the Lord, praise Jesus I'm following a path that will remove her from this rat's nest. I stagger to my feet holding her in my arms, and carry her to the bedroom.

"Settle down sugar, let's pick out a story to read."

Leaving the room, I sneak a peek at the jackalope, whose shiny boiled eyes are dancing beneath rattling antlers. Why, that nasty critter's just as pleased as he can be.

Watermelon Salad with Feta and Mint
by
Mallory Lakes

Swollen with the promise of endless days, if summer were a fruit it would be a watermelon, which seems to yield an infinity of pieces, then, as the season itself, vanishes.

Before air-conditioning transformed how we cope with summer's heat, there was watermelon. Mark Twain described watermelon as, "...chief of this world's luxuries, king by the grace of God over all the fruits of the earth. When one has tasted it, he knows what the angels eat".

Low in calories, high in antioxidants and other good stuff, what's not to like about this much-adored fruit? My shopping cart autopilots to watermelon crates at this time every year; watermelon is as essential to summer celebrations as are fireworks.

You'll relish the salty, tangy taste of feta in this recipe; and fresh mint is the perfect herb to tie the flavor of sheep's milk cheese and melon together. It's a sophisticated salad that wowed my friends at a recent potluck.

I purchased a seedless melon for this recipe; picking out the seeds in this salad makes me crazy. But I also loaded a seed-in melon into my cart. Like a bone-in steak, seed-in watermelon has a sweeter flavor than the seedless varieties.

Tomorrow I'm making my annual pilgrimage to my brother's lake house, and the seed-in melon will accompany me. Much is to be made, rightly, about the art of seed spitting, and our traditional seed-spitting contest is not to be missed.

Mallory

"**M**allory. You and that f-ing screen. You've been at it since you got here. Get your sorry ass off the couch and help me with the barbecue."

I turn off my tablet, stand, stretch, lazy and content. My brother, Clay, is the only person I let insult me or make demands of my time. I cinch my hair into a twist and secure it with a clip. Eyeing my smart-phone, I grab it, glance at a new message then shove it into the back pocket of my shorts.

"And get rid of that thing; keep your thumbs still and look your family in the eye when you're speaking. You've never even met the folks you're texting."

"One more line to this persistent dude. He's going to torch his chicken if he doesn't cool his jets. Then I'm done. Promise." I retrieve the phone from my pocket and plop back onto the sofa. My limpid body belies the pads of my thumbs pecking the keys like baby chicks at scattered grain.

Foodfiend: Those coals are too hot for your chicken. I've written an article that offers tips on how to barbecue chicken without burning it. Here's the link: http://bit.ly/DFnoburn Happy Fourth!

Tossing my phone into my bag, I stand and extend my arms to the side, vulnerable to Clay's barbs, shots and ultimatums. "Fire away, bro. I'm all yours." He gives me the finger and I shoot him a peace sign, smiling at his brotherly charms while wiggling my toes into flip-flops.

"Pork's on the pit and the fire needs smoke. There's dry and seasoned hardwood in the woodshed out back."

Clay's an attorney in Atlanta and lives with his wife and son in Buckhead. He and his family spend most summer weekends at this house on water's edge, Anderson Lake. The woods behind the lake house are filled with white oak and hickory, the finest hardwood for smoking pork. For his barbecues, Clay uses two parts hickory, which delivers a bacon flavor, and one part white oak, which wields the smoked punch. He incorporated a massive stone barbecue pit, central to every meal, on his back deck overlooking the lake, a hand-hewn bench wraps around the grill.

True to the Lakes family name, and as far back as we can trace our genetics, water flows through the topography of our DNA. Papa Lakes', my grandfather on my father's side, ancestors were from the West Country in England. They lived by the shoreline of lakes or streams, and in those days, Lakes was the name for English families who lived by water. Since coming to America, our family moved inland, to Atlanta, but we've always managed to have a family lake house in driving distance of the city.

Growing up, Mama, Clay and I spent our summers with Papa Lakes at his cabin near Lake Blue Ridge in the Chattahoochee National Forest, in northwest Georgia. Papa Lakes built the rustic cabin himself, situated close to *the ass-end of the Appalachian,* as he was fond of saying. Daddy drove up most weekends and after he settled, the cabin felt tiny with his scattered gear so Clay and I slept on the screened-in porch, snuggled deep into red flannel-lined sleeping bags.

I remember the symphony of summer dusk, the chorus of katydids and crickets commandeering the buzzing cicadas, swelling the air with their chanting melody; my half-closed eyes sliding down Mama as she sang a lullaby about making a wish on the last spot of sunshine before it disappeared behind Blue Ridge Mountain; her soft whispered breath and powdered scent as she knelt for a hug, the astringent smell of nail polish, and the flash of diamonds as her fingers trailed along my chin before stroking my hair. Everything was safe, protected, and I felt loved, wishing I could freeze that exact moment, like a photograph, and that Mama, Daddy, Papa Lakes, Clay and I could live there forever.

Walleye fishing excursions with Papa Lakes are memories chiseled into my soul. After catching a flapping shimmering string, we'd scale, gut and season them with salt, pepper and lemon juice before dredging them in crushed pecans and flour. I watched them—the first lusts of my life—as they shuddered in fat in the ancient iron skillet. That nutty crunch giving way to sweet citrusy flesh still haunts; this was the first food I learned to cook and I have never sunk my teeth into anything finer.

I never knew my grandmother, Papa Lakes' wife, who died giving birth to my daddy. After her death, Papa Lakes took more interest in whiskey than women. Mama made Papa Lakes her pet project, and tried cleaning up his vulgarities and bad manners, but to no avail.

One evening, while heavy into Kentucky bourbon, he was eating his beloved Portuguese sardines from the can. Edge-level oil dribbled onto his frayed brown bathrobe as he pried a fish from the tin, then raised the slack creature to dangle above his thrust-back head and gaping mouth. Releasing the fish into waiting jaws, he clamped them shut then chewed with relish, flecks of silvery skin dotting his chin, black veins and pin bones affixed to the corners of his lips. Mama's eyes bulged and her hand darted to her mouth as she stared at this performance then she threw up her arms exclaiming, *I give up,* but kissed his grizzled head before fetching him a napkin.

My parents inherited the cabin after Papa Lakes died, but Clay and I quit making the trek; we were in college, and there were more enticing amusements then the rustic house on the water. After Mama's cancer diagnosis, Daddy sold the property. Within a year, Clay purchased several acres on Anderson Lake and built his family's vacation home, two hours north of Atlanta. The Coosawattee River feeds the lake and the water is the color of moss and clean, but it doesn't hold a candle to the mesmerizing azure of Lake Blue Ridge.

Lulu is his wife of fifteen years; Robbie, named after Grandpa Lakes, is their twelve-year old son, and my only nephew. God, how I yearn for a family, even one child would be a blessing; a first cousin for Robbie. My breath catches, hope churning through my chest—*Cooper called.*

"Rob and Lulu took the pontoon down the lake," Clay says, interrupting my thoughts. "Lulu's got some friends from Tri-Delt visiting down at the Weatherly's. They've got a boy Robbie's age, and a bundle of fireworks they're organizing for tonight. Weren't you here last Fourth for the big blow-out?"

"No. I was at Itchy's parents. You remember. They've got that house on Lake Lanier and live there when they're not on Sea Island."

"Well, you missed a pyrotechnical hallucination. Tom Weatherly almost burned up their dock but the water put out the flames. Lately it's been so dry they're tapering back and cut out the most dangerous explosives. Won't be as exciting. Speaking of firecrackers, how's Itchy?"

"I don't know. Maybe you should ask Tony Grasso."

"That guy who owns the grocery chain?"

"That guy indeed. He seems to be making a lot of demands on her time since she started working there."

Tipping his chin, he shoves his hands in his pockets, narrowing his eyes. "I hope you're not saying what I think you're saying. Phil's a damn decent fellow, just treading rough water. Haven't seen much of him since they resigned from the Club."

"Itchy was irritating me so I've been avoiding her. But it's too much work. I'll give her a call her next week, I've big news to share. I'll keep my distance, though. She's changed, so let's change the subject."

"You're the boss. Can't stomach the thought of her cheating on Phil, if that's what you mean, but she once was a favorite. Y'all were quite the duo back in the days. I hope you two work things out." My eyes sting; I hope so too. It feels as if half the core of who I am is lost.

"So what's your big news, if you don't mind my asking."

"Well...you may remember Cooper."

"Oh no, honey. Don't tell me he's back. That prick hurt you big time."

"He's not a prick, but yes, he hurt me, he most certainly did. But I share the blame. I was too intense; too eager to get married and have his child. I scared him off."

"You? Intense? Scary? Nah, not my Mallory." His words ooze sarcasm and he laughs, swatting me with a *Golf Digest*.

"Stop that." I grab the magazine and bop him back. "He didn't come crawling to my door on his hands and knees like he should have, but yesterday he did call. I was too shocked to hear all he said but I'm clear on one thing: He wants to see me. Talk."

"*Talk?* Buyer beware. Your response?"

"I said it was a busy month; that I'd call after I organized my calendar."

For once I'd been thinking straight and kept my voice calm, not betraying the absolute joy and relief I'd felt that he'd called; it was as if my world changed from black and white to color the second I saw his name flash on my phone. I arranged my tone to sound friendly but not eager. Cooper taught me a lesson and I've taken it to heart: He can chase *me* this time. Maybe he only wants to be friends; he sure was hot on that blond. Still, it's hard not to get my hopes up.

"Take it slow, Mallory. What's the hurry?"

"Cooper's the love of my life, and you may recall I turned thirty-nine last month; time clock's a ticking. So that's the hurry. But I *will* slow down. I'll take it from a gallop to a trot."

I met Cooper four years before my parents died, when I was thirty-three. Later into the relationship, deep into the languid, wine-drenched hours of night, we spoke of the beautiful babies we'd make. I've come to the conclusion I made too much of that, making up baby names, pointing out cute kids in shopping carts. He must have been repelled by my scent of desperation. If I had any indication he was going to bolt, I'd have quit taking the pill, stolen his sperm, and had his child, with or without him. At least I'd always have a part of him, whether he wanted me or not.

Clay grabs his keypad from the mantle. "Need to grab something from my golf bag." We walk out the back door towards his car. "Lulu and Robbie will be at the Weatherly's for a couple of hours then the brigade comes here for watermelon and vittles. They've got the fireworks scheduled for ten-fifteen, when it's good and dark. We'll take the pontoon out on the water and watch the show from there."

He pops open the back of his SUV. Digging his hand into one of the long zippered pockets of his golf bag, he pulls out a plastic zip-top bag containing dried clumps of herbs. Must be the secret ingredient in Lulu's pasta salad. Why's it stashed there? I take the bag and note the greenish-yellow, fungus-like mounds then sniff the herbaceous, skunk-like aroma.

"God, Clay. This is pot." I hand over the bag in a flurry, as if it were contaminated. Clay was a pot head in high school back in the eighties, but I'd assumed smoking dope went the way of his cassettes.

"Not just any old pot. This here's Santa's Jingle, three-time winner of the Reefer Cup." He pulls out rolling papers and constructs a thick joint on the hood of the car. "After I quit drinking, I re-acquainted myself with the ganja. I get it from a buddy of mine in Arizona; medical marijuana's legal there and he smokes it to relieve his *back pain*." He cocks an eyebrow and winks.

"I only indulge on weekends and holidays. Lulu says she prefers a friendly stoner to an obnoxious drunk, but Robbie doesn't have a clue. I never hid my drinking from him, but this stuff's illegal, at least in the state of Georgia. Until they change the cannabis laws, he'll never catch his daddy ripping up a doobie. It's role reversal: I'm the kid and he's my father."

"Planning to share?"

"That's the idea." He rolls the joint back and forth, compressing it into a thin cigarette between his palms.

I arrange my face into a neutral expression, hiding my surprise at this proclivity. It would make sense for someone like me to be a toker, but Clay's so conservative. He inherited Mama's patrician groomed looks, her wispy blond hair, which he combs to one side, and her small, tapered nose. His madras shirt—red, white and blue, in celebration of the Fourth—is tucked into beige khaki shorts, and hints of a bourgeois belly push over his belt. It's odd watching Clay, a card-carrying Republican, roll a joint. I change the subject.

"Give me your nine iron so I can scare away snakes. They're camouflaged under leaves." A seven-foot rattler was shot a few years back in these woods. The three-inch bitter brown rattle, now displayed in a glass box frame at Big Timber Grill down the road, gives me the heebie-jeebies when we stop by for a burger. "Maybe we should take a gun."

Clay rolls his eyes, then roots out the golf club, leaning it against the car. Lighting the joint, he inhales and passes it to me.

"I haven't smoked dope since college. I'm more enamored with the alcohol buzz; it's not as mind numbing." I place the tight paper roll between my lips and inhale; my lungs expand with smoke, and then contract in a fit of coughing. I recall the second reason why pot never became a habit.

"I don't know, Clay." I gasp for air, trying to clear my windpipe. "Mama died of throat cancer, and this stuff's way harsher than tobacco." My throat, clotted with resin, burns and I hand him the joint.

"Back home, I smoke with a vaporizer; moist air is easy on my throat. So's ice cream, my other new vice. *Ben & Jerry's Chunky Monkey*, to be precise. Since I've quit drinking, I've developed a sweet tooth." He pats his gut with affection. "Don't give me that slant-eyed look. I only smoke twice a week, tops, and the payoff's huge: no more hangovers, no more regrettable drunken performances."

Touché. I think of that night after La Cueva, back at my loft with Nick, Tommy and Marselina. The memory haunts and my face reddens, but I keep that sordid misadventure to myself.

142

"I haven't had a drink since May fifth," I reply. "It's been sixty-one days and, *ohhh*...about twelve hours. But who's counting?" I follow Clay down a path into the woods, our feet crunching through tinder-dry leaves and twigs.

Nick called a couple of days after that evening. We met for coffee and I learned his last name: Papadopoulos. He was all about his work on *Atlanta Alert*'s upcoming Bin Laden feature, and he never once asked a question about my life. Tommy said it was nerves, but inflated egos annoy me. I'm mortified we had sex, and never returned his calls after coffee. Marselina and Tommy, on the other hand, are a frequent duo hitting the clubs about town.

Clay's lips circle around the joint. He inhales then sputters, "Sixty-one days, huh. Good for you. They say blood is thicker than wine, or is it water? The point I'm trying to make is alcohol triggers bad behavior in our gene pool."

"Maybe. But I've never been so bored in my life. I never said I was *quitting* the juice, I'm only taking a break so the booze knows who's boss."

"Good luck with that." He takes another puff then passes it to me. A few embers flicker into the leaves and he stomps them out. "The only good news is our livers are thicker than cow hide; toughened up from generations of abuse in the bucolic English countryside."

I chuckle then swallow, clearing my throat. Taking a smaller hit, I hold it in my lungs for several seconds then exhale. Like coils unfurling, every nerve in my body loosens and unravels. We continue through the woods, knocking through dead sticks and leaves with the nine iron.

"I do feel better since I've been off the sauce. Mellow would be the verb. Or is mellow an adjective?" I mull over this a minute and can't decide; my brain's in a fog. "Daily yoga also helps. There's that vinyasa studio close to my loft. The classes calm my nerves."

"So, Mallory, you're one of those downward dog chicks. A walking, talking, barking cliché. I didn't notice your tie-died mat bag strapped across your back, or your batik sarong. Did you leave them at your loft?"

"Down, boy, down. I've been practicing yoga for twenty years and my bag is black, thank you very much. The timing of the classes is perfect, six to seven-thirty, which interferes with cocktail hour."

"Thank God for small mercies. May I make a couple more comments, Mallory, without you jumping all over me?"

"Oh, Clay. Don't spoil our moment." I hate it when he's serious.

"Listen to me, just one minute." He spits on his thumb and forefinger, plastered with brownish-yellow calluses, and presses them into the burning joint, snuffing it out.

"You've replaced booze with your fan club. Jesus, Mallory, I read your blog and readers' comments everyday. Are you *ever* unplugged? Do your fans hold you hostage? Some of those readers are assholes, yet you invite them into a chat room. Is your every thought electronically externalized? What ever happened to introspection? Your writing sounds as if you're possessed, not to mention you're Twittering your life away, informing your audience with philosophical insights like: *Bacon's so good.*"

"Wow. Thanks, Clay. Your perception's enlightening, but you've never sent or read a tweet in your life. Writing about food just happens to be my vocation."

"Since when do you forage in back yards for salad greens? You know lawns are sprayed with herbicidal chemicals. Since when do you cultivate bacteria for fermentation food projects? Ever hear of botulism? And now I'm reading you're planning to slaughter that pig you purchased. You don't live on a farm, there's no need for that." His blue eyes, usually clear and bright, are bloodshot. "That's some weird shit, sis. Get a grip. Some distance and perspective."

Irritation at my brother is ruining my high. My fists clench. "Her name's Lilly-Belle, and I won't slaughter her myself. I'll just assist in butchering the meat. My readership has shot through the roof since I started writing about that hog; thousands of people follow my tweets and blogs. Through my words they're learning the real cost of factory farming versus ethically-raised animals."

"Seems to me you hide behind those words *ethically-raised* so you can feel OK about eating meat. At least I'm honest. I don't apologize for enjoying a good steak, whether it lived an ethical life or just whored around the feed lot."

"What a wit, Clay. Mind if I quote you?" I knock a splintered wedge of bark from a tree with the club then turn to face him. "Farm-to-table is only a portion of what I write about. Most of my writing is light, humorous even. For pity's sake, you're acting like I added cilantro to Mama's cheese grits. My readers would be bored, wouldn't follow me, if I didn't push the envelope now and then. Practice saying: *Gee, Mallory, it's notable you took a break from drinking.* Or, *gosh, Mallory, it's fantastic you're balanced with yoga.* Or how about, *I'm so proud of your success, Mallory; you command a lot of power with those finger-tapping Twitters.*"

He rests his hands on my shoulders and looks into my eyes. "I *am* proud of you. But I want you to think about this: Is it *you* who's writing your blogs or are your blogs writing you? This social media stuff, to my mind, is bullshit mediocrity. It dissolves the boundary between the person and their persona. At least today, this one day, be the real Mallory, unwired and present with your family."

He pinches my cheek. "I confess your blogs are addictive and you can count me as one of your followers. I even purchased the pork we're barbecuing, upon your recommendation, from the Coryville Hog Farm." I smile up at my brother, glad this conversation is ending. "But," he adds, "I had to take out a second mortgage." I roll my eyes as he folds me into a cushy hug. "I'm always here for you, little sister. You know that."

Something is nagging me; I push from his embrace. "Aren't we forgetting something?" Clay returns my thick gaze. The thought rises to sea level. "Weren't we supposed to be collecting wood for the smoke?"

Sitting cross-legged on the floor of the deck, my top vertebrae pressed against the bench by the barbecue pit, I watch the sun sink into the lake. The American flag, raised on a pole, is centered on the lawn below the deck. Distant booms, sporadic and celebratory, reverberate and the flag hangs limp in the heavy, humid air. Lulu pulls the watermelon from my cooler then places it on a picnic table covered with newspaper; our seed-spitting contest will soon begin.

With prongs and a long fork, Clay turns the pork over, mops it with his special sauce, throws additional wood over the smoldering coals then covers the grill. He flips a switch on a stone grid beneath the pit and the outdoor sound system blasts an inspired mix of bluegrass and Southern rock bouncing off the canopy of trees.

The pot has rendered me speechless, yet hungry, and Clay's pork smells as legendary as the song that just began: "Burning the Strings Down in Georgia". The Billy Temple Band lyrics tell the story of Jessie, a musically talented man, who has stolen the heart of Billy's lover, and how Billy challenges Jessie in a guitar-playing duel. If Jessie triumphs, he claims Billy's musical fame and wealth as his own; if he loses, no woman will ever desire him again.

Clay, prancing in smoke around the grill, bends to crank the music louder, picks up a grill pan, and pretends playing it as a guitar. I stand, stretch my hands to the heavens, and they twirl in crazy circles with a mind of their own as my feet pirouette towards my brother in the crackling billows of porcine. We clasp hands and dance a two-step to the frenzied guitar playing. Clay spins to the right then raises me off the floor, lifting me as high as he dares without spoiling my rhythm and step. While dancing, our voices accompany Billy's singing in shouts:

> "Jessie's a dude down in Georgia,
> Best guitarist his town's ever seen.
> Money up in smoke and gettin' mighty toked,
> He was lookin' for a change of scene."

The faster Clay spins, the greater the centrifugal force, and the easier it is to lift me; I always land on the beat. *Go Jessie go...but watch your back.... Billy's on your tail. Go, Jessie, go Jessie....go go go. Watch the sparks fly from those quivering strings.*

I'm twirling like a mad woman, whipping hair blinding, but my arms and legs are possessed by some fierce and crazy energy so there's no need for vision.

> "Jessie, grab that pick and watch your back,
> You play that guitar hard.
> I'm on your tail just about to cut loose,
> Our time has come to spar."

Our favorite verse is next, and we let it rip from the gravel in our guts to the top of our lungs:

> "Burning the strings down in Georgia,
> You'll never know true love again.
> Burning the strings down in Georgia,
> Stealing my lover will be your last sin."

The guitar spirals into a crazed crescendo and the lyrics send send something thrilling, something dangerous, something deep from the belly of the universe shivering straight up my spine. There's a fire inside me, and it's starting to smoke. Fat drips from the pork into the wood and flames leap, licking the grill grates. Clay releases me to grab a water spritzer, sprays the flames then moves the pork to a cooler side of the grill. My body quietens but the fire pit spins in circles. Breathless, I collapse onto the bench to get my bearings. As my breathing slows, my eyes wander from Clay to the horizon.

Robbie secures the pontoon to the dock then jumps into the lake, a perfect canon-ball—dead center into the reflection of the flag—which just caught a breeze, and the Stars and Stripes cast red, white and blue ripples across the mercurial waters, and then vanish. Cooper's image flickers across the landscape and I smile, so in love, so relieved he called. So why, when I'm feeling so happy, does the same wave of unease swell between my eyes, dark and unexplained, pushing him away?

Smoked Pulled Pork Sandwiches with Hot Slaw
by
Mallory Lakes

Eating a slow-cooked smoked barbecue sandwich is as close as I've come in this life to transcendental bliss. With a respectful bow to my yoga instructor, I can't tumble into the same state of ecstasy in meditative poses as I do when I sink my teeth into a perfectly constructed pulled pork sandwich.

The hedonist in me revels in pork basted and smoked over white oak and hickory then tossed in a lip-smackin' sauce, topped with a mountain of Hot Slaw and sandwiched in a plushy (I'll repent tomorrow) white bun.

There is nothing quick about this recipe; it requires that precious commodity-time-to smoke the pork to perfection. This Fourth of July holiday weekend may serve up a slower pace, allowing you the hours required to keep a watchful eye on the pork as it smokes. You may, indeed, forgive the time commitment when biting into this tangy taste of heaven.

Let's begin with the sauce. What to use. Damn. That topic's more loaded than a double-barreled shot gun. There are hundreds of regional sauces, tweaked and nuanced through generations, savored beside the South's most esteemed pits. But I can't provide recipes; oh no, their secret ingredients are kept better guarded than the family silver.

My brother uses our father's recipe, a thin tomato-based sauce with a savory kick. Delicious, no doubt; and my peppery cider vinegar and lemon-butter mop also enhances the flavor of the pork, complementing the smoke. Whatever you prefer, avoid overwhelming the smoky pork flavor with excessive sauce, especially thick, sweet ones, which can burn the meat and blanket the nuances of the smoldering embers.

If you don't have the hours required for smoking pork, there are options for slow-cooked barbecue to-go. Shade Tree Barbecue, a Southern tradition, is making a revival in parts of Georgia. After the Civil War, freed slaves often found employment cooking barbecue on the side of the road under a tree to shade them from the heat. The tradition is making a comeback in the South; some entrepreneurs have set up mobile road side pits and picnic tables just outside Atlanta.

You can purchase the barbecue by the pound, smoked to perfection at Wilson's, a two-trailer operation just off I-75 at the Madison exit. Make sure to eat a sandwich at the picnic table under the massive hickory next to the grill. But you may want to bring goggles, there's a lot of smoke, and the essence of smoldering pork and wood burning embers will seep into your pores, perfuming you for days. Dogs go wild.

A slam dunk served with Mashed Potato and Pickle Relish Salad.

CHAPTER 11

Mallory

Time to decant the Zinfandel; Itchy will be here soon and we'll be eating in an hour, just enough time for the wine to breathe. I rinse the duck breasts, pat them dry, wash my hands and walk to the dinner table, which I'd set last night. A cut-glass vase is filled with Japanese irises. Picking up one of the sword-shaped blossoms that had dropped, I admire the regal shades of violet and the dappled yellow throat, which pick up the nuances in my table runner.

I push the sharp point of the corkscrew into the cork, revolve it deep into the rubbery mass and try pulling it out, but it sticks in the bottleneck. Feigning impatience, I shake my head at this misbehaving cork, but this is a battle I relish. I brace the bottle between my knees and wrestle; the cork emerges with a resounding *pop*. As I pour the wine, the garnet liquid sparkles and fans against the crystal lip of the decanter.

It's been over eleven weeks since I've had a drink; our local AA will have to do without my confessionals for the time being. The first couple of weeks were a challenge but, as giving up any habit, not hanging up clothes before bedtime or screwing on lids, I survived. There were no trembling hands or hallucinatory ants crawling on the ceiling, the sort of thing you read about.

I plan to join the world of social drinkers, people who don't rely on a daily fix of alcohol to self-medicate and calm nerves. I'll be the type of woman who, on occasion, sips from a glass of the finest Cabernet. God forbid the woman tumbling into the deep folds of night, gulping cheap Chardonnay.

The reasons for breaking this period of abstinence are twofold, actually threefold. I called Itchy last week, and she invited me to a Zinfandel-tasting tonight, some of the finest Zins, she says, California has to offer. The wine tasting is private and sponsored by Grasso's, a perk for their service staff; also educating them so they'll feel comfortable suggesting wines to customers. That's a respectable first reason for falling off the wagon. I adore rich and spicy Zinfandels, which taste like Mama's brambleberry jam.

The second, the unspoken, reason I'll be joining her is Tony Grasso will *not* be attending. Itchy's voice sounded strained when she mentioned this, and I wonder if they had some sort of falling out.

The last, the most significant, reason for revisiting the bottle, is celebrating my reunion with her. We haven't seen one another since our trip with Tony to The International Market. I never returned her calls after that outing, and quit going to the gym she frequents. I showed my disdain for her infidelities with silence, a more insidious weapon than words.

Three months have passed, and my interpretation of that day has wavered. My withdrawal from Itchy was, perhaps, a manifestation of my own arrogance. Perhaps I'm jealous of the abundant love bestowed at her feet. So little love in the world yet she has this excess with which to gamble. But I've missed her. Itchy is the only person who can look at me and I'm seventeen years old again, squandering time, believing everything good will happen.

Through high school, we shared the complications of lust and virginity. I remember our freshman year, sneaking out of my house after midnight to spy into Luke Leffler's bedroom. I'd developed an enormous crush on him after our make-out session parked by some abandoned railroad tracks, but he never called me after that night.

Luke lived a couple of streets down from my house and I began secret nocturnal visits, learning the location of his bedroom, studying his profile as he read books in bed. His nose was small and turned up at the tip. I fantasized our future children would inherit his cute nose. I suppose you could say I'd cased out his home, that I was stalking him. Believe me, there's nothing as deadly as a pubescent girl firing off rounds of hormonal angst using unrequited love for target practice.

That night with Itchy, under a full moon, we crawled through holly bushes to Luke's window, the prickly green leaves scratching our arms and legs. I moved a rock beneath his window and we balanced on it, grasping the window ledge. It was hard to suppress our giggles as we stretched and peered into that poor boy's bedroom as he lay sleeping. Itchy pointed to a *Boys to Boys* CD by his stereo system and a half-eaten box of coconut macaroons by his bedside. She snickered, whispering that if he listened to that sort of music while eating macaroons, he must be gay. I felt much better; no wonder he didn't call.

Budding narcissists, Itchy and I spent hours at the pharmacy agonizing over self-tanners and hair products, anguishing over the most effective blemish remedies. Our conflicted teenaged souls, however, were also tortured by the injustices, bigotry and racism surrounding our little kingdom of privilege. One Martin Luther King Day, back in the late eighties, we cut classes and marched at the head of the Peachtree Parade. I'm aware that doesn't make a statement these days, but back then it was enough to get us grounded. As it happened, our parents woke up to see our photo, arm-in-arm, white elbows linked with black, gracing the front page of the *Atlanta Sun* when we should have been at school.

Itchy is my best friend, and whatever she's up to with Tony Grasso, I'll compartmentalize elsewhere, far removed from our friendship.

Tonight's tasting is at Fox Hills Country Club, a golf and tennis club to which Tony belongs. It's situated twenty miles southwest of Atlanta in a remote area that remains verdant, untouched by construction crews and bulldozers. A developer from South Carolina was waiting for final approvals to build a swanky subdivision close to the club, and it was his good luck the housing crisis hit before the first stakes were laid.

Fox Hills is typical of private clubs that dot suburban landscapes across America. Its bloated uber-white, pseudo-Greek Revival architecture, desperate to emote old world Southern charm, is like a trumped-up hussy mispronouncing *bon chance*. Even with its grandiose fiberglass balustrades, its too new, too gold upholstery and tasseled swags, this mutton-in-lace would be forgivable if the club members weren't so pumped with vanity. They'll let anyone into this club, anyone like Tony Grasso who can afford the hefty dues.

The flip side to Fox Hills is The Buckhead Country Club—the BCC—the club to which my family belongs. The emblem for Atlanta's blue-blooded families, the BCC always makes the *Top Five List* of the most elegant American clubs in *Town and Garden* magazine. I spent my summers on the BCC swim team, and my young-adulthood attending debutante parties and wedding receptions in their well-appointed rooms, which smell of fresh-cut roses and silver polish. After our parents died, Clay took over the monthly dues, insisting I continue to enjoy the Club's amenities.

My mother's grandfather, a lawyer, was on the original board of directors and wrote the tenets of their restrictive membership policy. It's a club that would never allow flashy Tony Grasso entrance through their gates. The BCC oval insignia gleams in the center of the heavy wrought iron gates like a Scottish clan's coat of arms, serving as a back-off warning to those who can't claim membership as their birthright.

You could surmise my belonging to this club to be a paradox, difficult to justify to my politically correct friends. I am, incongruously, an outspoken liberal, the first to scoff at convention yet I embrace this irony, it being, after all, a part of my family's identity. It's worrisome that this character discrepancy harbors elitism, racism and privilege, but, by coincidence of birth, belonging to this exclusive tribe is a card up my sleeve, secret ammunition. When the occasion warrants, I pull it out, not to impress, but for shock value.

Over a year ago (and I replay this particular scene with relish), Cindy Pritchard stopped at my work station. She looked so smug and sanctimonious in her navy, poly-blend pantsuit, a brass button bulging at her waistline. She folded her fingers, festooned with cubic zirconia, and looked down her nose at my disheveled desk. Her smile was thin, like cracked ice, and her eyes flashed contempt.

"So what are you doing for Memorial Day, Mallory—after you clean off your desk?"

"Oh, the usual. Meeting my family at the Buckhead Country Club's annual barbecue. What are *you* up to?"

I took such pleasure at her loss for words. Her lips creased into a frown and her eyes narrowed as she puzzled over the possibility that someone like *me* could belong to the Buckhead Country Club. Then, no words spoken, she turned as white as her starched collar and marched away.

Itchy was always by my side at every BCC event, swimming in meets, batting tennis balls across nets, and walking down the aisles as we were presented to society, inspected by other members of our tribe. I'm making a festive dinner to commemorate our reunion.

I need one-third cup of Zinfandel for the sauce. Pouring the wine into a measuring cup, I inhale the aromas of ripe berries and tobacco. I can't wait a second longer and pour a glass for myself. I hear the buzzer. I take a tiny taste, and then rest the glass on the table. It's been so long since I've seen her. I buzz her in, pick up the glass and take another lingering sip, then a big gulp. Inhaling, I hold my breath…count to five…then exhale, unbolting the door.

And there she stands, blond hair shining like a shaft of August wheat, in sharp contrast to the peeling muddy paint in the outdoor hallway. I kiss her cheek and give her a long, tight hug. Pushing away, I look in her eyes. "God, Itchy, I've missed you." My hands fall to her hips. Lovely as always, but she *has* put on a few pounds. Her cheeks are fleshy; her arms don't feel as toned.

"Girl, you have no idea."

"Let me pour you a glass, yes? We'll be Zin-heads tonight. I'm even making duck with a Zinfandel sauce."

"You are too much. Sounds divine. And yes, of course I'd love some wine. What can I do to help?"

"How about trimming these beans while I put the potatoes on? The sauce will only take minute. I have my ingredients at the ready. My *mise en place*, don't 'cha know." I loop an apron over her head, and she presses her forehead into my shoulder and starts to sniffle.

"I'm sorry, Mallory. I'm sorry I let you down. Please love me anyway."

My throat tightens. She slept with Tony Grasso; her tears confirm my worst suspicion. How could she let another man touch her? How could she do that to Phil? Yet. Even so. I've shared so much of myself, of my life, with this woman. She needs my help to sort this through. Yes. Forgive. I drape my arms around her neck.

"I'll love you forever; till death do us part. We'll talk over dinner. Don't screw up your makeup with those tears." I give her a squeeze, hand her a tissue, and then grab the platter of duck breasts. "The fire's ready. I'll put these babies on the grill and will be right back." I climb the stairs to the rooftop garden. The giddy warm cloak of an alcohol buzz feels divine. I've missed how it hits my bloodstream, relaxing my limbs, cheering my spirit.

Dinner cooked, I assemble the plates, take a photograph for my blog, dim the lights and light the candles on the dining room table. "Itchy. This lighting is transcendental, let me take a photo of the two of us." I move the camera, secured to my tripod, a foot from the table, focus on Itchy, then adjust the F-stop so the candles are out of focus. I put the self-timer on ten seconds, bolt to the table and plop into her lap. Wineglasses clink, the shutter releases.

Phil dropped Itchy off at my loft on the way to a class so we take my car. The sun is setting as we drive to the club, catching up on the stuff of life: the twins, my job, absent the stuff of her and Tony. We didn't discuss him over dinner either. She said she didn't want to ruin our reunion, and she'd save it for later. I haven't brought up Cooper either, but I've been dying to share the news that he called. Not seeing him is making me crazy, but this time I'm sparring instinct and playing by the rules. I'll keep him at arm's length, ensuring his interest is piqued with flirty text banter until he's putty in my hands. But I'm worried about that blonde. Phil is friends with Cooper and I need to get the scoop.

"Cooper was at La Cueva on Cinco de Mayo dancing with some exotic babe," I venture, unsure of what her reaction will be.

She's quiet. Her lower lip protrudes in her pursed-lip pout.

"You know something. Tell me."

"You don't really want to hear about him, do you?"

"He called and wants to see me so, yes, I *do* want to hear about him."

"Oh honey, Cooper broke your heart. Are you sure you have the strength?"

"These days I'm as strong as a bull, and if I start seeing him again, I'll take it at a snail's pace."

She begins the story in a rush. "I got the story from Phil. Apparently Cooper was at his boss's condo, finishing up a project. He met the housekeeper, a blonde vixen, the one you must have seen at the club. She's from the Ukraine and is here on a green card. Get this. She doesn't speak a word of English."

"I knew I should have played dumb with that man," I say, miserable.

"OK. This story will make you feel better." She touches my arm. "You remember Laurence Reynolds from high school, right? He met a woman online who lived outside of Warsaw. She couldn't speak English and had a friend translate the correspondence. She was a serious hottie. You know the type, Mallory. One of those Bolshevik black-leather Natashas." I smile.

"Well, anyway, Laurence sent her a ticket to Atlanta so they could meet, and he went gaga over her. Phil and I were curious and invited them to go boating with my parents at the lake. Get this: She wore spiked heels, refused to take them off, and scratched up Daddy's teak deck. I thought he'd push her overboard. And you should have seen the skimpy outfit she wore.

"Laurence ended up marrying her; they must have had *one* language in common. She learned how to speak English from daytime television and, as it turns out, she's a raging bitch. She used Laurence for citizenry then framed him. She'd do things like burn herself with cigarettes, rush to the hospital and tell the orderlies: *"Me whosband did zies."*

Laughing, I swerve into the left lane, and then steady the wheel.

"He ended up giving her almost half his net worth to make her go away, but he asked for it. Cooper's smarter than that; he told Phil that dating the Ukrainian was like sleeping with his eyes open. She's yesterday's news so you can take that worry off your list." She squeezes my arm. "But maybe you should take him off your list, too. We all love Cooper, honey, he's a doll, but I don't want to see you hurt again."

Yesterday's news. The only words I hear. I'll text him tomorrow and arrange a meeting. The club looms into view. Taking a sharp right into the lot, I search for a space close to the front entry where it's paved; the back lot is gravelly and we don't want to scratch our heels. No such luck. The front section is packed with golfers putting clubs into the trunks of their cars, which probably cost more than my last year's salary. I pull into a space in the back. The 18th hole parallels the walkway to the entrance and we crunch through the gravel, following signs reading "Grasso's Wine Tasting".

A huge flower arrangement has been placed on a round wooden table in the entry corridor. I stop to admire the out-of-season daffodils in the arrangement then take a second look. Silk. Tacky, but they did fool me for a second.

We walk through the club to a small dining room lit with soft yellow lighting. A reproduction of an English hunt scene hangs in a gilded frame on the back wall, and a mismatched Louis XIV banquette is centered under the painting. Each piece, obvious fakes, could have been purchased from the recycle center.

Sixteen or so Grasso employees are seated at a long rectangular table. The men are wearing white starched shirts with shiny ties, and the women's legs are crossed, bound in nylon, even in this humidity. I've got a hunch they're putting their best foot forward; this club must be a big deal for them. Only two seats remain unoccupied; we must be the last to arrive.

A piece of bread and glass of water are at each place setting, for cleansing our palettes between tastes, and silver spittoons are scattered about the table to encourage spitting the wine after tasting. Though unseemly to the uninitiated, this practice is accepted wine protocol; it's difficult discriminating subtle nuances in the grape when one is inebriated, and Zinfandels are legendary for having prodigious alcohol levels. A wine vendor faces us at a separate smaller table, polishing glasses, and his table is filled with several dozen bottles of Zinfandel, many with impressive labels.

"Hey y'all. I've brought Mallory Lakes to take notes," announces Itchy. "If you misbehave, she'll write you up in her column." The participants regard me with tentative smiles, and I notice the raven-haired deli clerk who reads my column; the one who roasts the chicken. Her dress is lovely, and she's quite attractive without the cap and uniform; if she washed off that half-inch of eyeliner, she'd be a stunner. She straightens in her chair and stares, her eyes and mouth opening into round Os.

"Remember me? Shelby? From the deli? I'm the one who roasts those chickens you like." Her backwoods accent amuses me. I wonder which tobacco truck dumped her off in Atlanta.

"Yes. Shelby. I remember you. You make the juiciest chickens in town." Lord, woman, *do* quit fawning. And spit out that gum, it's about to fall out of your mouth.

The vendor dashes over to seat us, and as we settle into chairs, his assistant distributes thimblefuls of wine in oversized bubble glasses.

"This is an extraordinary little Zin with a great deal of character from the Russian River Valley." The vendor holds his glass to the light. "Note the rich, reddish-brown color of the wine. Now move it like this."

His practiced hand moves the glass in tight, quick circles. He pauses to regard the tableau of sparkling glasses swirling around him like maroon pinwheels spinning in a breeze. One man's wine spins out of the glass, splattering over his hands, dotting the bleached cuffs of his shirt. "Oops," he says, his face reddening. "I guess I'm over-eager." His co-workers twitter as he grabs a napkin and wipes his fingers.

"Now, sniff. Deeply inhale the aroma." The vendor lowers his expanding nostrils over the glass. "Next, take a sip and let in a little air. Do you taste fruits or spices?"

"I taste both," says a woman with spiked orange and yellow hair, who is sitting next to my *fan*. "I taste cinnamon and raspberries."

"Great observation. Does it feel rich or thin on your tongue?"

"It feels like soft, velvet dripping onto my tongue and down my throat when I swallow."

My fan slides her eyes away from me to regard this spiked-haired woman. She pushes her elbow into the woman's side and giggles. The evening progresses in the same manner. Wine to nose, wine to mouth; how many similes for describing a Zinfandel's character can this guy come up with? I'm done with spitting.

"Itchy. This is a sixty-dollar bottle. I'm going to swallow; it's a pity for it go to waste."

"OK, but just sip. The others can do what they want, but we need to set an example. Please. For once. Stay sober."

"For once? Tonight was the first time I've had a drop of alcohol in over two months."

"You're kidding. Good for you. What spurred that?"

"Too much tequila and a one-night-stand."

"Oh honey. We need to talk. The past few months have been a rough ride for me, too. My life is unraveling. Out of control. It's got to stop."

"Grasso?"

Her eyes moisten then slide to her glass. I rest my hand on her arm.

"Now is *not* the time," she whispers. "I'll stop by your place tomorrow. We'll have a long overdue heart-to-heart." She glances at me sideways. "Of course, only if you're free."

"I'm always free for you, Itchy. I'm so sorry; sorry about everything." She squeezes my hand.

I take a sip of the Zinfandel. The average person has ten thousand taste buds throughout their mouth, and I explore the fruit and pipe tobacco flavors over and under my tongue, then swirl it around the insides of my cheeks. A potent vintage, sweet and spicy. I swallow the black-ruby heat then take another sip.

As the evening progresses, Itchy and I misbehave, whispering our own inappropriate wine descriptors. The vendor finishes his spiel and he and his assistant tidy up their area and leave. Most of the *Grasso* employees exit with them, pushing against each other, peppering the men with questions. We chat a couple of minutes then realize the table is empty. No. Wait. Those two women remain, heads together, laughing like conspirators at the far end. I can smell the wine in the spike-haired woman's grin, and a bottle of Zinfandel stands, half-empty, as a soldier held captive between their elbows.

"Itchy, let's get going. It's after ten." I'm not in the mood for forced conviviality, or sharing that last bottle with deli clerks, the bottom of the professional food chain. My *fan* has been regarding me all evening; those kohl-lined eyes are unnerving.

Pushing the chair back to stand, my ankle buckles over the four-inch heel; I stumble into the table, bracing myself with my palms, and nod at the women. These shoes are killing me. Walking through the cavernous rooms, I see the club has emptied, except for the remaining Fox Hills staff, and their eyes crawl over me like worker ants, recognizing and appraising their queen. I straighten, pulling my mouth into a smile. Exiting the club, I kick off my heels and careen into Itchy, laughing, hugging her tightly then dig into my purse pulling out the keys.

A few cars are scattered across the vacated lot. Night has fallen. Trapped air steams over a pond on the 18th hole, and there are no streetlights, only the July moon and high-beaming stars. Swirling to the refrain of the whip-poor-will's chant, tiny lights of orange, green and yellow blink around us—fireflies flashing, flirting, luring their partner to the dance. A creature dives towards our heads.

"A bat," screams Itchy, ducking. Then, it reverses direction, lurching into the night, wind hissing through wing tips at the launch.

"That's a nighthawk. Papa Lakes called them goatsuckers. He said their oversized mouths suckled mama goats after they hatched."

"Bats, goatsuckers…creepy. Let's get out of here." Her tone indicates the night has lost all charm.

I pull at her sleeve. "No. Wait." The throaty cricket evensong offers tenor to the mockingbird's soprano, an innocent, pure vibrato, oscillating in moist heat redolent of freshly mowed greens. The outline of the club, now hazy lines, moves in and out of focus, and time seems to drift. I pick up my shoes. "Let's go."

Tip-toeing over gravel, my toes bruise walking to the car. Opening the door, I toss my shoes into the back seat, fasten the seat belt, turn the ignition then drive out of the parking lot. There are no street lights; damn, it's dark. I glance at the time on the console: ten-ten. Good. We'll be home early.

"The road is curvy," says Itchy. "Follow the center line. Exit 96 should be down the road a few miles then we'll hang a right onto the expressway."

The line glows and sinews down asphalt like a yellow corn snake; gnarled branches jut into the road. "They should cut these branches down," she comments. The air conditioner hums but it's no match for the humidity enveloping the car. Our legs stick to the leather seats, and we roll down the windows.

I guide the steering wheel, following the weaving line, and she looks at me and giggles. "It's like we're back in high school." I turn my head and smile. *Itchy.* My dearest friend. Itchy. I gaze into her eyes and swim in those turquoise pools, lovely as the ocean on a summer day. Eyes that have witnessed my life, shared my memories.

"Remember," she continues, "when we'd get stoned?"

I giggle at the memories. "And you'd always insist on stopping for a shake at....."

A blur outside the window. A heavy thump, *huhwump*, knocks against the side of the car, Itchy's side, the passenger side, shocking us into the present. I slam my foot into the brake pedal. A scraping, then rattling from the road.

"What the heck..." Shifting the gear to park, I unbuckle my seat belt, push open the door, and run behind the car to see what I hit. Itchy follows. A dark mass on the side of the road lies in front of me.

"Oh, thank God. It's just a bag of garbage."

My vision adjusts to the inky night. Moonlight flickers over something else, something collapsed over metal. I take several steps to the mound and kneel down. A boy. Or a small man on a bicycle. Eyes shut. A foot jammed into the spokes. Bile rises up my throat.

"Itchy—call 911—right this fucking second. Do you hear me? I hit a man—oh God—maybe a boy." I try swallowing, then gag.

The cacophony of whip-poor-wills and crickets strain the air. Their volume rises, menacing; their chorus predatory, bestial.

Itchy's face slackens, and her head turns to the side, to disbelief, as I stoop down. Matted black hair surrounds white oval baldness on the top of his head; a ribbon of blood seeps from this perfect egg. "CALL 911—*NOW!*"

She runs to the car, and returns with her phone. Standing above us, her shoulders heave, pressing the numbers on the pad. "Oh God. How bad is he hurt?" Her voice sounds shattered, like glass breaking. "Is he alive? Please tell me he's alive."

She cries into the phone. "There's been an accident. A terrible accident. Please help us. I don't know where we are. Cherokee Trail? Down from Fox Hills Club. Just get here. Fast. Someone's hurt. Bad. We need an ambulance. Now!"

Squeezing my eyes, green lights flash like fireflies behind my lids, swarming in blackness. I swat at the air, then collapse, pounding the pavement. I hoist myself up, onto all fours, to gaze at him—hands now paws—hovering like a beast over a kill. My mouth opens. I try to howl. Soundless.

"*Stop acting crazy, Mallory.* Feel his pulse." She crams a fist into her mouth to muffle a wail.

At that moment, his eyelids flicker, and he moves his head, groaning. "*Unhhh.* OK. I'm OK. Just my leg." His left hand slides down to his calf and grasps it. His face contorts and eyes squeeze shut.

"I'm so sorry," I cry. "So so sorry. Lay still. Don't move. We've called an ambulance."

"No. No ambulance. Really. I'm fine. Please." He speaks slow, in a deep Hispanic accent. Dark eyes peer into mine. "Lady, please. You. *You* take me home."

"Don't move. You have a head injury and your leg is likely broken. An ambulance will be here soon."

"No ambulance lady, *please. You* take me home." He tries pulling his foot out of the spokes then falls back, moaning.

I put my face into my hands and weep. A car's engine rumbles from behind. Brakes screech. Doors slam. The slap of feet, beating the pavement, running towards us. I turn my head from the man. Shadows dart through headlights. It's those deli clerks from Grasso's. Shelby?

She squats down next to me and peers into his face. "Oh sweet Jesus. Your head's bleeding." She looks at me. "What happened?"

"Please, miss," he says, lifting and extending his arm, touching Shelby's knee. "Help me up. Take me home."

I grimace, whispering between my teeth, "He says he's OK but I think his leg's broken. An ambulance should be here any minute." I don't tell her what happened. Isn't it obvious I hit him? The man tries to hoist himself up, and falls back on the pavement. Blood trickles, coming out much faster now, leaking behind his ear, down his neck.

"Be still. Please. You can't move. Does anyone have a towel I can press against the wound?"

Shelby's friend moves towards us, slowly, hands cupped to her mouth, as if terrified of what she'll see. Shelby stands, bends over, clutches her stomach, and runs towards their truck. I hear the door open and then a choking sound. She returns, head down, a cloth in her hand. Again, the man looks at us, eyes fluttering, pleading. "Please, no ambulance. Help me stand. Take me home."

"Where *is* that God-damned ambulance?" Itchy cries. "They're taking forever to get here."

Shelby stoops beside me, handing me a rag. "It's clean."

I fold it in half, then press it on the cut, which is centered on his bald spot. The man and I lock eyes. He's quiet, but his words resound in my brain: *Please, no ambulance. Help me stand. Take me home.*

A police car careens down the road, siren wailing, and screeches to a stop next to my car. Our bodies, as well as the entire landscape, are bathed in swirling red and blue lights. Everything appears to smoke, to be trapped in flames. A cop gets out of his car and the man closes his eyes.

"Officer, we didn't see him," says Itchy. "It's so dark and he didn't have headlights on his bicycle. My friend was paying careful attention to her driving. He must have swerved into our car."

"Is he breathing?"

I look up and meet his eyes. "Yes. He said he's OK, but I think his leg's broken. He's also bleeding from a head wound."

"Were you driving the vehicle?"

I nod and mumble, "Yes."

"Keep the cloth pressed against the wound," the officer says. "Help will arrive soon." He walks away and pulls out his phone. Meanwhile, the man lies still, eyes closed, as if he were sleeping. Blood pools from the wound, blackening the white cotton rag, and my right hand shakes as I press the cloth. I try to quieten it, holding it with my left, focusing on the movement of his chest, his breath steady, rhythmic—in, then out—my breathing shallow and rapid, an animal's pant.

At last, another patrol car screeches to the scene and an ambulance soon follows; the cloth is saturated and my fingertips feel moist and sticky. Paramedics leap from the ambulance and run to my side. "Hold his head steady while we apply a bandage."

I remove the cloth, drop it to the ground, and cradle his head as they kneel beside me, wrapping a crown of gauze over the wound. "That's it. Keep holding him steady while we put on a brace." They wrap a thick white pad around his neck and secure it with a Velcro strip. Then, they cut the spokes to release his foot, pull the bicycle away, and slide a gurney under his body.

The officer returns and helps me stagger to my feet. For a long second my vision goes to black and all sounds are muffled by the roil of an invisible wave. *Deep breaths. Must remember...breathe.* As they wheel the man into the back of their vehicle, the officer walks to the ambulance, leans into the stretcher, and asks his name. The man remains silent, his eyes closed. The officer checks his pockets and pulls out an envelope, which is folded over.

He turns and walks to us, raises his eyebrows and cocks his head at the other cop, who takes Itchy's elbow and guides her to his patrol car.

He turns to me. "I'll need to see your license, registration and insurance."

"They're in my car." My voice is hollow, echoing through my ears, my heartbeat pounding in my chest.

He rips open sanitizer tissues, hands them to me, and I wipe my trembling fingers, one at a time. He opens a plastic bag and I drop the bloodied tissues into the bag then wring my right hand with my left as though squeezing water from a sponge. I walk to the open door of my car, climb into the front seat, and grab my wallet from my purse. I remove my license, hand it to him, then fumble through the glove compartment for my registration and insurance papers. With shaking hands, I give these to him as well.

"Remain in the car and keep the window rolled down." I sit on my hands to stop their commotion, my entire body now quaking, and he closes the door and stands outside the car, staring down at me through the window. He pulls out a notepad and pen.

And now there is silence. How could there be silence? There should be keening. There should be wailing. Only the scratching sound of the officer's pen, like a predatory vulture, as he scribbles on his pad, clawing at my heart. I run the tips of my forefingers under wet eyes then wipe my runny nose against my knuckles, which smell like rust. He studies my face, taps the pen on his pad, and speaks in a slow, considered cadence, as a parent might to their disobedient child.

"Have you been drinking?"

"I was at a wine tasting at the Fox Hills Country Club, but it didn't involve heavy drinking. It was a Grasso grocery store function to educate us about wine. The rules are to taste, then spit."

I did spit, several times when I didn't enjoy the wine. The total sum of my alcohol intake couldn't have been more than a glass, maybe two, but I'm not drunk. My mind races, panicked. What is the blood alcohol percentage a woman my size should be under to legally drive? I figured this out once. Eight ounces? Did I exceed this? Should I ask to call Clay? Would that be an admission of guilt? I'll play that card if I have to take a coordination test, or whatever it is they do.

His nose twitches as he regards me, silent. Then, some indecipherable emotion, something close to amusement, passes his face.

I catch his eyes. "I may smell like alcohol, but I assure you, officer, I'm sober."

Sober. Yes. I *am* sober; that hazy buzz I felt after the tasting has been beat out of me. But what if I'd had more? I could have been driving faster, I could have hit that man dead on, I could have killed him. And what if he does die, later in the night? I shake my head trying to exorcise this nightmare.

"Well, I tell 'ya." He returns my license and paperwork, sliding his pad into his pocket. He stretches and yawns. "I tell you what. I'm sure he's Mexican and I'm sure he's illegal. A bunch of them in these parts. Been on our radar for some time now." He glances at my crumpled face. "Don't you fret, now. I'm not gonna breathalyze 'ya. One less wetback to deal with, so you, young lady, did us a favor." He smirks. "Those people blend into the night, staining the state of Georgia."

I got off. Just like that. But the initial pool of relief freezes into black ice, a frigid shale, cutting narrow and deep. I don't grace his cruel words with a reply and turn my head, gazing out the window, to the left of his holster. Itchy walks towards Shelby as the other officer strides towards the bicycle, a bolt of tape and camera in his hands.

Like me, Shelby is barefoot. Her face is in her hands and she sways, as if she were a branch, dangling from a bough. I feel her movements in my own body, and her misery, too, suffering my victim's pain to my core. I've always felt superior to people like Shelby, arrogant in their company, but our only difference is the circumstance of birth. I imagine her life, trying to make her best hand with the cards she was dealt. Then I think of myself, born with a silver spoon, capable of such destruction.

Shelby

The goats are wailing and groaning, their noise creeping up the walls, lurking around my dreams like panting ghouls. Half awake, my arms and legs thrash, tangling the sheets in sleepy terror. These aren't the lazy, carefree bleats I'm used to hearing from goats, sounds that make me smile. These are moans from the bowels of hell. Tracy must have forgotten to feed them.

Muttering a prayer with my head under a pillow, I touch my swollen eyes, caked with dried tears. My lashes are stiff and stuck together with old mascara; I didn't remove my makeup before falling asleep. Kicking off the covers, I rub out the bits of crust and crud in the corners of my eyes and open them. There's a clock on the dresser: eight thirty, already? I'm surprised I could sleep, much less sleep in, after last night's fright.

How could an evening that started off so fine end up in such a nightmare? I try turning my thoughts to something good, but I've got a feeling this memory will stick like ugly wallpaper that won't scrape off. It will never fade. Those dark eyes will always haunt me. He touched my knee, asked me to help, to take him home. He didn't want to be hauled off by that ambulance.

Tracy and I were the last to leave the wine tasting; we left a few minutes after Mallory and Itchy. Would you believe I've come this far, this fast. Six months after leaving Coryville finds me six chairs down from Mallory Lakes. She wore an off-the-shoulder embroidered shirt and green flouncy skirt, and with that thick auburn hair, she was more beautiful than I remembered. But three hours later, kneeling by her side, watching her copper bracelets jangle and her shaking hands on the man's wound, she seemed less God-like, not so famous.

Tracy was driving slow, focusing on the centerline, so I saw it first. A car stopped in the center of the road, with the doors open. Our headlights, like a spotlight on a dark-lit stage, streamed over two women, one stooped down, hovering over a heap. I screamed for Tracy to stop, and she parked the truck on the side of the road. I kicked off my heels and ran to see what happened.

I saw him before Tracy—a man knocked over on his bicycle. Silver metal gleamed in the moonlight, his foot jammed into the spokes, and blood oozed from a cut on the bald spot of his head. I knelt beside Mallory and she asked for a cloth. Jerking up to my feet, my stomach convulsed as I ran to the truck. I tried to hold it back but it was no use. Grabbing onto the side door with one hand, and holding my dress back with the other, I vomited. I tried regaining my composure as best as I could, and then found a hand towel in the back of the truck.

Returning to the accident, Mallory looked up when I handed her the cloth. Her eyes were cut to swollen slits and her face, wet with tears, was an eerie shade of greenish-yellow, luminous in the headlights. I felt bad for her and for the first time ever, I was glad I wasn't Mallory Lakes. But mostly, I felt terrible for that man. I stood and walked back to Tracy. The pupils in her pale gray eyes loomed large in the dark, like craters on the moon, and her round, white face was blurred, smeared over like a stranger trying to warn me away in a dream.

Waiting for help, we chewed gum to hide the alcohol on our breath. I'm still not used to the taste of wine so was happy to spit. Tracy swallowed but never seemed drunk, giddy maybe, but not drunk. Still, I was worried the cops would give her a breathalyzer and nail her for drunk driving.

Within minutes, a police car arrived. This is the second time in one month I've had encounters with the authority. Enough for one lifetime, thank you very much. After what seemed like eternity, another cop arrived, then an ambulance a couple of minutes later. Two people leaped from the emergency vehicle, tended to his injury, then slid a stretcher under his body. As they wheeled him into the back, the policeman checked his pockets and pulled out some paper that looked like a letter. Then, he asked Mallory for her license and as they walked to her car, the other officer escorted Itchy to his patrol car.

I stood on the side of the road next to Tracy, feeling helpless. She was sniffling, and I stared at my feet, wringing my hands. I was anxious to discuss the situation, but we knew better than to speak to each other. A few minutes passed then Itchy and the officer got out of the car and walked in our direction. I reckon this will be the last Grasso wine tasting we'll ever attend.

Itchy was teary-eyed but managed a tight smile. Mallory sat in her car, door closed, while the officer stood outside next to the window, looking down on her and asking questions. I couldn't hear their words but he never gave her a breathalyzer, and I know she wasn't spitting. If Tracy had hit him, with her hair spiked in defiance like a porcupine's quills, they would have given her a breath test for sure.

The other cop sectioned off the scene with neon yellow tape, and checked the bike and car with flashlights, probably looking for her car paint on the bicycle. Then, he examined the skid marks behind the car. He asked me and Tracy for our phone numbers, in case they had questions. We must have seemed sober because he sent us on our way. On the expressway, Tracy said she wasn't up to driving me back to the city so I was staying at Squash Blossom, like it or not. I didn't protest. We were tired, scared and numb. I asked Tracy what she thought about him not wanting an ambulance. She said that he was probably here illegally; I suspected the same thing. We drove back to the farm without speaking another word.

Tracy directed me to the guest room and said goodnight, too tired to smile. I turned on the light, slipped off my dress and folded it over a rocking chair tucked in a corner. The bed was soft and comfortable, and the air conditioner hummed quietly; no wonder I could fall asleep. I wish I could hide in this bed all day, but I'd best get moving and see what's in store for me next; this crazy weekend's slipped out of control and has a mind of its own.

I roll out of bed, fold the quilt back, and run my palm over a hand-stitched design of a white-winged dove. Shielding my breasts with crossed arms, I tiptoe across the room; the bedroom, like the house, smells of vanilla. The walls are painted the yellow-butter shade of morning light, and braided rugs of green and pale beige are scattered over waxed wood floors. Wouldn't you know, there's a poster of two squash blossoms hanging on the wall, their leaves matching the colors of the rugs. The name in the corner of the print reads Georgia O'Keefe. Huh, named after the state. I wonder if she'll be one of the artists at the festival this year.

Some arguing just kicked-up downstairs, even drowning out the goats. Must be Tracy and Clare. That's odd. Tracy told me Clare *never* raises her voice. I wonder what the ruckus is about? I crack the door, and listen, straining to make out their words.

"You didn't tell me you'd be out with the *coquette*."

"I work with Shall-be, it was an educational event for the staff and, in case it slipped by you, she happens to work for me. She doesn't have a car, so I gave her a ride."

"I saw the way you checked out her sweet little tush. You'd like a piece of that action. And that pet name, Shall-*be*. It's so contrived. So annoying."

"*Shhhh, Clare,* you'll wake her. She is *not* a member of faerie-land nor does she want to be. She's had a tough life and...please, Clare, this doesn't *sound* like you. We had a horrible experience last night and don't need you turning weird on us."

I close the door and return to bed. Now I've got even more bad stuff to think about: Clare is jealous of me. That's surprising. I mean, that always happens between men and women, but I didn't know women got jealous over other women. I wonder if she thinks I plan to turn into a lesbian and steal Tracy from her. I'd better think of something to say to make her calm down. Like it or not, it's time to enter the day.

I get out of bed and put on the dress I was wearing last night. Sandra let me borrow it; she's rolling in the dough she makes doing hair, spending her last nickel shopping Lenox Square trying to get the Coryville out of her system.

I slide out the door, padding down the hall and into a bathroom. My reflection startles me: Last night's eye makeup is smudged into black half-moons under my eyes; looks like someone smashed me up in a fight. I pick up a bar of soap and wash my face. I don't see a brush, so comb my hair with my fingers, walk out the bathroom, down the stairs and into the kitchen.

Clare must have been awake for hours. The counters are packed with vegetable-filled baskets, which she's organizing into crates. Must be for the Atlanta chefs. I muster up my nerve, look directly into her eyes, and try my best to sound cheerful. "Good morning, Clare. Thanks so much for letting me stay here last night. Tracy must have told you what happened."

Her eyes flit my way and she manages that forced smile. "Yeah, she told me. I'm glad it wasn't worse. And I'm also glad y'all didn't get nailed for drunk driving." Her voice is soft but gritty, like when I grate hazelnuts into silky chocolate mousse at the deli.

I want to tell her that I didn't swallow but figure it's best to keep quiet. Tracy sits at the table. Her head is down, and one hand thumbs through a seed catalog as she gnaws her nails on the other like they were kernels on a cob of corn. The flower jar is empty; the season for elderberry blossoms must have come and gone. She folds down the corner of a page in the catalog, and looks up as I join her at the table.

"Coffee?" She tips her cup at me. "Maybe you'd like to borrow more comfortable clothes, Shelby."

She doesn't say my name her special way, and it hurts my feelings; it's the same way I felt when Buck ignored me. Strange how painful emotions from the past well up and tangle with the present, making them worse than they should be.

"I'm not a coffee drinker, but I'd love to borrow some old shorts and a shirt if that's OK. I feel silly in this dress." I run my palms down the fabric of the pale pink dress, trying to smooth it out; one hundred percent silk. Sandra said it cost ninety dollars, even on sale. I'm lucky it didn't get blood or vomit splattered on it. Still, I'll have it dry-cleaned before giving it back to her. This dress must be sanitized, placed on a hanger then wrapped like new in a plastic bag. I'll never tell Sandra about what happened after the wine tasting.

Tracy stands. "I'll call the hospital and get an update on his condition. Later on, I'll drive you back to The Troubadour. Thank God I scheduled us the day off. In the meantime, I'll find you something to wear." Tracy walks out of the kitchen, and I remain seated racking my brain to think of something to say to Clare; I have to say *something*.

"You must be crazy busy seeing how this is the height of the growing season."

"Actually we're between the two main growing seasons: spring and fall." She takes the clipboard off the table, studies it, then removes several bunches of frilly greens from a basket. Tying them together, she lays them carefully into a crate as if they were a stack of hundred dollar bills. "But, yep, having a great year."

Head down, she peers at the board, removes a pen from behind her ear and makes a check mark. "I've even been commissioned by an Atlanta chef who's going to pay us five hundred dollars to grow him one perfect melon for some elaborate feast." She clicks her pen shut, puts it in the pocket of her shirt, and looks at me. "In this economy, seems absurd, doesn't it?"

"I can't imagine," I exclaim, delighted she's willing to make small talk.

"My dad never would have believed it, either. He almost lost this farm. He owned the land but not the equipment and was paying twenty-two percent interest to the bank. He went broke trying to compete with industrial farms while paying off the machinery."

"Growing up, I watched a lot of neighbors lose their farms. After all their sacrifices and work, it made us sick seeing their lives sold off at auction. At least you kept yours."

"By an apron string. I'm an only child and after my folks died, I inherited the farm. I sold off parcels, keeping the best chunk for myself, and spent a couple of years reworking the soil to meet organic guidelines. Then, I contracted primo restaurant accounts, and everything was coming up roses. At least until the flood hit. Torrential downpours flushed away the soil, lakes and streams overflowing, ruined all of our crops. Almost ran us out of business until the hamlet pooled resources and..."

"I remember that flood. September o-nine, wasn't it?" I say, interrupting her. "It washed away all of Mama's tomato and okra plants. They were at their peak, ready to pick then vamoose. Mama was so upset, like to die. I can only imagine how awful it was for *you*."

I must have hit a sweet spot, the corners of her mouth tip upward. You have to earn your smiles from this woman, but dimpled and kind, they are something to work for.

"You're right, it was awful. Tracy had to take the Grasso job so we could stay afloat. But now the soil has recovered and I got my accounts back. I don't mean to whine. That flood was nothing compared to the damage done by the Mississippi last May."

"Come hell or high water, disaster always seems to hit the folks who can least afford it."

"Amen to that. This summer it's all about the drought. We haven't had a good rain since the last time you were here for the potluck. But we're coping better than most. Organic farming conserves more water in the soil than the farms that rely on chemical pesticides and fertilizers."

"I never knew that. Organic's the way to go."

That comment earns another smile. Encouraged, I stand and walk to the next crate she's loading. "Your eggplants are beautiful. I don't see brown spots on *any* of them." Small, plump purple eggplants are so dark they're almost black; others are long and slender, their creamy skin striped with pale lavender lines. I lean over and remove one from the box. "I've never seen a white eggplant before."

"This varietal's an heirloom, my favorite of the white-skinned." Fiddling with the tip of her braid, she admires those eggplants as if they were newborn babies in a hospital ward.

"Believe it or not, my little girl loves eggplant. Most kids hate it, but she's what you'd call an adventurous eater."

"Maybe she could come visit the farm one day."

I look into her eyes, touched she would invite Miss Ann. Clare squats down to cut off several lengths of string from a roll of twine and the muscles on her tanned thighs, the color of sweet tea, flex and swell. On one rests a mosquito bite, dead center, a pink ring surrounding it like a bull's eye. I stoop beside her and a fold from my dress billows over the welt; queasy pleasure swells in my stomach.

"She'd love that, Clare; she'd get a kick out of your goats. A couple of weeks back, I took her to see the hogs at the Coryville Hog Farm. She went crazy over those pigs."

"Do you live by that farm? Most of the restaurants I supply get their pork from there." She measures a piece of twine then snips. "Cool."

"We live a mile or so down the road. And I appreciate your inviting my daughter to visit; she needs fresh air. Mama smokes non-stop and I think her cigs are making Miss Ann sick."

Clare ties the strands of twine together in a loose knot and stands. She extends her arm, takes my hand, and helps me to my feet. Her grip is strong and capable. It's the grip you'd expect from a woman who, all by herself, saved a hundred-acre farm from the auction block, a flood, and now a drought.

"The Squash Blossom Festival is scheduled three weeks from today; bring her along. Tracy tells me you'll be helping with the food; your daughter can pass plates to the guests. We'll outfit her in a Squash Blossom Farms T-shirt."

Tracy walks into the kitchen, holding a folded pair of shorts and shirt. My face burns as if Clare and I shared a secret.

"How's he doing?" I ask.

"The hospital wouldn't release any specifics, but said his condition is stable. I'll check to see if there's anything online."

"Why, do you think, was he riding a bike so late at night?"

"I doubt he has a car. He's Hispanic, that was obvious, and more than likely, he doesn't have papers."

"And that's why he didn't want us calling an ambulance. It would stir up trouble for him."

"It's a shame that..."

"Tracy," Clare says, interrupting our thoughts. "Are there any more T-shirts left in a child's size?"

I look at Tracy. A smile blooms across her face. "For Miss Ann?" She glances at me then Clare, so happy that her partner's mood has shifted; a thundercloud passing across a clear sky without releasing a drop of rain.

"Yep," I say, forcing my eyes to meet hers. "Clare said I could bring her along, and she could pass food to the guests. She'd love that."

"We'd be honored to have Miss Ann helping out at the festival," Tracy exclaims, handing me the clothes. I'd best ignore that churning feeling I felt with Clare. Must have been admiration for her fortitude, and gratitude she invited my daughter to the farm.

"Thanks, Tracy. I'll go change."

I return to the kitchen in clothes that must belong to her, and she is sitting behind a desk on a side table, her eyes moving across the computer screen. The faded orange shorts are a perfect fit, but the button down shirt hangs long so I knot it at the waist. This new me is pleasing.

"An accident report was posted...no names or details are provided...says the victim has a concussion and a broken leg." She turns to me. "That's it. Lucky dude. It could have been so much worse."

"Mallory must feel terrible," I say. "Thank God she didn't kill him. Do you think she posted her daily blog?"

"That would be cold, considering what happened. I'll check." She taps at the keyboard. "Oh. Come look. She posted something a few hours before the tasting. *Duck with Zinfandel Sauce.*" She smirks. "Zinfandel. Betcha' she downed a few before the tasting."

I walk to the computer. I stare at the screen.

Mallory

I awaken to cries and scratching sounds on the glass pane beside my bed. The figure of the cat, hair standing, back arched with claws extended, lurks outside my window. He must be hungry, but the mournful cries were mine. Visions from last night return in a flood. I should have downed a bottle from my inheritance of Mama's cancer-coping arsenal instead of those two piteous pills.

When the meds did their job, my dreams were delirious. I gave birth to twin daughters with fins instead of arms. We glided through ocean swells, our synchronized hips weaving, keeping time with the rhythm of the current's pull. As hunters, we were out for a kill. I pointed to a large grouper hiding behind a fossilized conch, and we unfurled a net and wrestled it over our prey; the angry fish thrashed, tangling itself in our web. I cautioned the girls to beware, never kill your fish in the sea: Blood lures sharks. They appear out of nowhere when you least expect it. Thrust forward by the relentless surf, we swam away with our struggling catch, planning to spear it on the safety of the shore.

Then the ocean heaved into a tunnel and the walls began crumbling. I couldn't breathe in a train going nowhere, whistle blasting. My cries for help were ignored by fellow passengers who didn't speak English, or didn't want to get involved. Mama, Daddy and Papa Lakes, all the people I had ever loved and lost, linked hands and circled me, praying in a monotone hum for my soul. I tried to cut in and join their ring, but they were braided together. My family, those who are dead, lived honorable lives and are in a sacred place; my lamentations are damned.

I know to be saved I must be willing to change, but there is no change I can make that will expiate me, no potion that will erase last night. I was sharing a moment with Itchy, looking into her eyes, not paying attention to the road. I could have killed that man. I *would* have killed him if I'd had more to drink; would have run right over him. The officer said he was here illegally, and I had done the state of Georgia a favor. What will become of him now, if he's not already dead?

Itchy's final words last night, after I stopped my car in front of her house, echo as if trapped in the base of a well. *"He wasn't wearing a helmet. Remember that, Mallory. It was dark, there was no light on his bike, and he was not wearing a helmet. He must have fallen into your car. It's his fault, Mallory, not ours."* Driving back to Cabbagetown, I felt the jolt of the car as I hit him—*huhwump.* It was my fault. I was looking at Itchy. I swerved into *him.*

Nine hours have since passed. I stagger out of bed, go to the cupboard and, with trembling fingers, pull out a tin of tuna, the pricey yellowfin from Spain; at least I can keep that cat alive. I open it, dump it on a plate then walk to the window. Always a struggle to open, in this dank humidity it won't budge. The cat regards the tuna and yowls as I push and tug at the window frame. No movement. I smash the plate of tuna onto the floor, and the sound of splintered glass scares the cat, who darts off the ledge. Everything I touch is lethal; every object, innocent in repose, awaits my hand for the infliction of damage. I fall into bed and sob.

Deep breaths. I need an answer, how to proceed. I text Itchy:

Come over. We must talk. I'm in hell.

An immediate ping.

I'll be there within the hour.

I get out of bed, pick up shards of the broken plate, and clean up the tuna. The strong odor of oily fish aggravates my headache and acid snakes up my throat. Retreating to the bathroom, I turn on the shower, choking on sobs in the gathering steam, then stand under scalding water, which pelts my body as recriminations until my reddened flesh feels blistered.

He wasn't wearing a helmet. Remember that, Mallory. It was dark, there was no light on his bike, and he was not wearing a helmet. He must have fallen into your car. It's his fault, Mallory. Not ours.

I towel off, step into jeans, button a shirt, then lie prone on Mama's sofa, waiting for Itchy. Several minutes pass and the bell rings; I bolt up, buzz her in and open the door. Her lips are chalky, cracked and, for once, bare of gloss; her oily hair is unkempt, and layers of pearls dangle from around her neck, serving as an amulet, I suppose, to ward off evil. She wears eyes of a one-hundred-year old woman, watery, pink and rheumy, and seems disoriented; I pull her body into mine, searching for solace, warmth, a safety net.

"Oh, honey," she murmurs, patting my back. "They filed an accident report. It was just a concussion and a broken leg, which will heal just fine. There was no mention of his name; thank God, they've kept our names out of the mess, too. At least for now. Most important, he's going to be fine."

A flood of relief. She grabs my shoulders as I stumble, straighten, and then nod. We sit at the kitchen island, and she taps her tapered fingernails on the counter; a tiny chip of crimson polish is missing from the tip of her forefinger.

"Fine. Just fine." She strokes my hand, and speaks without inflection, as if she were dreaming. "Hopefully this is his wake-up call. For starters, he needs to start wearing a helmet. And for God's sake, he should have lights and reflectors on his bike, especially if he's going to be out riding at all hours of the night. It wasn't your fault."

I bite the knuckle on my thumb. It *was* my fault; the wine made me fuzzy and I wasn't paying attention to the road. But if I vocalize my thoughts, they become the reality.

"I was barefoot," I say, instead. "Isn't it illegal to drive without your shoes on?"

"I don't think so, Mallory, I do it all the time. It's hard wearing heels when you're driving." There's a dimness behind her eyes as they shift from mine. "It wasn't your fault," she repeats, adjusting her pearls, her voice wavering, as if caught in a lie.

My body starts to shake, out of control; I put my face into my hands. "What if I'd had more to drink, what if I'd finished that bottle? I could have killed him." I'm blubbering; my face is saturated with tears. "I'd be sentenced to prison and they'd throw away the key."

Moisture leaks from my nose. I brush my sleeve against it then rub my fingertips under my eyes. *Steady, girl, steady. Through the nose.*

She shakes her head, as if bored watching a B-rated re-run, tucks my chin into her hand and turns my face so I'm looking into her eyes. "There's no need for melodrama; no one's going to prison."

I swat away her hand, straightening as if she'd slapped me. "*Melodrama?* Was last night a theatrical performance? I hit a man with my car. An ambulance came and carted him to God knows where, and you're telling me I'm melodramatic?"

"No, Mallory, no. I didn't mean it like that. Last night was awful and you, especially you, feel everything so deeply." She takes my hand, and squeezes it, as if in apology. "I guess what I'm trying to say is..." She presses her lips together in thought then speaks again. "Maybe your take-away from this mess could be to take a good long look at your relationship with alcohol. Maybe this is a wake-up call for you, Mallory, as well."

She leans forward, arms thrust in front of her chest, wiggling her fingers in a gesture to hug me, but I rear back, pushing her elbows away with my forearms.

"Now you wait, you shush. Yes, I like to drink. And sometimes I overdo it, like Mama and Papa Lakes. But I *did* quit; for two whole months I didn't touch a drop, and now I've got a grip. I'm learning to sip, and last night I just sipped. I am *not* an alcoholic. I'm a wine drinker. And wine is food, so in my profession..."

She brushes my finger away. "It's OK, girl, it's OK. You don't have to explain yourself; I won't mention it again. I'm not one to cast stones, not these days. Oh God." Her gaze drops to the counter. "*Phil.*"

"What did he say? You told him about the accident. Right?"

"Of course I did. And then...I ended up telling him...everything."

"Everything? What do you mean, *everything*?"

"About me, about Tony. Everything." She wears a peculiar expression—dazed, empty—as if she's confused about know who she is.

"Oh, sweetie. I wish you'd have felt comfortable talking to me about this from the beginning. I'm your best friend, I could have helped you sort through your feelings."

"Not being able to confide in you was awful, but you wouldn't let me in. I wanted to talk to you about Tony, and what was happening with Phil, but you never returned my calls. You've always judged yourself so harshly, Mallory. And since our outing that day with Tony, I felt you judged me, too."

I've been so naive about Itchy and what I thought to be her oh-so-perfect life. She's always been there for me when times are tough, and I hurt and abandoned her when she needed me the most.

"I'm so, *so* sorry, Itchy. You always seem to have life under control. I was only concerned with my feelings and was selfish and sanctimonious. My silence was borne of jealously, and I hope you'll find a way to forgive me."

"The grass isn't always greener, Mallory. I do forgive you, and we must never allow this to happen to our friendship again." She looks at me and a flicker of life returns to her eyes.

"It's such a relief to be getting this out. You know, Itchy, I feel closer to you now than ever before." I straighten her pearls. "So from the beginning. What happened?"

"It's a long story. We have so much catching up. Where to start?" She blinks and cocks her head to the right, as if puzzled. "I guess it began early last year, after Phil and I lost our money, all of our savings; vanished. And now our house is worth less than what we owe. Combine that with Phil's job on shaky footing, it was too much, Mallory, simply too much. Never in my life have I clipped coupons. And there I was, at the dining room table, clipping coupons."

She lifts her hair and ties it into a knot; tendrils of damp curls stick to the nape of her neck. "God, it's hot in here. Is something wrong with your air conditioner?"

I stand, walk to the thermostat, and turn the dial counterclockwise to sixty-two degrees.

"And through it all," she continues, "Phil refused to talk about the situation; said our finances were under control. Then, last winter, I found a notice from the bank saying we were several months behind on our mortgage. I confronted him, told him I'd ask my parents for help, and he shut me down, said not to get my parents involved. We became strangers to one another, detached, and he was always too busy to talk about our finances. And sex? What a joke. I lost interest, so did he."

She pushes back her chair, stands, and wanders to the dining room table. "Oh, the irises..." She picks up petals, tips browned and curling, scattered around the vase. Placing them in her palm, she gazes at them. "So lovely last night." Walking to the trash can, she stoops and brushes her hands together, the petals fluttering into the canister like falling wings.

She faces me. "I made out like it was no big deal. To you, my parents, my friends. Like canceling our membership at the Club, the girls not swimming on the team this summer, all of that, no big deal. And the twins, always underfoot. Last week I yelled at them for downloading seven songs. Seven dollars and I hollered as if they were drowning kittens."

Her head falls backwards and she speaks to the ceiling, twisting her pearls. "I may have seemed like I was taking things in stride, but I blamed Phil for everything. Couldn't stand the sight of him." Her voice rises in anguish. "My life was in reverse, until I took matters in my own hands, until I got that job. Then, one thing led to another. Tony, I suppose, made my life go forward."

She bends over, forearms crossed over her stomach, and lowers her head to catch my eye. "He gave me back what I thought I'd lost. I felt so alive with that man. But he's a player; he only wanted one thing from me, and my feelings for him were based on tinsel and glitz, nothing real. A charade." Her voice, a throaty whisper, punctuates each word as if trying to make me understand.

"I betrayed all of the people I love. What I did was terrible. I am a terrible woman." She straightens her back, bites her lip, and resumes her seat at the counter.

"No, you're not. You're a wonderful woman who got tangled up in a bad situation. I wasn't a good friend but girl, I'm here for you now. I'm surprised you told Phil. What did he say?"

"At first, when I was carrying on about the accident, he was so sweet. We were on the sofa and he scooched me into his lap, cradling me as if I were a baby. He held me so tight, as if he'd never let go. And I felt so much love for that man, so much love, and it's been such a long time. But it was late, and I was tired. Tired of the lies. Tired of sneaking around; it felt safe to confess. I told him I'd been confused—temporarily deranged. I explained it was over, that I was ashamed, and it would *never* happen again. I told him I loved him and asked him to forgive me. I thought the truth would strengthen our marriage. But I was wrong. Dead wrong."

She releases the pearls and puts her mouth in her hands, silencing a wail. "He choked, more like gagged, then pushed me away."

I strain my neck towards her head, now fallen into arms folded on the counter, trying to understand her words, muffled in tears.

"Watching his head shake, tears streaming down his face, broke my heart. I feel dirty, cheap and ashamed. I was weak. Selfish. I hate myself. For richer or poorer, a good wife stands by her man. For better or worse." She lifts her head to meet my gaze. "If only I could find the rewind button."

"How did you two leave it?"

"After a few minutes, he wiped his eyes, never saying a word, then went to the kitchen to get a beer. He returned to the sofa, turned on the TV, and pressed his body into the corner pillow, as far away from me as possible, staring at the screen. I don't think he even knew what he was watching. I tried talking to him, but his lips were sealed, wouldn't even look at me.

Finally, I went upstairs to bed. I may have dozed an hour or so. When I came down, he was still there, transfixed to that screen." She clutches her arms together, trembling, then braces her forearms into the counter, leaning her face into mine.

"I tried again. To talk to him. Told him I'd been depressed, that I missed him, that I'd acted out and was desperately sorry. But he sat there, no words, so I returned to bed. When I woke up, I found him asleep in the guest room. I closed the door so the twins wouldn't find him there, went to the kitchen, brewed coffee, and soon after the girls came down. I made breakfast. French toast with strawberries and powdered sugar. Their favorite meal. They thought we were celebrating something. Oh Mallory, how could I have let another man touch me? And why did I tell Phil, why? I want it to go away."

I squeeze her hands, kiss them, then drop my head onto my clasped forearms, nodding *yes*, make it *all* go away. Words are finished. There is nothing left to say.

We are both quiet for several minutes, re-scripting the events that led us to this moment, playing out the twisted, malignant maelstrom—in short, smoothing it out—as we try to grasp some meaning, some significance, some acceptable version that would cast a glimmer, even a flicker of hope over smoldering coals, pummeled promises, wrecked lives.

Itchy interrupts my thoughts. "Did you post today's blog?"

"I can't, Itchy. There's no way I can shop and cook today. I'll write Richard a note and tell him I'm sick."

"Oh honey, keep moving forward. You said you'd write a blog every day, you can't lose your job. Write something that sounds normal, sweet, something sentimental. Post an old recipe and photo you've already taken. Switch up the writing a bit." Rolling her eyes, a shadow of a smile, she shakes her head. "But don't *dare* reference that hog you're planning to slaughter." She brushes my hair away from my cheeks with her fingertips.

"Then, call Clay. The officer told me it's unlikely charges will be pressed against you, but your brother will know what steps you'll need to take. Let him make the calls, not you." Her eyes crawl over my face. "Especially in your state."

She glances at her phone. "Gotta run; Phil's home with the girls. I told him I'd be back in a couple of hours. Not that he gives a damn." We stand and hug each other, clinging and reluctant to release ourselves into these nightmares. "Friends forever, Mallory. For better or worse." We link pinky fingers, the dead weight of them pulling our hands down. "I'll call later." She walks towards the entry way and leaves, closing the door quietly.

I turn to sit, lose my balance and clutch the counter to keep from falling. I can't shake that man's face from my mind. He didn't want an ambulance, he wanted to go home. Where was home? The cop said he was an illegal; part of that shadowy sub-culture our state has been trying to expunge. Just last April, Georgia passed a bill opposing illegal immigration. They launched the biggest crackdown, next to Arizona, in the country.

My loft smolders in a dense fog of sorrow. I don't want to be alone, and imagine the comfort I might feel if Cooper were holding me in his arms. But I dare not contact him now; if he couldn't handle the old Mallory, I can only imagine the dust that would fly from his heels now. I'll call Marselina, tell her I need to see her, ask if she can stop by. She volunteers at that clinic in the Mexican community, and may have some answers. But first, I'd better speak with Clay.

I pop a low dose morphine tablet from my stash. Not enough to whack me out, just enough, as Mama said, to file a ragged edge. I call Clay, and we discuss the accident for well over an hour. He tells me to sit tight, that he'd make the calls and would manage the situation. He was relieved I'd been sober, almost sober, and there's no legal evidence proving otherwise. Breaking off a piece of the nightmare and handing it to him was cathartic, as if I were a priestess, tearing off a bit of bread from a loaf then placing it into his outstretched palms; the sign of the cross, the body of Christ. Then, I call Marselina.

Early evening shadows creep into my loft. Marselina has arrived and sits on Mama's sofa, curious, wondering what happened. I stand in front of her like an actress on a stage, rehearsing my lines. I turn my body to her in profile, and pace the floor, picking at torn cuticles. This is how Itchy must have felt last night with Phil; as an adulteress confessing her infidelities to her cuckolded husband, costumed in a blood-spattered gown, worn in last week's performance by Lady Macbeth. Recounting the accident, I tell Marselina everything, almost everything. I omit the scene where I lock eyes with Itchy—*huhwump.*

Marselina nods as I speak, her ebony eyes following my movement, until I am finished. Then she stands, wraps her arm around the back of my neck, and I fall into her shoulder. "You are not alone in this, Mallory. And the most important thing to understand is you can't blame yourself; you were a victim of circumstances beyond your control."

I'm no victim. I turned from the wheel; I was even laughing when I hit that man. But I can't admit this truth, and push away, wiping the tears from my eyes, directing my words towards the window.

"But that man? What will happen to that man?"

She places her hands on my shoulders. "In truth, if he's here without papers, he'll likely be deported. I'll see if any of my friends know of his situation. Tommy can dig around, too."

I meet her eyes. "*Deported?* Please God no, Marselina. You must find out what's happening to him. We shouldn't have called an ambulance. I should have done what he'd asked and taken him home. There must be something I can do."

Silent, she bends forward and takes my hand, touching her lips to the top of my palm. Her hair falls over my arms, tickling them, shooting up goose bumps. Straightening her back, she releases my hand and leaves.

And now I'm alone. I must find words, soothing words to channel comfort from my family; it's time to write my blog.

Fried Green Tomato BLT
by
Mallory Lakes

There are few things in life that would qualify me as an expert. But there is one discipline-dare I say art form?-in which I truly excel: making and eating fried green tomatoes.

I am, frankly, pedigreed in this particular field. My credentials stem from learning this craft from the pros. Growing up, I carefully observed my grandmother, mom and various aunts pull out the cast iron skillet, corn meal and bacon fat when green tomatoes were abundant.

I adore fried green tomatoes-when properly cooked they have a crispy crust with a tangy, creamy filling. And layering them in a sandwich with crispy bacon, arugula and homemade mayonnaise renders this sandwich a feast for the gods. I've never repeated a recipe until now, but this one begs I haul out the skillet.

This recipe is nothing fancy, and I'd prefer not calculating the calories. I simply enjoy country cooking when summer lays thick, heavy on the vine; when the sun blazes hot, and the humidity-indeed, life itself-has sucked me to the bone. This is a recipe that conjures memories of my family. But the recipe will never taste as good as Mama's because the missing ingredients are the people closest to my heart, sitting around the table, on a long-ago day in July.

I dedicate this recipe to the memories of my mother, and all the fine women who inhabit my Georgia family tree. And I can't forget Papa Lakes, who taught me the best mayonnaise doesn't come from a jar.

PART 2 | CHAPTER 12

Shelby

If ever there was a finer morning in August, I'd like to hear about it. Miss Ann and I have spent the past three days at Squash Blossom, helping the neighbor women prepare for today's festival. Last night Miss Ann was so excited, she could barely sleep. Her little feet kicking my legs and back, I may as well have been sleeping with a fresh-caught catfish, slapping and banging around a row boat.

Everyone woke at the crack of dawn to iron out last-minute details before the festival, which officially kicks off at ten o'clock. After last week's scalding temperatures and humidity close to 100 percent, we finally have a break in the weather. The forecast predicts a high of only eighty-four degrees with no chance for rain, not a cloud in the sky. Tracy just made the call not to pitch the tents; at least we can cross that off of our list.

We've been picking squash blossoms in shifts, round-the-clock, for forty-eight hours. Last count, close to one-thousand, four hundred blossoms have been collected, all reserved for the dishes we'll pass. Clare purchased five additional cases from nearby farms to ensure we'd have enough. Last night we stayed up past midnight, prepping ingredients for the salad, corn cakes, quesadillas, and what I'm in charge of: stuffed squash blossoms.

Clare sold five hundred and thirty-six tickets at twenty-five bucks a pop. Most of the tickets were online sales and the rest sold at the Atlanta restaurants that buy her produce. After she covers the costs, she'll donate the remainder to the Women's Crisis Center. All the labor's been volunteered so she figures she'll clear at least four thousand dollars. Six port-a-potties were installed yesterday; the septic system could never handle this kind of crowd.

Right now Miss Ann's with Tracy, helping her feed the goats, while Clare ropes off the vegetables so they don't get trampled. The artists will be arriving in a couple of hours and will sell paintings and jewelry from the back of vans and pick-ups. The Sunset Sisters, two guitarists from Atlanta, are scheduled to arrive by nine, and the gates open at nine-thirty.

Clare and Tracy tell me they love having a child bouncing about the farm, and Miss Ann's having the time of her life. Yesterday she told me the festival brings good *karma*. I asked her what the word meant and she said *luck*; if Miss Ann thinks she's strung into a bracelet of good fortune, it does my heart good.

I'm standing behind the butcher-block counter in the kitchen, trying to focus on my task. Hangdog tired, I still have it in me to admire the large wicker basket filled with squash blossoms, which are layered between sheets of wax paper, like a folded crepe curtain, designed in a swishy pattern of yellow, orange and pale green swirls.

I pick up the first blossom. Swollen with seeds and membranes at the base, it thins out as if it were a vase, twisting into a pig's tail corkscrew at the top. I run my finger against the blade of the paring knife, which is sharper than the ones we use at Grasso's. I can't get distracted or I'll cut myself. I push the pointed tip of the knife into the base then push the blade upward, making a slit through the center but leaving the back and stem end intact. The blossom feels papery and fragile, like a butterfly's wings between my fingertips. You can hold most butterflies by their wings without harming them, but you'll damage their scales if you press their wings tight; the butterfly may never fly again. I keep this in mind, and handle the blossom as if it were a butterfly.

I hear Miss Ann's laughter through the kitchen window when the goats bleat *baahhhh.* Today their noise is full of curious and rambunctious energy, so different from their awful moans the morning after the accident. I'm thankful that man didn't suffer more than a broken leg, but his eyes still haunt me. I wonder if he was deported. Nauseous, I put my knife down and close my eyes. Tracy and I never told a soul about what happened after the tasting, and the police never called us in for questioning; it's as if the night vanished. Mallory hasn't shopped at Grasso's since.

Itchy keeps to herself in her own little wine world, makes herself scarce as hen's teeth, inventorying racks like she's in a trance. She's seen better days since I've started working at Grasso's. She's put on a gut, her face is blotched and I don't see Mr. Grasso walking the aisles with her. Tracy says there's a new marketing director he's keen on; that man's lower than whale dung at the bottom of the sea.

Glancing out the window, sunlight splashes over Tracy as she hands Miss Ann a bunch of alfalfa. Her small outstretched hand clutches then thrusts the strands of green sprigs dotted with flowers through an opening in the pen. A nanny goat trots up and noses her fist; Miss Ann squeals, drops the alfalfa and jumps back. Tracy stoops down to hug her.

Miss Ann's Coryville doctor thinks she has an allergy that brings on symptoms of asthma, and instructed me to make an appointment with a specialist at the Children's Hospital in Atlanta, which I set up for next month. Since she's been at the farm, she's not coughing and sniffling so much. Clare believes the Squash Blossom honey we've been drizzling over her peaches is curing her. The women at the farm next door have a hive close to the squash patch, which provides nectar and pollen for the bees. Clare explained that honey bees are female, and have a special relationship with squash blossoms. After they forage the squash, drinking nectar from the golden cups of the trumpet-shaped flowers, they return to the hive, and perform a love dance of joy, shaking and wiggling their tails.

She says raw, unfiltered honey has antioxidants with strong healing powers. Also, the pollen in honey created in the Squash Blossom hamlet works as a vaccination, building immunities to local allergies. It wouldn't help Miss Ann's symptoms if she ate honey with spores of flowers from

Alabama, for instance, since she suffers from allergies in Georgia. Sadly, the honey doesn't seem to have a positive effect on her symptoms in Coryville, but she gave me another jar to take back just in case.

The taste of Squash Blossom honey is a journey, beginning with the scent. It's as if I'm on a morning stroll through a secret field of flowers, inhaling wild rose, lavender and peony. Then comes the taste, a rich spiced flavor hard to pinpoint. But it's the lingering aftertaste that traps me; a whisper of squash—raw and embryonic—before it was formed, a delicate bitter bee bite that balances the sweet, a fading persistence that leaves me yearning for more. If you prefer sappy sweet honey without an edge, Squash Blossom honey is not for you.

We're leaving the farm tomorrow, and it saddens me knowing I'm returning Miss Ann to hair dye and cigarette fumes. Mama says that at last she's trying to quit, wearing one of those patches, and says when she can't help herself, she smokes on our neighbor's front porch. Since the bust, his house is empty, so she sits on the front steps while Miss Ann jumps on the trampoline out back. But Mama says she's *still* coughing and her eyes, even the ruined one, are crusty, especially after she wakes up. Miss Ann complains that it hurts to wear her prosthetic now more than ever. She's not in school during summer, so Mama only makes her put it in when they leave the house. Maybe the house has mold. I never thought of that.

I pray that either the specialist or Squash Blossom honey will resolve this, but I can't shake the feeling she may be sick from missing me. I left home six months ago, a lifetime for a child.

The health department inspector just left, and the kitchen is full of women chattering like magpies, some chopping vegetables, others standing over the stove. They buzz around me like honeybees circling the hive; each person knowing her job and doing it. It's hard to concentrate, but my thumb works a rhythm, pushing the knife, and I'm speeding through the blossoms. Tracy says I have the quickest, most efficient knife skills she's ever seen. The next step will be to stuff each of them with one of the small balls of seasoned goat cheese I prepped last night. Then I'll dip them in flour, egg, and coat both sides of the blossoms with breadcrumbs. Tracy instructed me to arrange them on sheet pans then store them in the rented refrigerated trailer parked outside the kitchen. The second shift of women will fry them before they're passed to the guests.

I've been hunched over this table for three hours and am finally putting the last tray into the trailer. My back hurts and my neck's sore, but I'd best get moving; the festival's underway. Sun streams through the window and from the outdoors comes another peal of laughter. Removing my apron, I walk outside, the brightness stinging my eyes. Miss Ann's dancing a jolly little jig by the goat pen, and I press my fingers on her shoulders to quieten her. Hand in hand, we walk into the house, then trudge upstairs.

"I don't want to change clothes, Mama."

Her squash blossom T-shirt has dirt smudges on the bottom but she still looks precious. Clare outfitted her with a tiny apron and, just as Miss Ann promised, she hasn't popped out her eye all morning. We walk into the bathroom. I rinse her face and comb her hair, pulling each side into curly-que pigtails, grateful she hasn't had a coughing fit. Rimming my eyes with liner, I smudge the lines with a Q-tip. We go to the bedroom and I change out of my work clothes, putting on a striped sundress and sandals.

We walk down the stairs and into the hallway, where women, holding platters of food, are heading out the door to feed the growing crowd. The signs on the front and back door say to keep the doors shut, but no one pays attention; they're flung wide open. The Sunset Sister's are singing to the strum of their guitars, their voices amplified, and the air swells with melody.

"Go, go, it's time to let go,
Time's not what it first seemed to be.
Go, go, it's time to let go,
Let the water cleanse through her in dreams."

This music is beautiful and I hum along as renewed energy seeps into my soul. Miss Ann and I walk across the porch onto the side field then weave through the cars and pick-ups loaded with art and jewelry. Above the crowd, past the field, Tracy is jumping up and down, waving to get our attention. I lift Miss Ann towards her, acknowledging we see her, and she walks to us.

"We're off to a great start; the back field's half-filled with cars."

Most of the people are women, ranging in age, I reckon, from seven to seventy. A few men hover about as well, some breaking from the crowd to wander around the vegetable plots, stooping down to study the plants. Clare plans to give a couple of tours through the gardens during the day.

"The first two festivals were only for women," Tracy explains. "But most of the chefs Clare supplies are men, and they teased her, said she discriminated against them. They told her they wanted to celebrate sustainable farming, too. We decided it was no big deal for men to attend, and for the past few years, all are welcome."

A maroon truck's tailgate is open and large elaborate necklaces, similar to the one Tracy wears, are displayed on black velvet.

"They're selling necklaces like yours."

"Yep. What would a Squash Blossom Festival be without squash blossom jewelry? Squash blossom necklaces are traditional pieces of Navajo tribal jewelry; Clare bought this necklace for me as a souvenir from our first festival." Tracy unclasps the turquoise and silver necklace from her neck. I've never seen her without that bulky piece and she now appears vulnerable, fragile.

"See this?" She cradles the silver and turquoise ornament, shaped like a horse-shoe, at the bottom of the necklace. "This is the *naja*, the powerful symbol for an ancient, secret religion. It wards off evil and ensures our crops will be fertile." Tracy strokes the rocks leading to the naja. "When I touch the stones, it protects me. Isn't the beadwork lovely?" She bends down to let Miss Ann touch a bead, which is shaped like a daisy blossom then she refastens it around her neck, quickly, as if lighting would strike her if she wasn't wearing that necklace.

"Squash blossom necklaces are the armor of the spirits." She traces her forefinger over the crescent, dangling around her neck. "The naja is my talisman, and shields my heart from evil."

Miss Ann smiles at Tracy, hanging onto her every word. My eyes wander across the crowd then stop, transfixed to the side of her face. Oh dear heavenly Father; it's Mallory Lakes. Like a target at a shooting range, I could never, ever forget her silhouette. My palms tingle and my neck and forehead dampen, and I can feel my face glowing red hot. She turns her head and catches my eye, cupping a hand over her mouth. She takes several swift steps backwards, as if I were a snarling, wild-eyed dog sprung from its leash. I smooth my hair and try to smile.

The woman she is speaking with stops talking and follows her gaze, craning her neck in our direction. With that black hair, dark skin and eyes, she could be a Navajo Indian herself. She grins then grabs Mallory's wrist and leads her towards us, yanking at her arm to pull her forward. Standing in front of us, the dark-haired woman beams at Tracy but Mallory's expression is impossible to read.

"Hi. I'm Marselina; this is Mallory."

"Good to meet you," says Tracy. "We've met Mallory. Nice seeing you again."

Mallory laces her fingers together and one side of her mouth twitches, as if she's forgotten how to smile. "Hey y'all."

"I remember you from last year," says Marselina, speaking to Tracy. "You own this farm, right?"

"My partner, Clare, owns the property. I've lived with her here over six years."

"This is my third year at your festival. It's my favorite food event. Way more fun than Peachtree Food and Wine; more local." Her words come out excited, in a rush, and I'm grateful for the distraction, wondering what, if anything, I'm going to say to Mallory.

"I grew up in Mexico. Twice a week, my mother and I would go to the market and purchase great bunches of squash blossoms. In

Mexico we call them *flor de calabaza*. She'd stir them into many dishes, even filled the flower vases with them. Squash blossoms bring happy memories."

This woman isn't an Indian, she's Mexican, but worlds different from the Mexicans in Coryville. Mexican kids go to Miss Ann's school, and their parents don't speak English so their kids are their translators. I wonder how this woman learned to speak our language so well. A woman walks by passing small plates of salad from a tray; forks are set under the mounds of greens. Marselina picks one off the tray, and, with her fingers, pops a glistening clover-like sprig into her mouth.

"The salad you're eating is made with purslane, heirloom tomatoes, and pork rinds," Tracy says. "We grow the purslane and tomatoes on the farm, and the pork skin comes from the Coryville Hog Farm. It's topped with the piece de resistance: squash blossoms." Tracy's face glows with pride.

"Mallory, this salad's a masterpiece. We always made salads with purslane in Mexico, the greens are so peppery and crunchy. You should publish this recipe on your blog."

Mallory, standing at the edge of the group, doesn't respond. She seems to be concentrating on her breathing, nostrils expanding as her chest swells out, and then contracts in, like an accordion. After a few moments, she turns to Marselina.

"I told you about Shelby and Tracy. They were the women who stopped..." her voice trails off, unfocused and trembling, as if reliving the experience, "who stopped after the accident to help."

Marselina's eyes widen, startled. "I'm sorry, I didn't know. And here I am rambling on and on. What a horrible night—an awful set of circumstances."

Mallory's neck muscles flinch and she gathers her copper hair then pulls it over her shoulder. She wears oversized sunglasses so I can't read her eyes, and her body fidgets, like a spooked roped pony pressed against the edge of the corral. She inhales, purses her lips, then exhales, shaking her head like she's chasing off horseflies. I wish she'd remove those shades. You can learn a lot about a person by watching how their eyes shift. She holds out her hand towards Tracy, tentative, like she's afraid she might bite it.

Tracy takes Mallory's hand in both of hers and cocks her head sideways at me. "We weren't much help. It could have been much worse. It was so dark, and he should have had lights on his bike." Mallory gazes at Tracy's hands cupping hers, as if in a trance.

"But let's change the subject, shall we?" Releasing her hand, Tracy gestures to me. "Shelby begins chef school at the Robert Russell Culinary Arts Academy next month."

Mallory raises her head and is quiet a moment, as if deciding whether to speak or walk away. "That's a great program. It's where I got my associate's degree. But if you get Chef Tomas for pastry, beware. That class is a nightmare."

It's as if the smell of manure passed in the wind and I smile, tell her, *yes*, I will beware. We make small talk about the classes but my heart's flittering like a robin trapped in a cage. As Mama would put it, *there's an elephant in the room* and conversation waltzes around what weighs heaviest on our minds: the accident. I wonder if she knows what happened to that man?

Our words are spent and a brownish-orange flush crawls up her chest as her gaze falls to the ground. With the pointed toe of her sandal, she nudges a stone from the earth then lifts and tilts her head sideways, studying my face. My eyes, reflected and distorted in her oversized sunglasses, tell her to let it go, it wasn't her fault, but she rubs her neck as if to lessen the pain of a suffering man's fate clenched around her throat.

Miss Ann's laughter splinters the moment as she points to a chihuahua's nose peeking out from a basket; the spell is broken. Mallory pulls Miss Ann's apron string. "I see you have an important job. Who does this beautiful child belong to?"

"That's Miss Ann, my daughter. But you shush now, she'll get a big head if you brag on her."

Another woman walks by with a platter of stuffed squash blossoms hot off the fryer, moist air trapped in a tiny cloud clings above them.

"Would you mind if I take a photo of Miss Ann holding that platter? She's darling, and it would be great promotion for the festival."

"Mama, oh Mama, can I get my picture taken, *pu-lease*?"

"Of course you can." I turn to Mallory. "That would be the highlight of her day. After she sees her picture on your blog, it may be the highlight of her life."

"Tracy, would you share your recipe for the stuffed blossoms?" Mallory asks. "I'll give you full credit in my blog."

Tracy agrees, takes the platter from the woman and hands it to Miss Ann. I lick my fingertips and arrange spit curls around her face then step away. Mallory removes her sunglasses and hands them to Marselina; her dilated pupils look like tar pits sucked to hell. Bringing her camera up to her face, she clutches it like it was her lover, or a rope she's grasping, hanging on to it for dear life.

"Smile, Miss Ann. Say cheese, sweetie."

It's after five; the festival will be over soon yet there are a hundred or so people milling around, their radiant faces suggesting a reluctance to leave. Tracy is hitching two goats up to a kiddie cart painted with wiggly orange sticks and topped with squiggly green lines to resemble a child's carrot patch. Miss Ann is first in line, pigtails bouncing, jumping up and down like she's on a pogo stick. I hope she doesn't have to pee.

I take off my sandals and lean against the side of the house, away from the goat smells, separating myself from people. I want to listen to the music without interruption; they'll be putting away their guitars soon. I'm exhausted but in a happy way. More than anything, I'm glad the day is done.

A flock of starlings pass, flying in a lost world dust of wings, and Clare is standing in the distance. She lifts her hands to the heavens, braids her fingers into a fist and stretches. Her taut arms are as limbs sprouted from one of the pecan trees, long, sinewy and knotted with muscle, and her greenish-yellow shirt is the same shade as the leaves flitting in the sky. She notices me, releases her arms, and then walks in my direction, as a ship sailing across the sun, as queen of the squash blossoms—regal and proud— nodding at her comrades, encouraging them to bloom.

Standing next to me, leaning her upper back against the house, she digs her boot heels into the soil. We look at the sky, and, as she twists her hair into a knot, I inhale the smells of the day, crushed rosemary and a musky sweat sweetened with honey, clinging to her skin.

"It went well. Thanks for all of your help. Miss Ann's too."

Looking at her, I smile, folding my arms across my chest. "The day was perfect. The weather, food, art, people—all so perfect." I turn my head towards the music. "The music too. I love the Sunset Sisters. Their lyrics touch me."

"They kicked off the festival with my favorite song. I asked if they'd conclude the festival by singing it again." She blows then swats at a mosquito on her arm.

I study the duo. Their eyes are closed and they sit in lawn chairs, strumming guitars in wide-spread laps. Their voices rise, throats stretching and swelling in harmony, with the passion of two women who've fished their lives through sludge at the river's bottleneck then dragged back a bucket of jewels to share with the rest of us.

"Holding fast to the hand of my daughter,
We walked to this place down the stream.
She let my hand go as she leaned towards the flow,
I won't stand in front of her dreams.

Go, go, it's time to let go,
Time's not what it first seemed to be.

Go, go, it's time to let go,
Let the water cleanse through her in dreams.

Soon I'll open my hand to my daughter,
And it will stay open, I know.
She'll find her own truth
Time away from this youth,
I won't stand in front of her dreams."

Clare unfolds her arms and pushes away from the house; she has more work to attend before she can call it a day.

"Again, thank you. It was the most successful festival we've ever had."

She tries to brush a kiss on my cheek. Caught off guard, I turn my head towards her, and our lips touch, like a surprise. It's not really a kiss so I don't turn my head away fast, like I should. But I do turn my head. After a moment.

CHAPTER 13

Shelby

"Hoo-wee," Lester says, opening the car door. He slides behind the steering wheel then mops his brow with a wrinkled handkerchief. "Today's a real scorcher." He left the car idling while he was in the gas station so the air conditioner kept us from melting into the sticky vinyl seats. He swivels, hoisting his armpit over the seat, and hands Miss Ann a bag of pork rinds.

"I got you the original flavor this time, sweetie-pea."

"Thanks, Uncle Lester. I like salt and vinegar on tater chips but not on rinds." She shakes her head, a solemn look on her cute little face.

"As I live and breathe, Miss Ann, you're a food critic already." I hand her a paper napkin. We left the Atlanta Children's Hospital a couple of hours back and are on our way home. Lester hands Mama another Double-A scratcher, decorated with horseshoes, then slides a third Lotto ticket into his shirt pocket, next to the others he bought at the last two stations.

"Third time's the charm." He winks at Mama. All he'll talk about, until Friday night's winning pick, will be how he plans to spend his millions. I make a split decision to take the bus back to work on Friday; if Lester drives me, I'll have to listen to this nonsense for three solid hours. Mama picks up a quarter and scratches at the little squares on the ticket, silvery shards falling into her lap.

Straining his head to look over his right shoulder, he backs his car out of the parking space in front of the Lickity-Split gas station. He navigates between truckers and their sixteen-wheelers, admiring tricked-out rigs in the side mirror with a deep, long whistle. Exiting the lot, he turns his gaze to Mama's lap to see if she's scratched a winning match.

"Lester, pay attention," I bark. "You're going to run that man down."

He jerks his head to the road and slams the brakes, waving him across. The man passes, tipping his cowboy hat. Lester nods, hunches over the steering wheel, then presses the gas pedal; the car merges onto the expressway.

"My chances for winning are much better along the expressway than they are at the 7-Eleven. I study this, and know for a fact, these stations are the ones spitting out the winning numbers."

"Like one in a billion-trillion?" I say, stroking Miss Ann's shoulder. That was the third station we'd stopped at in the past hour; we'll never get home at this rate.

"My odds are better than that, Shelby. I spend a lot of time analyzing the winning numbers for the Mighty Million, and I know which stores and gas stations produce the most winners. One of these days I'll get lucky; I can feel it in my bones." I watch his scrunched-together eyes in the rear-view mirror perhaps fantasizing his dream trip to Vegas after winning all of those millions.

"You mean you'll have good karma," Miss Ann says.

"Where does she get such words?" Mama asks. She blows at the loose flakes on her card, shakes her head then turns to Lester. "Not a dime, hon."

"The Mighty Million's up to *two hundred and eighty million dollars.* If I choose the annuity option, for every million dollars I win, I'll receive almost forty thousand big ones a year for life. Multiply that million by two hundred and eighty and see what Lady Luck's got up her sleeve."

"Before taxes, Lester," Mama says, patting his leg.

"Dadgum government, rob a crippled man blind. The Coryville County Jail has more honest folks filling their walls than does the entire

United States Congress." He raises his brows at Mama and nods as if he's privy to top-government information.

"Slats chooses the easy pick," he continues; "lets the computer select numbers for him. But he's dumber than a box of rocks. I'm smart. Got the best numbers figured out upstairs." Clasping the vinyl-padded steering wheel with his left hand, his right taps a revolver finger at his brains.

"Both hands on the wheel," I yelp. "You're swerving. I think the Lotto's a waste of money."

"Did you know, Shelby," Mama says, in that know-it-all voice of hers, "the Georgia Lottery has given over twelve billion—that's billion with a *b*—dollars back to the state for education? I look at it this way. Even if Lester never wins a red cent, he's contributing to Miss Ann's education fund."

He should set up a bank account in her name and make the contributions there. I don't say this out loud; it's too hot to argue.

Miss Ann is strapped into her seatbelt, munching on rinds and playing with her puppet. We let her bring Woody along for a distraction. Her back was like a scratch card with the doctor putting potential allergens into all the little needle pricks. We waited thirty minutes to see if any of the marks produced a red blotch, which would indicate she had an allergy; not even one of them caused the skin to swell.

Next, they did a lung function test and had her breathe into a hose connected to a machine. She had trouble taking even one deep breath without coughing, so here's the bad news, the *diagnosis*: Miss Ann may have asthma. He gave me a prescription for an inhaler, medication and eye drops—and that's in addition to the drops she already uses for her artificial eye. The specialist said cigarette smoke may be a trigger, but smoke does not cause asthma. I'm mystified, have more questions than answers, and that familiar fear returns, swelling my gut: She's sick from missing me.

I open my book *Fundamental Cooking Theories and Techniques* and finish reading the last two pages about thickening sauces and soups. I've been taking three classes a week, two weeks now, at chef school. So far, so good. I even had a jump-start, earning four surprise credit hours. All I had to do was present the school with the SaniSafe Certification I'd earned at Grasso's; I can spot the difference between a rat turd and a mouse dropping a mile away.

After the written exam, we'll have a hands-on test demonstrating our knowledge of classical vegetable cuts. Once again, I lucked out because I get to practice these skills every day at work. A new girl was hired to run rotisserie operations and I've been promoted to the cold food prep station. I had my six-month evaluation last week, and Tracy gave me four out of five on all questions asked on the form. She said I deserved five out of five, but Human Resources frowns on that; as the deli manager, she must set goals so her crew will work harder. HR gave me a thirty cent per hour raise, which helps since I'm not reimbursed for school books.

I turn to the next chapter: *French Culinary Words and Phrases*. Skimming the first page, I'm already lost. The funny marks over foreign words look like chicken scratch. Maybe I'm not so lucky; chef school is harder by the minute. Feeling car sick, I close the book. Praise Jesus Lester's out of cash so we'll be home soon.

Pulling into the driveway, the thrill of simple pleasures, of making dinner for my family, washes over me. Tracy and Clare gave me a crate of produce—lima beans, okra, corn and tomatoes—as a thank you for helping at the festival, which will inspire a fine meal. Walking to the kitchen, I image Clare selecting vegetables for me. It feels like kudzu is curling through my stomach when I imagine her working the soil, tanned back straight and muscled, digging her shovel deep into the earth. And like the vine, when I pull away the thought, the snaky feeling returns twofold. This burning itch, invading my emotions: Am I in love? With a *woman*?

Last night lying in bed, I imagined holding her, loving her in a romantic way, and I knew exactly how she felt when I touched her. And—then. I stopped. Most folks say same-sex romance isn't natural, that it's a sin, and the mere thought will damn your soul. Something *is* wrong with me. An emptiness, a hunger, a restlessness; something's out there that I need but

I don't know where to find it. And what about Tracy? I could never hurt Tracy. I once had these same feelings towards Buck, and there's that guy at school with golden eyes and a strong square jaw who's been trying to catch my eye. I'll shift my thoughts towards him.

Sounds like a herd of cattle are trampling through the house and I bless the distraction. I cover my ears as Miss Ann and Mama about knock over the card table while chasing each other out the back door. Lester follows them, howling like a hunt dog, as they barrel over to the neighbor's abandoned property. They've claimed his back yard as their own, and Lester made an opening through the chain-link fence so we could crawl through. Mama's got two lawn chairs pulled up next to the trampoline so Miss Ann can tumble about. Early evenings they shoot the breeze while Mama hulls peas into a pan, with Lester keeping a bait cooler filled with beer and Co-Cola close by.

I lay strips of bacon in the skillet and turn on the burner. As the fragrance of sizzling fat fills the kitchen, I chop the remaining vegetables and pop an okra in my mouth. It has a furry feel on my tongue and the seeds are bitter; this is one vegetable that should never be eaten raw.

All of these colorful veggies will make a fine batch of succotash; Mallory just posted a recipe. I've got access to a computer and printer at chef school and have caught up on most blogs she's written. I especially enjoy reading her conversations with the readers. But I can't afford to make half of what she writes about 'cause *it's got to be organic.* Fresh produce is expensive enough, and vegetables from Squash Blossom Farms, the Atlanta Farmer's Market and Southern Green cost three times what they charge at The Pig.

I chop the onions and wonder what it is about this vegetable that makes folks cry. I grab a couple of paper towels, dab at my eyes, then smooth them over a plate, laying the fried bacon on the towels to drain. With the blade of my knife, I scoop up the onions and slide them into the bacon fat.

Mallory writes about *carbon footprint*s, meaning the energy used to get food from far-flung places to, say, the local Pig, is polluting and wrecking our planet. Her readers respond indignantly, everyone united in their fury that Mexican tomatoes, for instance, ripen in trucks. Deforestation, vanishing ozone layers, and acid rain are just a sample of their holier-than-thou word fall-off. Mallory describes big factory farms where vegetables are grown in chemical-packed soil, where chickens feet never touch the earth, and how animals wallow about suffering in their own excrement. I'm not hard-hearted, but a buck's a buck. In the end, something's going to get you, may as well be a poison apple. The only folks who can eat *farm-to-table* foods are rich folks like Mallory and most of her readers.

On the other hand, it's a good thing there are people who can afford to pay the cost to keep honest farming and food traditions alive, allowing Coryville Hog and Squash Blossom to stay in business. Sliding the lima beans and tomatoes into the pan, I'm reminded of the riches, the emeralds and rubies, Clare gathers from the earth. Maybe one day I'll be sitting in high cotton and can afford to buy from local farms myself. But boy howdy, five hundred dollars for a melon? That's a big seed to swallow.

I dip a spoon into the vegetables and taste; needs a kick. I grind pepper into the mixture and will stir the basil in just before serving. I hope Mama and Lester will appreciate where this dinner comes from; I know Miss Ann will. She's been begging me to take her back to Squash Blossom. Mama said she's smitten with farm-life, asking for plastic goats and pigs when they shop at Walmart. Speak of the devils, they're slamming through the back door now.

"Whew," Mama complains, fanning her armpits. "Even with dusk settled, it's hotter than two goats in a pepper patch."

"Dinner'll be ready in a sec; soon as I toss the corn into the mix." Pressing the blade into the tip of the cob, I push it down, removing the kernels in a golden sheath. "Yesterday's biscuits are in the oven. Get what you want to drink. Sweet tea's in the fridge."

We close our eyes as Mama mumbles grace then pass platters of succotash, steamed rice, biscuits and honey around the table to the rhythm of forks tapping and scraping across plates.

"Eating your cooking is like winning twenty-five dollars on a Scratch and Score." Lester sniffs, swipes his mouth with a napkin then shakes pepper vinegar over the rice. "As my heart belongs to Dixie, this food here beats the Cracker Box's meat-and-three without a contest." With a knobby, gnarled forefinger, he crosses an X across his chest, eyes glued to his plate. "Thought their fried okra was a slam dunk but this here's God's gift to a starving warrior."

Mama rolls her eyes but goose bumps prickle my forearms under the glow of his praise, and my hand darts over the smile creeping across my face.

"Mmm," Mama says, inspecting a forkful of vegetables before putting it in her mouth, "I couldn't find time this spring to put in my tomatoes and okra. It's a treat eatin' home-grown."

"She's been working her fingers to the bone with that beauty shop," Lester says.

Mama crumbles half a biscuit over the vegetables then takes a bite, washing it down with a swallow of tea. "I got a card catalog filled with all my clients' custom coloring preferences. I also got a salesgirl who stops by the house and keeps me stocked with permanent rinses, highlights, low-lights, color restorer and color remover. I put half of my profits back into the business. There's lots of miscellaneous expenses like scissors, razors, capes, brushes, timers, hair clips..."

Here we go. Woman chatters like a fox squirrel. Hates the air still and has to stir it up, rattling silence with words, detailing this or that, things of no interest to anyone except herself. But her prattle gives me time to think.

"*Mama*. Excuse me for interrupting but I had a thought. Do you think your hair chemicals are what's making Miss Ann sick? Maybe she's allergic to them. They weren't included in the allergist's scratch test." Miss Ann sniffs and wipes her nose with a napkin. She looks from me to Mama.

"Oh, Shelby, those smells aren't strong enough to hurt Miss Ann." Mama's jaw sags as if I just kicked the wind out of her. "The shop's my future."

"Maybe we can blow them out the window by the door going down to the cellar. Lester, could you go to Walmart and get Mama an exhaust fan? I'll give you forty bucks. Do you think that would cover a fan with enough power to get rid of those fumes?"

"Sure, Shelby. I'll get the best fan they carry. If it runs over, I'll take care of the difference myself."

"Thanks, Lester." Lester's not the sharpest knife in the drawer, but at least he's not cheap.

"Come along, sugar pea." I turn to Miss Ann. "Time for bed."

Miss Ann usually falls asleep in the middle of the bedtime story but tonight her fingers fold the corners of the pages and she fidgets in the crook of my arm.

"Mama, do you think MeMaw's hair dye's making me sick?" Her voice is tiny and squeaks with that sore throat.

"I don't know, but I promise you, I *will* get to the bottom of this, and you *will* get better. You need to close your eyes and go to sleep."

"You leave the room, and *then* I'll go to sleep. OK?"

Why, my baby is growing up before my eyes; she's never asked me to leave her bedroom before she fell asleep. I kiss her on her forehead. "OK, hon. May the good Lord bless and keep you, and I'll see you in the morning. Say your prayers, now." I slip out of her room, tiptoe to my bedroom, and fall asleep as soon as my head hits the pillow.

I wake up with a start. That smell. Lord, do not let it be what I'm sure it is. I glance at the clock: ten thirty; I've been sleeping an hour. I walk out of my bedroom, down the hall, and lo and behold, there sits Mama in Lester's lap, a lit cig dangling between her fingers. When she sees me, her back stiffens and she stubs it out with quick jerks. The butt is stained with a plum-colored lipstick, matching the ticking on her plunging neck-line, and in the dim light, the TV outlines them in a blue florescent glow. Smoke furs the room and bends around the cragged, fanged antlers of the jackalope, who's presiding over the scene, eyes dancing, eager to see my reaction.

"You promised me you weren't smoking in the house...."

"You heard the doctor. He said cigarettes weren't causing her asthma."

"He said they could be a *trigger*."

"This is the first time in over a month I've smoked in my own home. Smoking outside hasn't made a lick of difference to Miss Ann's cough, one way or the other."

Grinding my teeth, I growl low and deep, like a mama bear pro-tecting her cub. "I don't know how you could be so selfish. You only think of yourself. I don't give a rat's ass what the doctor says, either your smokes or your hair products are hurting my baby. Your—only—grandchild." I spit out those last words slow, like I was thrusting a knife deep into her heart. The jackalope's antlers rattle, as if applauding my performance.

She gives a sharp wounded cry like a crow's caw, puts her face into her hands then turns into Lester's shoulders. Static strands of red hair stand from her head like pins stuck in a cushion and Lester smooths them down.

"Now, I don't want you talking mean to your mama like that."

Rage swells my chest as my shoulders rise to my ears, fingers curling inwards, poised to jump at Mama, to claw out her freckles like a bobcat. I shake my hands then press them into my thighs, leaning over, trying to clear these crazy thoughts. One minute I'm in love with Clare, and the next I hate my own mother. Something *is* wrong with me. I'm not mad at Mama. She loves us and is doing the best she can taking care of Miss Ann so I can follow my dream, to carve us a better life. The jackalope snares me with his eyes, anticipating my next move, goading me on, urging me to attack her. I pull a chair from the card table, stabilize it against the wall, hop up, then pounce into the creature.

Weaving my fingers between his antlers, and with every bit of strength I can muster, I pull...wiggle...pull. Ripping sounds of tearing wallpaper fill my ears...bolts heaving from drywall...Mama crying *no, Shelby, no*... a puff of plaster dust explodes from the wall blinding my vision....as I lose my balance...as I fall to the floor...gripping the vicious, tormenting jackalope.

His antlers, like swords, puncture my palms, and my blood seeps and stains his gnarled, matted fur. I hurl him to the floor, stand, press my hands together and hold them over my head to stop the bleeding. Lifting my leg, I smash the jackalope with the heel of my foot, over and over and over, flattening his skull and crushing his eyes...until an antler cuts my foot...until Lester links his elbows under my arm pits, dragging me away.

Miss Ann is standing in the doorway, which frames her as if she was a portrait of an angel. She is wearing a white cotton nightgown and curls circle her head in a halo of glistening gold. Her blue eye stares at me, crusted around the edges, yet wide, shining with silvery light. Looking down at the shattered jackalope, my throat tightens, and I am proud, amazed by my bravery; both of his evil eyes are missing. Miss Ann and I are rescued. That creature's been done in for good.

CHAPTER 14

Mallory

Cooper is sitting next to me on Mama's sofa and I am facing him, knees tucked into my chest, studying the tapered slope of his nose, the classic elegance of his profile through the steam over my coffee mug. Late-morning light, the brownish-yellow of Dijon mustard, prowls into the loft beneath pulled shades, and hovers in a low-lying angle over his feet. It's the first time we've spoken since the day he left.

I recounted each detail to him about that night, even the part I've omitted to everyone else: The accident was my fault; I was looking at Itchy when I hit him. And then I confessed what I'm most loathe to acknowledge, even to myself: I was foggy from the wine. I should never have been driving. I am responsible for that man's fate. It was a relief to give voice to the guilt shrouding my subconscious like a thundercloud. Why play games with him now, ridiculous in retrospect. Expose the dirt, let the cards fall where they may, and let him run while he has the chance. But he remains still, and as I wait for him to speak—to tell me why he called, to tell me why he's here—he stares at my face, opening, and then shutting his mouth, shaking his head.

"Can I pour you another cup?" My voice is fuzzy, as if woken from a dream.

"That was my third; enough java to keep me jived through the day." His citrus smell and the thought of those muscled thighs woven through mine rattles my thoughts. Tiny lines are etched into the corners of his eyes and a few thin threads of gray are woven into his dark glossy hairline; he's aged more in the past nine months than our separation should have allowed, yet he's never looked so handsome. His eyes try catching mine, but I lower my head.

"What an idiot I've been." His shoulders tighten into blades as his forehead falls, eyes crushing into upturned palms, head moving sideways and back, in an emotion appearing thick with regret. After a minute he straightens and looks at me, the whites of his eyes covered in a pink film, his face shining in tears.

"I'm so sorry. Sorry and disgusted with myself. We'd become so close, and the force of my love knocked me off kilter. I'd never felt such passion, and was scared of losing control. I wasn't thinking straight."

He takes my coffee cup, places it on the table then strokes my knuckles with his thick forefinger. His touch shoots sparks up my groin like lightning, but what follows is a dry ache, reminding me of the joy those fingers once gave to a woman I no longer recognize. He bends his head towards mine.

"And when you weren't in my life, I started sinking, acting out, trying to fill the void of your absence with stupid crap." His eyes bore into mine, the green of his iris pulling at me, trying to drag me in, becoming as dark as a carpet of seaweed washing into the ocean.

"Nothing, Mallory, *nothing* could replace you. As days turned to weeks then months, I began obsessing over you, following your blog to see what you were doing. When someone spoke your name, I went crazy. Maybe I needed the space to understand the significance of what we had."

As he holds me in his eyes, his continence, each fiber of his being, quivers, as if trying to make me understand, to make me forgive him. But his words are meaningless, lost in the tangle of my despair.

"It's a relief to be next to you, hearing your voice. I've found my way home."

Home? Home should be safe; there's no safe haven here. I pull my lips under my teeth, biting them to halt any words that could stray, betraying my thoughts. It's as if some insidious beast has claimed my soul and built a smoking fire, making me numb to his words, and I must use all of my strength to keep the heat and ire of this demon within.

Squeezing his eyes closed, he threads his fingers into a fist, beating his chest. "I've rehearsed what I'd say to you at this moment a thousand times. Mallory, please, believe me. Believe that I am so sorry, and I will never leave you again. Believe that I will love you for a million years." Opening his eyes, he shakes his head as if trying to emerge from a trance. "Even more. I will love you through eternity."

His words are irrelevant, even absurd relative to the reality surrounding my situation—the accident. Irritation clouds my emotions. Opening his eyes, he looks at me with a new expression, as if reading my thoughts, and he pulls my hands away from my knees, pressing them into his chest.

"But God; this is about you. About what happened. I want to take away your sadness, re-light the candles in your eyes. Tell me how to do this, baby, tell me."

I can tell by the tone of his voice, by the pleading look in his face, that he is trying to erase my road map of guilt and recrimination. But I have no response. For no one, not even Cooper, can ease this pain. The position of my hands pressed into his chest feels awkward, and I pull them away, stroking his arms gently as I release them. We sit in silence, collecting pain, sifting through heart ache, and I mark time passing by shifting shapes and shadows until a blaring horn outside the window breaks the quiet. I jerk as if awakened from a dream.

"I've depressed you with my story."

Leaning into me, I feel his breath on my cheek as his words emerge in a river of passion. "What I want, Mallory, is for *your* story to be *our* story. I love all of you, your good stories, and those, well, not so good."

He straightens, shaking his head, the look on his face now as clear as the sky after a thunderstorm passes, the weighted shadows carved under his eyes and cheekbones easing as he presses his lips together in thought.

"I'm all figured out. I want to shoulder your pain, divide it in half." His words have now become clipped, precise, as if he were analyzing spreadsheet data. "A broken leg is most likely the worst of his problems. Heck. I've broken the same leg twice." He pulls my hands, once again, into his, resting them on his thigh. "The Georgia Department of Labor has bigger fish to fry than this, right?"

He wants to fix me, to make it all right, but I have no response, except to shake my head. His eyes move to the side, to regret, then back, and he removes his hands from mine.

"I'd take all of your pain if you'd let me." Dropping his head, he whispers, *I love you,* the words fluttering into his palms as bruised petals. Three simple syllables, powerful enough to soothe every ache ever felt in any human heart, breaks mine. My eyes, as weights, drag up from his hands, past his torso, to meet his gaze.

"You don't have to say the words, Mallory. I can read those beautiful eyes. I'm not trying to be flip, but what comes around goes around."

"Please, Cooper, understand that this has nothing to do with payback. I've been through, rather, I'm *going* through some sort of breakdown and need to dig my way out." I put my hands over his, which lie inert, and give a little squeeze. "*Alone.* But it's a comfort knowing you care, knowing you still want me, knowing you're here for me. Knowing all of this will help on so many levels." The sound of my voice confuses me; it's as if it belongs to a stranger.

With a heavy hand, he brushes my hair away from my face. "I need you back in my life. I've never been so certain of anything. There's nothing I wouldn't do for you, baby, and I'll continue contacting you. All you have to do is open the door."

"You're not afraid of me, are you?" I ask him, my voice unsteady.

"No, Mallory. I'm not afraid. Not anymore."

These are the words I've been pining for, and a part of me wants to grab him, clutch at him, make love with him, share love with him, and have him protect me from myself. But the vulnerable part of me is gone and might not return. I'm not the person I was before the accident. Yet. Somehow. Maybe he's right. Maybe nothing more will happen to the man. I'll find out soon enough. But resuming our relationship is too much risk, too much work, at least right now; my mind has to catch up to the yearning in my body. I stare into the void beyond the arc between his shoulder and neck.

He stands and I walk him to the door.

"Thanks for letting me stop by. I'll call you tomorrow." He cradles me as if I were a fallen bird, and his voice is husky, whispering into my neck. "I'm going to wait for you, Mallory, please don't let it be forever." His unshaven jaw scratches my nose like sandpaper as he touches his lips to my forehead, and my body hangs limp, rag doll arms at my sides.

And then he's gone, leaving me with fiery cheeks as I stare at the closed door, imagining a hell even more excruciating than this Satan's den should I decide to open it. Then I walk to the kitchen island and resume my post, peeling apples.

Sixty-seven days, eighteen hours, and—how many minutes have passed since the accident? With a Swiss watch's precision, some communication cable in my left brain has been ticking off the time, to the minute, since I hit that man. Yet, at this exact moment, the second hand has failed. What next will fall from time?

Who was this man of Latin descent? Did he see me smiling at Itchy before I hit him? I wonder. Did he stop to catch his breath? Was he thinking of the last place he'd been, or his next destination? What was inside his brain when my car lashed forth like a pouncing tiger? Perhaps the accident shocked him into the present, or maybe he was already there. *Accident. Accident. Accident.* Such an anesthetized word, but far preferable to *killing.* Because, in the end, it was a broken leg and concussion. But, with a flip of a coin, he could have just as easily been dead.

I drop my paring knife and place my head in my hands. So this is it, the last straw, the worst that could happen, the final act before the curtain falls. I've climbed down the last rung of the ladder and staked my tent on the edge of the cliff. Losing my parents, my savings, all of these losses culminating in harming this man. Marselina said if he was here without papers, he'd likely be deported. Clay confirmed he was an illegal. What did they do to him? I'm a menace. Lethal to what I touch, lethal to myself.

I force my mind to retrace the image of the bald spot on top of his skull; split, round and shining with blood, a full moon in a crimson sky. Itchy has always said I judge myself too harshly, but forgetting I almost destroyed a human being would be a sacrilege, a denigration. I straighten, pick up the knife, and resume peeling apples.

If someone were watching me, they would think me a calm, normal woman going about the motions of making a meal. But the demons are at bay, gathering arms, growing in numbers, waiting patiently until their full force has gathered to launch an attack. Meanwhile, I wait, peeling apples, a stranger in my own skin. A woman peeling apples, sitting at her kitchen island, cupboards filled with stacked china dishes and lined-up glasses, arranged in rows as precise soldier formations on a battlefront. These objects, in truth, are really not mine. Their surfaces are matted with the invisible fingerprints of ghosts that have preceded me. I am detached and don't recognize myself.

Raw porcine smells of sausage and bacon sizzling in beer permeate the air; an earthy odor of wet dogs, malt and simmering fat. My hog lolling about in her muddy pen must have an odor such as this. I receive monthly e-mail updates and photos of Lilly-Belle's progression. The apple peels surrounding my cutting board look like the curls of shaven wood chips she sleeps on at the farm. I've peeled three times the number of apples needed for my recipe, but, as if in a trance, I reach for another. Centering the fruit on my butcher-block slab, with my sharpest, Japanese blade, I slice the apple into precise quarters. I reach for the paring knife, and peel off the skin, aware that I am peeling apples, yet wondering—am I awake or asleep? Perhaps I am dreaming that I am peeling apples.

Strains from my *Single Lady* ringtone pulls me to the surface; if only a proposal were my only concern. I'll replace the ditty with a dirge. I decide not to answer but check the message after the beep. It's Marselina. She and Tommy are leaving, before the football game begins, to secure a table.

Marselina phoned yesterday. They have information about the victim, who he was and what happened to him. Tommy got the final details from some officer friends, and he'll share the story with me this afternoon. That is, as long as the football's not in play.

The University of Georgia is Tommy's alma mater and he's a rabid fan of their team. They're playing an away game at Ole Miss, so he chose The All-Star Sports Bar to meet; *Yelp* reviewers described the venue as *action-packed fun*. Readers have been requesting food that would complement remote-driven activities, in particular, college football, and I rationalize their menu could provide inspiration for my blog. In truth, I hate sports bars, but at least it will be noisy and informal.

It's ten minutes past one and I crush an OxyContin in a spoon then wash it down with beer. I know. God, I know. BOOZE+OPIOIDS = COSMIC NO-NO. But it's only ten milligrams and they expired last year. Not enough to incur damage. Just enough to deliver a dose of hopped-up vigor. And one would think I'd have put a halt to alcohol consumption. On the contrary, alcohol's my trap door; booze drowns this fearsome grief and allows only shallow emotions to bubble up. I take another gulp.

Lest you wiggle a righteous finger at me, keep in mind, I've quit driving. In fact, I donated my car to Vietnam Veterans of America. I tell friends and colleagues I've made a commitment to save fossil fuels by using public transportation. *Going Green*. In truth, I rely on a regular cabbie; the blur of swaying faces on the overcrowded buses are accusing.

Clay made some calls and said the case was dropped, just like that, off the radar. He said digging into the man's situation would be asking for trouble, that he was in America illegally, and that our tax dollars paid his medical bills. I should have been relieved by his words, but not knowing that man's fate sickens me. My only hope for reprieve, a blinking yellow light, is if Marselina has good news; that no one cares about his status. Then maybe, just maybe, this choking guilt will be mitigated.

I turn off the stove and dislodge the toothpicks that secure the bacon to sausage. With tongs, I remove the sausages from the simmering beer. Then I return to the island, open my laptop, and log onto my site. My readers are directing my script and telling me what to eat, even telling me how to *feel* about my food. Richard Wright sent a congratulatory e-mail last week. My analytics, the number of readers following me, is steadily increasing. Restaurants and grocery stores pay top dollar to be featured on my blog. I rustle myself together to shop, cook, photograph and write, which is the only time I'm able to creep into the flickering threshold of normalcy. In my blogs I reference imaginary friends who help prepare and eat my food when, in truth, it's just a well-fed cat, a cab driver and myself.

Speaking of which, my cabbie's outside the window. I fight my desire to wave him away, but I made a commitment to meet Marselina and Tommy, who have no idea as to the extent of my depression. The thought of leaving my loft frightens me, but it's time to learn of the man's fate. Soon enough the drug will do its thing: I will be brave, cheerful, the impersonation, the personification of my blog. The Mallory Before.

He honks his horn twice, steps out of his cab, and waves his hands beneath my window. I knock on the glass and indicate, with a thumb's up, that I'll be down in a minute. This is our signal, this is the driver I always request; he speaks little English. I wrap the sausages in Saran, place some in the fridge and others in a container to take to the driver. Grabbing a shawl, I cover my shoulder blades, bonier than ever.

The cab zigzags through streets packed with revelers in various stages of inebriation; some wearing the red and black team colors of Georgia and heading to bars to watch the game. Another football Saturday in Hot-lanta. I give the driver a generous tip, gesture three fingers for the three hours I wish him to return in, then walk into the bar. Boisterous bravado bandies about the knots of people sitting at tables and the bar. Some faces are illuminated by the purplish cast of the high-def flat screen TVs plastered into walls, and others lit with a greenish hue cast by their smartphones.

I spy Tommy and Marselina sitting in a booth. Tommy laughs and shakes his fists at the ceiling—the bulldogs must have scored a touchdown. Marselina is solemn, examining her hands, rearranging a collection of Aztec rings on her long, dark fingers. I weave amongst the patrons, waving my hands above my head; Tommy catches my eye.

"Ho, ho. It's Ms. Lakes," Tommy shouts, above the noise. "Sunglasses in a bar? You've been MIA lately. Hanging with Kid Rock? Thanks for crawling out from under that rock to meet us."

I remove my glasses and place them in my purse, wondering if I put on makeup. I knuckle his biceps. "Laying low, swamped with projects." I slide into the red vinyl booth as the waitress brings a pitcher of beer to the table and fills our glasses, a local brew Tommy says he's been anxious to try.

"At the moment I'm mining old recipes to see which would work in gluten-free diets. Seems like all of my readers have some sort of food issue these days."

"Growing up on chili peppers, I must have developed immunities to the afflictions that plague you waspy-types."

"Chili Peppers, Marselina. You said chili peppers." Tommy puts down his beer and grabs her hand, dotting little kisses up and down her arm. "I was hoping we could discuss chili peppers."

"Put on the brakes, cowboy," I say, taking several long gulps, clutching the mug to shutter my shaking hands. "I'm done with chili pepper tastings. Y'all can do that in the privacy of your own home."

"Nick still asks about you," Tommy says with a sly half-grin. The game's in half-time, his focus is off the screen.

"Oh, Tommy, he's not my type. I'm taking a break from men." Exhausted irony underlines the truth behind that statement. "I'll soak up enough testosterone from this randy scene to keep me celibate for months.

But I do need your advice. Seeing as we're into college football season, I was hoping you could help me with a tailgate blogging strategy."

"Oh no, Mallory. Not you too," Marselina whines. "Please steer the topic away from sports. Tommy is obsessed and if I hear one more word about the Bulldog's defensive strategy in next month's Florida game, I'll scream."

"Simmer down, Chiquita." I tap the plastic-coated menu on the table. "The fans are requesting recipes for tailgate parties and remote-driven activities. I need football-watching food inspiration for my blogs."

"But the food here's processed nasty garbage," Marselina quips. "Overly-salted, frozen then flash-fried to order. Look what that man's eating, the one wearing the Falcon's baseball cap: mozzarella sticks dipped in ketchup. *Ick.*" I follow her gaze to the bar. "I could write a thousand-word treatise on why I despise mozzarella sticks and ketchup."

A swollen fist knocks into a platter of brown-crusted cylinders. Thick fingers fumble, grab a stick, then smear it into a crimson pool, which drips on the counter as it rises from the platter to his mouth, vanishing in front of the baseball cap. Oh God, I didn't come here to discuss football and fried cheese. This banter is pushing me over the edge; the bar pulses in a surreal digital phosphorescence. I close my eyes, shaking my head.

"You have to be intoxicated to eat this crap," she continues.

I force my eyes to open. "Then drink up, girlfriend. You're right, of course, but my readers are requesting menu ideas and I aim to please." We've downed most of our beer, and it's still half-time. Tommy beckons the waitress to the table.

"So, Tommy," I say over the noise, toying with an empty straw wrapper, "Marselina tells me you've news about that man."

"It took a bit of digging but I got the *official* report this morning." He looks up at the waitress. "Hey, do y'all sell unfiltered Reds?"

"No, we quit selling cigarettes. These days, you're lucky we still let you smoke in here."

"The day that happens is the day you won't see *me* patronize this place. I support smoking bans in public areas, like buses and banks, but I'm against the government telling me where I can and can't smoke."

Oh God, he's off to the races. The waitress turns to me and points her pen at my face. "Hey. Aren't you Mallory Lakes, the food blogger?"

My eyes drift up to the woman. "That's me." I force a smile.

"I love reading your columns but I never have time to make any of your recipes. I plan to, one of these days." Her eyes, curious, flit around my face and I wonder, again, if I put on makeup. She walks away, scribbling on her pad.

Marselina looks at me and puts her hand over mine. "It's OK, Mallory."

"Spit it out, Tommy." I say. "What happened to him?"

"Well, girlfriend, they dug up his status: Mexican. Illegal Mexican. Marselina knows more about his personal life." His eyes slide to the screen. "*Yes*. The game's started." Wadding his empty pack of cigarettes, his neck cranes around the room. "Hey, hey. There's Ned. Give me a minute." He winks, sliding out of the booth. "I'm gonna go bum a couple of *cowboy killers* from my man."

Several men, sitting at the bar, slam beer mugs on the countertop, waiting for some official report, arguing about a pending review of a contested play. Tommy returns. Retrieving a cigarette from behind his ear, he lights it and regards the screen.

"Another commercial? Hot fire shit. We just got out of half-time. I should just go to the damn game." His eyes lower to meet mine. "Where were we? Oh yeah. The cops traced a piece of mail they found on the victim to a post office box for the Fox Hills Country Club. Apparently the club employed a dozen or so illegal Mexicans to keep the golf course maintained."

"Illegal? That's calling the kettle black. The Club broke the law too if they didn't check papers."

"Fox Hills claimed they knew nothing about their status; they contracted an outside employment services company, Quick Crew, Inc., to staff the green's maintenance team. It was up to them to check out the applicants. Quick Crew closed shop overnight, and that's when the police officially closed the books."

"How come none of this was reported?"

"As it turns out, the golf club's president and CEO is buddy-buddies with the mayor. He contributed mega bucks to his campaign in the last election. With the soured economy, Fox Hills lost a chunk of membership and is hurting, and called in favors to discourage bad press. It was corrupt political bullshit, business as usual. A sloppy mess. Combine that with the state's latest no-tolerance legislation towards illegals so after the initial accident report, the story was dropped and the man deported."

Marselina's jaw moves sideways, back and forth, as if she's chewing gristle. "So the club operates off the sweat off an immigrant's brow, and…"

"I wanted to write a feature but Wright told me to drop it. The mayor's always been a big promoter of *AtlantaNow*. Of course the man's wife and friends didn't make a stink; they're all illegals too."

"These *illegals*, as you refer to them—these *sin papeles,* people without papers—they *do* have names. And the man's story, by the way, *was* covered in detail by the local Mexican-American paper, *La Actualidad,* in its entirety."

Marselina shreds paper napkins, a mad glint in her eyes, as the ragged white strips thicken into a mound. "As the economy worsens, politicians use *sin papales* as their scapegoats, and the South is battling to see who can pass the cruelest immigration laws. Knowing this is the way America works doesn't give us carte blanche to turn a cold shoulder."

I want to stuff that mountain of paper into her mouth to force her silence as she continues, her words amplified, pounding in my ears, as if in contest with the cheers at the bar.

"His name is *Manuel Angel Hernandez,* and he's a devoted husband and father who is much loved in his community. Albeit his *illegal* community." Her face falls into trembling fingers and her rings glint in the surrounding florescence then she drops her hands to the table, resumes ripping napkins, and relating the story.

"ICE conducted a private investigation, which culminated in him, his wife and daughter being deported back to Mexico. Ciudad Juarez, no less; the most dangerous of the border towns." Her eyes, black and flecked with brown, are wide, glazed, as if she's looking at a crime scene. "And Manuel. Hobbling about with a broken leg. Trying to feed his family." She makes the sign of the cross. "With all of that violence. Those brutal beheadings. God save their souls."

"How old is the girl?" I bite my lower lip with such force a metallic taste swims through my mouth.

"A small child, five or six. They came to America the year after she was born."

Miss Ann's age; the darling child with a smile so bright it eclipsed the sun. I printed the photo I took of her at the Squash Blossom Festival and taped it to the shade on my desk lamp. Each time I turn on the light, a ray of innocence flickers about the shadows of my loft.

"A daughter, eh," says Tommy to Marselina, interrupting my thoughts. "You never shared that bit of trivia with me."

"Trivia? Their lives are your trivia, eh. There's lots I don't share with you, mi amor."

Tommy wraps his arms around her neck and nibbles at her ear lobe. Giving her shoulders a slight shake, he looks into her eyes. "Now come on, we've beat this mule to death, you exquisite, you sensitive, you *black magic woman*, you." His eyes dart past her bent head to the screen behind our booth. "Oh shit. I missed that last play. We're about to score." He shifts in his seat to face the other screen, raising his arms, shaking his fists, shouting, "Go Dawgs."

Marselina straightens, shaking her head. "Don't worry," she says to his back, "I have *my* papers. Remember, my last name was Miller before I changed it back to Rivera." She knuckles his spine. "Forget it. Watch the game."

She turns from Tommy and directs her words to me. "These people come over and work their asses off, ecstatic with any crumbs Americans—us *legals*—are willing to toss their way. This argument about stolen jobs is bullshit; even in this jobless economy, they do the disgusting, debilitating work Americans refuse.

"On the other hand, you have the Indians, the Koreans....the *Ukrainians* without papers." Marselina nods at me, smile tight. "They aren't so quickly deported. There's no convenient border to toss them over." She downs her beer, savagely.

Hang on now...hang on....*through the nose.* I look at Marselina, and her eyes, red-rimmed and glassy, swim in unshed tears. I can't hold back. Hiccupping, I drop my head into my folded arms, sobbing in great, thrusting heaves. She reaches across the table to touch my arm.

My tears provoke hers, teasing them to slide down her face. "It's not your fault, Mallory. You two were caught up in circumstances beyond your control. But he's the one who'll pay. It's us Mexicans who're tossed back like dogs. Us Mexicans so easy to discard."

Through my tears, beneath the slat of my bent elbow, the waitress's lower torso approaches us, a note pad tucked into the apron's pocket just below her waist. It stops, swivels, and I watch the back ties of her apron bow bounce across her butt as she retreats swiftly from the table.

Tommy glances in our direction. Eyebrows up, his head jerks from me to Marselina as he smolders his cigarette, crushing it into the ashtray with his thumb. Grabbing a wad of napkins, he passes me a handful then pulls Marselina's head into his chest. His mouth, moving to her ear, whispers, "Save it, baby, save it for later."

CHAPTER 15

Shelby

"Create a plate that's random and rustic, Shelby. Natural, as if the food just sprouted from the soil." My teacher, Chef Chen, was raised in China but attended culinary school in France. He apprenticed in kitchens across Europe before being hired to instruct us students in Atlanta.

"Here, use these." He removes a pair of tweezers from the pocket of his chef coat and we peer into the plate. "Tweezers allow precision." He places a tiny cilantro bud, tilted to the right, over a sesame-crusted orange square of fish. "I like the placement right here, angled just so, over the salmon tartare." He straightens his back then hands me the tweezers.

"This tool's a chef's best friend. It will help you build an exquisite dish of flavor profiles, giving you exact control over presentation and taste."

I study the plate, tweezers pinched between my thumb and forefinger, then arrange a yellow and orange striped nasturtium blossom, and a sprig of watercress against a small mound of shiny edamame beans. I shake my hand to loosen it then arrange salmon roe, bit by bit, as if it had dropped like pollen from beneath the nasturtium stem.

"You're a natural, Shelby. Excellent work as always." Chef pats my back and excitement shivers up my spine. He turns to another student, Shep, a new friend of mine, waiting by his side. "Out the door." He picks up the finished plate and scurries out the swinging doors into the restaurant.

Shep's handsome in a quiet, thoughtful way, and his sarcasm makes me laugh. He's smart too, and even received a degree from business school before entering chef school; one day he plans to own his own restaurant. We always partner in cooking assignments, and last week we met for coffee. He spent an entire hour coaching me on the pronunciation and meaning of French culinary terms. I aced the Basic Methods of Cookery test after his help. Next week he promised to help me with yeast dough hydration formulas; I despise math. I shiver when he brushes against me, consider our names—Shelby and Shep—just how right they sound together, then shift my focus back to school.

My calling could be Garde Manger, which is the chef who makes cold appetizers look beautiful. Last week Chef said he's never allowed Level One students to garnish appetizer plates until I came along; only seven weeks into the program and he uses my work, particularly my exactitude and speed with a knife, as an example to instruct others. It amazes me the things that are important in this new world: that the food should look like a painting, that it's a big no-no, for instance, if tomato repeats itself on the menu. And I'm happy in the structure of this discovered land. My troubles melt like fat over a flame when I'm holding a sauté pan, whisk in hand.

Every Wednesday from eleven-thirty until one o'clock, students mastermind and serve a meal at Heritage, the school's restaurant. Customers from Atlanta, our guinea pigs, make reservations to come here and enjoy a three-course fixed lunch. The twenty-five dollar price may sound high, but the students tell me the same meal would be double that at a downtown restaurant. We're training to be focused and productive in a short period of time, and to make sure the guests are pleased, not only with the flavors, but with our presentation and service. The diners in that civilized, temperature-controlled room have no idea how crazy and hectic our world is behind those swinging doors; my head's been spinning off its socket these past few weeks. This isn't a barbecue cook-off, I can tell you that. I was raised on boiled peanuts, collard greens spiced with pepper vinegar and hoecake dunked in potlikker, and now I feel like Alice after she fell down the rabbit hole.

There are eighteen students in my class, half women, half men, with one chef instructor and two student-assistants. I'm taking classes three nights a week, plus I work the Wednesday lunch; at this rate I'll graduate in a year and a half. At last I'll be a chef, and can make a new life for me and Miss Ann. We'll have an apartment in the city, and she'll enter fourth grade in a new school system, a promising future ahead of her.

It's two o'clock; the floors are mopped, and it's time to switch gears. Tracy's put me on the schedule to work half-shifts on Wednesdays so I can work the lunches at Heritage. I'm scheduled to clock-in at three-thirty, which gives me just enough time to take the bus back to The Troubadour, change into clean chef clothes then get to work; there's no down time in my new life.

On the bus ride back to The Troubadour, I think about Chef's praise. I am thrilled. I've made so many sacrifices, I deserve to feel a little proud. One day my daughter will be proud of me too. I'll be a chef. Maybe I'll contact Nina Bradley; let her know her work with me, after all, was a success. I can't help but hope. The bus drops me off at the stop, right on schedule, a half block down from The Troubadour. I jog up the street, and then skip down the walkway towards the motel. My head's in the clouds—a new feeling for me.

Turning the key, I open the door and walk through the room into the bath. My chef coat hangs on the shower rod, drying after yesterday's soak in bleach and detergent. I touch it; still damp. Most students wear soiled coats but it's important to me that my jacket always be spotless and white, at school and at work. I have three chef coats and on alternating days I soak one of them overnight.

Unbuttoning the jacket, I slide out of the stiff, long sleeves then drape it along the sink to examine; there's a grease stain midway up the front. I always get that exact stain in the same spot from leaning into the stove. I bought a little brush to scrub it out. A clean, dry coat hangs on a slender hanger ready to wear, next to the damp one. I remove it, put it on and regard my reflection in the mirror. The coat hangs heavy, erasing the curves of my breasts and hips; I'm two straight lines.

When I wear my chef coat and black trousers, there's no commitment to being male or female. Men don't leer at me because I'm protected by my suit of armor. I'm smart, fearless and sexless, and for the first time in my life, shown respect. Untying my hair, I brush it out then pull it back into a tight ponytail. I smear Vaseline over my lips, and that's it. I've quit wearing makeup; the world must take me as I am. Sprouts are stuck to a chef clog so I swat them with a washcloth, then done. Putting my keys, bus token, and a five dollar bill into my pocket, I walk out the door and head back to the bus stop; it's a quick ride to work.

Walking down the street, I stop to admire the Alexandria Hotel, a breath-taking tower of twenty-two white granite floors with rose marble trim, layered in tiers tapering up through the clouds like a wedding cake. But instead of a plastic bride and groom perched on top, there sits the most famous restaurant in Atlanta: Vendemmia. I've a few minutes before the bus arrives so I work up my nerve and edge closer to the hotel. I'll bet those folks next to the doorman think I'm one of the chefs; why wouldn't they? I walk closer to the front entry and admire the cut of a woman's suit as she waits for a cab.

Expensive cars glimmer in the side lot. I walk over to get a better look then stop dead in my tracks. Smack dab in front of me is a shimmering white roadster; the spitting image of Tony Grasso's car. There's one way to find out for sure. I bend over to look at the license plate: *Grasso*. Yep, his car—I thought he checked wine sets on Wednesdays. Straightening my back, I see a couple walking towards me. I back away from the car. Please sweet Jesus, don't let it be who I think it is…oh no—it's *him*. With his arm around the waist of the new marketing director.

When he sees me, he cocks his head and his brows furrow, as if he recognizes me but can't remember from where. I want to run but my legs are frozen, and I can't help but stare; I should say hello, but my voice feels strangled. A cloud passes over the sun and his face darkens, and icy eyes lock mine before disappearing into hooded slits. Not saying a word, he shakes his head, sniggers, and digs his fingers into the woman's back, pushing her away from me and towards his car. She is wearing stacked wedged sandals and her long, tanned legs are free of pantyhose. I thought nylons for female executives were mandatory at Grasso's. Honey-streaked hair cascades down her back in long wavy loops, and the thin material of her black dress fixes against the outline of her thong. Her butt, like two molded mounds of Jell-O, jiggles like panna cotta as she prances to his car in quick, tiny steps.

I turn away and stare at the sidewalk, immobile. My cheeks are feverish flames, my knees knock together and my stomach churns. That familiar feeling of life gone wrong settles into my gut, heavy as a stale round of sourdough bread. I've always heard this is how you get ahead in life, by fucking your way to the top. I know I'm better looking and a lot smarter than that tramp; but not *that* smart.

Did I honestly believe that happy feeling would last forever? Stupid, stupid Shelby, thinking I'd improve my life by working my fingers to the bone, sacrificing months with my child for all this nonsense. He's a married man and knows that I know what he's up to; what's in store for me now? I should have cut corners and seduced Tony Grasso myself; I could earn my degree without a care in the world. But I'd never let that snake lay a hand on me. I'd rather dig for food in Grasso's dumpsters, sharing a rusted-out shopping cart with that stooped, gnarled beggar woman.

I hear his car speed off, and then glance over my shoulder, not daring to breathe, double checking to make sure they've gone. Turning to the street, I force my feet to walk, dragging one foot in front of the other, almost missing the bus to work. All the seats are taken, and I stand towards the front, one hand gripping the overhead handle while the other clutches the pole. I dig my fingernails into my palms as my body sways with the rhythm of the bus, knowing, just knowing, what pot hole lies ahead; a message floating up in a magic ball after you shake it: *Forget your foolish dreams.*

The bus drops me off in front of the store and I clock-in with eight minutes to spare. Tracy runs towards me, breathless.

"I've got it," she says, waving a sheet of paper in front of my face. "I may have the answer to Miss Ann's breathing problems."

"What are you talking about?"

"Maybe she can't tolerate gluten. You know, the stuff that's in bread and pasta. Mallory's been writing about it in her blogs. I've been reading that gluten-intolerant people have all sorts of issues."

And now *this*. But my daughter comes first on my list of worries. "So what should I do?"

"She needs to be tested. But in the meantime, tell your mama to quit feeding her breads, pastas, cake, cookies—anything made with flour."

"I guess we're ready to try anything now. All that medication, even the Squash Blossom Honey, isn't worth a flip in helping her symptoms."

We've ruled out everything, including mold and asbestos, everything except the chemicals and dyes. I've another appointment with the allergist in two weeks, and am taking samples of hair products this go-round. It's been over a month since we saw the doctor; the same day I lost my wits with Mama, getting my revenge with the jackalope.

Lester patched up the hole in the wall where he was mounted, and I bought Mama a silk flower wreath to stick up in the creature's place. She finally started speaking to me again and admits the jackalope was a gnarly eyesore; she'd just gotten used to it. She says the flowers are pretty and feminine, a fitting memorial to a critter whose new home's at the county landfill.

"Here's a recipe for Gluten-Free Brownies." Tracy hands me a copy from Mallory Lake's latest blog. "She makes brownies using black beans instead of flour. Imagine that. Mallory says they're so good, you don't even miss the...."

"Tracy, I need to tell you something."

"Are you OK? You look like you're about to barf." In one breath I tell her the story about Tony Grasso and the marketing director, start to finish.

"Jell-O doesn't know what she's in for," Tracy says. "Remember what happened to Itchy? She packed on the pounds, piled on makeup to cover her zits, and was so spaced-out, she messed up each vendor's wine order. Some said the accident made her fall apart, but I think it was Grasso. Good thing she quit when she did; her neck was on the chopping block."

"I'm the one who's gonna get her head chopped off. Tony Grasso knows *I know* about his shenanigans."

"Well, Humpty is his henchman, and Humpty thinks you can do no wrong. Now if *I* was the one who saw 'ole Tony and Jell-O, you can bet your bottom dollar..."

I interrupt her. "Give me the prep list; I need to get busy."

The next three hours pass keeping time with the thud of my heart and my blade dicing vegetables. A dreary fog has settled over my cutting board. Will I lose my job? How could I afford to live, or go to chef school? Grasso needs to understand I know how to keep my mouth shut. Maybe I'll contact him, call him, or go upstairs and tell him it's OK, that we can pretend we never saw each other. Maybe....

My thoughts are cut short. Humpty is standing in front of me, looking for the world like he lost his last friend. My right hand is paralyzed, strangling the black rubber handle of the knife.

"Shelby, I need to speak with you in my office." Rivulets of sweat roll down his forehead, and he pulls out a handkerchief to mop his brow, dread in his eyes.

Tracy approaches us, fiddling with the bead work on her necklace. "What's this about, Mr. Davis? If it's about the rotisseries, we had them out at..."

He turns to her. "This doesn't concern you, Tracy." She straightens, staring at him, and a look I don't recognize crosses her face.

I follow him across the store to his office, which is across from the stairwell leading up to Corporate. Tony Grasso is climbing the stairs. He gives a hard look over his shoulder, his eyes now those of the jackalope—beads of impenetrable darkness—and his lips curl into an ugly grin. My face burns with embarrassment and shame. Grasso will have the final word, and now he can also gloat in the satisfaction of seeing the humiliation radiating on my face.

Humpty closes the door behind us and pulls out a chair, gesturing me to sit. This is the first time I've ever been in a professional office, and he sits behind a desk facing me then lowers his eyes regarding his pen.

"Shelby, you know we appreciate the job you've done here at Grasso's, but we're in a difficult economic environment and are forced to cut costs." He pushes the top metal cylinder of the pen—*click, click*—in, out. "I have no choice but to eliminate your job position." He glances at me then his eyes slide back to the pen—*click, click, click.* "Understand we're not firing you, just eliminating the position. I'm sorry it has to end this way, Shelby, I really am."

I want to ask if this is so, why is Grasso's advertising for deli workers on *AtlantaNow*? But I keep my mouth shut, hunching my shoulders to my ears and clenching my jaws in a silent choke; I'll be damned if I let this man see me cry.

"I wrote a letter of recommendation for you. You're a hard worker, and an excellent cook, but we can't afford to keep you on board." He hands me an envelope. "You'll have to gather your belongings and leave now, but I'll make sure you're paid through the end of the week." That beat down yellow dog can't even look me in the eye.

I return to the kitchen, and don't have to say a word; Tracy knows, she can read my face—flaming hot, firebrand red—and she's scrubbing her hands as if they were contaminated with rat poison. I stoop down to retrieve my notebook on the shelf under the stainless counter. Lately I've been jotting down recipes, thoughts and ideas, just like Mallory Lakes, but at this moment can't imagine anyone ever being interested in reading my recipes and feelings about food.

Tracy's face is dark, thunderous, and she stomps to my side. Her back stiffens, and her eyes widen as if a whip was being slashed across her spine. I've never seen an anger such as hers, even worse than Uncle Watley's, and it frightens me.

"You're scaring me, Tracy. He didn't fire me; maybe he told the truth. They had to eliminate my job position for financial reasons." I know that's a lie, but her anger's like a hurricane and I'm worried where next it will land.

"Bullshit," she spits. "That's just another one of their slimy tactics so you can't go after them for firing you without a warning, and for no just cause. And that dirt-bag Grasso bloody well knows you haven't worked here long enough to collect unemployment. I'll stop by The Troubadour after work. We'll put together a plan." Her mouth compresses into a sharpened blue blade.

"I'll have to leave The Troubadour after tonight. I can't afford to stay there if I don't have a job."

Tracy lifts her chin to the ceiling, closes her eyes, and her hands clasp together as if in prayer. Opening them, she bites at the cuticle on her thumbnail and nods, as if Jesus was whispering in her ear and she agreed with his plan.

"Pack your bags and tell the receptionist you're leaving for good. You can stay at Squash Blossom while we sort this through. Tony Grasso will get what's coming to him. I'll bring that prick to his knees." Leaning across the table, she looks hard into my eyes, and her words are spoken in a growl, like a truck passing through gravel.

"You mark my words, Shall-be."

Goat Cheese Panna Cotta, Poached Pear and
Arugula Salad with Maple-Bacon Dressing
by
Shelby Preston

Here's a recipe I just learned in chef school. It looks hard, but it's not if you read the directions three times before beginning. Most of the steps should be completed a day in advance, so make sure you plan ahead. Panna Cotta is usually made with sugar but this is a savory dish. The dressing lends enough sweetness, for my palate.

Tip: When making panna cotta, you need to get the gelatin to liquid to solid ratio just right. You don't want them too firm, but they have to be firm enough to hold their shape on a plate. They should taste light and be slippery when they slide down your throat.

But don't let what I wrote scare you from making them. Panna cotta is just fancy Jell-O, which should jiggle and wiggle when you move the plate around.

Chapter 16

Mallory

Misery kicks my gut, relentless, as a sledgehammer. Last week's bar room tear-fest with Marselina was disarming; since then, I've only trusted myself to leave the loft to buy booze and recipe ingredients to satisfy the blog. Cooper calls or texts daily, concerned, anxious to see me again. But my feelings for him have twisted into a coil of barbed wire; there's no room for him now.

Cooking, daily posts and online conversations with complete strangers in the cocoon of my kitchen are my escape hatch. Clay was more correct than he realized; I've created a puppet, Mallory Lakes, to entertain my readers. My truth is her language game; I feed her the words my readers want to read, and direct her motions, but she can't dance onstage with strings forever.

A couple of weeks ago, I accepted an invitation from Tah-dah, an underground supper club, to cater a five-course meal with Troy, an Atlanta chef. Underground dinners, which by-pass zoning and health department laws, are staged in various venues, their location not disclosed to the guests until a few hours before the event. These dinners often attract an odd, eccentric cast of characters so perhaps my strangeness will go unnoticed. But will tonight be too difficult a test—am I ready to handle the rigors of having my food, indeed myself, scrutinized by an audience and a chef I barely know? For two days I've avoided alcohol and drugs to stay focused so my environment is alarmingly intense. On edge and fragile, I'm in a lousy mood.

"All of this contrived espionage surrounding these dinners is a pain-in-the-ass," I mutter to Troy. He's walking backwards through the front door of my loft, gripping one end of the cooler, which is filled with ice and perishable foods.

"Careful down these stairs. Go at my pace, I'll guide you." Our feet, clad in chef clogs, clomp heavily down the stairs sideways, under our weight, plus that of the heavy cooler.

"It's adolescent," I continue. "Like I'm back in high school throwing a party at my parent's house while they're out of town. But these are adults, some middle-aged, for God's sake, boasting: I'm so hip, look at me. I host underground dinners. I stage freaky fantasies and invite my friends to watch." I push open the door with my butt. "Hoo-hoo. I pull fast ones over the health department and zoning authorities."

His van is double-parked in front of my building. He opens the back then wedges my cooler in between folding carts and prep tables.

"Give me a minute. I need to get something." I trot up the stairs, grab a lipstick and my toolbox. Sorely tempted to pop a couple of Xanax, I make the split decision to soldier the night clean, then exit my loft, bolt the door and dash down. I hand him the container filled with the knives, zesters, thermometers and other chef paraphernalia I'll be using through the evening.

Troy has a roguish bad boy look about him. A two-day stubble speckles his chin, one ear is pierced with a small gold hoop, and he wears a black bandana chef-hat, known in biker circles as a *do-rag*. His chef coat and pants are black as well. I only know him professionally, but by the way he shoved my toolbox into his van, I'm sure I've offended him. We need to work as a team so I'd best make amends. We climb into his vehicle and he turns his key in the ignition.

"OK. I admit it. I've never chefed at one of these dinners so I don't know what I'm talking about. But I *have* been a guest at a couple of undergrounds. And, granted, the food has been extraordinary, but the people are…"

"There's a reason why they're popular," he interrupts. "They're a win-win. The dinners are intimate and give adventurous diners a break from pricey, ho-hum restaurant menus." He taps his ring finger, adorned with a thick silver skull band, on the steering wheel, as if trying to refrain from punching me out.

"And as a chef, I earn money on the side and make a name for myself. I can experiment without having to invest in a restaurant. The main reason they're illegal is we don't operate under the nose of the health department. We can't call it a dinner party because we charge a fee, so we *have* to be secretive."

"Touché, Troy. I'm just jealous. I don't know how you have the energy; I can barely manage cooking for a cyber-audience." Placating this dude is tiresome. He turns the steering wheel, edging left into traffic. At the light, he turns toward me to make a right hand turn. Avoiding his face, I look out the window and knot my hair into a ponytail; I feel his eyes on my profile.

"Getting invited to chef a Tah-dah dinner is a culinary coup," he continues. "They attract a sophisticated audience of bold eaters who pay the bucks, yet don't mind if I screw up, as long as the screw up was made while taking a risk. The group does hang on to their odd traditions; I think they get a sexual charge from the subterfuge."

A sexual charge? Ick; what have I gotten myself into? I direct the conversation to a neutral zone. "So Troy, with all of the prep we've done, tonight's menu should be easy to pull off. I'm only concerned about the espresso-crusted pork; I'm worried the grinds won't adhere."

He navigates his van north through Cabbagetown. "A high-temp sear will seal them to the flesh. You know, I was in Buenos Aires a couple of months ago—that city has the most active underground dinner scene on the planet; they've been built into their culture for decades."

Oh crap, here we go.

"Wow, who knew? I thought the scene was born of leftist food fanatics bored with staging sit-ins at city hall." Tourette syndrome must be my latest malady; I can't stop throwing zingers at this man.

"Very funny, very funny. Keep talking; get it out of your system now, Mallory, so you don't offend the guests. Tah-dah provides me an escape from the entry-level, line-cook crap I regurgitate each night at Range. At the undergrounds, I can rework and re-imagine what I learned in chef school, giving it my own spin."

"I'm sorry, Troy. I'm being unfair; I know what you mean. I spent two years at Fleurion and never once got a break from what felt like KP duty. I've just had a bad week." And I haven't had a drink in two days.

"You should be flattered they invited you; they're picky about who cooks their food. The group's been impressed with your coverage of the local food scene. The Coryville Hog Farm, in particular."

"That's why I agreed to chef; to promote the farm and get new material for my blog. The hog we're using tonight is from their first slaughter. Next month, *my* hog will meet its maker on the chopping block; I need charcuterie inspiration for the beast."

In truth, I accepted the invitation to test the waters; if I can make it through tonight without drowning, perhaps there's hope I can venture forth as a cog on the rotating wheel of humanity. But the world outside my loft seems fraught with danger, as if I'm capable of inflicting catastrophic damage on every person and every thing that I encounter. *Two women driving a car. A shared memory. A distraction. Eyes connect. A man crashes into asphalt. A family is ruined. And the fireflies. Always the swirling, flickering fireflies.*

Itchy has stopped by my loft several times since that night; the evening of the accident and her confession to Phil. She said they are like ghosts passing in the hallway, but she's moving forward; rather, going backwards. Itchy is starting over with herself, by herself, from the beginning. She's begun therapy to gain the courage, as she put it, to study her blind spots;

to understand the character traits that have made her who she is, and influence how she behaves. She's concerned about me, encouraging me to do the same.

But I can't bear the thought of a confessional to a stranger; they'd lock the door and throw away the key. Sedatives ease anxiety, opiates give energy, booze numbs depression, and sleeping pills lure me to sleep. Self-medication is my only relief, and the guilt that was consuming me is being trumped by grief, and the unsettling knowledge that my journey has just begun.

"I've enjoyed reading your blogs about that pig you purchased," Troy says, interrupting my thoughts.

Switch gears, the guy's trying to be civil.

"Thanks. Tonight's *Snout to Tail* theme should be great inspiration for future blogs; I appreciate that the entire anatomy of the pig will be eaten. Tell me about the kitchen set-up."

"I don't have a clue. I didn't even know where the event was going to be until a few minutes before I had to leave; thank God for GPS." He pats the navigation system suctioned to his windshield. "We don't have time to get lost. As I'm sure you're aware, they never disclose where the dinners are held until the last minute. It's part of the intrigue, the subterfuge, the..."

"The total bullshit?"

"That too."

At last. He's loosening up.

"Tonight's venue is set in an old train station on the MARTA red line close to the warehouse district. It was built around 1918, and shut down several years ago. They saved it from demolition by renting it out for special events; there have been spotty renovations to get it functioning."

A train station? I roll the window down and stick out my head. The wind blows against my face, relieving the nausea churning about my stomach.

"What's wrong, car sick?"

I lean back into my seat. "Oh, let's just say I'm not fond of trains."

This must be some sort of cosmic joke, the gods devising a torture chamber to tick one more check off the scorecard. But I'd best pull myself together. It's obvious I'm a mess.

"I had a bad experience on a train as a child and make a special effort to avoid them."

"A derailment?"

"Something like that."

"The dinner won't be in a train, it will be inside the station, so you'll be fine. Great timing; there's the station up ahead." I follow the direction of his gaze and regard the old station, paint peeling around the ornate molding beneath the roofline. "We can unload at the side street next to the back entry, and then I'll park elsewhere. We've been instructed to park at least a block a way from the station, so as not to draw added attention to the dinner."

Rolling my eyes, I unstrap my seatbelt.

We haul our equipment and food onto the back platform facing the railroad tracks. Troy parks the car and returns. The door to the station is unlocked, and we enter the room. Two large banquet tables have been set up horizontally so all of the guests are able to view the platform, which, Troy explains, will serve as a stage for the evening's entertainment. Classic old-school wooden benches peek out from under white linen tablecloths; each table is set with gothic candelabra, diamond-cut stemware and sixteen place settings of creamy bone china, edged in gold.

I flip switches, turning on elegant globe lights hanging from a high vaulted ceiling, which cast a soft gold glow over the surroundings. Trailing ferns dangle from pots hanging from brass chains, and large plants with leaves the size of elephant ears sit about in hammered bronze urns. This appears more a conservatory than a train station. Yes. I'll be fine. Troy walks in as I'm rolling up the shades to allow more light to filter through the dimly lit station.

"Don't do that; keep the shades drawn. I told you, Tah-dah doesn't want anyone to drive by and see what's going on. There's enough light coming in from the platform." Biting my tongue, I roll them back down.

There's a small, separate area for cooking, which at one time must have been affixed to a concession stand. It has a dated, but professional gas stove, a large refrigerator and enough space to set up our prep table. I stick my thermometer into the fridge to make sure it temps below forty degrees. Drat—forty-four—the food will be safer in my ice chest. The freezer, thankfully, is in working order.

"I'll put the chocolate-bacon sorbet in the freezer; then wash the greens." We've done most of the prep work in our home kitchens, so the next few hours, until the guests arrive, should be enough time to organize the five-courses.

We work side by side, heads lowered, hands moving in sync with our knives. Troy checks his watch. "We're making excellent time; your knife skills are impressive."

What did he expect; I spent just as many hours as did he in chef school.

"Thanks." I keep my eyes on the cutting board, chopping seeded tomatoes into a precise, quarter-inch dice. With my knife, I scrape them into a bowl, and then grab a rag from the sanitizing bucket. I wring it out then use it to swipe the seeds into the trash.

He smiles, and dips his head towards mine, trying to catch my eye. "You're an attractive woman. You should post more photographs of yourself on your blog; I'll bet your audience would double." No, not this, he's coming on to me. If there were any romantic feelings left to wring from my heart, they would be for Cooper. Not this jerk.

"It's not about me, it's about the food and readers," I snap, speaking in a tone reserved for waiters slow to bring drinks to the table. He doesn't respond. I pissed him off. He snatches a bunch of cilantro from the cooler, takes it to the sink, and turns on the faucet. I shunned him. *The fragile male ego.* How can I stop his flirting without offending him?

He returns to the table. "*You* should write a blog, Troy. From a working chef's perspective. You're so talented, it would be a fascinating read." No response. "I'd follow it," I venture. He begins chopping, oblivious to my attempt at flattery. "I'd even recommend it to my readers; I've got thousands of followers." He looks up, the shadow of a smile crossing his face.

"I might take you up on that." He straightens his jacket, resumes his task, and we make small talk about his ambitions; at least he's cooled his jets towards me.

As we make the final touches, peeling baby turnips and carrots, we hear the animated voices of guests trickling into the station.

"Let's get the pork cracklings out." Troy hands me several silver bowls lined with white linen. We arrange the fried pork fat, which we'd seasoned with hot, smoked Spanish paprika, over the napkins, wash our hands, then take the cracklings into the station. The first guests arrive as we are arranging the bowls beside the candelabra.

They are escorted in via the platform entry, two at a time. Wearing blindfolds, they clutch the arms and hands of a puffed and balding man, perhaps in his fifties, who guides them into the station. He stops at the entry table. The guests drop their heads back, and their nostrils and chest expand. Then, he unties their blindfolds and lightly frisks them to ensure compliance with Tah-dah's no-recording device rule.

"Let me introduce you to Harold. Tah-dah is his brain child and he organizes these events with his wife." Troy guides my elbow to this mastermind of underground intrigue whose white tux pads a portly girth.

"Good evening, Harold. This is my co-chef tonight, Mallory Lakes."

"It's a pleasure meeting you, Harold." I glance at the basket of blindfolds, willing my mouth to stay shut; he catches my eye.

"Of course. The famous Mallory Lakes. I know there's no need for blindfolds, the guests know we're in a train station." He pronounces *I*, like *ah*, his lips molding around the word as if savoring a fine Cuban cigar. "Blindfolds are part of the ritual, rather the *tradition,* to which we've become accustomed." He closes his eyes, inhales and sighs. "When blindfolded, we can concentrate on the aromas of your fine cooking; tonight's gustatory pleasures should arouse all of the senses."

His laconic drawl resonates with the confidence of a man immersed in life's finest indulgences. Two King George hunting spaniels, perhaps, pounce about his Greek revival estate, which houses an unrivaled expressionist art collection and wine cellar stocked with first-growth, world-class Bordeaux. He's a man of rarified affectations, bored with fine dining, even the revered Michelin-starred ilk, and is always on the hunt for the next Bacchanalian adventure. I am familiar with his breed; I grew up surrounded by men such as this, though not as extreme.

"Our dinners are all in good fun. This is my wife, Melissa. She selected and will be pouring the evening's beverages. Ah, as always, am master of ceremonies."

Melissa smiles and extends her hand. I take it; it feels like bones and feathers. Her lips are painted red, to match the backless, chiffon dress that cinches her tiny waist then billows out like an open umbrella, fluttering about her ankles. Her face is as white and shiny as the waxed marble floors on which her small feet, clad in dragon-festooned Chinese slippers, sashay. Harold resumes his task of meeting guests at the platform, blindfolding them, then leading them into the station.

Melissa hands each arriving guest a Lillet Blanc aperitif from a black lacquered tray, then encourages them to find a seat and sample the pork cracklings, which she correctly refers to as *chicaronnes*. After all of the seats are filled, Harold strides up to the platform, nodding his head from side to side, the king amongst his subjects. The doors separating the station from the platform remain open and fresh air flows into the station, lending a festive, al fresco feel to the evening.

"Good evening, good evening," he says, his voice booming over the crackle of crunching pork fat. "Ah am delighted you could attend Tah-dah's seventeenth dinner party. As we're all aware, pork is the essence, the heartbeat, the very soul of Southern cooking, where exists a strong tradition of savory thrift. Therefore, the theme presented for tonight's meal is Snout to Tail, every course following the body of a hog." The guests clap with enthusiasm; applause for the cracklings, applause for themselves.

"There's something sacred and primitive about the experience shared eating a whole-hog dinner, and tonight's hog lived a contented, and now realized life. We will honor this noble pig, his farmer and the method by which he was raised, ensuring nothing on him goes to waste."

The accolades this hog is garnering are absurd. It's a pig, for heaven's sake. This man is annoying me, but maybe I'm jealous; the feeling a parent of a C- student has listening to another parent rave about their child's acceptance to Harvard. I'll make sure Lilly-Belle receives the same consummate praise in future posts.

"With pleasure, ah turn the stage over to our chefs for this evening, Chef Troy and Chef Mallory."

Troy whispers, "I'll do the talking." We walk toward the platform then stand next to Harold.

"Thank you for inviting me back. I've chefed several Tah-dah dinners and am honored. For those of you who don't know me, I'm Chef Troy, currently working at Range on Peachtree, and this is Chef Mallory, who, as most of you know, writes the popular real-time food blog for *AtlantaNow*."

The audience applauds as I crank a smile, sliding my eyes from side to side, canvasing the guests. Several men, thirty-something urban hipsters, wear tight black jeans and wide leather belts. Their skinny ties, roped in a noose around their necks, peek from under silk jackets. Their partners, sleek-haired divas, wear belted sheaths and opaque black stockings, which stop short at wide, studded leather straps swaddling their ankles, affixed to sadomasochist, six-inch pointed heels. Subdued suburban-types are outfitted in stylish hemp designer clothes. All of the guests, armored in their garments of the noblesse oblige, revel in the smug satisfaction that they are the anointed ones, that they are, indeed, Atlanta's cutting edge.

"The first course we'll be serving in tonight's pork-centric menu is head cheese," Troy continues. "Head cheese is a misnomer as it's not a cheese at all, but a jellied paté made from the head's meat, fat and other organs from the animal. It's often maligned, which perplexes me. Its marvelous juicy flavor has a seductive gelatinous mouth feel; you won't find a country in the world without some version of this delicacy."

A woman taps her knife against a glass. Her cropped, bleached hair is parted to the side revealing jet-black roots, coordinating with dangling ebony earrings. Her plump body twitters in a twisted taupe body scarf, which wraps around her as if she were sausage stuffed into a casing. She taps relentlessly until the room quietens.

"Chef Troy. Chef Troy. Would you share your recipe with us?" Her voice, rasping and adenoidal, suggests she has a bad cold, allergies or is, in a word, obnoxious.

"Absolutely," he replies. "Though it's quite involved. The meat and fat from the head, the heart and the tongue were removed and marinated for twenty-four hours. They were then chopped, combined, wrapped in cheesecloth and rolled into a roulade. I poached the roulade with the hog bones in seasoned stock for hours, then chilled it overnight before cutting it into thin slices."

"It sounds exquisite." The woman sniffs, claps her hands, and beams, nodding at the guests seated at her sides. How could she not know about her outfit, that garish black lipstick, those oversized frames; how could she not know how ridiculous she looks?

"Exquisite, indeed," Troy says. "The head cheese will be accompanied by wild greens, drizzled with Georgia Pecan oil, and salt-rising croutons from Carroll Street Breads. The greens were donated by Neighborhood Foraging, which is a local bike club. The group follows a road map, taking members on a fifteen-mile loop, foraging for edible wild vegetables, fruits and nuts found in participating homeowner's yards. If you're interested, pick up a pamphlet on your way out." He gestures to a small table piled with brochures and handouts.

"Now, if you'll excuse us, we must get on with the show, and serve the first course."

Harold stands and applauds. "Tally-Ho, Chef Troy, Chef Mallory." He nods at the guests, encouraging their applause. We walk to the kitchen and load the pre-arranged plates onto stainless carts. Harold's thundering voice resounds through the walls into the kitchen.

"I thought this dinner was top secret; all of Atlanta can hear that guy."

"Now, now, Mallory. Behave. Let's get this cart rolling."

We wheel out the loaded cart and begin passing plates. Melissa joins Harold on the platform. Holding up a bottle of wine, she sweeps it across the audience so all can admire the label. "The tannins in the Cotes-de-Rhone I'll be pouring deliciously complement the rich fat in the head cheese."

"Thank you, dahlin," Harold says. As she walks to the first table, his eyes transfix upon her swishing derriere, following her movements as she bends then pours a thimble of wine into an oversized tumbler. He clears his throat and several seconds pass in silence, except for the whisper of chiffon and the trickle of wine poured into glass.

He takes a deep breath, shakes his head and clears his throat a second time. "As you're aware, Tah-dah dinners always include some aspect of performance art." In an effort of supreme control, he raises his brows and his gaze slides from his wife's derriere and returns to the guests.

"The performance reminds us that dining should be an experience that appeals to all the senses, including the intellect. Tonight ah have commissioned an artist, a Porcine Poet, if you will, majoring in English at the University of Georgia to entertain us." He gestures toward a young man I hadn't noticed prior to now, standing in a shadow in a back corner of the station. Harold removes an index card from his jacket and begins to read.

"Tonight's guest grew up with pigs, his father owns the Humble Hog Farm in Macon county, and he romanticizes them in his original... *sonnetish*?" He looks up from the card to address the young man. "Sonnetish? Is that the right word?" The young man nods. "Sonnetish it is. It is my great pleasure to introduce you to Alexander Theodore Allen, who prefers to be simply referred to as—*Zan*."

Harold takes a seat as the tall slim man crosses to the middle of the platform. He stops at the edge, his back facing the tracks, then casts rimless-glassed eyes about the group. His chin rises and protrudes; a thin goatee, trimmed as a sharp dagger, grazing the top brass button of his worn, vintage, military-styled jacket. He pushes up his sleeves and folds his right arm over his chest, revealing a pig tattooed to his forearm; papers flutter in his left hand, which is flung out to the guests. His voice, sonorous and thundering, rises and falls with the cadence of his verse.

> "Oh my swine, my sow, my hog, my small piglet
> My substantive amour and my whistle-wetting druid,
> 'Tis not bristled housing yet how well it doth treateth
> Hospitably so, the meats I oft eateth."

Time has misplaced this man; he should have been born in the Elizabethan era of Shakespearean bards. All he's missing is a circular ring, like that used on a pig, pierced into his nose. For the first time since the accident, I'm seized with laughter, but glance at the guests; they are taking this porcine poetry quite seriously. I look down at the floor, cover my mouth, and retreat to the kitchen.

Troy is ladling the second course, Pig Trotter Soup, into cups.

"Have I landed on Mars?" I giggle.

"I think it's cool; his verse gives beauty and dignity to pigs. That poet has thousands of *Facebook* fans and he's made quite a name for himself."

"Oh my God. Zombies have possessed you and have stolen your soul."

"Here," he says, handing me a towel. "Behave. Wipe off the dribbles."

Zan has retreated so we wheel the soup to the platform. Troy claps his hands over his head to get the group's attention.

"The next course served will be Pig Trotter Soup with Roasted Chilies and Tomatillos. Trotters are another name for pig's feet and, as is the tradition of classic soul food cookery, not one porky shred is wasted on this evening's hog, right down to his feet."

After wheeling the soup to the floor, we begin serving, and the poet resumes his post, continuing his recitation.

"...Every belly's pearly secret: sultry, animally viscous.
O what succulence so forbidden, and is hidden, ah such mischief.
My want to share your bed ne'er be evanescent.
The sniff, the taste, the gulp, the mm...coquettishly deferent.
'Tis time I crossed over this fence of barbed wire, to be everything and selfish,
Ay, sate this desire."

This guy must get off on screwing pigs, the real barnyard variety. Maybe they'll be wheeling in a couple of sows after dinner; a porcine orgy, complete with piggy porn, for the guests to partake. Nothing would surprise me tonight. Zan's verse, however, reminds me to finish the Pork Belly Tacos; they need an avocado garnish.

As Troy helps Melissa fill wine glasses, I return to the kitchen. I remove six avocados from my crate; when diced, they should be sufficient for thirty-two tacos. I slide my knife into the black-green fruit—avocado *is* a fruit—then glide the blade from pole to pole, cutting it in two. Pressing the blade into the pit, I wiggle it out, pit attached to knife; this is the most efficient way to pit an avocado. I dice it in the shell, and with a spoon, scoop the pale green emeralds onto my cutting board, and then arrange them over five tacos.

The next avocado is larger; I spread my fingers wide to hold it in my palm and rub my thumb against the bumpy skin. Most avocados I buy are from central Mexico; perhaps Manuel's family left the border town and found jobs picking avocados. I've read many Mexican children, out of necessity, work the fields instead of attending school.

Manuel and his wife would have to use fruit pickers, which are lined wire baskets opening at the top with picking hooks attached; the hooks pick the fruit then it falls into the basket. Their daughter would stand close by with a strong cloth bag, filled with avocados. I imagine an avocado missing the basket and the girl catching it with both hands. *Bueno, bueno,* her parents might shout as she places it into the bag. It takes several months for broken legs to heal. How would Manuel get about the fields? Would his leg be encased in a cast; would he be hobbling along with a crutch? I envision them wearing patched, torn clothing and mud-crusted sandals, and worn, wide-brimmed hats would shield their lips from the parching sun. But twelve-hour workdays would be a better fate than life in Ciudad Juarez, drug-infested and racked with violence.

"Mallory. You can't put avocado on the tacos," Troy says, startling me from my reverie.

"Why not? They're traditional and expected in tacos; their cool texture is the counterpoint to the heat in the salsa."

"No one grows avocados in Georgia. They're not local. Spoon them off."

"God, the locavore police have stepped up their militancy. I'm all about shopping local when it's possible, Troy, but I love avocados, will continue to eat avocados, and they are great in this recipe." My voice is rising. "Practice what you preach. How big was the carbon footprint you spread in the sky when you flew to Buenos Aires to explore their underground scene?"

"Please, Mallory, *shhhh*. Keep your voice down. You sound absurd. The guests have expectations that the ingredients used for tonight's dinner are locally sourced."

"That Cotes du Rhone wasn't locally sourced. Why didn't they select a beverage from a Georgia winery? I'll tell you why: They don't like Georgia wines, that's why. I'm going to shout it out, publish it in my blog: Tah-dah Supper Club discriminates against local wineries."

Troy pushes my wrist into the cutting board then removes the knife from my hand. "Go out the side door, away from the guests. Chill. I'll finish the dinner myself."

"Fine." I stomp outside, kick open a metal lawn chair leaning against the side of the station, and sit. I look at the stars in the black sky and wonder...do *they* see the same stars...do they pray each night to return to America? Somewhere a family is shattered because of me. And, then, I think of avocados.

A woman's laughter pierces the air. I'd better get back to the kitchen; the demons lurking in my soul are far worse than these people's foolishness. Standing, I kick the chair over then kick it again, then kick it hard as if it were a football, watching it tumble then land beside the railroad tracks. I return to the kitchen, head pounding, craving Xanax, damning myself for trying to do this straight.

"I'm sorry," I say to Troy as he loads the tacos, without avocados, onto the tray. "I'll shut up and work."

It's not, after all, these people who are the object of my scorn. I've projected the disdain I feel towards myself onto them. It's me who's the absurdity: *Chef Mallory.* My journey to culinary excellence, the rigors of chef school, accepting the hierarchy and control of a professional kitchen, culminating in the exquisite pleasure, the personal gratification of serving each guest a perfect plate, has degenerated into a mime of doped up, digitized drivel.

Troy jerks me to reality, his voice clipped and strained. "Carve the pork into three-quarter-inch thick medallions and return them to the oven; I have it set at two hundred degrees. Then, reheat the Red-Eye Gravy. I'll ask *Melissa* to help pass the tacos."

He wheels the cart into the dining area then turns to close the kitchen door. I return to my cutting board and it has been cleaned; the avocados, even those uncut, are lying in the trash.

A train streaks by, its piercing wail catching me off guard, and the knife on my cutting board rattles, as the kitchen spins, blackening into a tunnel. Grasping the edge of the table, I manage slow deep breaths as the whistle fades. A flicker of light. The kitchen returns to focus.

I failed the test. I can't do this. I'm going insane. Mad. Crazy as a loon. Will I ever find some understanding, some glimmer of meaning to cast about the wreckage, pulling me out of this despair?

With tongs I remove the tenderloin from the oven, place it on a platter, and return to the table. Centering it on my cutting board, I hold it in place with my thumb and middle finger, firm yet gentle, so not to dislodge the coffee bean crust. I pick up my knife, and with one sharp thrust, wedge it into the tender flesh of the pork.

"Pork Belly is the essence of oozing flavor," Troy rhapsodizes from the dining area. "Layered in textures of melting, unctuous fat, it's sandwiched between shreds of rich and savory flesh." His pork belly soliloquy slides under the door, as does my knife, soft and wielding, through the meat. A puddle of pale juice seeps out, napping the medallion.

"For this course we dine on the belly of a superior breed of hog, a pig of profundity, born, humanely raised and sacrificed for our dining pleasure at the Coryville Organic Hog Farm."

Wiping my hands onto my apron, I back from the table, spin around, and escape into the night.

Pork Belly Tacos
by
Mallory Lakes

Food fads are often followed by a backlash: an opposite, yet equally fashionable, trend emerges balancing the former. An example: A friend of mine, who previously eschewed anything with an iota of fat, recently extolled the sublime pork belly dish she enjoyed at Range on Peachtree.

I have to agree with my buddy; Pork belly is wonderful. The best taco I've ever tasted, bar none, was a three-dollar pork belly taco enjoyed at Timothy's Taco Cart (whereabouts updated daily on Facebook, Twitter and their website).

The past decade in America has witnessed a food culture smitten with anything to do with the pig, porcine enthusiasts staging snout-to-tail dinners, and bacon being infused into everything from ice cream to bourbon. All parts of the hog, including the squeal, are quite fashionable. Atlanta could rightly be named capital of this pork-centric nation; local food shops offering us a plethora of porkishly salivating treats that blaze a trail across the city.

But I'd beg to argue that this is no trend. Charcuterie is a form of cooking and preserving meat, particularly pork, and the craft has utilized every scrap of the hog for centuries. Indeed, records regulating charcuterie date back to first century Rome, and I look forward to utilizing classic techniques of charcuterie with my superior specimen of hog, Lilly-Belle, after she is slaughtered.

Arguably, the most popular charcuterie in our country today is bacon, with most brands of American bacon coming from the pork belly before it's cured. The closer you can get to purchasing pork from humanely-raised, small-farm hogs-such as the Coryville Organic Hog Farm-the better the flavor. The following recipe calls for braising an uncured pork belly, which is essentially layers of fat and beef, but if you don't enjoy a juicy, well-marbled pork chop, it's unlikely you'll enjoy pork belly. Conceding to its cholesterol count, I savor it in moderation.

I washed these tacos down with a Chardonnay from the Piedmont region of Georgia. This award-winning Chardonnay's prominent notes of peach and pear balance the pronounced Southwestern flavors in the recipe.

Tip your glasses towards mine in a toast to our local Georgia wineries.

CHAPTER 17

Shelby

"Don't be sad, Shelby. Open your eyes. We're surrounded by beauty. It's paradise."

Clare's arms float up into the brilliant colors of an October sky, and her head tilts back as the tip of her thick silver braid sways, flitting across the top edge of her frayed jeans. Late day sun fills the air, painting her torso in yellow and orange streaks, changing to splotched reddish-brown shadows as she turns, facing me, speaking with a passion that glistens her face.

"The earth's bounty nourishes our body, and her wisdom, our soul."

Yeah, right. Not if you're Shelby Preston. If you're Shelby Preston, you know the world's as healthy as an apple, rotten to the core. Yet, her presence comforts me, as if she's channeling spirits on a Ouija board; my neck tingles and scalp burns. Her words trace every plant and blade of grass, soothing the air she inhabits; clumps of cauliflower beam up at her face, fronds of chard tremble in the breeze, fanning her feet.

"Her truths are simple. Ancient, really. Inhale her sweetness, Shelby, as she flings her fragrance; all the earth asks is that we love her and be gentle with her soil."

"I know, Clare, I know." My voice is thick, snorting back tears threatening to spill over and taint the landscape. "Your farm is so peaceful and lovely, but I'm out of place here. My life's a heap of stinking compost."

"Listen to what you're saying, Shelby." Her eyes lower from the sky to my face. "Compost doesn't stink; compost nourishes the soil, which nourishes us. Compost gives us energy to grow."

I crouch onto the soil, resting my butt on the ground, pulling my thighs into my chest. I yank at weeds as if they were Tony Grasso; as if getting rid of them would banish that man from the earth and I could pick up my dreams from where I left off. My chef coat feels hot and heavy under the sun. I've worn the same jacket for two days straight now, and it reeks of despair. Who am I kidding—a *chef*?

I shall be a red-dirt woman raising a red-dirt child. I shall be groveling for change under threadbare cushions in a backwoods racist town. I shall be white trash; a woman broke down, balled up then thrown away. I release my fists, clenched with reeds, brush them together, and look up at Clare.

"You can spin fancy words however you like, but the reality is my life's worth crap. So many wonderful things were just beginning to happen, and I was finally figuring out the person I wanted to be, even daring to believe that one day I could provide a better life for my child."

I break out in a new burst of tears; how could there possibly be more to shed. "But all that's ruined. My dreams have been smashed, wrecked, flushed down the toilet into a sewer pipe. My plan failed. Failed because of *me*. The plan wasn't the failure, it's *me*. *I'm* the failure. And now I've failed my daughter, too." My vision is fogged; I'm waterlogged from all these blubbering tears.

Clare is still, and between our words, above the rounds of my knees, I watch her mud-crusted boots sink into the damp dirt. A rock glints from the ground between my feet. I dislodge it and turn it over in my palm; a perfect oval. She kneels, in union with the earth, facing me. Lifting my chin with her fingertips, she runs them consolingly under my jaw, which tickles, and through my tears, I smile. I feel protected with her so close. Then, she pushes her forefinger and thumb into the soil, sorting through sprouts, and works out another weed. Cradled in her cupped palms, it pulses in an otherworldly shade of green; the universe is intense, vivid, drunk with delight beneath her gaze.

"Don't ever embrace failure as an option. You're not a failure now, and you never will be. Weeds will always grow in your life, and, sometimes, when you pull out one weed, two spring up in their place. But you must be persistent, Shelby. Keep pulling at the weeds, they're competing with your space for growth and happiness." Her breath feels soft, warm on my cheek.

"I wanted something better from life, something more for me and my child. I wanted to be important, someone my daughter could respect, someone I could respect. I wanted to be a *chef.*" The word tastes bitter on my tongue. "And just when my dreams were becoming a reality, this comes along to whop me broadside. My world is chaos, and I'm so confused, turned inside out. Maybe getting fired was a sign telling me to forget my ambitions and return to my daughter."

"That could be. Work within your landscape, never struggle against it. Wisdom is recognizing your reality, your truth, and going with it. Passion, chaos and confusion are entwined and they're everyone's reality, what it means to be human. In this crazy world, how could it be otherwise? Don't be afraid of your feelings, Shelby. Embrace them, and in the jumbled-up ball of yarn, find the thread of goodness and follow it, follow its possibilities, even when it breaks your heart."

I try to respond, but my throat's too clogged to speak. Beads of sweat dotting her flesh smell of turned soil; her indigo eyes, fringed in dark lashes, are so soft, so kind; I want her to comfort me, to love me; I want to voice my feelings and feel their heat as they swirl from my lips in a cry of love.

"Stay confused and follow my truth? Clare. Is that what you're telling me? I, umm, the passion and confusion...umm, the truth is—I'm in *l-l-l-love* with you." The words slip out in a stuttered whisper, not conveying the sincerity of my emotion, but they're out there and there's no taking them back. The rock is clinched in my fist, fingernails digging into my palm, and she is silent.

"But Tracy's my best friend and I feel terrible. I don't know what to do; I don't even know how you even feel about *me*. Oh, my life's a mess."

She places her hand on my knee; amber and silver glint in the sun's rays, the same ring Tracy wears on her left ring finger. "I've given you a lot of thought, Shelby. I wasn't sure what I was feeling. At first I didn't like you and, in retrospect, I was jealous; I was attracted to you, and upset that you and Tracy were friends."

She digs out another weed and dangles it in front of my nose, the roots, as her fingernails, are caked with dirt. "I had to *root out* my anger. Become soiled. That morning when I spoke with you in the kitchen, I put aside my jealousy. That was a gift I gave myself because after I got to know you, I discovered your kind and gentle soul. You and Miss Ann have enriched my life."

I scrape the dirt from around the rock. I can't meet her eyes, and am mortified under the weight of her gaze.

"So what I'm saying is yes, l love you, Shelby, *yes*. But I don't love you in the way I love Tracy. Examine your feelings for me, as I did for you, allowing our relationship and your feelings to have this pain. But you also may feel joy and gratitude for finding a sister, one who loves and cares about you. Your emotions may trigger sexual feelings but they could be, they *should* be, redirected towards a meaningful friendship with me, instead."

A meaningful friendship; maybe she's right. Before I was fired, my desire for Shep grew each time we met for coffee, each time we partnered in class. The way his hand felt, as if he were stroking a kitten, when he positioned mine around the knife. The way his face reddened, just like mine, when I brushed against him at the stove. I think he shared my feelings, much more than friendship. Am I some wrung-dry sponge, soaking up love, falling for anyone, male or female, who's kind to me?

Growing up, Sandra was my best friend but that relationship seems shallow now. I'd never had true friends until I met Clare and Tracy. *It's OK to be confused.* I look into her eyes—Clare, my sister—and feel safe; a cocoon marooned in milkweed pods, poised to turn into a butterfly. I try to smile but the sides of my mouth tremble. I return my gaze to the rock, spit on it and rub it clean against my sleeve, soiling the jacket. The rock is smooth and black, with silver and white specks dotting its surface. If I squint, it looks like a map of the solar system, like wishing stars. I slip it into my pocket.

She stands then pulls me to my feet. "Tracy will be home from work in an hour." She brushes her hands together then straightens the collar of my chef jacket. "Oops, sorry. My fingers are grimy; I smudged your collar."

"That's OK, Clare. My jacket's a mess."

She smiles. "*Chef* Shelby. What do you say we surprise her by cooking dinner. You're dressed for the job. The ingredients can be the treasures we find in the ground."

"I'd like that. Tracy must be having a tough time, they're one worker down."

Clare walks to a row of feathery leaves emerging from the earth. "*Aha.* That's where you're hiding." She pushes the tip of her long-handled pitchfork into the earth, a couple of inches away from a plant, wiggles it into the soil, and works the prongs back and forth, digging them into the ground.

"Roots are the underground edibles of the vegetable world; there's a subterranean world of nourishment hidden right beneath our feet." Bending over, she grips the plant by its base, eases out a parsnip, and shakes it; black soil falls away from the plant in clumps.

"A baby, my favorite." She brushes the dirt away from its roots. "We had a touch of a frost last week, which sweetened them up. I'll also dig leeks, turnips and carrots, then you can work your magic in the kitchen."

Clasping my palms together, I stretch them to the sky, glad to be returning to a sharp knife and cutting board. But I'm especially happy we're done with that heavy conversation; cooking dinner, I can fold into myself and consider my options. Clare said to work within my landscape. These days my landscape is Atlanta, a big city, and there are other grocery stores, even restaurants, where I could apply for a job, some that may even pay for chef school.

It's six-thirty. We're sitting around the kitchen table and my gratin rests on the counter next to the stove. Joining hands, we bow our heads: "Peace," Tracy says. "Peace," Clare follows, the word spoken in a sigh. I squeeze their hands but remain silent, trying to feel the word inside, turning it over, praying that one day I will find a fit.

Outside the window, the sun sinks below the edge of the fresh plowed farmland, casting a golden glow that spreads like oozing honey over the western field. A force rooted in my soul—God?—pauses from brush and canvas whispering: *Follow the thread of goodness.* The sky blooms in hazy puffs of red, purple and yellow; the same shades as the blossoms in the vase.

Touching a petal, my eyes turn to Clare. "What types are these?"

"Don't ask me, I'm the vegetable expert. Tracy's in communion with the flowers."

Tracy beams as she admires her arrangement, her cropped yellow and orange hair electrifying her head in radiant spikes, and the Squash Blossom necklace glimmers like a medal of honor against her chest. "The pale purple are asters, and the bright yellow ones, coreopsis."

Tracy's a flower, too, but not something you'd buy from a florist. She's a field flower that wilts moments after picking. Girls like Tracy should never be plucked, but left wild, wind-blown and wandering; sapphire bluebells, diamond anemones, ruby bee balm, shimmering across open meadows as far as you can see.

I get up, retrieve potholders from the counter and pick up the gratin, which has a musky earthen smell. Returning to the table, I set the dish next to the vase and look at Tracy. "I hate bringing up a sour subject, but...how's work?" A storm cloud settles over her face, even the flowers droop beneath her grimace; I wish I'd never opened my mouth.

"It's not the work; it's the evil atmosphere Grasso creates that contaminates the store. I can't eat didly at lunch, my stomach's so tied in knots."

Clare smiles and places her hands on top of hers, patting and massaging them. "Create air to breathe around his cruelty. Forgiveness and compassion for him begins with you, then your peace will follow." Tracy gasps, yanks her hand away and points an index finger into Clare's startled eyes.

"Compassion for Grasso? Clare, are you out of your mind?" Pushing back her chair, she lurches to her feet, eyes rolling back into sockets, chest thrust like the rear of a stallion come across a snake. "You've been in the sun too long—or hanging out *way* too much in the meditation center." Grasping her arms across her chest, she sways back and forth, rocking herself, trying to calm down, then leans her face towards Claire, eyes wide.

"*You*...don't have any idea what it's like dealing with that man and his pathetic, saggy-jowled henchman." She speaks slowly, punctuating each word with an exclamation point, desperate with irritation, insisting Claire understand. "Tony Grasso is evil. Amoral. He's got a contract with the devil. It's not just the shit he pulls with women, though that's bad enough. I'm discovering some under-the-radar activities going on in those stores."

Her jaw clenches and she pounds her fist into the palm of her hand—*thwack, thwack, thwack*—glaring out of the window. "The Grasso story is just unfolding."

"I worry about you, Tracy." Clare reaches for her clenched hand, pulls her towards the table, and strokes her knuckles. "Don't get mixed up in his negative energy. We've had so much business lately, you should quit and work on the farm."

Tracy's eyes glint, snap from me to Clare, then she collapses, hangdog and deflated, into her chair. "I've got business to attend to first. So let's change the subject, shall we?"

She picks up her fork, stabs a piece of turnip molded into a crackling of cheese, then glares at it as if it had claws. Bringing it to her open mouth, she clamps down, chews, swallows, bats her lips with a napkin, and the lines in her forehead unfurl, the clouds part. She tilts her head at me, smiling. "As always, Shall-be, food for a goddess. You're such a talent. What will you do about chef school?"

"I called Chef Chen and told him I didn't have money to continue. He said he was disappointed; that I passed Level One with flying colors." I pick at the golden flecks of herb-embedded crust. "I don't know, maybe school's not part of my plan after all."

"Trust yourself, Clare whispers, her voice as soothing as a summer breeze. "Be patient. Move in the direction of your intention."

The sun has set, and the sky is streaked with the same deep blue striations of her worn jeans. I rest my fork prongs against the edge of the plate and stare into the fields, keeping to my thoughts, and then my eyes return to the vase of flowers. I imagine picking flowers such as these and placing them in a jar beside Miss Ann's bed. Putting my hand into my pocket, I rub my fingers against the cool stone and turn to Tracy.

"Could you drive me back to Coryville, tonight, after dinner? I want to go home. I want to go home to my daughter."

Root Vegetable Gratin

by

Shelby Preston

Baby vegetables can be difficult to locate, unless you grow your own or shop at the Farmer's Market. Expensive. The following recipe calls for regular-sized vegetables; the kind you'd find at Piggly Farms. If using baby vegetables, you'll need to double the amounts I listed below.

Tonight I hit pay dirt. The babies I used were freshly dug and sprung from the ground a couple of hours before we ate them.

(Please excuse the sloppy hand-writing. I'm writing this as my friend drives me home, and we're weaving down curvy roads, bumping over pot holes.)

CHAPTER 18

Mallory

Sleep is elusive. Every nerve ending on my body is pulsing, every gesture, exaggerated. I stir the soup and turn off the burner. Sleep, sleep, so desperate for sleep. If sleep ever finds me, maybe I'll awaken to discover the past three and a half months have been one hellacious nightmare. I shake the orange, translucent cylinder of pills—a rattler's warning on a diamond-back snake—and swallow an Ambien, and then another, nudged down with wine, finishing the glass in a mercurial gulp. Then, lying on my bed, I trudge towards the slope and slide down the ledge into my dreams.

My eyes glide through darkness, which is complete but for the dozen blue and yellow flames trembling in glass that surround my bed. Bright, flickering spirits of the dead. I lit the candles to honor the departed souls in my family, for this first of November is a most sacred Mexican holiday—*Día de los Muertos*—the Day of the Dead. I lie prone, with the patience of death, my arms resting by my side, a corpse waiting for the embalmer's tool.

And, now, here you are. *Manuel.* In my bed. How strange that you're in my bed. I study your face, your eyes, half-hidden, in a fold of the sheet. I push it back and touch the vulnerable white eggshell of your head, smooth and glistening. Candlelight spins a design, painting shades of darkness, wavering shapes of light, over this most sacred spot. My body spasms, feeling the jolt of the car—*huhwump*—as it strikes your body. Blood seeps from the crack. I never knew a head, holding every hope, every dream, could be as fragile as an egg.

I am so sorry. So terribly, terribly sorry.

Rivulets of sweat leak around my ear lobes, down my neck, dribbling between my breasts. Lurching out of bed, I yank off my shirt and regard my reflection, cheeks deepened into gullies, eyes sunk into sunless skin, dim in the windowpane. My hair is wild, disarrayed, and the proportions of my body have changed: my stomach caves inward, and my arms are like fractured sticks, razor angled, dangling limbs from a tree. Without a struggle, and with super-human strength, I push open the window. A gust of wind blows out the nightstand votive; a curling cloud from burned wax dampens my eyes.

Millions of stars pulse, clogging the sky as a shimmering one, and then the moon rises, breaking up their cluster as a porcelain disk, brilliant and bright.

"Manuel. Come look at the moon. Come. Join me at the window."

Silence.

"No? Too tired? Or do you find me abhorrent." I grab a shawl, cover my bare breasts, and my voice emerges as a rasping hiss.

"Fine, remain in bed. *Manuel Angel Hernandez.* Not an American name. And *you* are *not* an American. You are no one; a shadowy menace. I'm an American, and dance over shadows."

My mouth and eyes twitch as if confused as to the source of the words I just spoke. He cowers beneath the sheets, which are covered with the snapping green and yellow lights of flickering fireflies as if in armor to protect him from my bullying. Bile, sour and sulfuric, rises up my throat and I shake my head ferociously, contradicting myself, the tips of my hair feeling as brittle as a broom, pricking my neck.

"I don't blame you for your fear; I frighten myself. From what source came those words—so cold, cruel? They weren't my words. And I *am* sorry. *So, so sorry.* You see, you must remain a shadow, my shadow, because I need you to be a part of me. Please." I patter my chest, a flutter of fingertips. "Join me."

Then, quiet. Stillness.

"I know your story, the journey of the *sin papeles*, no fresh lands to explore, no new continents to conquer. Only a twenty-first century America: discovered, decadent, and now decayed, yet surely a better world than the one you left behind." Trembling, I tighten the shawl around my shoulders.

"And look at yourself, in my bed, a mound of quivering shapes and shadows. You hurt me with your silence. Why won't you acknowledge that I feel your suffering? Why are we locked together, you and I, and what is becoming of us?"

Sadness fills me, the utter sadness borne of empathy that confounds all reasoning, all language, which finds its source at the genesis of creation, back to that first ignited spark, uniting me, Manuel, and all souls thereafter on some craggy, prehistoric stone. I struggle to find words, and I do; they emerge slow, gain momentum, and are carried into the night, echoing around jagged cliffs, crawling over the bed sheets, and then tumbling down precipices of darkness.

"You are one of the brave ones who crossed the night-time desert—gauntlet of death and fear—knowing your wife could be raped, knowing you and your family could be killed. But each day in your homeland, tasting the rotting poverty that fed your anguish, your courage grew. You, Manuel, were never afraid."

I walk three steps towards the bed, directing my words towards the mound beneath the sheets.

"You risked your life, searching for signs along the path, following the throngs of other moving shadows, whispered stories lost in the wind. All this for the American dream of a minimum wage, which would allow primitive provisions for you, your wife and child. And when you arrived, after your family was settled, you vowed you'd never take the dream for granted."

At the bed, I rustle the sheets. "It was this dream I took from you."

The fireflies vanish, and my voice softens to a whisper. "But there were simple pleasures you did take for granted. The expectation of new mornings, of inhaling the fragrance of your wife's neck as she lay in the suspension of sleep, nestled in feathers of her long-ago life. The expectation of pink on your daughter's cheek, rising and swelling as dawn's first sky, when she ran into your arms. A new morning was the one expected thing, the one pleasure taken for granted. At least, Manuel, you have the morning." I pull back the sheets and push away pillows. "Or do you?"

My bed is empty. *I'm talking to an empty bed.*

I return to the window and stare at the moon shining full and bright, her white beam giving way to a coppery, luminescent orange glow. Constellations of stars disband, twinkling and glinting across an infinite sky as if they, too, were candle flames calling the dead, beckoning me to join them.

I awaken with a start. I've managed to surface—frightened, shaken, dim with drugs—yet oddly restored, as if I've pushed through invisible borders and planetary fields. I haven't eaten since yesterday and am famished. I made a soup that Manuel would enjoy. I'm ready to join the living and write, my antidote to madness.

Dipping into shadows, fading to the kitchen, I reheat the soup, and then ladle a cup of the thick, gold-beige liquid into a bowl. I sit at the island and dip a spoon into the brew. It tastes of fetid stalks and fermented fruit, soiled and unclean, and it smells like the whiff of a candle, just snuffed out.

Butternut Squash Soup with Apples and Chipotle
by
Mallory Lakes

Today, this Day of the Dead-Dia de los Muertos-is a holiday celebrated in Mexico and by Mexican-Americans living in the United States. It's a day for family and friends to gather and pray for friends and family who have died. Traditions connected with the holiday include building altars honoring the deceased and making the favorite foods the departed enjoyed then visiting their graves with these gifts.

This evening I made a soup that a Mexican friend of mine might enjoy. It's an autumnal soup of intense fragrance, lingering heat and otherworldly flavors. So heavenly, I also plan to serve it on Thanksgiving.

In fact, I plan to shake-up the traditional Thanksgiving dinner. Putting chipotles and cumin into a Butternut Squash and Apple Soup is just the beginning. I'm craving the flavors of Mexico; Corn Bread, Chipotle and

Smoked Paprika stuffing, for example, will stuff my Adobo-Rubbed Roasted Turkey.

My intention, however, is not to upset the apple cart. The Thanksgiving recipe wheel does not need more spokes, much less an additional spin. I'm simply bored; I've been making the same dishes for almost fifteen years, and good food knows no borders.

Recipe ennui may not be enough to appease you. Hispanic-inspired recipe twists could be interpreted as treason amongst your troops. I need further ammunition, defaulting to history to defend the Thanksgiving upset.

Hear me out. Think Thanksgiving, and you're reminded of pilgrims and Plymouth, Massachusetts, right? According to the Texas Almanac, the first North American Thanksgiving tradition was celebrated by Spanish explorers in northern Mexico in 1598. (Keep in mind that back then, borders between Texas and Mexico were a bit sketchy.)

At that time Spanish King Felipe II created an incentive for explorers to launch expeditions into Mexico. The Spanish called Mexico the "New Spain," and they went to seek wealth for the Spanish crown. The survival of the expedition sparked this celebratory feast; possibly and arguably, the first Thanksgiving.

And what would I be most thankful for this Thanksgiving? That America was a country where borders were meant to be crossed, and, most important, we'd savor the ride.

CHAPTER 19

Miss Ann

I am so scared and I am so mad, both at the same time. I lie under my bed, squeezing Pouch and her puppies into my chest as I figure out a plan. MeMaw was so angry at me for dumping all her hair chemicals down the sink she like to go crazy. Long red marks on my legs sting from her switching.

So I will tell you the whole story start to finish. This morning I woke up and felt sicker than ever. Mama had gone to work at The Pig. She got herself a job last week as a cashier. She works the early shift during the workweek, but has afternoons and weekends off to be with me. Today is Saturday, but her boss asked her to work since the store'd be extra busy with a chicken sale.

At lunch I couldn't eat my peanut butter sandwich 'cause it stuck in my throat and I was having trouble breathing. MeMaw was in the front yard visiting with a neighbor lady who was pointing to her head of pink sponge curlers, must have been asking for hair advice, so I had plenty of time to put my plan into action. If Mama, MeMaw and the doctor can't make me feel better, then I have to make me feel better myself.

Mama said MeMaw's hair chemicals is what's making me sick so I went down to the cellar and dumped them down the sink before MeMaw even knew I was missing. She came down the steps just as I was dumping out the last bottle of Violet Moon. I planned to throw the bottles away before she caught me, but I never had time. Empty jars were scattered all round the floor and under the sink.

When I saw her face, I was real sorry I done it. It twisted purple and white, and then she started crying. She ran upstairs and I heard the screen door slam—*kabam*—so I hid under her hair style table, quiet as a mouse 'cept for my chattering teeth. Then the door squeaked, slammed, and her clip-clocking shoes came marching down the steps. From around the table legs, all I could see were her legs and hands, which were holding a switch; long and skinny with buds, the kind that hurts the worst.

She told me I ruined her business and what would she do now? She asked me where did I think she'd find the money to buy new hair supplies? Did I think dollar bills grew on the black gum tree? She cried and cried swatting my legs and I cried and cried jumping up and down like a grass-hopper. After the switching, MeMaw left me alone, and she never leaves me alone. She told me she was driving to The Pig to tell Mama that I ran her out of business, and that I was to go to my room and stay there till she got back.

I will show MeMaw and Mama. I will run away. MeMaw will come home to an empty house and Mama will leave work and they will be sorry. MeMaw will be sad she ever switched me, and Mama will be so mad at MeMaw for switching me, she will hate MeMaw too. I'll also show Mama what it feels like when someone runs away. Mama ran away from me and now I will run away from her. I hate MeMaw and I hate Mama.

From under my bed, I see a straight yellow line of light beneath my closet door. MeMaw gets mad at me when I forget to turn that light off so I will get my jacket, remember to turn off the light, then Pouch and I will run away. I keep Pouch under my bed and every night after story-time, when I'm alone, I pull her out. Keeping this doggie a secret is the hardest thing I've ever done in my whole life but if MeMaw found out Mister gave me this dog, she would take it away.

MeMaw says Mister is a devil-man. I know he is not a devil-man 'cause he loved his doggies and had a little girl too. Maybe she'd kill Pouch and her puppies, just like the police killed Mister's doggies. Just like Mama killed the jackalope. I don't know what would happen to me if they took away Pouch; Pouch is the only one who loves me. Woody's mad at me too 'cause I love Pouch and her puppies more than him. I roll out from under my bed and brush the dust balls off my dress. I look at my clock: twelve-thirty-four. I am in second grade and can tell time.

I hold Pouch tight, walk into the closet, and pull the pink jacket from the hanger. Next, I go to the bathroom and scrape the crusty gook from around my eyes with my fingernail and a Q-tip. Used to be only my blind eye gave me problems, now both 'ems do. I stuff my pockets with toilet paper 'cause my nose is always running. My inhaler don't do much good so I leave that behind. I won't put in my prosthetic 'cause it hurts, and besides, Pouch only has one eye. I forgot to turn off my closet light so go back and finish that business.

I stop to take one last look at the circle of flowers where the jackalope used to be. I miss him and our home feels empty, but I'd best get moving 'cause MeMaw said she'd be right back and Lord only know what's in store for me next.

Pussy-footing out the back door, my feet take off flying, fingertips tracing the clothesline, past the clothesline, past the swamp, past the bus stop, past the crooked post. Now I'm running alongside the cattle fence like I'm being chased by the devil. My feet know the path and they are taking me to the hog farm, which is the last place I had fun with Mama. After that, Lord only knows where I'll go; maybe I'll dig me a hole to China.

I start to cough and the cough turns to a wheeze and I can't breathe. I plop down on a burnt-out stump, catch my breath, and blow my nose. I unzip Pouch's pocket and stick my nose into her puppies, relaxing my jitters. Pouch and her babies always make me feel better. I'd best *walk*, not *run*, away from home. I slow down because even walking, I can't keep my breath straight, the ground pulling at my chest, sucking at my windpipe. I get up, wipe my nose, and drag my feet down the road.

I smell the farm before I get to it. *Pee-eww*, those pigs sure make a lot of stinky-poo. Since that last time we was calling pigs, Lester began singing a song, trying to make MeMaw smile. I miss my MeMaw. Singing will keep me walking. Singing will make me feel better; singing always keeps me from crying. I sing under my breath, but only the first part.

> "Let's sing a little rhyme about three pink pigs,
> Fat snout noses just made to dig.
> Curly wigglin' tails they'd dance a little jig,
> Won first prize at the country fair gig."

When Lester sings the second part, MeMaw tells Lester to shut his mouth. I quit eating MeMaw's hot dogs, ham and bacon after he sung the words. So I don't sing the words, just think 'em in my head.

> *Flatten to bologna, carve 'em into chops.*
> *Ham is made from hind legs, don't forget their hocks.*

I never knew all that food came from pigs. It was chilly when I left the house, but I'm warmed up now. And scared. I work on my karma, walking six steps, then stoppin'...six steps...stop. I'm still scared. I try singing: "Let's sing a little rhyme about three pink pigs...hmm, hmm, hmm, hmm, hmm…"

I hear real pigs squealing now. And look at all those cars. The last time I was here, we were the only ones. Lots of folks must be out hog-calling today.

One of the cars is bright yellow with black writing on the side. I sound them out: *Ci-ty-Cab.* I've never seen a cab before, 'cept on TV. There's a man in the car humped over the steering wheel. Must be sleeping. I'd best keep to myself. I don't want no one to see me 'cause what would they think of a little girl all by herself with a doggie. Maybe I'll hide in that bush and peep out from 'neath the branches.

Crawling into the leaves, the prickles scratch my legs, still stinging from the switching. I wonder why Brer Rabbit's mama made a prickly briar patch their home. Their fur must protect them from scratches. My legs hurt worse than ever so I climb out and cry. My face is soaked wet. I'm gonna stop this foolishness; I'm a big girl and have already cried once today. I kneel to the ground, hiding behind a patch of Butterfly milkweed.

This grows in our yard, gets orange flowers that come and go, and I learned the name from Mama. They are Mama's favorite plants 'cause the butterflies eat at them and hatch their baby caterpillars in the leaves. Mama and me loves butterflies and watch them flutter in the milkweed. I wish Mama was holding me now. She came back home to take care of me and what was I thinking running away? I curl into a ball.

There's a truck with a big silver trailer attached to it. Lester would surely love to have that trailer. Looks brand spanking new. Some woman wearing overalls like a field hand is bent over pushing a giant pig up a ramp. A group of folks are standing around and watching, real quiet-like and shaking their heads. A lady with thick long hair has her back to me, and is pulling a tissue from her bag.

The pig don't like walking up that ramp. It chews at the side, turns around, then trots down to the water bucket for a sip. Then, a man comes out of the trailer, calling *sue-we, Lilly-Belle, sue-we.* Her snout turns away from the bucket, and she goes prancing up that ramp and into the trailer just as merry as can be. He closes the door.

Sun's hiding behind a cloud and I'm starting to shiver, even with my jacket on. A wheeze is crawling up my chest and I'm sorry I left my inhaler. I unzip Pouch and stick my face into the puppies to muffle the cough. Pouch don't like it when I cough into her puppies, so I pull 'em out then cough into their mama; I can't let those folks hear me.

Behind the farm, from off to the side, I see a tiny little house with smoke curling out the chimney. It must have a fireplace. That house is too small for grownups but it's big enough for me and Pouch. Maybe a little girl lives there.

I'm sicker by the minute, coughing and coughing like I'm fixing to choke. I want so bad to warm up by that fire. Everyone's eyes is fixed on the trailer door. The lady with the tissue has her head down, and it shakes, like she's crying. That pig is squealing and squealing—*wee....r...bree.* The coast is clear. Now's my chance to run to the house without them noticing me.

Trying to make up my mind what to do, a shot, like a firecracker—*ka-pow*—explodes. *Oh Mama, oh sweet Jesus, come help me, please.* I jump up. Stuff the puppies into Pouch. No time to zipper 'em safe. I dash down the road, cross the yard, running as fast as my feet will carry me. I'm at the little house but my chest is rattling and my heart is jumping, jumping, jumping like a bullfrog. Can't catch my breath...*help me, Mama, help me!* Pull open the door. Step in the house. Split pigs hang from hooks. A fearsome fire. I'm wrapped in smoke—*enh, enh*—can't catch air. Stumble. Fall. Hogs spin 'round and 'round...fire's fading...*Mama, please...*

Mallory

Scanning the panorama of the farm, I zip my jacket; a cold front's coming through and tangled, low-lying clouds, typical of a November sky, wrap the weathered silo. A thorny, gnarled oak tree sprawls next to us, just outside the fence, and singed orange leaves cling, shivering on the branches, lending the only color to the soot-gray landscape. Martha-Mae and I stand in the pigpen, looking down at my hog.

"Lilly-Belle. Such a sweet name."

Martha-Mae, the woman who has nurtured my pig for the past seven months, kneels to rub her back.

"Lilly-Belle's clever and has a cute personality. Likes to have her back scratched with a stick." I kneel down and rub between her ears—one pink, one gray—same as her piglet photo, which I still carry in my wallet.

"I've always heard pigs were smart."

Martha-Mae looks up at me, spread nostrils flaring. "It's no accident Mr. Orwell cast pigs as the rulers in his book, *Animal Farm*. What ticks me off are folks who call them dumb. These creatures are intelligent, smarter than dogs, and you can even teach them tricks. The more time you spend with a hog, the more you get to know their personality."

Martha-Mae has a scrubbed, fresh-milk complexion, chapped pinkish-red. She's no-nonsense solid, robust and plump; beautifully, brilliantly plump in a generous-spirited way. She stands up then bends to pat Lilly-Belle up and down her bristled sandy girth, mottled with blackish spots.

"Pigs have always been misunderstood. In the Book of Leviticus, God says they're unclean, that we should not eat their meat or touch their hide. But the Old Testament was written by men, not God, and experts agree that those views have no place in today's world. Back then, folks didn't understand their physiology. Pigs get a bad rap as dirty animals because they roll in mud. The truth is their sweat glands don't work well and they're just trying to cool off. Hogs actually prefer a clean environment."

Martha-Mae, wearing worn brown denim overalls and a pink thermal shirt and cap, resembles a pig herself, which, in this world of charming and winsome animals, is the ultimate compliment. I wish I'd gotten to know my hog better. Then again, maybe not. Today will be bad enough. My stomach's cramping.

"I can't believe she sprung from a little piglet to this huge porker in six months."

"She's a big girl all right; gained near two hundred pounds since that photo of yours was taken. Today's the perfect weather for the slaughter; air's chilly so there won't be so many flies, stench will be minimal, and it's dry so her carcass will be easy to wash."

"Don't you ever want to keep your favorite hogs for pets?"

"We hold onto two female piglets each year for breeding, and on Valentine's Day we bring in a boar for the ladies. But Genesis says God gives man dominion over inferior creatures, which still holds true today. Not to say pigs are inferior to humans, but as charming as they are, it's not practical to keep pigs as pets. They don't produce milk or lay eggs, they don't have wool, and they can't chase away varmints. The reason we raise piglets is to turn them into food, but that doesn't make slaughtering them any easier."

"Can you take a picture of me with Lilly-Belle?"

"Sure, hon; show me how your camera works. I'll get you a handful of feed at the Pig Palace." She waves her hand in the direction of the silo. "Food'll get her attention. She's hungry 'cause she hasn't had a thing to eat since yesterday. Her digestive tract should be as clean as possible, but one last bite won't be a biggie."

Martha-Mae unlatches the gate. We exit the pig pen and walk to the silo, which, Martha-Mae explains, was converted into a shelter for the hogs. Lilly-Belle trots by our side. The air in the silo smells of damp turned hay, and Martha-Mae bends over into a pen to grab a feed pan, shaking out all but a handful.

I walk to a rounded edge of the enclosure. "The lighting here is lovely." Bathing in the soft golden glow, I take a meter reading, adjusting the F-stop and shutter speed so the focus will be on me and Lilly-Belle, the background a blur. Standing, I show Martha-Mae where to press the button, and she hands me the feed pan. Sitting on a bale of hay, I shake the barley, oats and corn into my hand then sniff the musty scent of dried grains. I extend my cupped palm to the pig.

"Come here, Lilly-Belle. Come eat a little snack."

Lilly-Belle nudges Martha-Mae's knee with her snout.

"It's OK, Lilly-Belle. You go on over and visit Miss Lakes." She pushes the animal towards me. "The hardest thing about slaughter is the betrayal. These pigs trust me; I'm their Judas."

The hog snuffles softly, trots to my hand, and her snout feels soft, wet in my hand—a shock of primal sensuality—burrowing into the grain.

"She's quite a rooter." Martha-Mae laughs. "Pigs have a keen sense of smell; that's why they're used for sniffing out truffles in France."

My palm is damp, licked clean. I drop my hand and run it under her snout, which feels warm and nubbly, like a burlap feed bag filled with corn. Lilly-Belle catches my eye, holding it in a way I've never before experienced with an animal.

Unsettled, I dodge her scrutiny and wrap my arms around her neck, which smells of fresh raw sap. She nudges her snout into my collarbone as if to inhale my essence. Her ear folds over like the back flap of an envelope and I lift it, leaning my lips to the small canal on the side of her head. "Thank you, Lilly-Belle. And *goodbye*. It's been one hell of a ride."

The shutter releases with a click; I stand and brush straw from my jeans. She hands me my camera, which I place in my bag.

"Well then. Time to lead her to the unit. If it's important to you, you can watch the slaughter, but I'd advise against it. It's best you let my husband, Eli, and the inspector do their job without distraction. They'll close the door before they shoot her."

"Shoot her? Isn't there a gentler way?"

"Eli will shoot her between the eyes with a twenty-two rifle, which numbs her nervous system. Then he'll slit one of the main arteries in her neck so the blood loss brings about a swift, less painful death. There's an art to a proper slaughter, and we believe this is the most humane method."

A *humane slaughter*. Could there be a better oxymoron? How to express my feelings. Well, now…hmm. The guilt of a murderess. That resonates. Or perhaps I'm just disgusted with my cowardice and blind hypocrisy. After all, I've eaten pork without remorse all of my life.

Tears well in my eyes as I bend to scratch Lilly-Belle's back. "I understand how you'd get attached to these animals. I hate the thought of her suffering."

"Our method of killing shows respect and allows for a better quality of meat. After they bleed her, they scald her carcass, scrape away the bristles, and hang her. Then you assist in gutting her, and you take what innards you want back to Atlanta. The caul fat's especially good. Then she'll cool for twenty-four hours or so. In a couple of days, you return and help with the butchering—as long as you've got the stomach for all of this."

I'm tempted to tell her I'm now a vegetarian and to donate Lilly-Belle's meat to a needy family. "That won't be an issue," I say instead, the knuckles of my forefingers swiping the moisture under my eyes. "I butchered a hog in chef school."

"Let's hop to it." Martha-Mae glances at her watch. "It's after two; we're running late. Lilly-Belle's first on the list, with more hogs to follow." Exiting the silo, the hog trots behind us like a well-trained dog.

"That's the smokehouse between the pecan grove and peach trees." Martha-Mae points to a small wooden hut set on a slab foundation tucked into the sloping land behind the farmhouse. A plume of blackish-gray smoke feathers from a metal pipe on the roof. "If you want, you can schedule it for your hams and bacon."

We walk towards a large silver housing unit mounted to a trailer. "The township just passed an ordinance allowing us to bring in mobile slaughter units. In the past, the most traumatic part of the hog's life was when they were taken away from their home and separated from the clan. Hogs are gregarious, social animals. The unit's self-contained and comes to our farm when we need it. It's cost-effective and easier on the pigs." She kicks an empty metal bucket with the tip of her boot, and her voice is quiet, directed to the ground. "Easier on us, too."

Several people mill around the trailer, looking as forlorn as myself; I'm not the only one witnessing an execution.

"OK, Lady Lilly-Belle. You go first, march on up that plank." Martha-Mae gets behind her rump and pushes. "Go on up now, go see daddy." The hog trots a few feet up, stops to sniff the floor, then wanders right and begins gnawing the side of the ramp. Grunting, she turns and prances down the plank, heading to a plastic tub filled with water. "It's OK, baby girl," Martha-Mae says as the hog slurps water. She turns and gives a little shrug in my direction. "Take your time."

A heavy-set man, who must be her husband Eli, emerges from the unit. He stands in the open door, cups his hands over his mouth and calls, "Sue-we, Lilly-Belle, sue-we. Come on up here girl." Without further ado, Lilly-Belle turns from the bucket then trots up to the man, her trotters banging against the steel. She takes a dainty hop through the door and Eli pulls it shut. Its clang reverberates through my spine.

I remove a tissue from my camera bag and close my eyes. Visceral grunts and squeals sound like Windexed towels being rubbed against a glass pane; Lilly-Belle's high-pitched whirring whine—*wee...r...bree*—feels like my teeth being drilled and ricochets between my eyes. *Forgive me, Lilly-Belle, forgive me.* The sudden crack of the rifle: *ka-pow.*

A twenty-two gauge damnation on my soul.

The pig noises stop. Silence. Tears splash from my eyes and I dab them with the tissue. It's time. Gritting my teeth, I walk around the side of the trailer, to the front entry, climb the platform steps, and open the door. There lies Lilly-Belle, facing me, a small black hole tunneled into her forehead, a slit along her neck. Bleeding from the wounds, she appears calm, as if any minute she'll roll onto her trotters with a grunt, then prance down the ramp for another sip of water. As the blood squirts out, a large blackish pool spreads across the floor.

My hand pressing the cloth...blood leaking from a crack...the air saturated with blood and fireflies...blood and fireflies...and the thick silence of shattered dreams.

Eli comes out of the trailer. "Next step we hang her up, then break her down."

Turning my head towards the road, a streak of pink flashes past the corner of my eye. A small figure scurrying down the road as if being chased by a demon. Careening. Stumbling. A little girl running around, now disappearing behind, the farmhouse. Everyone's eyes are fixed to the door; no one seems to have seen the child but me. Or am I totally mad?

"I need a minute." I turn then stumble down the steps. The atmosphere changes from a memorial service to a business operation, and my departure goes unnoticed. I walk to the road. *Steady, steady; through the nose...*

An old beat-up sock lies beside the road, almost buried in the pecan-studded grasses. I bend over. A little stuffed puppy. I pick it up, shove it in my pocket and quicken my pace, grabbing other identical puppies, following their trail. The chill taste of wood smoke burns my throat. Something's wrong. I'm running now. The smokehouse door is open gasping sponges of soot. A child lies limp, curled across the threshold, eyes closed, lips blue, smoke blanketing her as a shroud. I drop to my knees, wedge my hands under her body, and drag her out of the smoke, screaming, "Help, quick. A little girl. She may be *dead!*" I stand and slam the door shut. A bunched stuffed dog lies at my feet.

Grabbing my bag, I fish out my cell phone. 9-1-1. No reception. People crowd the smokehouse. Faces twisted. Panting. A man bends down, props her limp body over his knee, puts his fingers over her pulse, and leans his ear into her mouth.

"Is she breathing?" "Barely." He gives her mouth-to-mouth resuscitation. A minute passes. Silence. "This isn't what she needs." Fumbling in his pocket, he pulls out an inhaler, pries open her mouth and squirts the medicine down her throat. "Let's get her to the hospital. Immediately."

Martha-Mae scurries to our side. "I've called the ambulance, but they've been known to get lost in these parts."

"Is there a doctor nearby?"

"Yes. There's a clinic on Route 6, fifteen minutes away, if you tear up the road."

"Listen up." I bark orders. "Eli, get in the cab and direct us; navigation doesn't work out here. Martha-Mae, call the clinic. Tell them to be prepared." She runs towards the farmhouse. "You," I point to the man who is saving this child's life, "bring your inhaler and come with us. If we can't keep her breathing, nothing else matters." I grab the stuffed animal, a wrinkled, deflated sack, then run to my driver, who is waiting beside his cab. His mouth moves in time with the beads he slides on his rosary, which usually dangle from his rear-view mirror.

"To the clinic. *Now.*"

The man helping the child is trotting towards us, a pink bundle cradled in his arms, her legs dangling to the rhythm of his gait. The cabbie nods, jumps into his cab, and turns on the engine.

Eli hops in the front seat. "Take a left and head down the road. Turn right on Beemus, which takes us to Route 6." He points to the left and swishes his hands forward as if to say: *Hurry, hurry.* The cabbie presses the accelerator into the floor. We lurch to the left, then fly down the road.

I sit next to the man cradling the child, and her legs, lined with red lashes, lie across my thighs. I remove the stuffed puppies from my jacket pockets, place them into the dog's pouch, and zip it shut. I had a stuffed dog with puppies like this when I was a child. We must be driving one-hundred-miles per hour and my body jerks about, yet is confined in the seatbelt as I hold the girl's legs steady. She's breathing in short rasps in sync with my pounding heart, and her yellow hair, plastered around closed eyes, is crusted in sand. I try to settle my breath; there is nothing more I can do. I turn to the man, perhaps in his late-twenties.

"She wouldn't be alive if it weren't for you. I'm Mallory."

"Mallory Lakes. I knew that was you. I've been following your blog; it was my incentive for purchasing a pig. I'm Jackson; *you* discovered her; it was a team effort. I've suffered from asthma my entire life, and that smoke could have killed her in another minute."

His greenish-brown eyes are soft, kind. Cooper's eyes. A flicker in my chest. At once, I regret turning down his offer to join me, so afraid of opening that door, even a crack. I knew today would be difficult, but how could I have known it would turn into this? I ache with longing, yet I'm not ready. I have to find my way through. Alone.

My gaze drops to the child tucked in the wing of Jackson's jacket, and I feel as if this child were my own. With a start, I remember—*The Squash Blossom Festival*—I took her photograph. This is Shelby's daughter; this child is Miss Ann. Her image, taped to the shade of my desk lamp, has been the sole sliver of light guiding me through canyons where the darkness is the deepest.

Eli rolls down his window and points his index finger out the window in the direction of an old country church. "We're coming on Beemus Road by the church. Take a right, take a *right*." The cab slows down then careens sideways as a cloud of dry dust billows through the window.

"Eli, shut the window; the dust will clog her lungs."

Jackson bends his torso over the child's head to shield her from the dust, now blooming through the cab, and removes his inhaler from the pocket in his jacket. We pass the slash of a church half-collapsed into itself, and a regimen of tobacco stalks in a desolate field, as defeated troops on a battlefield, defrocked of their leaves. Eli rolls up the window as a weathered sign passes in a blur: "NO BURIAL'S WITHOUT WRITTEN PERMISSION."

Thoughts sink beneath the girl's rattled breath, her quivering chin, into a place that defies articulation, a place of portent. What is this: this child, this church, this sign. What does all of this mean? My teeth are gritty with dust, and I try moistening them with my tongue but it lays thick, inert, like a wad of cotton.

A beckoning, a realization rises from the pit of my belly to the top of my skull, splashing to the surface. Moisture dribbles from my head and crawls down my neck as a fever breaking.

The meaning of this moment, all that is filling this moment, unspools inside me. I won't continue down this highway to hell. I won't. I will face down my demons—the pills, the booze, this self-loathing guilt—and I will face down what I've created myself to be: my persona, the black-lit box I've drawn around my soul, the puppeteer twitching, yanking at strings, now rotted and tangled around me.

There's another life to save. And that will be my own.

Shelby

"Afternoon, Stella. Chilly out there, huh?"

I turn to face the register. Land O'Lakes, that gal's sure packed on the pounds since high school; I can't let myself slip now that I'm home for good. I close the cash drawer as she loads the belt with potato chips, onion soup mix, sour cream, a cut-up chicken, Oreos and milk.

"Nippy, all right. See you're back in Coryville."

"Yep. Come home to take care of my child."

"Must have been hard leaving your girl and this friendly little town in the first place."

Unclasping her hands from the shopping cart handle, she nudges it forward then swivels her girth to face me, chubby little hands swaying in front of a hefty bosom. She begins humming verse, shrill and off-key, to "Midnight Train to Georgia", head bobbing to the beat, and then belts her own version of the song:

"Shelby's going back to find...da da da da da...the child she left behind... she told her that she would. She said she's boarding...yeah yeah yeah yeah... that ole' beat back bus to Coryville." Palm fisted, she tugs at a pretend bus cord, elbow pressing into belly folds shouting: "Next stop, Bus Man!"

Sweat beads dot her nose at this exertion and she smiles at me, breathless, eyes darting to the cookies as if embarrassed. "Our choir's just joined the Gospel Circuit." She shrugs and lowers her head. "Who knows where that will lead?"

Instinctively I want to add another verse: *And I surely learned the hard way, that dreams are just mirage and smoke.*

Her bowed head, wrapped in a fleece of wooly sheep hair, tugs at my heartstrings.

"You've always had a pretty voice, Stella," I say instead. "Maybe one day I'll see your group on *America's Got Talent*."

She looks up, eyes glittering with possibility. "You think, Shelby? What a nice thing to say. Thank you." She bags her groceries and rolls the cart out the store, words spoken over her shoulder. "I know your mama's glad to have you back."

The next customer is one of Mama's clients; I forget her name. She can't miss mine:

Shelby

Piggly Farms

I always forget to remove my nametag after work, but leave it to Mama to tell me she doesn't need reminding of who I am. Oh now really, here she comes again, second time in an hour. She's flying around the register like a witch, looking like something the cat dragged home. She cuts in line then squeezes sideways around the woman's cart.

"Oh Mama, *please*." Her face is so white the freckles have disappeared. "What's wrong? What's happened?"

"Miss Ann's missing. Get in the car. Help me find her."

"What? You sure?" I shout to the cashier next to my lane. "Judy. My girl's missing. *Help me*."

Judy leaves her line of customers, which is doubling up as the folks in my lane are turning their carts and pushing them into hers. "Get moving, Shelby. I'll lock your drawer and page the manager."

Mama and I scurry out the store. She parked in a handicapped space in front, leaving the door wide open, keys dangling in the ignition. We jump into the car; she turns the keys and presses the gas pedal. The engine catches a few seconds, shakes, sputters then dies. Taking a deep breath, she turns the key again and the engine catches in a rumbling idle. Ancient piece of junk needs to run a minute before it can drive. Lurching sideways in the seat, she faces me.

"After I told you she dumped out my dyes, I went straight home. First thing I did was check on that child, but she was gone. Her jacket's missing too. I checked around the swamp and trampoline. I must have looked under every bush in a one-block radius and she's nowhere to be found."

"Jesus Christ. With all the crazy loons around town, you should never have left her alone in the first place."

"I couldn't have been gone more than fifteen minutes. I told her to stay put in her bedroom; that I'd be right back."

"What in God's name did you *do* to her to make her run away?"

"I was so upset, I gave her a switching, then drove here to tell you what she'd done."

"Fine, just fine. Beat her with a stick then leave her alone. I'll never leave her with you again, ever, not even a minute. How could you, how *could* you?"

"I did not beat her, Shelby. I gave her a switching, just like my Mama gave me, and like I gave you when you was a child acting up. I called the police and they got a car out looking for her." Mama's knuckles protrude, bony, white and veined; fisted around the steering wheel.

"OK, OK. Calm down. Think. She couldn't have gone far. Where would she go? Maybe she's headed to Serenity's. She could be there already."

"I thought about that and called her mama. She said she wasn't there but she'd go out looking for her."

"Did you check next door? There'd be lots of hiding places in a vacated house."

"I went through every room and she was nowhere to be found. She wouldn't hide there, stinks like the sewer backed up."

"She asked if I'd take her hog-calling again. Drive to that pig farm. After that, we'll check the woods."

"Wherever she's gone, she didn't take her inhaler, I stuck it in my purse. She left the prosthetic at her bedside, too."

Mama taps the gas and the car revs, at last, ready to drive. She pops the gearshift to reverse, backs out the parking space, and then slams on the brakes; our heads lurch backward. Then, she ratchets the wheel to the right, navigating around abandoned shopping carts like she's at the Atlanta

Motor Speedway, almost running down some dude carrying a bag of groceries as she guns out the lot.

My hands are splayed against the dashboard, steadying myself as the car
careens through back roads. The side mirror reflects my face: pinched eyes,
blotched skin, mouth drawn into a chalk line. We land at the farm in minutes. The lot's filled with cars and off to the side, a pig's hung up, split down
the middle, red guts dangling from its belly. No one notices. Folks mill about
the farmhouse, hands in pockets, and the mood is solemn, like at a funeral.

Mama pulls up in front of the farmhouse. I jump out and run to a
heavy-set woman wearing overalls. "My daughter's missing. She's wearing
a pink jacket."

Her eyes, runny, dart from mine.

"God, what's happened?" I grab the bib on her overalls as an unbridled
crimson terror crashes into my body. My voice rises into a shriek: "What's
happened to my baby?"

Bloodshot eyes stare out from a white moon face. "We found her in the
smokehouse. She wasn't conscious, but still breathing when they rushed
her to the clinic."

"The clinic off Route 6?"

"Yes. They should have been there thirty minutes ago." She checks her
watch, voice unsteady. "I was just about to call and get an update on her
condition."

I squeeze her hands then run to the car and jump in, heart pounding
in my throat. "She's at the clinic on Route 6. *Hurry.*"

Mama, who was waiting in the shuddering car, shifts to drive then
flattens the accelerator.

"They found her in the smokehouse. She must have had an asthma
attack; the lady said she wasn't conscious." *Don't let her die!*

We fly down the road. At this speed, the car rattles like a time bomb,
empty Co-Cola cans roll back and forth over my feet, my hammering
heartbeat filling my ears. In the side mirror, I see a cop tailing us, his red
and blue lights flashing.

"Sweet Jesus. Pull over. Keep the car in park but don't turn off the engine; let *me* explain."

The officer walks to the car, scribbling on a pad. Mama rolls down the window and I lean into her, craning my head towards the officer.

"I clocked you ladies at eighty-two miles an hour. Where's the fire?"

Panic rises up my throat and I swallow a sob. "My daughter's sick, barely breathing; a stranger took her to the clinic. We need to get there. *Now.*"

He closes his pad, looks at me, then Mama. His badge catches a glint of sunlight, peeking between a mass of clouds, and splinters my throbbing head.

"Must be the child I'm looking for. Both of you will be killed driving crazy like that. I'll turn on my lights and siren to clear the way. You follow me; I'll lead you there. *Safely.* It's the place on Route 6, right?" I nod.

He turns on his siren, a slow growing wail, pulls into the road and drives around our car. The sky is lost through my tears and I try focussing on the back of the police car but all I see is the smashed-in eye on my china doll. She trusted me. I betrayed her. I didn't nurture or protect her the way a mother should. What kind of mother would leave her daughter? I squeeze my eyes shut and pray harder than I've ever prayed before in my life: *Punish me, punish me, not my baby.*

The short drive to the clinic is an eternity. At last Mama pulls up, stopping behind the police car at the entrance. I tear out and trip on the front entry mat, falling through the door as it opens automatically. Hoisting myself to my feet, I hobble to the front desk.

"Was a girl admitted?"

"She arrived half an hour back," the receptionist says. "They have her in the back room on an oxygen mask."

"Is she breathing? She's my child. I must see her now."

"Yes. She's breathing. A woman brought her in; she's with your daughter. There were also some men accompanying her." She points to the back of the clinic. "Over there."

Three unfamiliar men sit silent, pressed into black molded chairs lined against the wall. One man looks my age and the other appears foreign; the older man has blood splattered across his overalls and rubber boots. A chill attacks me like a knife and I scream.

"Now! I must see my baby *now*!"

"Let me talk to the doctor. He must do everything he can for your child without interference."

Mama collapses into a chair, puts her face in her hands, and sobs under the humming buzz of fluorescent lights. A minute passes and she looks up. Her hair is flattened, crushed on the sides. All the air has been sucked out from under her skin, and black mascara streams following the creases from her eyes paint old age on her face.

"I'll sit right here until somebody tells me the next horrible thing that is happening to my granbaby. I'm so sorry, Shelby...so, so sorry." Staring at me with wide, stunned eyes, she spreads her arms out to her sides, crying, pleading: "Just get a gun and shoot me." She howls like a dog in heat then folds herself into a crumpled heap, misery shivering down her spine, face grinding into trembling hands. Her wailing pleas blur into nonsense so I cover my ears and begin rocking, tumbling into a grieving stupor. I want to blanket her in my arms, comfort her, tell her it's my fault, that I take blame. But all the words have been beat out, and a fluttering sickness swells my gut.

A hand touches my shoulder. "Come. Your child is stable."

Mama looks up. "Stable? Stable?" She jerks, flinging her arms to the ceiling. "Thank you, Jesus, thank you."

Joy surges through me, an unimaginable relief, and I gasp, which explodes from my throat as a hiccup. I turn, stumble, and the nurse grabs my shoulders to steady me. *A second chance. Yes, sweet Jesus, a second chance to make things right.*

Taking my arm, she leads me down a narrow white hallway; a drawing of a smiley-faced stick family under a broccoli tree is tacked to the wall. She opens a door, and there lies Miss Ann, an oxygen mask affixed to her face. A woman is standing at the bedside, holding her hand. She looks up. How could this be—

"Mallory?"

"Yes, it's me. She's exhausted but her breath is steady now."

I rush to the bedside but the doctor blocks me with his arm.

"Don't jar the mask. We must keep her on oxygen another thirty minutes. We gave her a corticosteroid medicine, which decreased the swelling and tightness in her airways. I'll give you a prescription for prednisone to reduce her risk of having a second attack, and she'll also need to take an antibiotic to fight off infection. We've put a healing ointment on the scratches on her legs; she must have been walking through brush. There'll be forms to fill out before you leave."

Swaying, arms clenched across my belly, I nod at the doctor. Miss Ann's good eye is open, and her blind eye is sealed with a sliver of crust. I take her hand and squeeze gently, trying to draw heat, draw up some life into her cool, limp fingers. Wearing a gown patterned with tiny pink and pale blue butterflies, she tries to squeeze back, and through the mask, she smiles. I patter her hand with kisses, and her tiny fingers taste salty, soaked with my tears.

"I love you, sweet baby, I love you so much. I will never leave you again. *Ever.* Mama promises you that."

Mallory strokes her other hand, watching us. Then, head caving between trembling shoulders, her hair falls forward, covering her face as a veil. She places Miss Ann's hand over a ratty stuffed animal, turns to remove several tissues from a dispenser, blows her nose, reaches for more tissues and hands a wad to me.

The doctor faces me. "We've checked her pulse and other vital signs; her responses are normal. She's able to articulate sentences. A lucky girl. She got here just in time. I'll get your paperwork organized."

"Could you tell my mother and the others not to worry; that she's going to be all right?"

"Of course. But your child needs rest. You ladies have a seat outside the door in the hallway. Or you can stand. I'll open the shades so you can watch her in the room." The doctor pulls the cord on the blinds and they fall to the windowsill. He walks out the door and I turn to Mallory, who gestures to the open door.

I kiss Miss Ann's hand once more. "I'll be right outside this room, sugar plum. You can see me standing through the window. But try to close your eye. You need quiet time. Another thirty minutes with the oxygen." Miss Ann nods; so brave is my child.

We walk out the door, close it behind us, and stand next to the window, watching her chest move in time to the squiggling lines on the ventilator.

"Tell me everything, Mallory, how you found her; *please,* leave nothing out."

She presses her palms into her temples. "I'll start by going backwards, beginning with the car accident, if that's OK with you."

I nod and then Mallory unravels the events leading up to this place. She tells me what happened after that night, about the man she hit, and how he, his wife and daughter were deported to Mexico. She says the months following the accident have been dark, that she's been wracked with grief. She stares at Miss Ann a minute or two then tells me she has a long road ahead. She puts her forefinger over her lips and shakes her head, as if to say it's so personal, so intense, she can't discuss this further. She then describes how her driver took her to the farm today to say goodbye to her hog. I told her I knew about her intentions; she'd written many stories about that animal. I always wanted to write a comment on one of those blogs, to tell her the farm was in my hometown, but I could never work up the nerve.

She explains how she saw Miss Ann dart down the road after the slaughter, how little stuffed puppies lying on the ground led her to the smokehouse, about the man who gave her the medicine, and how they rushed her to the clinic. She turns her head from the window to look at me.

"So here we are; your little girl's safe. But, if you don't mind my asking, what was she running from?"

My eyes drop to my feet. I describe the symptoms of her illness, my suspicion that Mama's hair products were a catalyst, so Miss Ann dumped them down the sink. I told her about the switching, which made her ran away. Then, I found myself telling Mallory my entire life story, at least the part beginning with Buck, and why I left my child to move to Atlanta. As I spilled my guts, she nodded her head, not saying a word. I told her about Miss Ann's eye, how her daddy left, and how much Mama loved and helped us. I told her how hard it was leaving my child to pursue my dream of going to chef school, and how she developed an unexplained illness after I left. I told her about Chef Chen, and that just when my life was turning around, Grasso's fired me.

"But I'm glad. It was a sign telling me to return to my daughter. Now I'm in Coryville for good. No dream that involves leaving my child is ever worth pursuing."

The pupils in her eyes are dilated, glassed over with a wet look. She smiles and touches my nametag. "I see you found yourself another job in the food business."

"Only part-time." I flick the tag with my forefinger and she unpins it from my shirt, places it in my palm, and her fingers wrap around my cupped palm. I rest my other hand over hers.

"I don't know how I'll ever repay you, Mallory. You saved her life."

She shakes her head. "No, not me. There's a man in the waiting room, Jackson, who saved her. If he didn't have his inhaler…oh God, let's not go there."

"I'm surely indebted to him. But Mallory, if you didn't see her, if you didn't go looking for her, if you hadn't seen the puppies on the road…"

Folding together, our heads bump then collide into each other's shoulders, which are so heavy, so heavy under the weight of what we've risked and lost, so heavy bearing the load. Her body, now broken with tears, is drowning us both, and I see to the bottom of the well from where hers is sprung. My tears are in gratitude for Miss Ann returned to my arms, but I suspect hers are for that man she hit, so I draw up a bucket of tears to lend to *her* grief. Weeping, clinging and entwined, we share what's left, shifting the weight, gathering strength from each other to put the next foot forward.

The doctor walks towards us with papers clipped to a board, and taps his watch. "Thirty minutes; I'll remove the oxygen."

Untangling ourselves, we walk into the room. Mallory pulls out several tissues then brings me the box. I grab a couple, rub them under my eyes then blow my nose.

"Well then," I say, clearing my throat. "When will you be posting your experience with your hog? You wrote you'd be sharing your thoughts and feelings."

She flinches, bringing her hand to her mouth. "I left my camera bag at the farm." She shakes her head, blinking back tears. "Never mind, I'll get it later. I've decided to take the day off, my first since I began the blog. I'm not going to post any photos or write about my experience with that animal. Saying goodbye was too painful. It was also too real."

The doctor bends over Miss Ann and removes her mask; I look at him and he nods. I bend down and gather Miss Ann in my arms, not holding her tight, but as if she were a butterfly for she is so fragile. I kiss her forehead, straighten my back, and reach for the stuffed animal on the bed; one of its button eyes is twisted off—another chip off my heart.

"Where did you get this animal?"

She turns her head away from my gaze, and strokes the stuffed dog's ear. "Promise you won't take her from me if I tell you?"

"I promise you anything and everything your little heart desires."

She tucks the dog next to her, folding the sheet under its paws. "Mister gave it to me before they took him away and killed his doggies."

"That man next door?"

"Yes ma'am. He said it belonged to his little girl, but she's gone away so he gave her to me. Her name is Pouch. I hid her under my bed, but sleep with her and the puppies every night. I was scared that if I told you or MeMaw, you'd take her away. I had to keep Pouch a secret. She has no one but me to take care of her and her babies."

I turn to the doctor. "Our neighbor was busted in July for running a meth lab in his house. He must have given it to her before he was arrested."

The doctor taps his pen on a prescription pad looking at Miss Ann with troubled eyes, biting the side of his lower lip. He turns to me. "We need to run a test on the material to check for contamination."

Then he leans his head down, looking closely into her face. "Ann. We must examine this dog and her puppies to make sure they're not sick. If one of them is ill, we need to help them get better. Just like we did you." Miss Ann pulls the animal towards her, clutching it to her chest.

"It's OK, baby. Letting Pouch see the doctor is the best way you can take care of her and her puppies."

"I need to kiss them goodbye or they'll be afraid." Her chin shakes and her eye brims with tears.

"All right, sugar plum. You tell your dog and her babies goodbye."

She kisses Pouch, unzips the animal and pulls out four little puppies. She kisses each one of them.

"Don't be scared. Y'all have to leave me for a while 'cause you may be sick. But I'm gonna wait for you. You'll be coming home to me soon, as soon as you get better."

CHAPTER 20

Shelby

"WALTERS, LAKES AND REED. ATTORNEYS AT LAW." Must be the place. I peck Miss Ann on the cheek, open the door and step out of the back seat of Lester's Zeplen. Mama rolls down the window. "Call me when you're done. And spit out that gum, hon. Looks like you're a cud-chewing cow."

"Will do." A cow, huh. Mama sure knows how to push my buttons, but I let her comment slide. Aunt Mama's in the back seat and turns from Miss Ann to smear a fresh coat of lipstick over her mouth. Lester says something to Mama, causing her to kick back her head and laugh, probably that stupid joke about cows. Left blinker flashing, the car weaves into traffic, and then vanishes as a Southern Freight truck, belching fumes, pulls up beside them in the next lane.

I spit my gum into a tissue while studying the sign; the black plaque affixed to the tall stone building turns my stomach. I've never spoken to a lawyer before. The raised block letters appear to be carved from gold, and there's a picture of an old-time measuring scale beneath them.

Chef Chen called a week before Christmas. After speaking with him, I waited three days to let Mama in on his offer; it took that long to register, even though his words rang hopeless. Then Mallory called the day after Christmas, and told me she and her brother had an additional proposition for me to consider, and requested that we meet. I check my watch: 9:45; fifteen minutes to spare.

Inside the building, a directory indicates the office is on the sixth floor. I take the elevator up, cross the hall, straighten my skirt and push the silver handle on a heavy glass door. The reception area is dimly lit, and a couple of charcoal leather sofas and several chairs are arranged over a plush gray carpet. A receptionist sits behind a shiny island, the counter surrounding her is black as midnight with silvery flecks sparkling about the surface like stars.

"Hello. I'm here to see Mr. Lakes, please. His sister Mallory will be joining us, too."

"Mallory hasn't arrived yet." Her white-blonde hair, ironed straight, swings about her shoulders as she swivels to pick up a clipboard. She could be a model in *Glamour*, and I try not to stare. Handing me a pen, she requests I sign my name on the roster.

"Can I bring you coffee?"

"No, thank you. Is there a water fountain?"

Teeth as perfect as Chiclet gum glisten and spread across her smile. "I'll get you a bottle."

I select the smallest chair, taking up the least amount of space, and thumb through a *Garden and Gun* magazine, not reading a word. Each minute feels like an hour until a pair of fresh polished shoes—dress shoes that tie—shine up from under the bottom edge of the magazine. Raising my head, cool blue eyes meet mine; this must be Clay Lakes, Mallory's brother. His eyes and hair color are different than Mallory's, but their crooked half-smiles are the same.

"I've been looking forward to meeting you, Ms. Preston." I put down the magazine then stand to shake his hand. He glances at the door. "Perfect timing. Here's Mallory."

I haven't seen her since that day at the hospital, and my pulse quickens as she walks through the entrance. She looks healthier; her eyes are luminous and wide, and it appears she's gained weight. I extend my hand but she brushes it aside, folding me into a hug.

"Merry Christmas, Shelby. Happy New Year."

"Oh Mallory. I've been so curious, nervous is more like it. I'm just confused and don't know what to say."

"There's no need for words. At least for the moment. All you have to do is hear us out."

"Ladies," Clay says, with that half-grin, tapping his watch, "you're paying me by the hour."

Following him to his office, I admire the cut of his frame in his dark suit. Black and white landscape photography lines the walls down the hallway, and Mallory cuts a fine figure herself, wearing slim black pants and a gray shawl. It strikes me the only colors in this office are white, gray and black. Except for me. I'm wearing a bright green corduroy skirt with a red-and-white, candy cane shirt; an outfit I thought was festive for the holiday season. But now, as usual, I feel silly and out of place in such a slick office. He closes the door, sits behind his desk, and motions us to have a seat in chairs facing him.

"Mallory told me of your wonderful news. Congratulations; that culinary academy produces some of the finest chefs in the nation."

"I may be prejudiced, it *is* my alma mater, but Clay's right," Mallory says. "The fact that you were offered a full scholarship is really something; the competition's stiff. I was thrilled when Tracy called and filled me in on the details."

A smile crawls across my face as heat snakes up my neck.

"Chef Chen also offered me a part-time job. He wants to hire me as one of his assistants. Pay's not much but it's something. Of course I'm thrilled and would love to put the pieces together, but life is expensive, and my schedule's complicated, caring for my daughter."

"And that's why Clay and I wanted to talk with you. Tracy spoke of your dilemma and, as I mentioned to you over the phone, we may be able to help."

Mr. Lakes taps his forefinger on a deck of papers. "We'd like to discuss your leasing a loft in Mallory's building."

My shoulders sag; like I'd be able to afford that option. We live on different planets, and these two haven't got a clue. I'd barely be able to afford The Troubadour on a chef assistant's wages and next-to-nothing child support. My palms are damp, folded in my lap, drowning in a sea of kelly green. I wish I'd worn my chef coat and black and white checked chef pants.

Shuffling through the papers, he clears his throat, and I look up to regard him. He appears to be Tony Grasso's age and obviously has money, but that's where the similarities end. Mr. Lakes' hair is sandy blond and wispy; Grasso's scalp looks as if it were plastered with seal skin. Mr. Lakes' jewelry is simple; only cuff links and a silver wedding band. Grasso wears a massive ring, chunky diamond watch, and a thick gold chain loops around his neck like a dog collar. He always reminded me of that pimp who hung out by The Troubadour. I'm sure Grasso's jewelry is real, but that pimp sported some mighty fine fakes. Dude tried to hustle me before I started wearing chef clothes.

Mr. Lakes makes another "*ahum*" sound as if trying to get my attention. Oh Lord, I've been staring at his hands like a crazy fool. I meet his eyes and force a smile.

"Over the past couple of years, my partner and I've been purchasing properties around town, many of which are in foreclosure. Most are in the Old Fourth Ward neighborhood, but we've purchased several condos at The Stacks. The loft you'd lease is one of them." He looks at Mallory and nods. "That is if you decide to move. The previous owners left overnight after their loft was repossessed, abandoning most of their furnishings. Your only financial responsibility would be to cover gas and electric. The water bill is....."

"Excuse me for interrupting, Mr. Lakes. I'm sorry for cutting in, but I must tell you, I don't understand what you're saying. I wouldn't have to pay rent? There must be a catch. Seems crazy generous. Why?"

"Actually, it was my sister's idea. The loft is in Mallory's building. We don't want properties to remain vacant, so we offer reduced rates on many of them. In your case, my partner and I agreed to waive the rent and association fee. So..." His voice falters, at a loss for words.

"But, as I said, you'd pay gas and electric."

He fumbles with his cuff links, affixed to a shirt as stiff and bleached white as my chef jacket. His thumb and forefinger are yellowed and calloused, the one imperfection on this perfectly groomed man.

"My turn, Clay," Mallory says. I swivel in my chair to face her, and raise my brows, nodding, as if to say: *Yes*, go on. She sighs as she crosses her legs.

"Don't let him kid you. He's doing *me* the favor. Where to begin." She shrugs, raising her palms to the ceiling, then drops them with a sigh. "Ah yes, when life was interrupted. I can't erase the accident and what happened to that man and his family, and nothing I do will ever even the score."

Body slackening, her composure dissolves, and she's suddenly flustered, afraid, unsure, and all of these emotions I read in her face as she folds her lips under her teeth. Her eyes move to her brother, who smiles, winking at her, and then she straightens, takes a lingering breath, and returns my gaze.

"But I can try to make some good come out of that night and its aftermath. I'd like to begin with you and your daughter. Getting to know you has helped me reclaim who I am, or at least who I want to be. You'll never know how grateful I am for that. I identify with your passion and desire to be a chef. I, well—" she glances, once again, towards her brother, "Clay and I were products of dumb luck, being born to parents who could afford to give us so many opportunities. When Tracy said you were offered a scholarship but couldn't afford living expenses, we concocted a plan." She clasps her hands together, holding them to her heart, beating them into her chest. "It would make us so happy if we could help *you* with *your* dreams."

I lower my chin. All my life I've heard about miracles, mostly of a religious nature. Crippled limbs released by the Holy Spirit enabling legs to walk, cancerous tumors disappearing, that sort of thing. Never been caught up in one myself. Until now. But the voices in my head are unconvinced...*Miss Ann.*

I look up and meet her eyes. "With respect, and don't misunderstand me, describing my gratitude would be like plowing a field with a butter knife, but Miss Ann goes to school in Coryville, and I can't leave her behind." *Never again.*

"Certainly not," Mallory replies. "There's an excellent public school, Cabbagetown Elementary, in walking distance of the loft. I've contacted the principal and have some names for you. The second grade teacher, in fact, is my yoga instructor. I spoke to her about Miss Ann."

Do I dare hope? My thoughts fly and heart races, words tumbling from my lips. "Coryville schools lost federal funding, and the board can't agree on a plan for boosting our kid's pathetic test scores. I've always wanted to get her out of that system, get us both out of that town, but the situation seemed hopeless."

"The Cabbagetown primary and secondary systems are, in my opinion, the best in the state," Clay says. "Far superior to the school my son attends in Buckhead. An academy of wealthy brats who..." He shakes his head, as if trying to clear bothersome thoughts. "Excuse me. I digress."

Mallory grips the armrests on her chair and leans into me, pleading. "Oh Shelby, please consider our offer. You'd be attending classes while she's in school. You'd have your associate's degree before you know it. Chef Chen told me you have an innate brilliance with food. The man's well respected and with his endorsement, there's no doubt you'd have job offers that were only a pipe dream for me."

It feels as if hot liquid were being poured into my veins; I hate them seeing me turn this scarlet. I try composing myself, pulling my hair off my damp neck and tying it into a knot. Mallory and Clay are still, awaiting my words, but if I speak, I'll cry. My lower lip begins to tremble and as Mallory regards me, her eyes brim with tears. She clears her voice and continues, her words in a rush.

"You'd love the loft; it has the same floor plan as mine. We've had it cleaned and I've checked it out; turnkey, ready to go. And if you have a night class, if you ever need me to help out with Miss Ann, anytime, for any reason…" She falls back into her chair, as if worn to a frazzle. Her next words are whispered, and I must lean forward to hear what she says.

"It would mean so much if you'd let me help you with her."

Since returning to Coryville, my ambitions had faded. First my ankles, then my knees, up past my waist, sinking in quicksand. As I brushed my dreams beneath the distant city sidewalks, I told myself Miss Ann would be enough; that this was a test of love. Now here is this woman and her brother unfurling a rope to drag us back to shore. *A miracle.*

Mr. Lake gives another one of his "*ahum*" sounds, catching my eye. "I have the name of an excellent pediatrician in Cabbagetown. Mallory described your daughter's special needs, and that she suffers from asthma."

I swipe the moisture beneath my nostrils and sniff. "I guess she told you. I mean…about that day."

"She did indeed."

I turn to Mallory. "But you never heard the end of the story. Miss Ann's health started improving right after that attack. Come to find out, it was that stuffed animal you found that was causing her asthma. Since we got her away from that dog and those puppies, her symptoms have vanished."

"Come again?"

I turn to Clay. "Our next door neighbor had been cooking meth in his house for years, but we didn't have a clue. He gave Miss Ann the stuffed dog with a zipper-lined pocket full of puppies. She must have had it for months, but kept it a secret because she thought we'd take it away from her."

"No doubt you'd have done just that."

"You bet your life. It was a filthy old thing and the man was scum. As soon as she began sleeping with the dog and puppies, her symptoms developed. Mallory found the stuffed animal by the smokehouse and brought it to the clinic. After Miss Ann told us where she got it, the doctor became suspicious and sent it out for tests. Sure enough, meth was all over that critter, especially coating the inside pocket, which contained the puppies."

"Dear heavenly Father," Mallory says, touching my arm.

Clay's upper lip curls almost touching his crinkled nose, and he lets out a soft whistle. "That's appalling. You've got to be kidding."

"I wish I was. The animal's pouch was used for hiding meth. The doctor said she'd been inhaling low dosages of the drug. She did have asthma, but it was chemically induced. She's been away from that dog over six weeks and was sick at first, but now she's almost fully recovered."

"What a relief that must be for you."

"Mr. Lakes, you have *no* idea."

He regards me, the crease between his brows furrowing into a deep V then he straightens his tie: black and gray pinstripes.

"Whew," Mallory says. "Ready for prime-time." Her eyes flicker across my face as if she'd just finished digging a deep hole and was uncovering, and at last discovering, my roots; the depths from where I came. Her face softens, as if she's meeting me for the first time, and she smiles, delighted to make my acquaintance.

"A happy ending. I thought beginnings were the only happy part of a story."

I turn to Clay. "There's something else you need to know." He straightens a paper clip into a line then bends it into an S shape, staring at that clip as if he'd like to use it to hook my mouth shut, scared of what's going to come out next.

"Your sister saved my child's life; she was the one who found Miss Ann and had the quick sense to rush her to the clinic." I raise my brows towards Mallory. "I'll bet you never told him that part, did you?"

Mr. Lakes flicks the clip into the trash. "No ma'am. She never told me that part." He folds his arms across his chest, shaking his head at his sister. "Did you now, Mallory."

"Don't forget Jackson." Her face flushes. "I guess we can debate who saved whose life, but for once, I'll spare y'all the drama. So what do you say, Shelby? Will you and Miss Ann be packing your bags?"

"You don't have to ask twice," I reply, not missing a beat. I turn to Clay. "Though it will only be temporary. Of course I'll pay rent, even start paying you back, as soon as I'm out of school. As soon as I get a job."

"I have no doubt." He smiles.

Mallory wraps her arms across her chest, hugging herself then catches my eye. "You're going to be one of the most sought-after chefs. There's no telling where you'll go. And Miss Ann, why, I guarantee she'll be the happiest little girl in all of Atlanta." Her head cocks as if puzzled by something. "Odd. It's been such a long time, happiness feels strange." Shaking her head, her eyes sparkle and dance. "Let's get down to business."

Clay's hands are folded on his desk and he grins, his head darting back and forth from me to Mallory. Then he slides the top drawer open. Pulling out an envelope, he rips it down the middle and a jangle of keys fall onto the desk.

"Here are two sets of keys; three keys on each set. The red one gets you through the front door on the lower level; the other two unbolt your loft, which is on the second floor; the loft two doors down from Mallory."

I finger the keys and think of the low life that hung around The Troubadour, but I only needed one key to get into that room.

"Don't worry," he says, sensing my concern. "Cabbagetown is in one of the safest sections in Atlanta. Mallory's a nervous Nellie and insists on multiple locks. She had the locksmith put them on your door too. There's an efficient public transportation system in the area so you won't need a car. It's faster to take the bus than drive."

He glances at his watch. "The week between Christmas and the New Year is slow around the office. I'm driving Mallory back to The Stacks after our meeting, and I'd be happy to give you a lift. You can inspect your new home."

"Well, as much as I'm dying to see it, I need to re-group. My family dropped me off; they're looking for a screen door at the recycle center. After I call, they'll come get me then we're heading back to Coryville.

I need time to explain things to Mama; she was teary-eyed when I told her about the scholarship. But Mr. Lakes, thank you so much. Thanks so much for everything."

"Please, call me Clay. Here's my card." He removes a business card from a holder next to his phone and hands it to me. "Don't hesitate to call me with any questions or concerns. It would please me to keep up with your life. Maybe you and your daughter can come out to the lake house this summer."

"We'd be thrilled." My eyes meet his, then dart to my lap, suddenly shy.

"Now then." He slides some stapled papers towards me. "Take a few minutes to read through the rental agreement. After you sign the bottom of the last page, the loft is yours."

Picking up the pen, Mama, Aunt Mama, Nina Bradley, and all of the people I've met in the past year, all of these people who've helped me get to this place, crowd my heart. I bite my bottom lip and squeeze my eyes shut, trying to stop the seeping tears. *Thank you. Thank you.* After a moment, I open my eyes, place the pen on the papers and turn to Mallory.

"I think I'll have a New Year's Eve party, the evening after we move in. Nothing fancy, just family and friends, but I'd love for you to come. Feel free to bring a guest."

Mallory nods, and her eyes, also rimmed in tears, meet mine, as if to say *nothing would give me greater pleasure.*

DECEMBER 31, 2011

Mallory

The intercom rings: Itchy. I buzz her in, and then open the door. She is wearing jeans and a camel pea jacket. Her look is soft, toned down, and if she wears makeup, it's minimal. This understated Itchy is lovely.

"Hey you." I skim her cheek with a kiss. "Have a seat; I'll brew a pot of tea."

"You're a tea drinker?" She slides from her jacket and tosses it on the sofa. These days she's quit wearing pearls; all jewelry, in fact, except for her wedding ring.

"My latest thing. Have you been to the Peach Blossom Tea Room? It opened last month on Carroll. The interior's done up in bamboo and you sit on these cute floral cushions and order teas from around the world. They also sell leaves in bulk." I open my cabinet and remove the accoutrements of my new tea service.

"All the teas they sell are sustainably grown." I shake then open a glass bottle of leaves, inhaling the scent. "Umm. Green tea with tangerine. Here, take a whiff." I hand it to Itchy. She puts the jar under her nose and sniffs. "Smell the citrus; how's that for aromatherapy. Last week I brewed an extra strong batch with ginger and scallions, then used it as a poaching liquid for snapper."

"Oh Mallory," she says, elbowing me in the ribs, "what am I going to do with you?" She hands me the bottle. "How do you come up with this stuff? I can barely manage PB and Js for the girls."

She sits at the island while I stand, spooning the greenish-black leaves into the metal infuser. I place it into the small, plump pot—black cast iron embossed with Sanskrit symbols of peace—then pour hot water over the leaves.

"There now." I secure the lid into the pot, set the timer, and slide a chair next to her, taking a seat. "Five minutes to nirvana."

Itchy tilts her head to me, scrunching her brow. "Where did you say Manuel's living now?"

"Valle del Fuerte, an agricultural region outside of Los Mochis. Mexico's bread basket."

"There must be a hundred-million Manuel Hernandezes in Mexico. How on earth did you get his address?"

"Turns out, Marselina tracked him down without a problem. He has friends in Atlanta and they keep in touch. His leg must be healed, or at least he's walking. He's a laborer in a sugar cane processing plant. Marselina has cousins in Los Mochis and they know the facility where he works." I place two tea cups beside the pot and slide a chair next to Itchy.

"You agonized over that letter. Did you ever send it?"

"I did, indeed; Marselina translated my words into Spanish. It's been a few weeks, but no response. I'm not sure if he received it, and if he did, if he'll contact me, but I won't give up trying to connect. Of course he hates me...but maybe, with time, if we ever do begin a correspondence..." Eyes wide, I clasp her forearm. "Who else in his life is in any position to help him? Marselina's been digging into his immigration status, and says she could facilitate the process for a visa. We could even help on his end, go to Los Mochis and stay with her cousins."

"That's extreme. Are you sure it's safe?"

"Safe? Where's safe? You were in Cabos, you showed me pictures of the resort y'all stayed in; the one with the infinity pool melting into the horizon."

"I wiggled around on my stomach like a snake taking that picture; scratched up my belly to get the perfect shot. Four years ago. Huh." She rubs her temples. "Seems like forty."

"Los Mochis is just across from Cabos; a short flight over the Sea of Cortez. The dangers for tourists are way overblown. Clay and his buddies have gone duck hunting there for years. Odds are better I'd be gunned down on Carter Street than getting caught in some drug lord's cross-fire."

"Mallory, how that night has haunted me. And not just what happened with Phil. *God*. How insignificant our issues are compared to what happened to that man." She drums her nails on the granite, pressing her lips together. "But I've discussed these feelings in counseling and now feel, to the bottom of my core, there's no debt to be paid. I've separated my emotions from the reality. You, me, Manual...we come from different worlds. The collision was circumstantial, the outcome a tragedy, but culpability should not be attached to this sadness. It was his fate, which doesn't have to determine ours."

"But it can influence it, at least mine. I feel that some sort of reparation will be a part of my healing. You may think this sounds whacked out but my destiny is linked with his and his family." They entwined when he asked me to take him home. I'm trying to get home, too. Home is the place I can live with myself, without hating myself.

"Well, I guess my destiny will be repeating this phrase for the rest of my life: It wasn't your fault. You were a victim of random circumstances. Would you have been responsible if his bike had been struck by lightning?" With spidery quickness, her eyes dart from mine then return to catch my gaze. "It's the same thing."

I look at her, silent. We never voiced the truth: I'd been drinking and wasn't watching the road. Cooper's the keeper of my pain. But she knows; she just loves me and understands some words should rest unsaid.

"I applaud you, Mallory," she says, breaking the silence. "Figure out a way I can wire him some money. I'm sure Atlanta dollars go further down there."

"I'm sure he'd prefer cash to letters from me." I shrug. "How are things with Phil?"

"I had a few sessions with the therapist on my own, and now he's joined our meetings. Phil and I are finding a middle ground; a place where we can forge a new relationship. Believe it or not, he shares some of the blame for what happened in our marriage. It's a start."

"Honey, that's a huge start. I'm so happy for you both."

"Oh, more good news. Southern Green is paying me almost double what I made at Grasso's."

"You'll be rich. When does the new store open?"

"Officially in early February, but I begin ordering and stocking the wine department in a couple of weeks."

"I'm so proud of you." The timer dings; I pour us each a cup.

"You know, Itchy, the way you've tackled your problems has been my inspiration."

"Here's to best friends," she says. "And to the new year." We tip cups, and she takes a sip. "Whoa. A tongue scorcher." She blows at the smoking beverage, and then places it down.

"Here's my news. Pat me on the back; I haven't had a drop of alcohol for seven weeks and two days. More important, I got rid of the sleeping pills and the last of Mama's drugs; the devil and his potions have left my side."

My eyes slink to my collection of glassware, twinkling in the sunlight, then back to Itchy.

"I'll resume sipping lessons tonight. Cooper's bringing bubbly to Shelby's dinner party. But I'll stop after one glass." A cut crystal flute catches my eye. Winking. Flirting. "Heck, champagne glasses are half the size of wine goblets and it's New Year's Eve. Maybe I'll have two, but that's it. God knows I'll never get behind the wheel."

Itchy shakes her head, lips pressed together, then the corners of her mouth tip up in a wry smile. "You've nothing to escape from, Mallory. Nothing."

"The thing of it is, Itchy, the big, brilliant, beautiful thing of it is, is that I have no *desire* to escape from anything. I've faced down my demons, or at least I'm working to that end. Herbal remedies help." I clasp a formula of dried licorice root, jujube and lily bulb tabs that a local Chinese medical practitioner made for me and stroke the vial as if it were a kitten. "And Cooper, such a support. Who'd a guessed? He even goes to yoga classes with me. You should see his quivering legs in those balance postures." I chuckle at the thought.

"Cooper in a yoga class? You've got to be kidding. I can't wait to tell Phil."

Itchy takes a sip of tea then looks up, brows raised. "This is marvelous. Must be the first time I've had tea that didn't come from a bag or bottle."

"Thanks. Another new addiction. Keeps me jazzed."

"At least it won't kill you." She takes another sip. "So where do y'all stand now?"

"I'm not ready to pick up from where we were before he left me. How can I? So much has changed; so much has changed about me. Cooper tells me he loves me, he'll always love me, and he'll continue to wait. The human heart's a mystery. A pounding muscle everyone has, but no one understands."

"And there lies the challenge." Her smile lights my eyes. "Cooper would be lucky to get you back. You're magnificent, Mallory, and I'm your biggest fan." She sips her tea.

"It's hard to believe that this time last year you were writing for the paper." Her forehead crinkles as if bewildered. "And I was working for *Grasso*. How did I stumble into that hornet nest?"

"What a hellacious year. Seems like it lasted an eternity." I shake my head. "It's hard to believe that through everything I've managed to keep my job."

"And through everything, I've managed to keep my husband." She stares into her cup as if the answer to life's most burning questions could be read in the scattered tea leaves.

She looks up, eyes clear as the new morning, then reaches into her bag, pulling out a box.

"Here's the twins' souvenir from last summer's beach trip; they want you to have them." I look at her, curious, and rip away the tissue paper wrapping. "Not pearls, honey, not this time."

I remove the top of a cardboard box and two effervescent shells, swirls of coral and flint, glisten on a bed of cotton. "Oh, Itchy."

"They washed up on the beach in Sea Island. Much prettier than pearls, don't you think?" Her eyes catch mine. "You're their godmother, Mallory. They adore you."

I bite my lower lip, holding back tears. "Those precious girls. Give them each a kiss."

She finishes her tea in a gulp. "I'd best skedaddle. I'm lapping up every second enjoying them while they're out of school. I've also got to box up Christmas ornaments and get the house organized before starting work." She stands and heads towards the sofa. After a few steps, she stops. Turns.

"We don't always know the path we're supposed to take. Sometimes we lose our direction, we get lost." She walks to my chair and raises her pinky finger; I link mine into hers. "But we've always had each other to help find our way back."

Unlatching our fingers, we embrace in a fierce hug. After a moment, she pushes away and leans back, gazing at me, twisting her ring with a smile. Then she turns, trots to the sofa and grabs her coat, glancing back at me over her shoulder.

"Don't forget to think of me at me at midnight." The door closes yet her words linger, filling her void.

I carry the box to the entry hall table and arrange the shells among favorite pictures, all framed in silver. I pick up a photograph: Itchy and I toasting the moment. *Wineglasses clink as the shutter releases. A purple splotch of iris; warped candlelit smiles.* The Mallory Before. My eyes, like fireflies, flit across the image.

There's another step I've added to my healing process: carving out a plot of hours, alone, where I can tend and weed through this year. I've tried writing about my experiences but, as of yet, words ripen, rot, then fall to the ground. I can't even conjure the first sentence that would grow and shape the past twelve months into something with meaning.

Writing would be purging, and another act of contrition; my words as ashes, sprinkled into the wind, with a fervent prayer that in some astral stratosphere, absent analysis and erudition, the lives I've torn apart will be mended. But what combination of words, sentences and paragraphs could possibly describe a handful of strangers, caught off guard by chance; no divine intervention, merely circumstances, then bound together through eternity?

I stare through the window, which frames a mass of thick grayish-black clouds; it is, after all, the last day of December. I walk to Mama's sofa and sit, hugging my thighs into my chest. So tired. So tired. Snuggling into the corner, I lay my cheek against the arm rest and inhale her powdered scent.

She is in me. Mama's in me.

Turns out Itchy and I are both right. Life is random, a deck of cards shuffled, collapsed then dealt to its players with blind oblivion; sperm to egg, roll of the dice, quirky fate. Yet some of us—those fortunate to have been birthed into nurturing families, those lucky few with prescience to find hope in despair—can coerce, twist and reshape the odds into something redeeming. Make your best hand, high card wins the trick.

I cut deals with the devil, learning just what he can do and precisely how he does it, huddling in his abyss as the fear of living devoured me. But light seeped through, tracing the contours of darkness; he couldn't steal my soul.

Closing my eyes, I round the bend to the place where the year began, and now is ending, and all of the events in between; everything that occurred the day of the accident, and my unraveling since. Nothing that happens in the universe vanishes, and our past is not a dream; our past is our story, which lives forever, somewhere, and is limitless, attaching itself to what follows, and it's this thing that follows that is the dream. Some dreams drown in booze, some come crashing down on asphalt, while others dissolve in a backwoods Southern town. Yet, for some, the dream persists. Shuddering. So you pick yourself up, retracing your path, but only if—and here's the burning truth—only if you've got the guts. I've seen the face of courage. In the past six months, I've seen this face on a man, woman and child. Next time I'll recognize it sooner. Next time it will be my own.

And here I am, at this moment, and it strikes me that this moment, too, is eternal, wedged in the chasm between the story and the dream. My story belongs to me, and tells me who I am and why I'm here. But it isn't shameful, a tale best long forgotten. My story is one of forgiveness. Of forgiving myself. And this is a place that is glorious, this is a place that's rare, this is the place I shall be, indeed.

Shelby

This *it*, Shelby. *The Stacks*—your new *home*? Dear heavenly Father, who'd a guessed? Since Mallory Lakes lives here, I thought it'd be someplace fancy. Looks like the movie set for Dracula." Mama clutches her arms in front of her chest and shivers, as if the fanged phantom were walking up to greet us, black cloak flapping in the breeze.

She's been working my last nerve ever since I crawled out of bed this morning, hurling zingers towards me at every opportunity, but tiptoeing around the fact that after last night Miss Ann and I will never call Coryville home. The corners of her mouth tick down, and her eyes are ragged and glassy; she must have cried herself to sleep. The smokestacks, outlined against the sky in the hard morning light, remind *me* of a mythical city in some futuristic fairytale; a place where wishes are made and always granted. With a drawn-out sigh, I collect my thoughts so I can defend my new home without upsetting her more.

"Some would call the lofts *re-purposed chic* and, frankly, they're fabulous. I researched them online and lots of artists live here. Used to be a cotton mill but burned down, and all that's left of the old mill are smoke-stacks. It's an example of industrial architecture and even listed on the National Historic Register."

"That's some gussied-up talk, young lady. All I can say is it's too bad you destroyed the old jackalope. He'd a fit right into this landscape; would'a loved the place."

"That nasty creature would put a curse on me. Let's end the year saying pleasant things to each other."

Lester opens the trunk and pulls out five boxes. Two of them are mine, my entire life wedged into eight corners of cardboard; Miss Ann has three, mostly filled with books and toys. Mama removes the cooler.

"Let's get this food into the fridge; meat should be thawed by now. What else are you making besides stroganoff?"

"Nothing, it's a potluck. Mallory said the kitchen has a gas stove, and is stocked with pots and pans, but I don't want to fuss with more than the main course. She says the square footage is ideal for us, almost identical to hers; anything would be a palace after The Troubadour. Tonight's more about toasting our new life in the new year, rather than making some elaborate feast. I just want to show the loft to my friends; they were struck dumb when I said I was moving here."

"Remind me who's invited. Besides Mallory Lakes, of course. Having dinner with her will give me bragging rights till kingdom come."

"Mallory's bringing an appetizer: Pork and Bacon Pinwheels with a Mustard-Dipping Sauce. Oh, and her boyfriend, I forget his name, is bringing champagne. I also invited Tracy, the woman I used to work with at Grasso's, who's coming with her partner, Clare. They're bringing salad and dessert."

"They own a business together?

"Clare owns Squash Blossom Farms, and Tracy helps her manage it. But understand this, Mama, they're also partners in life."

"Oh no, Shelby. You're not telling me they're *lesbians*." Her nose crinkles as if she was chewing a bitter pecan.

Lester and Aunt Mama quit jabbering and set the boxes on the ground; Aunt Mama's jaw drops towards her chest and Lester's eyes bulge like a bullfrog. Mama taps her foot and her eyes thin, regarding me with distaste. Miss Ann breaks the silence, circling me in a little jig. "What's a lebian, Mama? What's a lebian?"

"A lesssbian," I say, wiggling my eyebrows at her, sounding out the *s* like I'm hissing as a snake, "is a woman who prefers living with a woman, instead of a man. And it's no big deal, unless you make it one." Face burning, my eyes bore holes into Mama then move to Lester and Aunt Mama, daring them to make some smart-ass comment.

"Tracy and Clare are my best friends, and I would not have survived this year without their help." I can't let my friendships be tainted by Mama's bigotry.

"I'll keep my opinion on that to myself. I thought Sandra was your best friend."

"We haven't seen much of each other, we're both so busy. When I'm settled, I'll call her. I've also invited Jackson. He and Mallory were the two that rescued Miss Ann. We've kept in touch."

Mama's pursed lips ease into a smile upon hearing there's a man in the picture. Relief washes through me at her approval, yet I'm irritated she has such power and control over my emotions.

"I told him he didn't have to cook, but he said he'd pick up some bread from a bakery around the corner."

"Sounds like a crowd."

"There'll be ten of us. Hopefully we'll have enough chairs."

Picking up the boxes, we carry them to the side of the building; I unlock the door with the red key then we haul them up the stairs. Brown paint peels in scales from the walls, as a snake shedding its skin. Maybe Clay will let me sand and paint it.

"This must be it: 4-C West." My fingers fumble, trying to get the keys to turn the right way in the locks. With a click, each finds a fit, snapping to the right. Holding my breath, I turn the knob, push the door and a warming glow of golden sunlight floods the entry as we walk in.

"Ho-wee, Shelby," Lester howls, shoving boxes into a corner. "Even a blind hog finds an acorn now and then."

"It's beautiful, Shelby," Mama whispers. "So spacious."

"Oh my," I whisper, releasing my breath, tying my hair into a knot. The back wall is floor to ceiling windows, which makes the open floor plan appear enormous. I walk around the living, dining and kitchen areas dazzled, tip-toeing over purple and rose rainbows made by the afternoon sun striking a glass prism dangling in the window. A half-wall separates a large bedroom from the rest of the loft.

"I'll speak to Clay about dividing this area so Miss Ann and I can have our own bedrooms. Lester, maybe you can help me install walls; I'll leave the rest open." Reaching into my pocket, I pull out my stone and kiss it, making a wish to protect us. I place it on a bedside table then crack open a window to let in some fresh air. Running my forefinger against the wall, *my* wall, I trace it back into the living room.

"Miss Ann can sleep on the sofa until her bedroom's set up."

"Sheets and blankets are in one of them boxes," Mama says, busying herself, taking the mushrooms, dill and sour cream from the cooler and organizing them in the fridge.

She swats a mean fanny in the kitchen, bound round, tight and confident in latex capris, and she hums a tune under her breath. She claims she hasn't had a smoke in over a month, and is also back in the hair business. Her sales rep restocked the entire line of products Miss Ann dumped down the sink and took twenty-five percent off the top of the bill; Lester put the balance on his credit card. I told Mama I'd pay it off—after all, it was Miss Ann's doings—but she shushed me quiet, making me swear to Jesus not to mention that day again.

I walk to the kitchen. "Dang. Forgot flour for the stroganoff. Maybe there's some in one of these cabinets."

"Over in that corner closet." Mama points her elbow to a door by the fridge. "There's oils, spices and canned goods; must be where they kept the pantry staples." Mama removes the venison from the cooler, slaps it on the island, and regards the liver-colored meat. Her face beats warmth, as if this meat were a long lost friend.

"This here's the venison from Sam's last kill. Been frozen close to two years but it was vacuum-packed. That butcher on Linville Avenue does a great job processing meat; I'm sure it'll be fine."

Aunt Mama pulls out a counter stool and sits, wiggling into the seat, making herself at home. "Seems like yesterday Sam was at the house. Hard to believe him and Watley are gone."

I brush my fingertips across the stove. The glimmering stainless has been shooting sparks in my direction since I walked through the door, flirting at me from all angles of the loft, like some guy checking me out across a crowded bar.

"I guess it's time to break in the kitchen." There's a sticky note stuck on a grill grate. I pull it off.

> "Hope is the thing with feathers
> That perches in the soul,
> And sings the tune without the words,
> And never stops at all." (Emily Dickinson)

The table's set, candles lit, and everyone claps as I set the stroganoff on the table. I'm proud, yet I shrug, like this dish, my new life even, is no big deal. There's barely space for nine chairs squeezed together so Miss Ann sits on Jackson's lap.

Mallory's boyfriend, a handsome man introduced to me as Cooper, pops a bottle of champagne then edges around the table, his tall frame stooping to pour a golden stream of bubbles into everyone's glass; there is sparkling cider for Miss Ann. Mallory clinks her glass with the tongs of a fork then stands.

"I'd like to propose a toast to welcome the new year; a good luck toast to Shelby, Miss Ann and their new life in Atlanta."

"Here, here," Tracy says, standing, looking at me with rosy pride blooming on her cheeks. "A toast to Shall-be; an extraordinary lady who makes her own luck."

My face feels ablaze as everyone cheers, Lester mortifying me in front of Mallory by wolf-whistling through two fingers shoved into his mouth. Mama elbows Lester, trying to silence him, then bows her head, nodding at me to follow suit. After saying the peace, we pass dishes around the table.

"Shelby, this is delicious," Clare exclaims. "I haven't eaten venison since I was a kid; I never liked the taste until now. Too gamey, or something."

"Thanks. It's as free-range, local and organic as you can get."

"Biggest buck ever shot in Jeff Davis County," Aunt Mama clucks. "I know my family's tired of hearing me ramble on about that day, but the story behind this venison bears repeating; most of ya'll ain't heard it." Mama raises her brows at me, and though we've listened to this tale many times, we put down our cutlery and nod politely at Aunt Mama.

"Watley was at a cockfight, for no good reason, when Sam stopped by. He saw Watley's new rifle on the gun rack and asked if he could borrow it. Said he was thinking about buying the same gun and wanted to test it out; knock off a few rounds. Sounded innocent enough to me.

"So off he went; he was back in a couple of hours with the biggest buck you ever seen strapped into the bed of his pick-up, long snout hanging over the side with its tongue dangling down. I declare, that animal was wearing his twelve-point rack like a crown." Aunt Mama slaps her thigh and chuckles.

"Weren't more'n a minute passed when Watley drove up. When he saw that animal the expression on his face woulda' woke the dead. Why, that was the exact whitetail Watley'd been scouting all season; talk of the county. Watley'd set his sights on the buck, said he discovered where it was hanging out, and bought the new rifle just to shoot him. Lord a mercy, when he saw Sam pull that very gun from the car, he 'bout broke his arm yanking it from his hands; lucky he didn't shoot Sam's head off. To make matters worse, Sam left the house and drove his truck all over town, honking his horn and showing off his trophy."

She leans her forearms into the table and turns to Mama. "Mercy, Noreen. Watley never calmed down after that day. Never spoke to Sam again and always blamed me, purple-faced, a screamin' and a yellin', which ended up killing *him* in the end. Wonder if those two ever met up? If so, wonder if it was in heaven or hell?"

Mama turns and winks at me, *let sleeping dogs lie,* but her eyes are glassy and she dips her head, dabbing her napkin around the corners of her lids. It's been a year since we buried Sam's ashes with Uncle Watley's but she's not over him; that man's heart is zippered to her soul. Lester studies her profile then places his arm across her shoulder. I wonder if she told him about Sam's remains.

Mama's sadness pierces my heart and my nose tingles, like it does when I'm fixing to cry. Blinking back tears, I change the subject. "I hear a new Southern Green is moving a couple blocks from the downtown Grasso's."

"Keep it local," Mallory says, grinning that half-smile of hers. "These days that's the only place I shop." Cooper rests his fork against the plate and pulls her into his side.

"The new competition must be ruffling Tony's tail feathers," I remark, pleased with anyone, anything or any enterprise that could hurt Tony Grasso.

"That store's nothing compared with Grasso's other headaches. I've been itching to let you in on the drama; a Greek tragedy for the grocery chain, a comedy for the rest of us." Tracy shakes her fists towards the ceiling, ferocious and victorious, as if she's won a battle.

"Bottom line: Business is down by half and shrinking every day. I can hardly wait to get to work; having the time of my life watching the performance. Every day a new scene unfolds."

"Tracy, what did you *do*?"

"I didn't have to do a thing. Humpty and that marketing director, Miss Jell-O-Butt, did all the dirty work. Actually it was 'ole Jell-O who started the fire; Humpty just fanned the flames." Tracy giggles behind her napkin. "She got canned. Like all Grasso's women after he's done using 'em." Glancing at Mallory then Miss Ann, her face flushes. "Oops, enough of that talk.

"As they say, hell hath no fury like a woman scorned. She took revenge by Facebooking and Tweeting to the entire Grasso customer database that the Grasso meats labeled as prime were from distressed cattle. Even attached the suffering animal's photos. That little chickadee was more adept at social marketing than Grasso realized."

"Distressed cattle? I'm scared to ask."

"Sorry, Shelby. I shouldn't talk about this over dinner, and I'll spare the gory details, but distressed cattle are abused and not given decent food and shelter. Because of this, some are sick when they're slaughtered and their meat's sold off cheap. Grasso's been cutting deals with Georgia Meats then packaging the product as prime."

"So gross."

"But true; I knew about the scam all along. The butcher at the south side store—that scraggly mullet dude, the one who used to work for Georgia Meats—has loose lips, especially after a couple of rum and Mountain Dews. I was going to leak the story but 'ole Jell-O beat me to the punch. She contacted the health department and they confiscated meat for testing. That prime was slime, so they shut down Georgia Meats and red-taped Grasso's meat departments, fining them up the wazoo. They had to restock and reapply for permits, but by then, Grasso's reputation was shot. The health department's set up shop in all their butcher departments."

"I only trust meat from Piggly Farms myself," Lester comments, eyeing the piece of venison attached to his fork prongs with suspicion. I smile to myself; Lester's jealous of Sam.

"Grasso fired Humpty and made him the fall guy, issuing a press release saying Humpty was supposed to monitor the meat buyers and neglected his responsibilities. But Humpty had his revenge; filed a grievance with the Georgia Department of Labor. Said Grasso broke labor laws firing people for no just cause."

"No just cause was the best thing that ever happened to me." I wince at the memory of Grasso and his jackalope eyes smirking down at me from the stairwell.

"Unh, unh. Lord have mercy." Mama shakes her head at me. "That store's trouble. Sounds like those scalawags did you a favor."

"What happened to Humpty?" I ask.

"Before leaving, he said he was going to apply for a job at Southern Green. That grocery chain focuses on stocking foods sourced from the South; Grasso's would have tanked anyway with their emphasis on Italian and French imports. Humpty wasn't evil. Just carrying out orders.

"Southern Green hired Itchy on the spot; she begins stocking the wine department next month." Cooper's arm is still wrapped around Mallory. He is forking food clumsily with his left hand, his right arm holding her into him like he's afraid she might vanish.

"Well I hope they hire Humpty, but I doubt it," Tracy says. "He's too old-style grocery for their hip cliental. Needless to say, work is the highlight of my life. And look..." She holds out her nails for my inspection; filed into precise half-moons. "I've quit biting them. I'll collect paychecks until they bounce or the stores close for good. Tony Grasso's karma is fulfilling its destiny; a beautiful thing to watch—especially from a distance."

"I don't put weight in karma, good or bad," Clare says. "I strive for balance." Tracy turns her head away from Clare and mouths the words: *Make her stop.*

"Could someone *please* tell me what karma means," Mama says.

"Luck," Miss Ann pipes.

Jackson smiles and looks around the table; it's the first time he's had a chance to work in a word all evening. "Karma means different things in different cultures. In Miss Ann's world, it means luck. In the Buddhist and Hindu faiths, karma means the action in this life determines your destiny in the next." He tickles Miss Ann. "If you're not a good little girl, you'll come back a monkey." She shrieks; he stops and hugs her. "We're born with the freedom to choose between good and evil; God doles out the consequences of each decision."

Tracy stands and waves her glass. "A toast to karma; Tony's next life will be spent feasting at the slop buckets on the Coryille Hog Farm. Wait, no. Pigs are too fine an animal for that creep. Let's toast to him coming back as a cockroach."

"I'll drink to that." I stand, tip my glass to Tracy's, and the chair falls backwards behind me. Mama puts her fist to her mouth, fixing to die laughing.

"Lester, it's close to eight. We'd best be hitting the road. There's a tangle of New Year's Eve traffic and we won't be home till past eleven." Aunt Mama's shoulders sag into the pull of gravity as she hoists herself from the table.

"Hate leaving the party but I reckon you're right."

"But you haven't had dessert," I say in a soft whine, sad to say goodbye, reluctant to feel their absence. "You'll miss Tracy's famous Squash Blossom Honey Cake. It's too bad you can't stay to bring in the year, but I'll wrap a hunk for you to take home."

"Two-thousand and twelve." Aunt Mama yawns. "Never dreamed I'd make it this far."

Lester and Mama push back their chairs. "It was such a pleasure meeting all of y'all nice folks. You watch after my daughter and granbaby. Make sure they *behave*."

I stand and my smile lands on Tracy, slides to Clare, travels to Jackson with Miss Ann curled in his lap, onto Cooper then rests a lingering moment on Mallory. "I'll be back in a few."

Picking up their plates, I walk to the kitchen and stack the dishes by the sink. I rinse my fingers, cut a large wedge from Tracy's cake, wrap it in Saran then place it in the cooler. Securing the top, I hand it to Mama, who lowers it to the floor and pulls me into her arms, her voice a whisper in my ear.

"I'm sorry 'bout what I said this afternoon. I really like your friends, honey."

I lean back, fingertips trailing down her synthetic-slicked arms and a fingernail snags on a frayed cuff of lace. Loosening it, I weave my fingers into hers.

"I knew you would, once you got to know them."

She looks at me, not as an adult looking at a child, making sure the seat belt's buckled or the vegetables are eaten, but as one adult who admires another. And in her face I see my own. "You got a lot of cheek, girl. So brave. Not a lick of fear of getting shot down."

"That's because I knew I could always go home."

But home's not Coryville, the place I was raised. My home is this woman, home is my mother, and all the roads she's had to travel that made her who she is. I rest my cheek on her shoulder; so tired, so very, very tired.

After a moment I raise my head and turn towards the kitchen island. A leather-tooled bound book inscribed to me and Miss Ann from Mallory is open, its rough-cut pages left blank for us to fill, and it lies next to a hammered nickel vase filled with the woody stems of wintersweet, dotted with yellow petals surrounding hearts tinged in purple moons, a gift from Tracy and Claire.

"This life, Mama, so lovely is this life." I squeeze her hands, shaking my head in wonderment that we made it to this place. But the journey's just begun, and I regard the counter covered with pots, pans, and the food-crusted plates beside the sink filled with glasses. "But there's always a mess of dirty dishes to wash."

"There sure is, honey, that there is."

Mama, Lester and Aunt Mama gather their bags, jackets and cooler, and walk out the door. Miss Ann skips towards me, arms flapping, cheeks splotched pink in excitement.

"Mama, there's a kitty outside the window."

Towns like Coryville get under your skin. Their desolation eats at you like a maggot and, for most, it's something you never think about; you become the place. Atlanta won't define me either. There's so much more of me waiting.

"I want to keep it, Mama. Can I take care of it, can I?"

My eyes thin at the silhouette of a large cat, scraggly fur framed in moonlight. "That's no kitten, child, it's an old raggedy tom."

My forefinger loops a curl around her ear and silver-blue eyes look up to me in a way that breaks my heart. I'm her mother, the center of her universe, and for a split second, the vision of the woman she'll grow to be flits across her face. Maybe that beat-back stray can take up some of the slack the stuffed animal and her puppies left behind.

"Here now. Give me just a minute and I'll rustle up some table scraps."

Yet this, after all, is enough. The place I want to be is here, right now, my daughter's arms wrapped tight around my legs.

The cat yowls, the sound as sharp and fierce as a newborn's wail, sliding into a love cry, then collapsing into night like an old woman's dying moan. A sound as old as time.

I smile down at my angel, smile down upon those eyes, eyes as lovely as a pair of fresh launched butterflies.

"Seems to me, sweetie pea, you've got yourself a job."

Venison Stroganoff
by
Shelby Preston

I love venison and appreciate this lean, flavorful meat. To my palate, there's a lot of flavor, texture and chew, which I expect results from the muscles they develop running free in the forests. I've seen recipes using wild boar, ostrich and elk, which sound exotic, but no one ever writes about venison. It's strange that folks snub the most local and organic meat to be had in Georgia.

Slicing the steaks, I admired the meat, without an ounce of fat. This was an animal that foraged in Georgia forests, grazing on acorns, wild apples and corn. You can bet there were no feedlots or growth hormones in this animal's life, not to mention "carbon footprint" left on the land.

I started out using Mallory Lake's recipe for Stroganoff, but switched up her seasonings and sub-stituted venison for sirloin. The final dish reminds me of a cross between her Stroganoff and a Paprikash I once made in chef school.

My friend, Sam Cox, provided the venison for my family and friends. I'll bet he's smiling down on us now.

The End

THE RECIPES

HOPPIN' JOHN

Yield: apx. 8 cups
Soak Time: 8 hours
Active Time: 25 minutes
Cook Time: 45 - 75 minutes (depending on heat level and type of pea used)
Rest Time: 1-2 hours

INGREDIENTS

1 pound (5 cups) dry Sea Island Red Peas or black-eyed peas

6 pieces raw bacon, chopped into 1-inch pieces

1 small white onion, coarsely chopped

3 stalks celery, sliced

6 cups chicken stock

1 bay leaf

1 teaspoon dry thyme

3 tablespoons extra virgin olive oil, Georgia Olive Farms oil preferred

3 tablespoons cider vinegar

1 small red bell pepper, seeds and membranes removed, diced

1 small orange or yellow bell pepper, seeds and membranes removed, diced

4 scallions, white and light green parts only, chopped

Cayenne

Cooked rice, Carolina Gold preferred

DIRECTIONS

1. Rinse peas, picking out and discarding cracked and yellowed. Soak 8-12 hours in 8 cups water. Drain and rinse.
2. In a large cast iron skillet or sauté pan, fry bacon until crispy. Reserve fat and drain bacon on paper towels.
3. Transfer bacon fat to a large pot. Over medium heat, sauté onion and celery in fat 3-4 minutes, or until just tender and fragrant. Add drained, soaked peas, stock, bay leaf and thyme to pot. Bring to a boil then reduce heat to simmer and cook, with lid slightly ajar, until peas are just tender, 45-75 minutes. Turn off heat, cover pot, and let peas sit in cooking liquid 1-2 hours or until tender and creamy, but not overly soft and mushy. Drain.
4. Whisk together oil and vinegar. Discard bay leaf from peas and toss peas with vinaigrette, peppers, scallions and reserved bacon. Season to taste with kosher salt, freshly ground pepper and cayenne. Serve with rice.

CRISPY ROSEMARY
CHICKEN BREAST TENDERS

Yield: 12 pieces

Time: 20 minutes

INGREDIENTS

12 chicken breast tenders*

1 tablespoon chopped fresh rosemary (or

1 1/2 teaspoons crushed dry)

1/2 cup white flour

1 extra-large egg, beaten

1 cup panko, Japanese bread crumbs

Grapeseed, peanut or canola oil, as
needed

Honey mustard or other dipping sauce,
optional

*The tenders, easily pulled away from the breast, are a particular part of the breast
meat called the tenderloin, which has a single tendon running through it.*

DIRECTIONS

1. Season chicken with kosher salt, freshly ground pepper and rosemary.
2. In each of three shallow dishes, separately place the flour, beaten egg and panko.
3. Coat each seasoned chicken tender in flour, then egg, then panko, pressing the crumbs to adhere.
4. Add enough oil in a cast-iron skillet or sauté pan to 1/2-inch depth. Heat oil until a drop of panko sizzles in pan, or thermometer reads 300-325 degrees. Working in batches, fry chicken until golden brown, about 4-5 minutes per side, adjusting heat if necessary so the chicken sizzles but doesn't burn before it's cooked through.
5. Drain on paper towels and serve with dipping sauce, if using.

SWEET AND SAVORY CHEDDAR MEATLOAF

Yield: 1 loaf (6 servings)
Active Time: 20 minutes
Bake Time: apx. 60 minutes

INGREDIENTS

1/2 cup panko (Japanese bread crumbs)

1/2 cup milk

1 large egg, lightly beaten

1 cup grated sharp Cheddar cheese, an English farmhouse Cheddar preferred

1/4 cup minced parsley

1 teaspoon minced garlic

1 cup finely chopped white onion

1/2 cup finely chopped carrot

1 1/2 teaspoons kosher salt

1 1/2 teaspoons freshly ground pepper

2 pounds ground beef*

1 cup (Heinz) chili sauce or ketchup

1 cup brown sugar

1 tablespoon Dijon mustard

In general, good meat loafs incorporate several grinds such as pork, veal, beef, or turkey. With this recipe, however, using 100% beef tastes best with the flavor of Cheddar. I use an 80/20 grind.

DIRECTIONS

1. Preheat oven to 350°.
2. Soften bread crumbs in milk until milk is absorbed; result should be paste-like. With a fork, combine crumb mixture with egg, cheese, parsley, garlic, onion, carrot, salt and pepper. Combine ground beef into mixture.
3. Liberally grease a loaf pan. Form mixture into prepared pan and cover with parchment paper or foil. On middle rack of oven, bake 45 minutes.
4. Remove meat loaf from the oven. Slide a rubber spatula along edges of loaf pan then invert onto a foil or parchment-lined baking sheet.
5. Combine chili sauce or ketchup, brown sugar and Dijon and spoon over exposed top and sides of loaf; return to oven for 20-30 minutes or until a thermometer inserted into the center registers 160°. Let sit 15 minutes, cut into 3/4-inch slices and serve.

CHICKEN GUMBO YA-YA

Yield: 8-9 cups (without rice)
Time: 2 hours

INGREDIENTS

1 cup canola, grape seed or vegetable oil

1 cup all-purpose flour

1 1/2 cups chopped white onion

1 cup chopped celery

1 1/2 cups (seeded) chopped green bell pepper

4-5 cups chicken stock

1 bay leaf

1 teaspoon kosher salt

1/2 teaspoon paprika

1 teaspoon dried thyme leaves

1/2 teaspoon garlic powder

1/4-1/2 teaspoon white pepper

1/4-1/2 teaspoon cayenne

1/4-1/2 teaspoon black pepper

1/2 pound andouille sausage, or other spicy sausage, cut into 1/3-inch pieces (1 1/2 cups)

4 cups cooked and chopped or shredded chicken

4-6 cups cooked rice (Louisiana white rice, preferred)

Chopped parsley &/or chopped green onions, optional garnish

Your favorite hot sauce

*I simmered a chicken the day before making the gumbo. I pulled the meat from the bone for the recipe and made stock with the resulting carcass. The meat from a purchased rotisserie chicken would save time.

DIRECTIONS

1. Make a roux by heating the oil over medium heat in a large cast iron skillet, heavy-bottomed pot or Dutch oven. Gradually add 1/3 cup flour to oil, whisking or stirring constantly, and cook 30 seconds; add another 1/3 cup flour, cooking and stirring 30 seconds, then stir in final 1/3 cup flour. (Note that it is critical to continuously stir or whisk the flour to incorporate into the oil. This keeps the flour from lumping and burning.) Stir flour-oil mixture often for 25-35 minutes, or until your roux is a rich red-brown color.

2. Add the onions, celery, and bell peppers and continue to stir for 4 to 5 minutes, or until the vegetables are wilted. (If you are using a cast iron skillet or shallow-lipped pan, you will need to transfer the mixture to a pot.) Gradually add 4 cups of the stock to the roux, stirring or whisking constantly to prevent lumps. When mixture has thickened and is smooth, add additional stock if it appears too thick.

3. Add the bay leaf, salt, paprika, thyme, garlic powder and 1/4 teaspoon each of the white, cayenne and black pepper. Continue to stir 3 to 4 minutes. Bring to boil, then reduce heat to medium-low. Stir in sausage and cook, uncovered, stirring occasionally, 45 minutes. Add chicken and simmer 15 minutes. Season to taste with kosher salt, and additional ground pepper(s), if desired. Serve with rice and garnish with chopped green onions, if using. Pass the hot sauce.

PIMENTO CHEESE SANDWICHES

Yield: 12 small sandwiches

Time: 40 minutes (includes time to make Pimento Cheese)

INGREDIENTS

24* slices good white, wheat or pumpernickel bread

2 1/2-3-inch circular cookie cutter

1 recipe for pimento cheese (recipe follows)

12 frilled toothpicks, optional

12 green pimento-stuffed olives, and /or cherry tomato halves, optional

DIRECTIONS

If desired, cut slices into circles with cookie cutter. Spread pimento cheese over 1/2 bread slices. Top with remaining bread. Spear sandwich rounds with an olive and/or tomato half, if using.

*For double-decker sandwiches, as pictured, use 36 slices of bread

PIMENTO CHEESE INGREDIENTS:

Yield: 2 cups

Time: 15 minutes

1/3-1/2 cup your favorite mayonnaise

1-2 dashes Worcestershire sauce

1-2 tablespoons minced scallions

2-3 tablespoons diced pimentos with juice

1/2 pound extra-sharp Cheddar cheese, grated

Cayenne

DIRECTIONS

1. Combine 1/3 cup mayonnaise with one dash Worcestershire sauce. Stir in 1 table-spoon of scallions and 2 tablespoons of pimentos with juice and combine.
2. Stir in Cheddar. Taste, then add additional mayonnaise, Worcestershire, scallions and pimentos as desired. Season to taste with cayenne and kosher salt.
3. Refrigerate 3 hours, stirring once, to allow flavors to combine.

HOT POT WITH KIM CHEE

Yield: 12 cups

Time: 45 minutes

INGREDIENTS

2 tablespoons sesame oil, divided

1 tablespoon chopped shallot

2 tablespoons fresh ginger, cut into matchstick, julienned slices

8 cups chicken, vegetable, or beef stock

2 tablespoons-1/4 cup soy sauce

1-2 cups kim chee*, coarsely chopped

2 bunches baby bok choy, washed, cored and sliced into long, 3/4-inch-thick strips

3 1/2 ounces shiitake mushrooms, woody stems removed and sliced (2 cups)

14 ounces extra firm tofu, sliced into 1 1/2-inch x 1 inch pieces

3 tablespoons chopped cilantro

6 ounces uncooked soba noodles (buckwheat noodles)

2 pounds raw chicken breast, cut into thin slices

1 large bunch watercress, long stems removed and washed (3 cups)

You can make your own or purchase it ready-made. Select hot or mild kim chee, according to your palate. I select mild kimchee and let individuals add chili paste or red pepper flakes according to individual taste.

DIRECTIONS

1. In a large pot or wok, heat 1 tablespoon oil over medium heat. Add shallot and ginger and cook 3-4 minutes or until just tender and fragrant.

2. Put the stock, 2 tablespoons soy sauce, 1 cup kim chee, and bok choy into the pot, and bring to a boil. Reduce heat and allow the broth to simmer for 10 minutes or until bok choy is just wilted. Add mushrooms and tofu and additional soy sauce and kim chee to taste, if desired. Simmer an additional 5-10 minutes or until mushrooms are tender. Stir in chopped cilantro.

3. While soup is simmering, bring a pot of salted water to a boil and cook soba noodles according to package instructions. In another large sauté pan, heat remaining tablespoon sesame oil to high heat. Quickly cook chicken in hot oil until just cooked.
4. Add the noodles, chicken and watercress to the soup before serving; or divide the noodles and chicken between six bowls, pour steaming soup over noodle-chicken mixture and serve, garnishing each bowl with watercress.

BLUE-CHEESE CHICKEN SALAD STUFFED IN ENDIVE

....

Yield: 4 cups chicken salad; enough salad to stuff apx. 40 endive leaves

Time to poach and chill chicken: 3 hours

Active Time: 1 hour (most time spent stuffing leaves and arranging platter)

INGREDIENTS

1 bay leaf

1 tablespoon dried herbs, such as basil, oregano, thyme or rosemary

6 black peppercorns

1 1/2 pounds uncooked, boneless, skinless chicken breast halves

1/2 cup your favorite mayonnaise

2 tablespoons walnut oil

2 tablespoons snipped chives, divided

Chopped orange zest and juice from 1 orange

8 ounces crumbled blue cheese

1 ounce dried cherries, chopped

3-4 heads endive (about 40-45 of the large outer leaves, washed and spun-dry)

40 whole pecans, toasted (Georgia pecans, preferred)

Nasturtium blossoms, optional garnish

DIRECTIONS

1. Bring a pot of well-salted water, seasoned with bay leaf, herbs and peppercorns, to a rolling boil. Let water boil at least 15 minutes to season. (There should be enough water remaining in the pot to cover the chicken by 1-2 inches, but not too much water to dilute the flavor.)

2. Carefully place chicken in boiling water, stir, and when water begins to simmer, turn off heat. Cover pot and let chicken sit in seasoned water 25-35 minutes or until chicken is totally cooked. Refrigerate and chill. (Chicken may be poached and chilled up to 24 hours in advance.) Cut chicken into 1/2-inch pieces.

3. Make a dressing by whisking together mayonnaise, walnut oil, 1 tablespoon chives, and orange juice, reserving zest for garnish. Combine diced chicken, crumbled blue cheese and cherries and thoroughly combine with dressing. Season to taste with kosher salt and freshly ground pepper. (Chicken salad may be made up to 24 hours in advance of spooning into endive leaves.)
4. Spoon chicken salad into endive leaves and garnish each with a toasted walnut, orange zest and remaining chives. Arrange on a platter garnished with nasturtium blossoms, if using. (May be made up to 3 hours in advance to serving.)

CHICKEN MOLE (THE EASY WAY)

Yield: 8-10 servings
Time: 40 minutes

INGREDIENTS

8 ounces prepared mole*

2-4 cups chicken stock, heated

2 tablespoons of creamy peanut butter

1/4-1 piece disk "Abuelita" Mexican chocolate

1/2-1 cup of tomato sauce (fresh tomatoes, peeled and pureed or canned)

2 cooked rotisserie chickens, meat removed from bones and shredded

3 tablespoons of lightly toasted sesame seeds

3 tablespoons fresh cilantro plus extra sprigs for garnish

I purchased a freshly made mole and Mexican chocolate from Bandera's

INGREDIENTS

1. Discard excess oil from top of mole paste and place mole into a large heavy-bottomed pan. Add 1 cup of heated stock to paste and, with a whisk or fork, break down paste until it has a smooth, medium-thick, gravy-like, consistency; add more stock as needed.

2. Place pan over medium-low heat and stir or whisk in peanut butter. Add 1/4 piece of chocolate disk to sauce, whisking to incorporate. Taste and add additional chocolate as needed (I prefer using 3/4 of the disk).

3. Stir in 1/2 cup tomato sauce. Taste and add additional sauce as desired; the more tomato sauce added, the less spicy the sauce will be.

4. Stir mole often, scraping the bottom of the pan and sides. As the mole heats, it will thicken; add chicken stock as needed for desired consistency. Be careful not to add too much stock, which would result in a watery mole.

5. Spoon mole on the bottom of a large platter or individual plates. Place shredded chicken over mole and spoon or pipe mole over chicken. Sprinkle toasted sesame seeds and cilantro over chicken and serve.

WATERMELON SALAD WITH FETA AND RED ONION

Yield: apx. 8 servings
Time: 25 minutes

INGREDIENTS

1/4 cup champagne or fruit-enhanced vinegar

1/2 cup extra virgin olive oil

1 tablespoon honey

2-3 tablespoons chopped mint, plus extra leaves for garnish

1 seedless watermelon, about 8#*, rind removed, sliced and cut into large chunks

1 small red onion, thinly sliced

4-6 ounces crumbled feta cheese

* For easy carving, slice off the tip of one end of melon. Set the melon securely on the tipped end. With a sharp knife, carefully carve away the rind and white pulp. Slice or cut into chunks as desired.

INGREDIENTS

1. In a large bowl, whisk together the vinegar, oil, honey and 2 tablespoons of the mint.

2. Toss the watermelon chunks and onion into the vinaigrette. Stir in 4 ounces of the feta. Add kosher salt, freshly ground pepper and additional chopped mint and feta to taste.

3. Serve in small bowls with a garnish of fresh mint sprigs. (I prefer serving in bowls as watermelon juice accumulates as it sits.)

SMOKED, PULLED PORK SANDWICHES WITH HOT SLAW

....

Yield: 12-15 cups barbecue: 25-30 sliders (or 15 regular-sized barbecue sandwiches)

Cole Slaw Time: (should be made 24 hours in advance): 40 minutes

Rub Rest Time: (unattended): 6-24 hours

Smoking Time: (mostly unattended): 7-9 hours

Note: Smoking times vary so allow yourself a couple more hours than you think you'll need to smoke your pork. You can always wrap your pork in foil and keep it in a warm oven until ready to serve; freezes well up to 1 month.

PORK RUB INGREDIENTS

2 tablespoons paprika

2 tablespoon brown sugar

1 tablespoon kosher salt

1 tablespoon garlic or onion powder

2 teaspoons cayenne

INGREDIENTS FOR SANDWICHES

6-7 pounds Boston butt (pork shoulder)

1/3 cup rub* (recipe above)

1-2 disposable aluminum or metal drip pans for placing under the pork butt

1 kettle (charcoal) grill, smoker or Big Green Egg

Charcoal, as needed

4-6 cups wood of wood chips (I prefer 2 parts hickory to 1 part white oak)

Cooking thermometer

4-6 cups your favorite barbecue sauce

25-35 small rolls or 15-20 regular-sized hamburger buns

1 recipe for Hot Slaw (recipe follows)

There are dozens of prepared barbecue rubs on most grocery shelves in town. You may have the ingredients to make your own signature rub just by using what you have on hand. The recipe above is a guideline and makes a flavorful rub.

DIRECTIONS FOR SANDWICHES

1. Combine rub ingredients: paprika, sugar, salt, garlic or onion powder, and cayenne, and massage 1/3 cup into pork. Wrap in plastic wrap and place in refrigerator 8-24 hours

2. Remove from fridge and let sit at room temperature 30-60 minutes, prior to grilling.

3. Place 1-2 water pans in the bottom grill grate. The pans should use apx. half the space at the bottom of the grill. Fill pan(s) halfway with water.*

4. Surround the pans with charcoal and, with a chimney starter or lighter fluid, heat coals to hot heat. Coals should be red hot and lightly covered with white ash. Sprinkle several handfuls of soaked wood chips over the hot coals.

5. Place the top grill grate on the grill. Position the grill grate so if you are using a hinged grill grate, one of the hinged areas lifts up over the coals so you can easily add coals when needed.

6. Lay the meat over the water pans as far away from the coals as possible. Do not let the meat rest directly over the coals, or the fat will drip into the fire, causing flames, which would burn the pork.

7. Cover the grill, positioning the vent on the cover directly over the meat. This helps direct the smoke over the meat.

8. Close all vents, including bottom vents, to keep the temperature low. If your vents and cover are extremely snug, open one vent. If your grill lid has a thermometer, it should read about 300°. Ideally you want the temperature at the meat level around 225-250; heat rises and a lid thermometer will show the temperature at the lid, and not at the meat level. If your kettle grill does not have a thermometer built-in, put a meat thermometer into the cover vent and check it occasionally.

9. If the temperature rises higher than 325°, open the lid and let the coals burn off a bit. Then add some more soaked wood and close the lid again. If your temperature begins to drop below 225 degrees, open the vents. If the temperature does not rise, open the lid and add more coals and soaked wood.

10. Regardless of temperature, add additional soaked wood, charcoal and rotate pork every 60-90 minutes.

11. Your meat is ready when it temps at 200° and is easily pulled apart with a fork. Wrap in foil and allow it to sit in a 200° oven until ready to serve. Then remove from heat, and in a large bowl, shred with a fork and thoroughly mix pork with barbecue sauce, adding sauce to taste.

12. To serve, place barbecue pork in a slider or bun and top with Hot Slaw (recipe follows).

*This step is not necessary if using a Big Green Egg ceramic plate setter for indirect smoking.

HOT SLAW INGREDIENTS (SHOULD BE MADE 24 HOURS, AND UP TO 48 HOURS, IN ADVANCE)

4 cups cabbage, diced into 1/2-inch pieces

1 ½ cups shredded carrots

½ red minced bell pepper

¼ cup minced sweet or red onion

¼ cup cider vinegar

1 tablespoon firmly packed brown sugar

1-3 teaspoons prepared brown mustard

Your favorite hot sauce*

1/3 cup canola or vegetable oil

HOT SLAW DIRECTIONS

1. Layer the vegetables in a large glass bowl in the following order: Cabbage, carrots, bell pepper and onion. Do not combine.

2. Whisk together the vinegar, sugar and 1 teaspoon of the mustard. Add additional mustard, hot sauce, kosher salt and freshly ground pepper to taste and pour over the layered vegetables. Do not combine.

3. Heat the oil in a sauté pan until it begins to smoke. Carefully and evenly drizzle the hot oil over the slaw. Do not toss. Let sit 10 minutes for the flavors to combine. Toss well and refrigerate until serving.

*Most Hot Slaw fans prefer it extremely spicy so I take a heavy hand with the hot sauce. However, you can put it in, but you can't take it out. My suggestion would be to add enough hot sauce so the slaw lives up to its name, then let your guests add more according to their palate's endurance.

GRILLED DUCK BREASTS IN ZINFANDEL SAUCE

Time: 40 minutes
Yield: 2 servings

INGREDIENTS

1 tablespoon unsalted butter

1 tablespoon minced shallot

1 tablespoon coriander seeds, lightly toasted then crushed*

1 teaspoon finely chopped jalapeno pepper

1/3 cup Zinfandel

2/3 cup unsweetened cherry or pomegranate juice

2 teaspoons cornstarch

1-2 tablespoons brown sugar

1 cup pitted ripe cherries, halved**

1/2 teaspoon finely chopped orange zest, plus extra for garnish

2 (6-8 ounce) duck breast halves, skin attached

I crush the seeds with a mortar and pestle or mallet.
**Thawed, frozen cherries may be substituted*

DIRECTIONS

1. In a medium-sized sauté pan, heat butter over low heat. Add shallot, 1 teaspoon of the crushed coriander seed and chopped pepper; sauté 3-4 minutes or until shallot is translucent and mixture is fragrant.

2. Whisk Zinfandel into pan and increase heat to high, whisking. When mixture is bubbling, reduce heat to low and let reduce a minute. Whisk cherry or pomegranate juice, cornstarch and 1 tablespoon brown sugar together. Add juice mixture to sauté pan and cook, whisking, until just beginning to thicken. Add additional brown sugar to taste, if desired.

3. Add cherries and orange zest to pan and simmer, occasionally stirring, until cherries have softened and sauce has thickened and coats the back of a spoon, about 10-15 minutes.

4. Preheat gas or charcoal grill to medium-high heat.
5. With a sharp knife, score duck breast skin in a criss-cross pattern. Rub remaining coriander over scored duck skin. Season both sides of duck breast with kosher salt and freshly ground pepper.
6. Grill duck, skin side down, 6-10 minutes or until skin in golden brown and crispy. Do not leave duck unattended as fat will likely cause flare-ups. When flare-ups occur, transfer duck to another side of the grill. Turn duck over, flesh side down, and continue grilling 1-2 minutes for medium rare (155°). Cooking times vary: The thickness of the duck breast and heat of the fire will determine cooking time.
7. Let duck rest 5-10 minutes. Spoon a little sauce onto 2 plates. Thinly slice the duck breast and fan out over the sauce. Drizzle with additional sauce, garnish with orange zest, if desired, and serve.

FRIED GREEN TOMATO BLT

....

Time: 45 minutes

Yield: 3-4 sandwiches

INGREDIENTS FOR SANDWICH

6 slices uncooked bacon, cut in half

4 large green tomatoes, cut into 1/2-inch slices (discard ends)

Peanut, canola or grape seed oil, as needed

2/3 cup yellow corn meal

1/3 cup white flour

1 extra-large egg, beaten

6-8 slices bread, your choice of bread (toasting optional)

2-3 tablespoons homemade mayonnaise* (recipe follows)

1-2 cups leafy lettuce or arugula

*Duke's or Hellmann's mayonnaise is a good substitute for homemade.

DIRECTIONS FOR SANDWICHES

1. In a large cast iron or non-stick skillet, fry bacon until crisp. Remove bacon, drain on paper towels and reserve, leaving drippings in the pan.

2. Liberally season both sides of tomato slices with kosher salt and freshly ground pepper. Place on paper towels and let sit at room temperature for 15 minutes.

3. Re-heat bacon fat to medium-high heat (360 degrees) adding additional oil to make 1-inch depth of oil in pan. Combine corn meal and flour. Dip the tomato slices in egg, then dredge in the corn meal mixture.

4. Fry the tomato slices in hot oil until golden brown, approximately 4-7 minutes on each side. (If the oil becomes too hot, it will smoke and the tomatoes may burn; if too cool, they won't develop a crispy crust.)

5. Drain tomatoes, uncovered, on paper towels. Taste and add additional salt if necessary.

6. Spread mayonnaise on one side of each bread slice.

7. Divide and layer bacon halves, lettuce or arugula, and fried green tomato on half of bread slices. Top with remaining bread and serve.

INGREDIENTS FOR MAYONNAISE

3 large eggs

3 cups canola or vegetable oil

2-3 tablespoons lemon juice

Worcestershire sauce

DIRECTIONS FOR MAYONNAISE

1. Place eggs in the bottom of the blender or food processor bowl. Pour 1/4 cup of oil over the eggs.
2. Turn on blender or processor and pour oil into bowl in a slow steady stream until oil has emulsified. Turn off blender and add 2 tablespoons lemon juice; process to incorporate. Season to taste with additional lemon juice, kosher salt, freshly ground pepper and a slight dash, or more, of Worcestershire sauce, to taste.

PAN-FRIED SQUASH BLOSSOMS STUFFED WITH GOAT CHEESE

Yield: 12 fried blossoms

Time: 45 minutes

INGREDIENTS

8 ounces soft (spreadable) goat cheese

1 tablespoon minced shallot (snipped chives may be substituted)

1/3 cup chopped fresh herbs, such as thyme, tarragon and basil

12 fresh squash blossoms

1/2 cup white flour

2 eggs, beaten

1 cup panko (Japanese bread crumbs)

1 cup grape seed or peanut oil, for frying

DIRECTIONS

1. Combine goat cheese, shallot and herbs and season to taste with freshly ground pepper.

2. Form 12 rounded teaspoons of goat cheese. Carefully make a slit through each blossom, leaving the stem intact. Stuff each blossom with a teaspoon of the herbed cheese. Gently twist to close and set aside.

3. In each of three bowls place flour, eggs and panko. Coat each blossom in flour, egg, then panko.

4. Place oil in large sauté pan pan and heat to medium-high heat. Oil is ready when it sizzles when a bit of panko or water is added.

5. Gently transfer each blossom to the hot oil and cook until golden brown, turning to brown all sides, about 4 minutes. Transfer blossoms to paper towels to drain. Serve.

SUCCOTASH

Yield: 4 servings
Active time: 15 minutes
Simmer Time: 40-45 minutes

INGREDIENTS

5 slices raw bacon

1 medium sized sweet onion, Vidalia preferred, chopped

2 cups fresh okra, cut into 1/2-inch pieces

2 cups freshly shucked lima beans

4 medium tomatoes, chopped

1/2-2 cups chicken or vegetable stock and/or white wine

4 cups (4 ears) fresh corn kernels cut from the cob

1 teaspoon minced garlic

1/2 cup torn fresh basil

DIRECTIONS

1. Cook bacon in a large skillet over medium high heat until crisp. Remove bacon, reserve, and add onion to bacon fat. Sauté over medium heat, stirring, about 3 minutes.

2. Add okra and sauté, stirring, an additional 3 minutes. Stir in lima beans, tomatoes and 1/2 cup stock &/or white wine, and simmer mixture until vegetables are just tender, about 20-30 minutes, adding liquid in 1/2 cup increments when mixture becomes dry.

3. When vegetable are just tender, stir in corn and garlic and simmer an additional 5 minutes. Season to taste with kosher salt and freshly ground pepper. Stir in basil and ladle into bowls, garnished with crumbled bacon.

BACON & BEER-BRAISED BRATS WITH APPLE-KRAUT

Yield: 8 Bacon-wrapped brats and apple-kraut

Time: 60 minutes

INGREDIENTS FOR BACON & BEER-BRAISED BRATS

8 pieces uncooked bacon strips

8 uncooked bratwurst

8 skewers or toothpicks*

4 cups your favorite beer

2 tablespoons dark brown sugar, optional

8 hoagie or brat buns (optional)

Mustards and ketchup (optional)

*If using wooden skewers or toothpicks, soak in water 30 minutes before using to help prevent flare-ups.

DIRECTIONS FOR BACON & BEER-BRAISED BRATS

1. Wrap bacon around brats and secure both ends of bacon with a skewer or toothpicks.
2. Pour beer into a large wide-lipped pan, and bring to a simmer. Taste and add sugar if a sweeter flavor is desired. Braise sausages, covered over low heat, in beer until bacon is limp and sausages are slightly firm to the touch, about 15 minutes. Remove brats and reserve 1/2 cup remaining beer (for using in Apple-Kraut recipe), discarding remaining beer or reserving for another use.
3. Bring a gas or charcoal grill to high heat. Oil rack and grill sausages, with bacon attached, 6-8 minutes on each side, or until cooked through (165 degrees) turning sausages to evenly grill and fry bacon. Do not pierce sausages while cooking as that will cause them to drain savory juices and become dry. Do not leave brats unattended; you may have flare-ups from the bacon fat. If flare-ups occur, cover grill or move brats away from flame to cooler portion of the grill.
4. Remove skewers or picks from brats before serving. Serve with Apple-Kraut (recipe follows) and buns and condiments, if using.

INGREDIENTS FOR APPLE-KRAUT

1 tablespoon butter or canola oil

1 large onion, thinly sliced

1 tablespoon brown sugar

2 apples*, washed, cored, then thinly sliced

4 cups sauerkraut (not from a can)**, rinsed

2 teaspoons caraway seeds

*I used Georgia Winesap, though any good cooking apple may be used. You may remove skin from apples with paring knife before cooking, if desired.

**Select locally-made or the store-bought refrigerated kraut.

DIRECTIONS FOR APPLE-KRAUT

1. Over medium low heat, heat butter or oil. Add onions to pan and sauté with brown sugar and a pinch of kosher salt 10 minutes, stirring occasionally.

2. Raise heat to high, then deglaze pan with 1/4 cup of the reserved beer from the brat recipe. Stir, let reduce a minute, then add sliced apples to the onion mixture.

3. Simmer an additional 10 minutes. Stir in rinsed sauerkraut, caraway seeds and remaining beer. Heat through before serving.

PORK BELLY TACOS

Yield: 6-8 tacos

Time to braise pork: 3-4 hours, mostly unattended

Active Time: 35 minutes

INGREDIENTS

2-3 pound slab pork belly

2 cups shredded green cabbage

Juice from 1 lime

4-6 tablespoons your favorite salsa, such as tomatilla or chipotle

6-8 (6-inch) soft, white corn tortillas

8 teaspoons crumbled queso fresca

2 tomatoes, washed, cored, seeded then cut into 1/4-inch dice

2 ripe avocados, diced

2 tablespoons chopped cilantro

DIRECTIONS

1. With a sharp knife, lightly score pork belly on the fat side by making 1/6-inch slashes in 4 places. Season both sides of belly with kosher salt and freshly ground pepper. In a dry heavy-bottomed pan or Dutch oven large enough to accommodate the pork, over high heat, sear pork until golden brown on each side.

2. Add water to cover up to 3/4 pork. Cover with a tight fitting lid or aluminum foil and simmer 1 1/2 hours. Remove lid, taking care not to let the steam burn you, turn pork over, and add additional water if depleted. Cover and continue simmering until pork is easily shredded with a fork. Let cool several minutes in cooking liquid then remove from liquid to carving board; cut or shred into small pieces, removing or retaining as much fat as desired.

3. Combine shredded cabbage with lime juice. Reserve. Toss pork belly with 4 tablespoons salsa, adding additional salsa and kosher salt to taste.

4. In a dry skillet, cast iron preferred, heat the tortillas over medium-low heat until they are softened. Wrap in aluminum foil until ready to use.

5. To make the tacos, in this order, divide the reserved cabbage, pork belly, queso fresco, tomatoes, avocados and cilantro over each warm tortilla and serve.

GOAT CHEESE PANNA COTTA WITH POACHED PEARS AND MAPLE-BACON SYRUP

....

Yield: 8 servings

Time to make poached pears and panna cotta (advance prep required): 75 minutes

Time to make dressing and finish plates: 40 minutes

INGREDIENTS

4 firm-ripe Bosc pears

4 cups fruity red wine*

1 1/2 cups sugar

2 cinnamon sticks

2 vanilla beans

1 1/2 teaspoons cloves

Parchment paper to cover pear while poaching

3 cups heavy cream (avoid ultra-pasteurized, if possible)

1 cup goat milk

8 ounces soft goat cheese, room temperature, coarsely chopped

1 teaspoon dry tarragon

Two pinches of cayenne

1/2 teaspoon kosher salt

1 tablespoon powdered gelatin, bloomed** in 2 tablespoons warm water

8 (1/2-3/4 cup) ramekins (molds), lightly oiled

1 packed cup of 1/4-inch diced uncooked bacon

1 cup maple syrup

Arugula, as needed, stems trimmed, washed and dried

Optional garnishes: Finely chopped parsley (for garnishing panna cotta) and raspberries.

DIRECTIONS

1. Peel pears with a vegetable peeler or paring knife and cut them, lengthwise, in half. Use a melon baller or spoon to dig out the core, and a small paring knife to remove the fibrous part of the core that extends to the stem, leaving the stem intact.

2. Combine the wine, sugar, cinnamon sticks, vanilla beans and cloves in your largest, heavy-bottomed saucepan or Dutch oven. Bring the mixture to a low simmer while stirring to dissolve sugar.

3. Add pears to the saucepan. Cut a piece of parchment paper into a circle that will fit over the pears in the pan. Place the parchment round directly on the surface of the liquid and pears. This will keep the pears submerged in the liquid.

4. Over low heat, poach pears for 20 to 30 minutes or until a knife tip is easily inserted into a pear. Turn pears over in the middle of simmer time to insure even poaching. Remove the pears from the heat and allow them to cool to room temperature in their liquid. Chill in the cooking liquid until cold, turning occasionally, at least 8 hours and up to 24.

5. Meanwhile, in a large bowl, half-fill an ice bath large enough to house the saucepan in which the panna cotta will simmer. Reserve.

6. Gently heat the cream and goat milk in saucepan. When just hot but not boiling, stir in the goat cheese and whisk until the mixture is smooth; stir in tarragon, cayenne and salt. Remove from heat and continue whisking in ice bath; whisking in the bloomed gelatin (see notes below) and continue whisking until completely incorporated.

7. Pour into oiled molds. Chill in the refrigerator for at least 6 hours and up to 24 hours. Fry the bacon in a skillet until crisp; deglaze pan with 2 cups of water and the maple syrup and reduce until 1 cup, or so, remains; about 15 minutes. Strain out bacon (reserve for another use), return the syrup to a small saucepan and whisk over high heat for 3-4 minutes, until the syrup thickens. Allow to cool, whisking occasionally to make sure the fat does not separate. (If refrigerated at this point, the syrup will thicken further; bring to room temperature before using.)

8. Unmold the panna cottas by running a knife along the edges of the ramekins and tapping onto 8 plates garnished with arugula. (If they don't slide out of the mold, place briefly in a small hot water bath and try again.) Slice the pears and arrange around the panna cotta. Drizzle with the bacon syrup, garnish, if desired, and serve.

A typical, 750ml bottle of wine is 3 cups; add an additional cup of water, if you don't want to open another bottle. That's what I did. A bit less of an intense red color, but lovely.

**Blooming gelatin is an important step to ensure a smooth texture. Sprinkle the powdered gelatin into water and stir to dissolve. Let sit for 3 to 5 minutes until congealed, then heat in the microwave about 45 seconds until liquefied.*

ROOT VEGETABLE GRATIN

Yield: 4-6 servings
Active Time: 20 minutes
Bake Time: 45 minutes

INGREDIENTS

2 tablespoons extra virgin olive oil, Georgia Olive Farms oil preferred

2 leeks, white and light green parts only, sliced and washed*

6 carrots, peeled and sliced into 1/4-inch rounds*

2 parsnips, peeled and sliced into 1/4-inch slices*

2 turnips, peeled and sliced into 1/4-inch thick rounds*

1 scant tablespoon chopped fresh thyme leaves

1 cup half-and-half or heavy cream

1 cup grated Asiago cheese

Onions, garlic, rutebegas and sweet potatoes are other root vegetables that are savory additions or substitutions for any of the ingredients used in this recipe.

DIRECTIONS

1. Preheat oven to 400°.
2. Heat oil in a large sauté pan. Sauté leeks with a pinch of kosher salt for 5 minutes. Add carrots, parsnips, turnips and thyme and sauté for 10 additional minutes. Season to taste with kosher salt and freshly ground pepper.
3. Transfer vegetables to a well-oiled ovenproof casserole or gratin dish. Pour half-and- half or cream over top and top with asiago. Cover with oiled foil (the oil keeps the cheese from sticking) and bake for 15 minutes. Remove foil and bake another 30 minutes or until golden brown.

BUTTERNUT SQUASH SOUP WITH APPLES AND CHIPOTLE

Yield: 10-12 cups thick soup
Active Time: 40 minutes
Roast Time: 25 minutes
Simmer Time: 20 minutes

INGREDIENTS

2 tablespoons canola or vegetable oil plus extra for oiling foil

2-3 medium-sized butternut squash (apx. 5 pounds), peeled, seeded and cubed

2 tablespoons unsalted butter

2 leeks, washed and cut into 1/4-inch coins (2 cups)

3 large carrots, peeled and cut into 1/4-inch coins (2 cups)

2 teaspoons cumin

1 1/2 teaspoons cinnamon, Mexican cinnamon preferred

1/2-1 tablespoon minced chipotle pepper in adobo sauce (1-2 peppers from can)

3-4 cooking apples*, peeled, cored and cubed

6 cups vegetable or chicken stock

Sour Cream or Creme Fraîche, optional garnish

*I used Georgia Winesap, though any good cooking apple may be used.

DIRECTIONS

1. Preheat oven to 375 degrees. Brush oil over two foil-lined baking sheets.
2. Toss squash with oil and spread a single layer of squash on prepared baking sheets. Roast until just tender, about 25 minutes.
3. Melt the butter in a large heavy-bottomed stockpot or Dutch oven. Sauté leeks and carrots until beginning to soften, about 5 minutes.
4. Stir cumin, cinnamon and ½ tablespoon chipotle into vegetables. Stir in apples and cook 1 minute. Stir in stock, roasted squash and bring to a boil. Reduce heat to simmer and cook until all vegetables are fork-tender, about 15 minutes.

5. Transfer the mixture in batches to a food processor. Process until smooth. Season to taste with kosher salt and additional chipotle, if desired. (This can be made up to 48 hours in advance, then reseasoned before serving.) Swirl creme fraîche or sour cream into soup immediately before serving, if desired.

VENISON STROGANOFF

Yield: 6 servings
Time: 40 minutes

INGREDIENTS

2 pounds venison chops or steaks

3 tablespoons plus 1/4 cup all-purpose flour

3-4 tablespoons unsalted butter

2 cups pearl onions, blanched in boiling water 1 minute, then peeled

1 tablespoon minced garlic

2 cups venison or beef stock

3 tablespoons Madeira (wine)

2 tablespoons tomato paste

3 cups sliced mushrooms, wild or domestic

1 cup sour cream

Paprika as needed

3 tablespoons chopped dill, plus extra sprigs for garnish

DIRECTIONS

1. Remove all fat and silver skin from steaks, if necessary. Cut meat diagonally into strips against the grain. Lightly season with kosher salt and freshly ground pepper. Dredge strips in 3 tablespoons flour.

2. In a large, heavy-bottomed skillet, heat 3 tablespoons butter over medium to medium-high heat. Cooking in batches, brown beef, about 1 minute on each side, adding additional butter if needed.

3. Remove meat with tongs; reserve.

4. Add blanched onions, garlic and a pinch of salt to pan and sauté, stirring, a minute.

5. Slowly whisk or stir in remaining 1/4 cup flour. (You may want to remove pan from stove when whisking in flour; if too hot, lumps could form.) Stir or whisk in stock, Madeira and tomato paste.

6. Bring mixture to a boil, stirring continuously, then reduce heat to a simmer, stir in mushrooms and cook until sauce is thickened, about 10 minutes. Stir in sour cream, 1 teaspoon paprika, chopped dill, reserved venison and gently heat. Garnish with a dusting of paprika, dill sprigs and serve.

A NOTE FROM THE AUTHOR

HI THERE!

Thank you for reading this story; I hope you enjoyed it. What's next for Shelby, Miss Ann and Mallory? Stay tuned because their final feast is yet to be served.

As Mallory noted in Chapter 2, today you, the reader, are in charge. As I channel my character's words, it's invaluable knowing what resonated with you; I would love your feedback. If you've the time and inclination, a review on Amazon &/or Goodreads would be tremendously appreciated; their links may be found on my Author Page.

In gratitude,

Peggy

Author Page: http://bit.ly/simmerandsmoke

ABOUT THE AUTHOR

Peggy Lampman was born and raised in Birmingham, Alabama. After graduating from the University of Michigan with a degree in communications, she moved to New York City, where she worked as a copywriter and photographer for Hill and Knowlton, a public relations firm. She moved back to Ann Arbor, her college town, and opened up a specialty foods store, The Back Alley Gourmet. After selling the business, she wrote under a weekly food byline in *The Ann Arbor News* and *MLive*. This is her first novel.

Made in the USA
Charleston, SC
27 August 2015